I, The King

BOOKS BY FRANCES PARKINSON KEYES

I, The King

The Explorer

The Old Gray Homestead

The Career of David Noble

Letters from a Senator's Wife

Queen Anne's Lace

Silver Seas and Golden Cities

The Safe Bridge

Senator Marlowe's Daughter

The Happy Wanderer

Honor Bright

Written in Heaven
(Revised and reissued as
Therese: *Saint of a Little Way*)

Capital Kaleidoscope

Parts Unknown

The Great Tradition

Along a Little Way

The Sublime Shepherdess
(Revised and reissued as
Bernadette of Lourdes

Fielding's Folly

The Grace of Guadalupe

All That Glitters

Crescent Carnival

Also the Hills

The River Road

Once on Esplanade

Came a Cavalier

Dinner at Antoine's

All This Is Louisiana

The Cost of a Best Seller

Joy Street

Steamboat Gothic

The Royal Box

The Frances Parkinson Keyes Cookbook

St. Anne: *Grandmother of Our Saviour*

Blue Camellia

The Land of Stones and Saints

Victorine

Station Wagon in Spain

Mother Cabrini: *Missionary to the World*

Frances Parkinson Keyes' Christmas Gift

The Third Mystic of Avila

Roses in December

The Chess Players

The Rose and the Lily

Madame Castel's Lodger

A Treasury of Favorite Poems

The Restless Lady and Other Stories

I, The King

BY

Frances

Parkinson

Keyes

McGraw-Hill Book Company · New York · Toronto · London · Sydney

Contents

Illustrations

Cast of Characters

PHILIP III, King of Spain

His children:

THE INFANTA ANA, later Queen of France

THE PRINCE OF ASTURIAS, later King Philip IV

THE INFANTE DON CARLOS

THE CARDINAL-INFANTE FERNANDO

THE INFANTA MARÍA, later Queen of Hungary and Empress of Austria

GASPAR DE GUZMÁN, Count of Olivares, later Duke of Sanlúcar, generally known as the Conde-Duque. (Chief Minister, known as *Privado,* to Philip IV)

INÉS DE ZÚÑIGA, Countess of Olivares, his wife

ANA DE GUEVARA, Nursery Governess of Philip IV

ISABEL DE BOURBON, first wife of Philip IV

CHARLES, Prince of Wales

GEORGE VILLIERS, DUKE OF BUCKINGHAM

ARMAND JEAN DU PLESSIS, better known as CARDINAL RICHELIEU, Chief Minister of France

DIEGO DE VELÁZQUEZ, Court Painter of Philip IV

MARÍA INÉS CALDERÓN, better known as LA CALDERONA, a young actress, later Abbess of Valfermoso de las Monjas, King Philip's "true love"

DON JUAN OF AUSTRIA, her son

BALTASAR CARLOS, son of Philip IV and Isabel de Bourbon

MARÍA TERESA, his sister, later bride of Louis XIV of France

MARGARITA, Duchess of Mantua, Vicereine of Portugal

JERÓNIMO DE VILLANUEVA, Marqués de Villalba, Secretary of State, Protonotary and confidential agent to His Majesty, Philip IV

DOÑA TERESA VALLE DE LA CERDA, his erstwhile fiancée, Abbess of San Plácido Convent

Sor MARGARITA, a beautiful novice at San Plácido Convent

DON LUIS DE HARO, nephew of the Conde-Duque and his successor as Minister

MARQUÉS DE AYTONA, briefly Provincial Governor of Flanders and, like Don Luis de Haro, a kinsman of Olivares, who remained close to the King after the Minister's fall.

Sor MARÍA, Abbess of the Conceptionist Convent at Ágreda, "guide, philosopher and friend" of Philip IV

MARIANA OF AUSTRIA, second wife of Philip IV

CARLOS, her only surviving son

THE INFANTA MARGARITA MARÍA, her only surviving daughter

LOUIS XIV, King of France

PART ONE

The Queen Consort

1615-1627

Spain was at war and a league of all liberal Europe under Henry IV of France was pledged to humble finally the inflated pretensions of the house of Austria; but just as . . . the prompt ruin of Spain seemed imminent, a circumstance happened that gave a new lease of life to the proud dreams of the Philips, and made the subsequent downfall during the reign we have to record the more complete.

In May, 1610, the dagger of a crazy fanatic ended the glorious life of "Henry of Navarre"; and the coalition against Spain broke down, and gave way to a struggle between his widow Marie de Medici and James I of England to secure the friendship of the decadent power which still loomed so large and asserted its claims so haughtily. The Queen Regent of France, papal and clerical as she was, succeeded where crafty, servile James Stuart failed; and in 1612 the eldest daughter of Spain, the Infanta Ana, was betrothed in Madrid by proxy to the boy King of France, Louis XIII, and young Philip, Prince of Asturias, became the affianced husband of Isabel of Bourbon, the elder daughter of Henry IV, the great Béarnais. . . . In 1615, King Philip III and his pompous Court travelled north in an interminable cavalcade to exchange the brides on the frontier.

Prince Philip remained at the ancient Castilian capital of Burgos, while the dark-eyed young beauty who was destined to be his wife rode, surrounded by Spanish nobles, from the little frontier stream through San Sebastián and Vitoria to meet her bridegroom. The boy and his father rode a league or two out of Burgos to greet the girl, who it was fondly hoped would cement France and Spain together for the fulfilment of the impossible old dream of Christian unity dictated from Madrid.

—MARTIN HUME. *The Court of Philip IV.*

Chapter 1

SHE was seated in a silver saddle, with housings of velvet and pearls, on a white palfrey, when she came riding into his life and into his heart.

She more than fulfilled every fond expectation, for she was not only pretty as a picture; she had paid her bridegroom's people the compliment of changing from her gorgeous French attire to the stiffer Spanish dress; and, though it was evident she was still not used to it, the complaisance which had caused her to wear it, made a most favorable impression. Besides, if her dress were stiff, everything else about her was delightfully easy: her smile, her glance, her bearing, all marked her as the true daughter of the great Béarnais; like him, she was engaging, like him, she was gallant, like him, she was debonair.

"It's all such fun!" she kept exclaiming. "Isn't it, Philip?"

"It must be, if you say so," he answered, all too inadequately, as he knew, and brought his horse a little closer to hers.

"Oh, but it isn't just because I say so! It's because it really is! And how kind and cordial everyone is. I'm sure I'm going to love Spain. In fact, I love it already!"

She burst into happy laughter and, impulsively, began to throw kisses right and left. No wonder that she charmed everyone in sight, from the beggars and burghers lining the dark narrow streets and the richly robed clergy awaiting her on the steps of the gorgeous cathedral to the pale, sandy-haired boy with the heavy underlip, who was almost speechless with the marvel of having so bright and beautiful a being become an essential part of his existence.

He was ten years old—two years younger than his bride—and

until she came riding toward him, that day near Burgos, very little which was bright and beautiful had entered his life. His mother, Margarita of Austria—delicate, devout, withdrawn—had died when he was only six years old. She had loved Valladolid and had grieved when the capital was moved, for the second time, from there to Madrid; she had never been well afterward. The boy's father, Philip III, who was also delicate, devout and withdrawn, had become a prey to moods of dark despair over his inadequacy as a monarch; and these alternated with mystic visions which gave him brief illusions of relief from his misery. More and more, except when his gay and charming favorite, the Duke of Lerma, was able to break through their barricade, he was surrounded by friars who dictated both the most trifling and the most important acts of his life; and it was these same friars or their counterparts to whom the little boy's supervision and education were entrusted. Prayers and lessons, lessons and prayers, relieved only by an occasional masque, were his portion; he had no companions of his own age, except for the young courtiers who acted with him in these rare entertainments, and he formed no close associations among them. This woeful lack made it all the easier for him to accept, as a friend, an Andalucian aristocrat, Gaspar de Guzmán, Count of Olivares, who was brought to him by the Duke of Uceda, the Duke of Lerma's son, to be his Gentleman of the Bedchamber, when he reached the age to begin dispensing with the services of his nursery governess, Ana de Guevara.

At first, he resented the intrusion of this huge, dark man, with his bold glance, loud voice and insolent manner; he was very fond of Ana and wanted to cling to her. But he was flattered at the suggestion that he was outgrowing apron strings and intrigued by the tall tales Gaspar de Guzmán, a superb raconteur, told about his childhood in Rome, where his father was the Spanish Ambassador, and his student days in Salamanca, where he had eventually become a lector. Little by little, Philip adapted himself to the change; when Ana was not at hand, he needed someone in whom he could confide and he found this increasingly easy to do when he and Guzmán were riding together—or when he was lying in bed and the Count of Olivares, as was fitting, stopped to make sure there was nothing more Philip required, before leaving for the night, just as Ana had always done and she was now doing less and less frequently. She had obviously resented Guzmán's presence from the beginning and finally the Count explained to the boy that her attitude was unbecoming in an attendant and, with reluctance, Philip consented to part from his old nurse.

"You'll still come to see me sometimes, won't you, Ana?" he asked tearfully, hiding his head in her comfortable bosom.

"Just as often as I can. I don't know how I'll manage, but never you fear. I'll do it somehow."

"Please do, because I love you better than anyone in the world now that my mother's dead."

"And I love you better than anyone in the world. What's more, I'll serve you better in the end than this—this interloper. He needn't have ordered me away—he could have given me different things to do for you. I know as well as he does that you're not a baby any more, but that doesn't mean I couldn't be of use. I'll never forgive him for what he's done to separate us and some day he's going to be sorry."

She could not say any more just then because Olivares came striding into the room and harshly told her to be gone. Philip was bewildered, as well as unhappy, too unhappy to say anything more then, when he was trying hard not to cry. But there were many other things that puzzled him and though, to do Olivares justice, he took some pains to explain these to the lonely boy, Philip's bewilderment and unhappiness persisted. For instance, he had also been very fond of the Duke of Lerma, his own father's *Privado*—the Chief Minister who was further officially recognized as the Prime Favorite. Lerma had dandled Philip when he was a baby and still romped with him as a youngster; he wept again when he heard that his "gossip" had been banished from Court. Guzmán, who was vehement and voluble, undertook to clarify this situation as he had the other.

"*Privados* sometimes become an evil influence on the monarchs who single them out for special privileges along with their ministerial responsibilities," he said. "They abuse their power, plunder the people to enrich themselves and end by ruling the country over which the King only reigns. That is what Lerma has done, what Uceda will do if he is not watched."

It did not occur to the ingenuous boy that this was exactly what Olivares, who was already sure his star was rising, would do himself, as soon as he had disposed of his predecessors. The Prince listened attentively and thought that he learned as he listened. But the lesson gave him no pleasure.

Now, at last, something had happened that did give him pleasure: the sight of the girl, still smiling and happy, riding on her white palfrey as they entered Burgos together. He and his father escorted her first to the Royal Monastery of Las Huelgas where, after Mass and breakfast, the Abbess, a near relative of theirs, offered the new Princess of Asturias a crystal goblet ornamented with gold and diamonds, standing on a golden salver, and several curios made of amber. That same day there were a banquet and a ball. At the ball, Isabel danced first by herself and then with the Prince, executing the stately Spanish *hacha* as gracefully as if she had been doing it all her life, instead of trying it for the first time that day. All the while she was dancing, she chatted merrily with her boy bridegroom as he remained almost speechless with wonder and admiration.

After the celebrations in Burgos were over, Isabel went on with him and the Court to Valladolid and Segovia for further celebrations and finally reached Madrid, which was now the capital. Triumphal arches had been raised over the narrow streets and the balconies were hung with flags and tapestries when she rode from the Royal Monastery of San Jerónimo to the Alcázar—that grim old palace on the cliff overlooking the Valley of the Manzanares. The way was crowded with people waiting to welcome her. She was less stiffly dressed now. Her robe was made of crimson satin, embroidered with bugles, her little cap was trimmed with diamonds and the girdle which encircled her slim waist was a diamond chain. Her pretty face was wreathed in smiles and, as she glanced in friendly fashion, first one way and then another, the populace caught the contagion of her friendliness and shouted with joy while Philip's heart contracted with it.

Of course, their married life, in the literal sense of the word, did not begin then; their apartments in the great gloomy Alcázar were widely separated and both had watchful bedchamber attendants; but they learned to "represent well" when called upon to play the parts of Prince of the Asturias and his future consort in public, and they were good companions when it was possible for them to be together in hours of relaxation. In fact, within five years, it was obvious that it would require nothing but a little extra—and unsupervised—propinquity to transform them from playmates into lovers. Philip was precocious, both physically and mentally, and Guzmán, now firmly ensconced in his affections and confidence, encouraged this precocity. Some of the forms the encouragement took were to sow the seeds of a sad harvest; but there was general rejoicing when Philip and Isabel were installed in the suburban palace of the Pardo to set up their independent housekeeping, and a day formally designated for the consummation of their marriage.

Even now, Philip was only fifteen; but Isabel, at seventeen, was already a woman, more than ready to satisfy his precocity. They tumbled into bed together as naturally as they had played at blindman's buff and acted opposite each other in a masque. Philip never needed to use persuasion, much less compulsion, to possess his wife. Indeed, her only complaint was that Gaspar de Guzmán put a curb on their lovemaking.

"Why should the Count of Olivares expect to be with you the last thing at night and the first thing in the morning?" she complained.

"Merely force of habit. He's been doing it for several years now."

"But that was before we came to the Pardo—before we were really married. Of course, we were supposed to be, but nothing counted until we came here. Now it does. And, as if his snooping weren't bad enough, then along comes his wife, as Mistress of the Robes. She's just as overbearing and arrogant as he is. Neither one of them seems to understand I have a right to keep you to myself."

"I think you're perfectly capable of putting the Countess in her place, darling. And Gaspar de Guzmán's very important to me."

"More important than I am?"

"Certainly not. And only in a very different way."

"Then please tell him to leave you alone when you're in bed—when we're in bed together. Carlos and Fernando don't intrude at such times or at any others. As a matter of fact, I'd be glad to see a little bit more of your brothers. I like them both very much. But if they have so much regard for our feelings, I don't see why Olivares can't at least come to see you later in the day when I'm doing something else."

"We're usually doing something together all day long. I don't very often leave you to do anything by yourself."

"Well, aren't you glad that we're usually together all day long?"

"Of course, I'm glad. But being a prince has a lot of tiresome duties that you can't be expected to understand. I'm not sure that I understand them so well myself. Gaspar de Guzmán explains them to me."

"Try to see if you can't make him keep his explanations shorter and give them at some more convenient time."

It would have been hard to find a more convenient time from Isabel's point of view. The Prince and Princess, if left to themselves, devoted their days to merrymaking with the same intensity that they devoted their nights to lovemaking. They were both pleasure loving and, since their idea of pleasure was much the same, life at the Pardo became one long sustained holiday. To a large degree, this holiday was uninterrupted, except for the visits from Gaspar de Guzmán, which became increasingly important to Philip and increasingly unwelcome to Isabel. This situation continued for six months. Then the condition of the King, who had been ailing for some time, deteriorated radically. Philip was summoned to the Alcázar and told to expect the worst.

Chapter 2

THE curtains of the great tentlike bed where Philip was lying parted slowly and the somnolent prince, at first only vaguely conscious that he was not alone, presently realized that his usher was announcing the arrival of a visitor; then, that this visitor was his Dominican confessor, Antonio de Sotomayor; and finally, that Sotomayor was kneeling beside him and saluting him in an unfamiliar way.

"Your Majesty—"

The boy burst into tears. He had loved his father dearly and, though the King had been seriously ill for several weeks, his eldest son had not been able to face the fact that the end was near, even when the dying man summoned his heir to his bedside to bid him a formal farewell. Young Philip had been overwhelmed, first by the horrors of a deathbed scene in a room encumbered with gruesome relics and crowded with grim mourners; and then by the long list of duties and responsibilities which he was told lay ahead of him. He was to strive for the happiness of his people; he was to cherish his sisters and his brothers; he was to avoid new counselors and stand steadfast to the faith of Spain. More specifically, he was to see to it that his sister María married the heir of the Hapsburg Emperor, Ferdinand Ernest, and, on no account, to allow an alliance with a Protestant.

Philip had left the death chamber badly shaken and had immediately sought the advice of Gaspar de Guzmán, who was not slow to take advantage of this for his own betterment and the downfall of others. The result was that, even before the King had breathed his last, the old order had begun to change, yielding place to new and alas! with no real assurance that one would be better than the other. At the bidding of Olivares, Philip received the Archbishop of Burgos alone that evening and instructed him to forbid the reentry to the palace of Lerma, whom the dying King, yearning for one more glimpse of his long-time favorite, had ordered recalled from his involuntary "retirement"; instead, he was to return to Valladolid and "await orders." The Prince, despite his reliance on Olivares, was by no means happy as he issued this command. He had not forgotten that Lerma, now a cardinal as well as a duke, had been one of his earliest friends and he was again almost as close to weeping as he was when he first heard that his "gossip" was banished from Court. In order to be sure of self-control, he gave his order tonelessly, though emphatically, and with a facial expression of complete impassivity. Hitherto, his countenance, though not handsome, had been open, mobile and pleasing; for the rest of his life it was to be masklike, except in the secluded presence of those whom he most loved and trusted.

After this interview with the Archbishop, which took place in a somber, paneled room as night was falling, the Prince had retired to rest and, after tossing restlessly about for some hours, a prey to personal grief and official apprehension, finally fell into deep slumber. It was from this slumber that he had been aroused with the information that he was the King. The tears which he had checked the night before now brimmed over and he asked that the curtains of the bed might be drawn again and that he might be left alone with his sorrow.

For a few moments, this request was respected; though the room had been gradually filling, most of those who had entered it were either silent or spoke to each other in whispers. Then Olivares strode in, flung back the curtains and summarily bade the new king arise and attend to his pressing duties. Disputes as to rights and privileges were already raging, according to Guzmán; and, appalled at this unseemly behavior, the new monarch ordered that no one else was to be admitted to his room until he was at least up and dressed.

Though the letter of the law was observed, as far as this command was concerned, the spirit was not; those who could not get

into the bedchamber did their wrangling in the antechamber, aware
that, as soon as the new king could be suitably clad for a public audience, he would have to come out. But preparations took some
time, for grief and excitement kept overwhelming him; after all,
he was only sixteen years old. It would help, he felt, if he could
see his brothers, Carlos and Fernando, to both of whom he was de-
votedly attached, as they were to him. Physically, they bore a close
resemblance to each other; all three were slim, pale, sandy-haired
and heavy-jawed; and all three were amiable and easygoing;
though Fernando was the cleverest and the most vivacious, their
temperaments and tastes were basically the same. There had never
been rivalry or jealousy among them and Philip knew the others
would do everything they could to assuage his sorrow, which they
should share. But, first of all, he wanted to see his wife. He
beckoned to Olivares, asked for a tablet and, tearing off a sheet,
wrote in his sprawling hand, the first of the communications which
he was to sign after the manner of Spanish monarchs from time
immemorial:

TO HER MAJESTY THE QUEEN OF SPAIN.
   *I want and need you very much. Please come at once to the
Alcázar.*
                                                        I THE KING.

His summons to the Alcázar had marked their first separation,
except during the royal progress which he had made with his father
two years earlier when the Portuguese Cortes had sworn to accept
him as heir to the throne; and that, after all, had been when they
were still only good companions, not husband and wife. Isabel had
clung to him as they said good-bye and sobbed that she would not
be able to rest at all that night.
   "I shall keep groping for you in the dark when I'm half asleep
and, when I don't find you, I'll be frightened."
   He did not take it amiss that she was more concerned about
her loneliness than his grief and he tried hard to comfort her.
   "I shall miss you just as much as you'll miss me, darling. I
shan't be gone a minute longer than I can help and when I get back

everything will be just the same as ever. Perhaps better, because we'll be so happy at having each other again."

He had known when he spoke that he was not telling the truth and this had disturbed him a little, because he had never lied to her before. Of course, when she came, he would not confess that he had hardly missed her at all, because he had been thinking of his father and his kingdom and not of her. But he would have to tell her that there would be no merrymaking for a long time, not even any lovemaking in the immediate future, for there would be a period of nine days' mourning reclusion for him and his brothers in the Royal Monastery of San Jerónimo. And, of course, they could not live at the Pardo any more; they would have to move to the Alcázar. He would have to try to explain all this to her, just as Gaspar de Guzmán had explained so many things to him. He could only hope that she would be better at understanding than he was. She must be made to realize that she was no longer merely his good companion, his love, his bride; she was his Consort. What was more, she was the prospective mother of his child. Their easy, impulsive union had been productive. Isabel was already three months pregnant.

Chapter 3

THE baby, a girl, was born prematurely and lived only a few hours. The next baby, also a girl, was born a little over two years later and lived only a month. Before she died, however, she was given a magnificent baptism.

The newborn child was carried down the great staircase of the Alcázar in the arms of a lady-in-waiting, the Count of Olivares walking backward with golden candlesticks as he escorted the new princess to the rooms of her governess, the Condesa of Olivares. The King with all his Court was in attendance at the Royal Chapel for the *Te Deum,* pontifically celebrated by the Patriarch and Cardinal Zapata. For three nights in succession, every balcony in Madrid was illuminated by a wax torch and a great masked equestrian display of one hundred and twenty nobles of the Court, with new costumes and liveries, took place, the Count of Olivares and Don Pedro de Toledo being the most brilliant and skillful riders. The great cavalcade paraded the principal streets of the capital and ran two courses, one in the Calle Mayor and the other before the Convent of the *Descalzas Reales,* which had been founded by the Infanta Juana, the younger daughter of the Emperor Charles V. The next day, the King rode in state with all the Court to give thanks at the shrine of the Virgin of Atocha, one of the most greatly venerated in Madrid. The baptism took place in the little parish church of San Gil, hung for the occasion with cloth of gold. There the Nuncio, with cardinals and bishops galore, made a Christian of the baby.

Physically, Isabel made a rapid recovery from both confinements and, mentally, was not unduly depressed by either. It was, of course, part of her royal duty to produce children as rapidly as possible, preferably at the rate of one a year. But once a baby was ushered into the world, most of Isabel's responsibilities were over and, next to her passion for her husband, her greatest passion was for pleasure. In the period between the two births, her tastes and Philip's continued to agree as to their pastimes and her growing resentment over the ubiquitous quality of Gaspar de Guzmán's presence in every aspect of their lives was their only source of discord.

Before the nine days of mourning at San Jerónimo were over, this upstart had been granted the wish, long denied, of becoming a grandee. After a sermon which extolled the merit of gratitude and the obligation of showing it, the new king was dining with a group of nobles and, when Gaspar entered the room, Philip hailed him with a significant salutation.

"Let us obey the good friar who preached today. Count of Olivares, be covered!"

The second sentence was in the form used to raise a peer to grandeeship and, thereupon, Gaspar de Guzmán was created Duke of Sanlúcar. He immediately put on his wide-brimmed hat and threw himself at the King's feet. Soon thereafter, he became Principal Chamberlain; and, though he pretended to leave politics entirely to his uncle, Don Baltasar de Zúñiga, as Chief Minister, the pretense was not very convincing, even while it lasted, which was not long, for within a year the poor old man was dead. Olivares was now universally addressed by his dual title—the "Conde-Duque"—and, in his capacity of official *privado,* was at the King's side morning, noon and night.

Isabel raged at this intrusion on her privacy. Inevitably, it meant that, before long, instead of sharing a room with her husband, as she had done at first and as she wished to continue doing, she was soon forced to accept the compromise of adjoining rooms. Philip came to her bed as soon as Olivares had left him at night, but he had to be back in his own before his minister arrived in the morning; for the Conde-Duque insisted that he and no one else should have the privilege of drawing the curtains and opening the window. He then sat beside the King while Philip drank his morning chocolate, meanwhile outlining his working schedule for the day. Next, he assisted the King at his ceremonial dressing—usually in brown velvet with silver trimmings—and remained for eleven o'clock dinner. After that, he absented himself long enough to undertake the ministerial duties he had mapped out and which he fulfilled with efficiency as well as dispatch; he had a tremendous capacity for work and could do as much in an hour as most men could do in a day and do it well. So, before the King's bedtime, he was back again, with dispatches—which he had already approved—for Philip to sign and some entertaining gossip to round out the evening. Isabel began to complain that she and her husband were lucky if they could get in a hunt or even a ride without him. Moreover, at all the public and semi-public performances, like bullfights, comedies, tourneys parades, balls and banquets, he was, of course, at the King's side. And this, though she hated the very sight of him!

"That bulging forehead! Those sunken eyes! Those bowed shoulders—it's no wonder they're bent with the weight of that great square head! And his voice—he can't say anything without bellowing! And his manner—he acts as if he were the king, instead of you!"

"I wouldn't know how to act like a king without him to direct me."

"You could learn. You'd better learn—before it's too late."

Gaspar de Guzmán was fast becoming not only a source of dissatisfaction to the Queen, but a source of such violent resentment and dislike that she harped on it constantly. If Olivares had been willing to take the trouble, he could easily have placated her, at least to some degree, by including her in some of his long discussions with Philip about the financial and military matters to which he was giving his zealous attention, and occasionally flattering her by asking her opinion on his decisions, even if this seemed to him inconsequential. But his attitude toward her, as to women in general, was inclined to be one of contempt; he regarded them as insignificant, except for successful childbearing, and the Queen had, so far, produced only two sickly, short-lived daughters. She was pleasure loving to the point of frivolity and to him she seemed empty-headed as well. Moreover, since his driving ambition for power was his greatest passion, feminine charms left him relatively unmoved and Isabel's personal attractions meant nothing to him. He himself had not married until he was over thirty and his alliance with Doña Inés de Zúñiga, the daughter of a Viceroy of Peru, had been largely one of convenience. Since royal marriages were arranged for reasons of state, without any consideration for the feelings of those who contracted them, Olivares saw no sound reason why Philip should be emotionally involved to the point of attaching importance, one way or another, to his minister's behavior toward his wife, provided it showed no actual disrespect to her as the Queen; and it was true that Philip, whose disposition was not only easygoing but peace loving, had no desire to quarrel with her about Olivares. However, quarrels began to occur, first on this score and soon on others; and, as Isabel had the more positive nature and the more animated spirit, Philip frequently came off second best in their arguments. In an effort to even things up, he began to complain in his turn.

His first enthusiastic attachment to his bride had been untinged by jealousy; he had been delighted that his admiration of her was shared by his subjects and that she responded so spontaneously and joyously to the tribute she received. Now he began to be annoyed, both by any special mark of homage and by any special response to it. As a matter of fact, his own conscience was troubling him a little and, as is so often the case under these circumstances, he was ready to suspect others, who were completely innocent, of committing the sins of which he himself was guilty. His undeniable devotion to the Queen was no longer strong enough to keep him faithful to her, especially during the advanced periods of her pregnancies; she had as much reason to believe that he was having an affair with a Court lady by the name of Doña Francisca de Tavara as he had to believe that Don Juan de Tassis, Count of Villamediana, who was Doña Francisca's more or less acknowledged lover, aspired still higher. Unfortunately, two episodes, though unconnected, gave Philip a pretext for showing resentment.

The Count had ridden into the arena at an early celebration of the King's accession to the throne bearing as his device a mass of silver coins—*reales*—and above them an audacious identification of them as royal. Perhaps, if Isabel had not remarked on the excellence of the Count's aim in the tourney, the latter's daring salute might have passed unnoticed, but Philip answered her crossly and his reply was audible to everyone in their immediate vicinity.

"Yes—but he aims too high."

Madrid, as always, was avid for gossip and this was a choice tidbit for the strollers on the so-called Liars' Walks—especially on the raised promenade which ran along the side wall of San Felipe's Church, opposite the Oñate palace. However, Philip himself was quickly ashamed of his pointed retort and proved that he realized it was unjustified when Isabel revealed a plan for a tentative feature in a series of festivals to celebrate his birthday, which were to take place the following April in Aranjuez, where they customarily spent the spring.

"Don Juan has written a comedy in verse which he would like to have presented at this time," Isabel told her husband.

"You speak as if this were a novelty," Philip replied drily. "As you ought to know by this time, Don Juan has been writing comedies in verse ever since he was in his teens and he is now well over forty. They are usually either dull or satirical. If the first is the case, they bore people and, if the second is the case, they offend people. What is this one about?"

"It is called *La Gloria de Niquea* and it is neither dull nor satirical. It is charming and the new theater in the island garden would be an ideal place to produce it. The heroine is the Goddess of Beauty."

"Oh! Is that so?"

"Yes and Don Juan wants me to take the leading part."

"So I imagined, as soon as you began to talk to me about this comedy."

"Have you any objections?"

He hesitated. He would really have greatly preferred that Isabel should do nothing of the kind. But to decline to grant a request which was, undoubtedly, no longer a secret would set tongues to wagging more furiously than ever; it would be assumed that he had a special reason for his refusal which, actually, he did not. Besides, a gracious assent would make amends to Isabel for his former unjust brusqueness, as far as Don Juan was concerned.

"Very well, if you have your heart set on it," he said; then, fearing that this time he had spoken if not brusquely, at least grudgingly, he added, "You will look very lovely in such a part. It is suitable for you. Come and give me a kiss or two before you send word to Don Juan that you will be his heroine for one evening. After all, you are mine all the time."

On the night selected for the comedy, the weather was perfect and the entire Court assembled to see the spectacle, with the King and his two brothers, Don Carlos and Don Fernando, sitting in the front row. The set, made of silk and canvas, was brilliantly lighted with wax candles and the prologue had just ended successfully when a piercing shriek from the rear, just as the curtains were being drawn, brought the spectators to their feet. A long tongue of flame was licking the draperies and spreading so swiftly that, presently, they were ablaze. In the panic that followed, the King fought his way to the back of the stage, searching in vain for his wife. However, when he reached the wooded garden back of the burning structure, he found her fainting with fright, but entirely safe; she had already been rescued by Villamediana. At the moment, he was too thankful to be jealous; but, as soon as he recovered from his first shock, he inevitably resented both the fact that anyone else had been swift and skillful enough to reach her before he did and the further fact that he had found Villamediana clasping Isabel in his arms to support her. Under the circumstances, the embrace was almost unavoidable; but it was also unavoidable that numerous persons in the terrified crowd, who had not yet made good their escape, had seen it and gossip became more venomous than ever. There was even a ridiculous rumor that Villamediana had set fire to the stage on purpose. Isabel and Philip quarreled again and, this time, Philip nursed his grievance. The fire had a sad sequel.

A few months afterward, when Villamediana was returning home after dark, the cloaked figure of a man darted from an archway in the Calle Mayor and discharged a bolt from a crossbow. It pierced Villamediana's chest and, though he leaped from his coach and drew his sword, immediately thereafter he fell, dying, to the ground. He had been noted at Court as a splendid and extravagant courtier, the most gallant among many gallant men; in a society of literary and artistic dilettanti, he was held to be the most critical and refined. His murder, almost at his own door, caused a profound sensation. Murders in the open street had, indeed, become scandalously frequent and they were mostly prompted by private vengeance and rarely punished; but the slaughter of Villamediana set tongues wagging and, as if by common consent, all fingers pointed at Philip as the instigator of the crime from motives of jealousy. The assassin was almost certainly one Alonso Mateo, an archer of the King; but neither he nor any other was ever prosecuted for the crime. "Whoever struck the blow, the impulse that guided it was the sovereign's," the people murmured and, characteristically, he made no effort to silence their murmuring. If they wanted to believe him guilty, they were welcome to do so, as far as he was concerned. But when it came to a question of the Queen, his attitude was less indifferent and hers did nothing to mend matters.

"You would not be so ready to believe the worst of me if you had not provoked me to do the worst," he told her angrily.

"I do believe you guilty of the worst, but it was not I who provoked you to it," she retorted.

"Indeed! And to whose door do you lay this provocation?"

"As if you did not know! You could not bear to think that a certain Court lady, whom you admire very much, should prefer Villamediana's attentions to yours! So you put an end to his gallantries."

"I should be more disposed to admire my wife, to the exclusion of any other woman, if she gave me more reason to do so. Not only do her glances incline to wander, but so do her thoughts and her speech. Otherwise, she would never think or say what she has just done and I can hardly be blamed for seeking consolation elsewhere. My disappointment—may I say my disillusionment?—is natural under those circumstances. After all, she has sworn to love, honor and obey me and I can find no evidence of such sentiments or such a disposition in her present behavior."

"Why should she go on loving a man or honoring him, either, who makes as light of his marriage vows as you do? And does she still owe obedience to him, whatever he may do?"

"Yes. I am still the King and I am still your husband. It would be better for you not to forget either the one or the other. You are not a queen regnant," he went on imperiously. "You are only my wife and you have not given me an heir, only one sickly daughter after another. At this rate, you will not even be entitled to burial among the mothers of kings."

Whatever his rights in the matter, Philip's expression of them was a far greater mistake than anything Isabel had said. She was still the true child of the great Béarnais—engaging, gallant and debonair, under normal circumstances. But she could no more be browbeaten or insulted with impunity than could her father have been. Philip, who had thought to put her in her place, found that his idea of this and hers were by no means the same.

"I can think of nothing more horrible than the prospect of entombment in that grim mausoleum your grandfather built," she said furiously. "I shall rejoice in the thought of escaping it and, as far as I am concerned, you are only my husband, for you are not much of a king or much of a man, either," she jeered. "You cannot rule Spain—you have to let Olivares do that. Neither can you beget a son. You have squandered your virility. Go and make futile love to Francisca de Tavara. And pray that Villamediana does not rise from his grave to lie between you."

Chapter 4

INEVITABLY, reconciliation was only a matter of time, a short time at that. The Queen was too fond of amusement to shut herself up in the gloomy palace, foregoing her accustomed round of bullfights, comedies, equestrian shows and pseudo-religious celebrations; and she could not attend these except in the King's company and as his consort. Philip enjoyed all such festivities as much as she did. Moreover, if he had appeared without her, there would have been fresh pretext for malicious gossip. Although, to use his own words, "he had sought consolation elsewhere," immediately after the disgraceful scene in which they had both behaved so badly, he had the good sense not to desert her bed for long and, on his return, to make more tender love to her than he had in a long while. He had not ventured to come sooner, he told her, when she turned her back on him and said she wondered how Olivares could spare him, because he knew he had offended her and he was afraid she would repulse him; that would be more than he could bear. Since her shoulder was all he could reach, he caressed this gently and presently murmured that he realized perfectly he had done wrong to remind her that all their children so far had been girls; he knew this was not her fault. But he begged her to believe it was not his, either; he was sure the next time they would have a boy. And, to make certain that time was not too far distant, after all, they both had the welfare of Spain at heart, did they not?

It was seldom that Philip spoke jestingly, especially about a serious matter, and Isabel loved a jest. Of course they must not disappoint Spain, she said laughingly, as she shifted her position to one more accessible and threw her arms around his neck. The rest was easy. The next day they appeared together at an unusually brilliant gathering, both in high spirits; and nine months later Isabel had another baby, unfortunately still another short-lived girl. But, meanwhile, there had been no more stormy scenes and no more reproaches on either side, when the arrival of two unexpected visitors eclipsed all other sources of excitement.

At first glance, there was certainly nothing world-shaking about the two disheveled young Englishmen, who gave their names as John and Thomas Smith and presented themselves at the so-called "House of Seven Chimneys," which was the residence of the English Ambassador to Spain, the Earl of Bristol, and demanded an audience with His Excellency. The guard at the wicket, after one swift glance at the unprepossessing strangers, very naturally replied that the Ambassador was extremely busy and that he could not receive them. They were insistent: they had been entrusted with a very important letter from their distinguished companion, Sir Francis Cottingham, who had been accidentally delayed on their long journey from England when they had nearly reached their destination; it was imperative that this letter should be delivered at once. At last the guard consented to admit one of the travelers, who shouldered the small valise which was the only piece of baggage the two had between them, and left his companion in the street to look after their horses, while he followed the guard into the house. As soon as he reached the Ambassador's study, he threw off his travel-stained cloak and hat and Bristol, to his amazement and consternation, recognized George Villiers, Duke of Buckingham, the daring favorite of King James. The next moment, his consternation mounted to terror at the announcement that Buckingham's young companion, who had been left holding the horses, was Charles, Prince of Wales.

In a state bordering on stupefaction, Bristol went hurriedly for Charles, who seated himself calmly after a brief exchange of greetings, and asked for pen and paper, so that he might get off a letter to his father by the first post, reporting his safe arrival in Madrid with "Steenie." They had outdistanced Sir Francis Cottingham, their official escort, and Steenie's secretary, Endymion Porter, the traveling companions with whom they had started out, he added casually, and had been only sixteen days en route from England. While this letter writing was going on, Buckingham stood non-chalantly by, enjoying the Ambassador's obvious discomfiture. For years, Bristol had been maneuvering to arrange a marriage between the Prince of Wales and Philip's younger sister, the Infanta María, and all his strategy had come to nothing. He had not guessed that the Count of Gondomar, the Spanish Ambassador to England, was also secretly maneuvering with the same end in view, and that Buckingham, who foresaw great personal advantage in furthering such a match, was aiding and abetting him. Acting on the advice of Gondomar, Buckingham had previously sent his half-Spanish secretary, Porter, who had formerly been a page of Olivares, alone to Spain with confidential orders to promise certain concessions, the lack of which had been an impediment to a mixed marriage, and to hint that the Prince might come to Spain as a suitor. As corresponding concessions were asked in return, Porter's mission had been un-successful; but a private message from Gondomar to Buckingham suggested that, if the Prince would only act on the "hint," so boldly and suddenly that his arrival would take everyone by surprise, the results might be altogether different. Buckingham lost no time in following the course indicated by Gondomar; and here he was, in poor Bristol's study, with the Prince in tow, ready for action!

By the time Charles had finished writing to his "Dear Dad and Gossip," as he always began his letters to his father, Bristol and Buckingham had agreed that they must send for Gondomar, who —somewhat to Bristol's puzzlement—had opportunely returned to Spain, and ask him to take the news of Charles' arrival to Olivares; a suitable plan for the royal visitor's reception and entertainment must immediately be worked out. Without troubling to send ad-vance notice of his visit, the Spanish Ambassador to England burst in on the Conde-Duque. The latter's labors for the day and his eve-ning conferences with the King were over and, with a sense of work well done, he was enjoying a quiet supper in his pleasant quarters, which were situated in a sheltered wing of the Alcázar overlooking an immense patio. Ordinarily, he would have been annoyed at such an intrusion on his privacy, but his mood was exceptionally genial, even though it did not match Gondomar's in exuberance; and, after inquiring agreeably to what he owed the honor of the visit, at such a late hour, he added jovially, "You look as merry as if you had the King of England himself in Madrid."

"Well, not quite that, but the next best thing—the Prince of Wales!" boomed Gondomar.

With his usual subtlety, Olivares managed to give the impression that he felt not only tremendously honored, but tremendously pleased to learn of the Prince's visit. As a matter of fact, he was aghast and, as soon as he could courteously rid himself of his unwelcome guest, he hurried to the King. He had just succeeded in reviving a moribund Board, known as the *Junta de Reformación,* and spurring it to action; a long series of ordinances had been passed, including strict sumptuary laws, designed to improve public economy and private morals; now all the savings he had visualized, all the sobriety he was advocating, would have to be sacrificed to provide for prolonged and lavish entertainment, on a scale immeasurably more extravagant and unprincipled than any that had previously taken place. And that was not the worst of it; any unavoidable accident to the Prince, even any imagined slight, might well be used as a pretext for war, for relations with England were in a precarious state. Somehow the Prince of Wales must be given the false impression that his suit for the hand of the Infanta was prospering. For the first time, instead of adroitly extracting submission from the King for a plan already made, Olivares not only wanted but needed co-operation in forming one.

Philip, like everyone else except Gondomar, was taken completely by surprise. But, to Olivares' relief, he also immediately grasped the gravity of the situation. For several hours, they conferred as to the best way of meeting a grave emergency; then Olivares left to put the wheels in motion and Philip belatedly withdrew to Isabel's apartment. He had lost all track of time, and it was not until he saw that she was kneeling at her prie-dieu in her dressing gown, already prepared for bed, that he realized it must be very late and that she would probably greet him with reproaches for his tardiness and complain that, at this rate, she would soon not see him at all, that Olivares was monopolizing his nights as well as his days. Instead, to his enormous relief, she rose from her knees and came toward him with outstretched arms.

"I've been terribly worried," she said fondly. "You've never been as late as this before. I was afraid something dreadful had happened."

"Something dreadful *has* happened. The Prince of Wales has come surreptitiously to Madrid, accompanied by that archfiend, the Duke of Buckingham. They arrived, looking like a couple of ragamuffins, at the British Embassy this evening and, somehow, forced their way into Bristol's presence. To do him justice, I believe he's almost as upset as I am, though of course he's been trying for years to engineer a marriage between my sister and his prince. But he's an honorable man; he wouldn't stoop to the measures our own traitorous envoy and Buckingham have adopted."

"You mean these insular wretches think they can force your hand by surprising you this way?"

"Yes, that's exactly what they think. Of course, they couldn't be more mistaken. They've not only shown very poor taste; they've shown very poor judgment. I won't let them force my hand, but it isn't clear to me yet how I'm going to prevent it. Somehow, we've got to play up to them. Olivares and I have been trying for hours to figure out how to do it. That's why I'm so late. We've not only got to observe all the amenities and save their pride; we've got to give them the impression that they're more than welcome; that we're very much honored to have them here. And all the time we'll be hating them and fearing them."

He sank down in a chair, the image of harassment and discouragement. Isabel went over to the table where a bowl of fruit and a decanter of wine stood in readiness, should they be desired during the night, and filled a goblet with Valdemoro. When she brought it to him, Philip looked up and shook his head, but she pretended not to notice.

"You're exhausted," she said gently, "and this will make you feel better. Do drink it—just to please me!" She waited beside him, showing no sign of impatience and, after a few moments, he took the cup from her and began to drink very slowly, a sip at a time.

When he had finished, he bowed his head again and she retrieved the cup and set it back on the table. Then she drew up a chair and sat down beside him, taking his hands in hers.

"Do you suppose there is anything I could do to help?" she asked.

He raised his tired eyes to look at her in astonishment. Such an idea had never occurred to him and, now that it was presented to him, it gave him no solace.

"What could you possibly do to help?" he asked incredulously.

"Why, I don't know, but it seems as if I ought to be able to do something. But I need to understand the situation better than I do. I understand why you hate these people, who have intruded themselves upon us, but I don't understand why you fear them."

"Because they may force us into war."

"How, if we don't want to go to war?"

He sighed. He was, indeed, exhausted and the last thing on earth he wanted to do just then was to attempt an explanation of conditions so complicated that it would be next to impossible to make Isabel understand them. But, after all, she had not only failed to reproach him because he had kept her waiting so long, without even sending her any kind of a message, she had tried her best to cheer and comfort him. He owed her at least some kind of an answer.

"The reason might be that England and Spain both want the Palatinate," he said slowly, as if he were trying to find the simplest explanation.

"The Palatinate? That Bavarian province?"

"Yes."

"Is that so terribly important to Spain?"

"Yes, for several reasons. One is as a thoroughfare. We need to have free access to every part of our heritage, so that Spanish Hapsburgs and Austrian Hapsburgs may be able to get together and work together for political unity. But, in 1618, there was a revolt in the Valtelline—the Valley of the Adda, north of Lake Como, which is inhabited by Catholics, but misruled by Protestant Grisons, the easternmost canton of Switzerland, to which it has belonged since 1512. This provided a pretext for the Duke of Feria—the Governor of Milan—to establish Spanish garrisons in the valley, which links Milan to Austria. Then, the same year, there was a revolt in Bohemia and that enabled General Spínola to occupy the Palatinate and secure control of the Rhine passages. These two successful strokes on the part of our commanders have made it possible for us to consolidate our vital 'Spanish road' and send men and supplies all the way from Milan, via Austria, to Flanders."

"I see," said Isabel, nodding her head.

"Another very important reason is that the Palatinate is an electorate of our Holy Roman Empire and its reigning prince has a right to vote on the succession. We Hapsburgs need that vote. If James could get the Palatinate back for his son-in-law Frederick, *he* could control it with the help of France."

"I see," said Isabel again, pressing his hand.

"And that shifty fool, James, actually has the effrontery to suggest that, because of certain concessions which he claims, quite without foundation, England is prepared to make, Spain will hand over the Palatinate!"

"What sort of concessions?"

"A compromise about religion." To his immense surprise, Philip was beginning to feel a certain amount of release and comfort in talking to her. "Privately, both he and his sons have Catholic leanings, but they do not dare to proclaim themselves publicly, nor can they force the English Parliament to reverse the policy of half a century, merely to placate a foreign power. But they are graciously willing to overlook the fact that my sister is a Catholic, on the assumption that, somehow, an amicable adjustment will be made between bride and groom. *Overlook!* The very keystone of her spiritual life and both the spiritual and political life of our empire! I promised my father when he was on his deathbed that María should never marry a heretic, that she should be given to the Emperor's heir. I not only promised, I swore to keep that promise. And this very night, I have taken the same oath in the presence of Olivares! I shall keep it, at all costs!"

Philip had risen from his chair and begun to pace restlessly up and down the room, as he spoke with a vehemence completely alien to his usual calmness. Isabel had never seen him so excited and so distraught. She also rose and, halting him, linked her arm in his.

"Of course, you will keep your oath," she said, speaking even more soothingly than before. "I will send for María the first thing in the morning and tell her that she need have no fear of being forced into a marriage that I am sure would be as unwelcome to her, in a religious sense, as it is to you, even if she does not understand all the political reasons that would make it perilous, any more than I did. Perhaps it would be better if you discussed these matters with us more. I will also caution María that she must keep up appearances, whatever happens. I feel sure she will listen to me. You know we are very close to each other."

"Yes—yes, I do know that," Philip answered, looking more attentively at his wife. "It is true that you might be of some help with María. Tomorrow will be given over to official calls: in the course of a morning ride, Olivares and Buckingham will meet 'quite by chance' and exchange compliments; then Olivares will lead Buckingham 'secretly' into my presence and more compliments will be exchanged; next Olivares will go to salute the Prince at the 'House of Seven Chimneys' in my name and that will bring the courtesies of the day to an end. Meanwhile, since you will not have to appear in public anywhere, you would have plenty of time to talk to María and prepare her for her part in the program. Day after tomorrow, a cavalcade will take place in honor of the visitors and she will have to ride in the royal coach with Carlos and Fernando, as well as myself, to give the impression that all three of her brothers are supporting her. You will accompany us, too, of course," he added, almost as an afterthought. "Some time in the course of the ride, again presumably quite by chance, our coach will pass the one in which Charles and Buckingham are riding with Bristol, going in the opposite direction. María must wear a blue ribbon around her arm, so that Charles may not be in the least doubt which is she. Probably the two coaches will pass each other several times before the cavalcade comes to an end at the Prado and María must sit close to the window all the time. But nothing will be required of her tomorrow. Yes, tell her that. It will reassure her. And afterward we will decide what to do next."

He had used the word "we" quite unconsciously. If he had been asked to define exactly whom he meant, he would have said no one in particular, it was a natural form of speech, that was all. But Isabel chose to interpret it differently.

"Of course, we will," she said fondly. "Between us, I am sure you and I can manage beautifully. But now, don't you think it would be a good plan if we tried to get some sleep? We will be able to plan much better when we are rested."

Chapter 5

WHEN Isabel sent for María the following day, she found the poor girl already in a state bordering on hysteria. News of the travelers' arrival and of their identity and their purpose had spread like wildfire through the city; and, early in the morning, the Infanta's confessor had come to her with terrible warnings about the consequences of marriage with the Prince of Wales. He had painted such a lurid picture of what it would mean to lie by a heretic's side and to bear heretic children that she was convinced hell itself would be preferable to such a fate; and she had forthwith sent her lady-in-waiting, Doña Margarita de Tavara, to Olivares with a message to the effect that she would immediately seek refuge in the Convent of the *Descalzas Reales*, preparatory to taking the veil, if the proposed negotiations should result in a marriage contract. When the message was delivered, the Conde-Duque was already involved in a conference of great importance with the King's Dominican confessor, Antonio de Sotomayor, and the entire Council of State—of which Gondomar had that morning been made a member—as to the most effective means of making the Prince's visit, for which public prayers would promptly be offered, "a great and very signal service to the Church." Understandably, Olivares had neither the time nor the inclination to pay much attention to anything outside the Council Chamber. But at the time of María's arrival, Isabel appeared to be completely at leisure. She was informally dressed in a lounging robe of richly embroidered silk and seated at ease on a velvet cushion, as she sipped chocolate, which she invited her visitor to share. It was unusually good this morning, so thick she could hardly stir it and the cinnamon flavor was perfect. She listened patiently and attentively while María poured out her heart and, when the latter collapsed in a flood of tears, the Queen efficiently mopped these up with a fresh handkerchief and spoke with equal practicality.

"I'm sorry you didn't come straight to me, dear, instead of bothering the Conde-Duque when he's so busy, especially as you haven't the slightest reason to worry about what he's going to do. He isn't in favor of this betrothal—that is, not the way things stand. Neither is your brother. They are both faithful sons of the Church. Of course, if Charles should be converted, that would be quite a different matter."

"But there isn't any chance of that, is there?"

"Why not? My father, who was a very great king, was a convert to Catholicism. He said that Paris was well worth a Mass—which, of course, was just a figure of speech. Charles might say, 'María is well worth a Mass,' meaning, because of his love for you, he might decide to take instructions in the Faith; and very probably, when he had done that, he could easily be persuaded to renounce the error of his ways. This, in turn, might lead to many other conversions and more kindly treatment of the English who are already Catholics. I am told there are a great many of them, that it is a mistake to suppose everyone in the insular kingdom is a heretic. But, apparently, the heretics are in power and have treated their Catholic subjects very badly. If a Catholic were in power again, all that would be changed and you would have been an instrument of great good."

María, whose sobs had ceased by this time and whose tears were rapidly drying, blew her nose and returned Isabel's fine, lace-bordered handkerchief.

"I have one of my own," she said, producing this from her sleeve. "But I was so upset I forgot about it. It isn't very pretty, anyway."

"It might still be useful," suggested Isabel. "But never mind—I'll see that some prettier ones are ordered for you. And not just handkerchiefs. You'll need a great many new clothes for all the fiestas that are being planned in honor of the Prince. There's no reason why you shouldn't have anything you want. I've already heard the new decrees prohibiting lavish embroidery and gold tissue and so on have been suspended for the period of Charles' visit. We'd better take advantage of this suspension promptly, before the Conde-Duque restricts us again. Suppose we make a list, before you go back to your rooms, of what you'd like to have. But first, let's talk about tomorrow afternoon. The cavalcade has been planned on purpose to give the Prince a chance to see you, apparently by accident, while you are out taking the air with your family. I understand he's very attractive and he's already expressed his desire, in the presence of the Conde-Duque and the Duke of Buckingham, to reveal himself as your suitor; and though, of course, he must do that gradually, with due regard to propriety, his first impressions of you may have a lasting and important effect. So you must look your very best tomorrow and behave like an Infanta of Spain. In that way, you will put him in his proper place as the heir to an unimportant throne, who is very much flattered that you should condescend to receive him. At the same time, you must make him aware how greatly blessed he would be if he could call such a lovely girl his own, under whatever conditions."

By the time the sisters-in-law parted for the day, María had very successfully dismissed from her mind the horrible prospect of going to bed with a heretic and begun to visualize herself as the chosen instrument for the happy conversion of the English prince, who was her suitor and who must be impressed and fascinated by her importance and elegance before she could begin her good work. Isabel was careful to see that nothing impaired this vision before the following afternoon. Ensconced in the door-seat of the King's great gilded coach, drawn by six mules, María was the very pattern of coy and blushing maidenhood, best calculated to awaken ardor, tempered by respect. Her golden hair was becomingly arranged and uncovered except for a knot of roses which confined her curls; her pink and white complexion was unobscured by cosmetics; her rose-colored dress, cut in the latest fashion without a ruff, was modified in its severity and made in such a way as to do full justice to her budding figure; her bearing was at one and the same time modest and self-possessed. She held herself erect and, every now and then, she raised her eyes which were, for the most part, discreetly downcast, so that she might have a brief glimpse of a coach passing in the opposite direction; but she veiled her glance hastily, with fluttering lids, if she had reason to believe it had been observed.

The results of this beguiling appearance and behavior were more than satisfactory to all concerned, including María herself. After the cavalcade, she spent the evening in conversation with Doña Margarita de Tavara, chattering complacently, not only about the cavalcade which had just taken place, but about the public entry of the Prince into Madrid which, she understood, was to take place a week later. (A long time to wait!) The cavalcade, while showy, was of course quite unofficial, even though the Nuncio, the Spanish and English Ambassadors and all the grandees and Court ladies had taken part in it, and the streets had been filled with soldiery, guards and common people. But on Sunday, the 16th of April, the Count of Gondomar was to give a great banquet and, afterward, all the Council Members would ride out in state, accompanied by full escort, to pay their respects to the Prince. María further understood that he would receive hundreds of important persons while standing under a canopy of silver tissue in the throne room of the Royal Monastery of San Jerónimo; and that later there would be another great parade, with pipes and drums heralding the coming to the monastery of the Spanish and Austrian guards, with dignitaries of every degree following in pairs. The prospect of such a sight was, indeed, exciting, María concluded with a contented sigh.

Isabel, meanwhile, spent the evening alone, with a distinct sense of achievement and happy anticipation of Philip's return, but without anxiety because of his prolonged absence. After congratulating her, in a quiet aside, at the close of the cavalcade, on the success of her strategy with María, he had added that he was to meet the Prince for a private interview; he would come and tell her about it afterward, but he might be very late. When he entered her apartments, he had hardly closed the door behind him when he took her in his arms, kissing her fondly and, as he raised his head, she saw that he was smiling.

"This time, I was the one to take others by surprise," he told her. "It had been agreed that I was to meet Olivares and Buckingham in the garden back of the palace, to arrange the details of the interview; and when the coach drove up to the appointed place, I was already there. I walked forward with my cloak masking my face. I have gathered that these people seem to like concealed identities. As the door of the coach opened, I heard the Conde-Duque say to Buckingham, 'There comes the King.' After all he had heard about the formality of our customs, Buckingham could hardly believe either his eyes or his ears. He leaped down and kissed my hand and then we all rode away together to meet the Prince, who was waiting for us in another coach at the Prado, with Gondomar and Bristol. The Prince and I both alighted and embraced warmly and, afterward, we talked together for more than half an hour."

"About affairs of state?"

"Of course not. Just amiable banalities. The affairs of state can come later—the later the better. It is obvious that Charles' first impressions of María were very favorable. Naturally, he spoke of them only guardedly and respectfully, but he told me he had already written his father how pleased he was with his reception—apparently, he is quite a letter writer. If you had not coached María to play her part so well, we would not have got off to the smooth beginning, which will mean smoother progress—in the right direction. Charles has requested the honor of another interview, so that we may go on from where we left off tonight—that is, with compliments. And I shall arrange one or two hunting parties for the next week—Carlos and Fernando will join me at the *Casa de Campo* and act as joint hosts. In that way, the days will pass pleasantly and noncommittally until the public entry of the Prince, planned for next Sunday. Time is our ally and James' enemy. The English understand and accept the absolute necessity of a dispensation from Rome and we can stress the fact, without giving offense, that often it takes quite a while to secure this. Letters have duly gone forward to Cardinal Ludovico, nephew to His Holiness, but he will not submit them to his uncle until he thinks best. Meanwhile, James is in a hurry to get the Palatinate and the money he would get from María's dowry—he is always short of funds. If he becomes impatient and therefore irritated, it may be that he himself will be the one to call off negotiations."

"But would that be an advantage to us? It might hurt his pride."

"He can't have much pride or he wouldn't have let the heir to his throne and his Lord High Admiral come straggling into a foreign capital alone at night."

"No, I suppose not. But then, he had tried more dignified means of furthering an alliance which he wants very much, through his ambassador and ours, and that had failed. So he decided to try a kind of coup d'état. Those do succeed sometimes—at least, I've heard so. On the other hand, if they don't, the people who have tried to engineer them are apt to be aggrieved, aren't they? And perhaps try to hurt the people they wanted for friends and allies in the first place? Isn't there any danger that England might do something of that sort?"

"You talk as if England were an important power—as if it might hurt Spain if she took umbrage."

"And it couldn't—not if she had help from another important power?"

"That isn't even a probability. France would be the power to which she'd naturally turn, if she were looking for help, and we've got a double safeguard there. The King of France is your brother and the Queen of France is my sister."

"Yes, but my brother would always do what he thought best for France. And you've told me yourself that your sister has felt and acted like a Frenchwoman ever since she was married—just as I've felt and acted like a Spaniard. I believe she'd do just what I'd do in her place—put her adopted country first. Is it all my imagination that France might have an interest in the Palatinate, too?"

Philip looked at his wife with surprise, but he hesitated before he answered. "Now you speak of it, perhaps they might," he said slowly. "Or, rather, the new minister, Cardinal Richelieu, might. I wouldn't put it past him to favor a Protestant Elector in the Palatinate."

"A Cardinal of the Church?"

Philip shrugged his shoulders. "The Church in France and the Church in Spain don't operate in the same way. If they did, your father never would have become King. Richelieu would do anything he could to spite the Hapsburg coalition. Besides, he is all in favor of keeping on the right side of the Huguenots, who are becoming as powerful in France as the Lutherans in Germany—politically. So a return of the Palatinate to the Protestant fold might just possibly be a point on which France and England would have an interest in common. But, if it were a point likely to do us any real harm, the Conde-Duque would certainly have taken that into consideration in his attitude toward the English marriage."

Philip was afraid that this last statement might bring about an argument and he had no desire to argue. So far, he had greatly enjoyed his long intimate talk with his wife, as he had the one the night before; it was a new and pleasant experience to discuss his problems with her at the end of an exhausting day and to make fresh discoveries regarding her intelligent interest in them. But he was very tired and he knew it would be impossible to convince Isabel that an accomplished statesman like Olivares never made mistakes in policy, much as she would like to have believed this. To his great relief, after appearing to ponder his theories quietly for a few minutes, she changed the subject to one he was much more willing to talk about.

"Have you been able to form any kind of an estimate as to the general feeling about the marriage?"

"Of course, the Nuncio is raising all sorts of objections and the grandees disapprove of the Prince's informal approach to it. But Olivares and I both believe the people are very much pleased with the Prince's visit. The most hopeful—or perhaps I should say the most credulous—already visualize Charles' conversion and the return of England to the Church, and the Conde-Duque is busily presenting this as a possibility to the public, just as you so ably presented it as a possibility to María. And, I believe, quite as sincerely."

His smile had become slightly satirical. Isabel calmly disregarded the imputation.

"What about the people who are not so hopeful or so credulous?" she inquired lightly.

"Oh, they are so pleased with the suspension of regulations about extravagant tissues and the prospect of all the fiestas which have been planned that they are not giving thought to anything else!"

Isabel smoothed her dress. "I am having the same difficulty myself," she said. "As a matter of fact, I've spent a large part of the day trying on new clothes. Incidentally, I took the responsibility of sending Charles a little present."

"A present! What kind of a present?"

"A supply of fine linen, for both personal and table use," she said demurely, "also a dressing gown, very elaborately embroidered, and several scented coffers, fitted with golden keys and filled with toilet requisites." Then, as Philip gave a half-suppressed exclamation of mingled annoyance and amusement, she added, still more demurely, "I cannot imagine that a fashionable young man like the Prince of Wales enjoyed traveling for over two weeks with no more equipment than could be carried in one small valise, which he shared with the Duke of Buckingham. I think you will find he is very much pleased with my gift."

Chapter 6

ISABEL lost no time in exhibiting her new finery. The first entertainment planned for the Prince after the ceremonial of his public entry to Madrid was a royal bullfight, magnificently staged by the municipality in the Plaza Mayor, which was admirably suited for such spectacles; and she appeared in the royal box wearing brown silk embroidered with gold and covered with gems. At the masked ball given by the Admiral of Castile on Easter Sunday, she first wore white satin, adorned with precious stones, and changed to a dress of black and gold when it was time for Charles to lead her formally into the ballroom. And on these and all other state occasions, she kept María, attired with equal elegance, at her side.

During Holy Week, there had been fewer opportunities for Isabel to cut a dazzling figure and to see that María did the same, because there had been a slight curtailment of sumptuous display in the form of special secular parades and spectacles and more stress had been laid on the customary elaborate religious observances, none of which, contrary to some expectations, had proved distasteful to Charles. After all, his father had often privately confessed to Catholic leanings, and he himself had no strong religious convictions of any kind and was already very much attracted to María and more than willing to do his share toward removing any obstacles which might prevent their union. He listened respectfully and willingly when the Conde-Duque turned the subject to the Faith, which was at every possible opportunity. Buckingham was less amenable to listening, but then he was less amenable about everything; whereas Charles, who was uniformly gracious and gallant, was making a favorable impression everywhere, Buckingham, who was frequently insolent and presumptuous, was making an equally unfavorable one; while the numerous English courtiers, who were fast arriving, now that all pretense of anonymity on the part of the Prince had been discarded, were considered noisy and disorderly by the grave and polite Spaniards. The first reaction to the English visitors, as Philip had told Isabel, had been one of hope and enthusiasm; it was soon evident that a real effort might be required to keep it up to that level.

On Easter Sunday, the Admiral's masked ball marked a resumption of galas and the beginning of the Prince's personal visits to the royal family. The day provided a logical occasion for him to pay the King and Queen the compliments of the season, by wishing them a joyous Easter. He was conducted first to the King's apartments and thence, accompanied by a suite of grandees, to the Queen's, where she and the Infanta, attended by all the Court ladies, received him. The entire company remained standing, with great formality, except for the royal pair, the Infanta and their guest, who were seated in a row, with the Queen and the Infanta in the two middle chairs, the Prince on the right hand of the Queen and the King on the extreme left of them all. Such an arrangement was hardly calculated to facilitate conversation; but the Prince managed to address the suitable felicitations to the Queen and to add the proper remarks of appreciation for the hospitality he had received. Then he asked for permission to rise and speak directly to the Infanta who, in her turn, rose to receive him. This was the first time they had actually spoken together and, considering the number and distinction of the onlookers, most of whom were within earshot, it was extremely important that nothing they said or did should be judged unworthy of them. The obstacle of unfamiliar languages, which the capable Bristol could only partially overcome, was another handicap, but Charles, with his impeccable urbanity, surmounted it in triumph. He made a graceful little speech, to the effect that he could not be thankful enough that the firm friendship between the Infanta's brother, His Catholic Majesty of Spain, and his father, the King of England, had made his visit to her country possible; and now that he was privileged to meet her, on such a glad occasion, he begged leave to kiss her hand and tell her that he was completely at her service for whatever she might honor him by asking of him. María extended her slim white fingers and murmured softly that she highly esteemed all he had said to her. Neither Charles nor anyone else who heard her felt that the brevity of her response and the low voice in which she spoke were inadequate to the occasion; she had not faltered, she had not said the wrong thing and her manner had been one of composure and dignity; Isabel had reason to feel proud of her pupil. Charles next ventured on a more personal remark: he had been sorry to hear that the Infanta had not felt very well during Lent; he hoped that Easter Day might mark her complete recovery. Speaking with more assurance than she had the first time, María thanked him for his solicitude, said that she was now indeed well again and that she was at his service quite as much as he could be at hers. After bowing to each other, they resumed their respective seats and, when Charles had exchanged a few more compliments with the Queen, the audience came to an end.

Several similar visits were wedged in between the series of bullfights, tourneys and excursions, and Charles also attended the weekly theatricals at the palace, which seemed to him slightly less forbidding than the formal audiences. To be sure, the royal family and their princely guest were the only spectators provided with chairs; but the plays were light, amusing and well acted and the Court ladies, instead of standing stiffly behind them, as the grandees were required to do, were seated on cushions scattered over the floor and not only presented a charming picture in themselves, but gave at least an illusion of more general ease. This arrangement seemed to promise an opportunity for getting in a few words edgewise with the Infanta sooner or later. However, Charles' hopes of this were defeated and he was obliged to listen to bitter complaints from members of his entourage, who were already beginning to refer to María as the Princess of Wales and to feel they were entitled to closer acquaintance with her. Rumors had reached them that England had agreed to every condition imposed by Spain, that King James had ordered the fleet to stand at readiness to convey the bridal pair to England and that the dispensation was actually on its way from

Rome. On the strength of these rumors, the Earl of Carlisle, designated by certain Spaniards as "one of the insolent crew" who had followed after the Prince, felt especially affronted when, "after much importunity," he was "brought into a room where the Infanta was placed on a throne, gloriously set forth with her ladies about her . . . she remaining all the while as immovable as the image of the Virgin Mary."

This description of the audience, sent in a letter to England, was duly shown to Charles, who did his best to soothe the injured feelings of his retainers by explaining the vast difference between Court etiquette in England and in Spain; but he himself was beginning to feel slightly irked. He had done his best, as a prince, to conform to customs which were alien to him and, as a suitor, to be patient and respectful; but there was a limit to everything. The dispensation had, indeed, finally arrived, qualified with many conditions which Buckingham claimed could be overcome without difficulty; but Olivares had insisted that it required additional study and had appointed a commission to go into the matter further. When these studies threatened to be indefinitely prolonged, Charles, prompted by Buckingham, wrote to his father asking for a blind pledge to support whatever concessions he, Charles, should make and received a reply which, as far as he could see, must remove the last Spanish objection; for James had immediately responded: "We do hereby promise by the word of a king that whatever you, our son, shall promise in our name we will punctually perform."

Provided with this unlimited guarantee, the Prince, with Buckingham and Bristol, hopefully met with the Olivares commission and still the sessions dragged on and on. Could the English prince and his associates also promise that the English Parliament would be as co-operative as the King, that religious tolerance should be decreed forthwith? Alas, they could not! Charles decided that all this had gone far enough, that it was time for another bold stroke, which would have nothing to do with theology. Despite all the obstacles to his courtship, he had reason to believe that María was as much in love with him as he was with her and, having learned that she often went to spend her mornings "a-Maying" at the *Casa de*

Campo, one of the royal pleasure seats on the Manzanares River, where he had several times been invited to hunt, he decided to pay her a surprise visit.

He did this with the same lighthearted disregard of its possible consequences that had marked his anonymous arrival in Madrid. No impediment was placed to his entrance to the park, as the guard at the gate recognized him and saluted respectfully; and, without being stopped, he skirted the small menagerie where lions, tigers and a few other wild animals were kept and the large pond encircled by tall trees. It was still quite early and no one seemed to be abroad except the animal keeper and two or three gardeners. When he reached the perron, there was a slight delay before a *mayordomo* appeared at the door, so it was obvious that no visitor had been expected at such an hour. Quite unabashed, Charles turned over his horse to the groom who had been hastily summoned and, with well-feigned surprise, asked if the Infante Carlos had not yet arrived.

"No, Your Highness. But he will surely be doing so at any moment, if he were to meet Your Highness here. Would Your Highness care to partake of some refreshment while he waits?"

"A cup of chocolate would be very welcome."

The *mayordomo* bowed and withdrew. As soon as he was out of sight, Charles took a hasty look around and assured himself that the drawing rooms were empty. He then stepped out into the walled garden, which was also empty. At the rear of this was an orchard, where Charles had been on previous visits and which he decided to try next, as it seemed to be the only place left where he might be likely to find his ladylove. He tried the gate and, finding it locked, did not hesitate an instant. He scaled the wall, balanced himself briefly on top of it and dropped down on the other side. When he landed, somewhat unsteadily, he instinctively and quite blindly put out his hand to seek support until he could gain a firmer footing. It was, of course, a heaven-sent coincidence that the Infanta was standing so near the wall that it was her shoulder he touched. He drew her closer and enfolded her in a fond embrace.

If she struggled at all, it was so slightly that he was not conscious of it; she seemed to fit so naturally into his arms that he felt she must have known she belonged there. But she gasped with surprise and the gasp became a little cry, not of fright or pain, but of rapture. Soft though it was, it could still be overheard by anyone near at hand and the Infanta was never left alone; but, fortunately, the only person very close at the moment was the Queen. Doña Margarita and two other ladies-in-waiting had strolled further into the orchard and were partially obscured by trees. Isabel did not lose a second. She stepped quickly to the gate, unlocked it and spoke in an imperious whisper, giving Charles a slight push as she did so.

"Get back into the garden and wander around there," she ordered. "You must go on pretending that you are waiting for Carlos or Fernando, which is what you must have done in the first place to be admitted. I'll talk to you about this later. Just now, there isn't time."

Fortunately, an excursion to Aranjuez really had been planned for that same day. Tongue in cheek, Charles apologized to the King and his brothers for the stupid mistake he had made. Oh yes, he had been most courteously received by the *mayordomo,* who had given him chocolate; and he had taken the liberty of strolling around for a while and visiting the menagerie after he realized that he had not kept his engagements straight. Perhaps a wish had been father to a thought; he enjoyed the *Casa de Campo* so much that he was always glad to go back there. Not that he didn't enjoy Aranjuez, too, and the menagerie here was even more remarkable. Camels that they could use for beasts of burden, instead of mules! Ostriches of all sizes! Even an elephant by way of contrast! No, indeed, he wouldn't allow his kind hosts to rob themselves; he must learn to be silent about the things he admired. Well, if they insisted—the elephant and one ostrich and not more than five camels. They would cause great excitement when they arrived in London.

The outing was alfresco in character, the kind Isabel had always most enjoyed, and she contrived, without any great difficulty, to draw Charles aside on the pretext of showing him her favorite fountain, which had not been playing the last time they came to Aranjuez, and which was really something to see—a marble Cupid whose quiver released jets of water like arrows, surmounting a basin encircled by the Three Graces. She chose a moment when the attention of practically all the other guests was riveted on a marble "Mount Parnassus," in the center of a small lake, which was a much more elaborate structure; and, when she was sure they would not be overheard, the haste with which she spoke in no way impaired its effectiveness.

"You must have completely lost your senses," she told him scathingly, without bothering to use formal terms of address. "I take it you did not really want to risk the responsibility for a murder; but if it were so much as suspected that you had been able to reach the Infanta when she was alone, the *mayordomo* who admitted you would already be as good as dead. Even her ladies-in-waiting would not be safe, if suspicion rested on them—at best, they would be dismissed from Court and sent to convents or remote country seats and, at worst, they would be skillfully poisoned, in a very unobtrusive but nonetheless fatal fashion. It is certainly fortunate for them that María did not scream, though it is a marvel she did not. You must have bewitched her. It was hard enough to handle the situation before. Now she is persuaded you really are the legendary Prince Charming who awakened the Sleeping Beauty with a kiss and, of course, she is delighted at the idea of playing the latter role herself. She is quite ready to risk her immortal soul by going off to your island realm and sharing your princely problems. The difficulty will be to keep her from saying so to anyone other than myself. She is now in bed and has been given a strong sedative by the physician I summoned when I took her back to the palace—because she had succumbed to a touch of the sun. There is no danger that she will talk today, but how much longer I can keep her quiet remains to be seen. I shall not draw another easy breath as long as the negotiations are hanging fire—indeed, not until you leave for England, taking María with you. As far as I can see, that is the only solution for what has happened this morning."

"Then my surprise visit wasn't such a bad idea after all, was it?" Charles inquired audaciously.

Chapter 7

ISABEL had never kept a secret from her husband and she had never deceived him about anything; now she was doing both. And she had never been sufficiently interested in affairs of state to question whether their management was wise or disastrous. Her dislike for the Conde-Duque had at first been based wholly on her resentment at the lack of delicacy he and his wife showed about intruding on her conjugal life and their generally oppressive and dictatorial attitude; she considered these an abuse of the prerogatives of his position as *Privado* and of the Condesa's as lady-in-waiting. After Philip's accession to the throne, Isabel had more or less successfully put the Countess in her place by saying that, as the daughter and the wife of kings, she did not propose to take orders or accept interference from the daughter of a mere provincial viceroy and the wife of a man who had been obliged to angle for the rank of grandee; and the Conde-Duque's general contempt for feminine intelligence and his opinion that women had only one sphere of usefulness did not become a personal matter to her until she ventured, in his hearing, to hazard a casual opinion on state affairs; he interrupted her with his customary brusque remark that nuns must be kept for praying and women for childbearing. Ever since then, she had hoped in her heart that some day she might find him in error when she had been right about a matter of policy; now she believed that the moment was, perhaps, unexpectedly at hand. Through no initiative of her own, she had been drawn into the network of international intrigue and found her sympathies involved because of her real affection for her sister-in-law. Gradually, she became more and more convinced that her husband's blind confidence in Olivares was misplaced, that the delay in negotiations for the English marriage was fraught with danger and that there would be still greater danger to her adopted country if the final outcome was not a happy one, as far as the young lovers were concerned.

For a week or so after the "bold stroke" which had accomplished nothing in the way of smoothing their course, Isabel managed to keep María in seclusion, on the ground that the touch of sun she had sustained at the *Casa de Campo* was more serious than had at first been realized; a slight, intermittent fever indicated caution. María was a difficult patient, frightened, rebellious and sulky; she brightened only when some small delicacy, such as a cinnamon-flavored posset, presumably beneficial to fevers, arrived from the "House of Seven Chimneys" with the compliments of the English Ambassador, the Earl of Bristol, and solicitous inquiries for her health. Occasionally, a tiny missive or an inconsequential gift was enclosed in the formal note; and Isabel decided that she might safely disregard the origin of these if the messages were destroyed and the keepsakes promptly locked away.

Having conceded this much, further indiscretions were averted for the time being; but Isabel gave thought both to the next move which she might possibly make in María's behalf and to certain aspects of the general situation, which she longed to have further clarified. When Philip told her the people were delighted that the restrictions on luxuries had been suspended, he had not added that perhaps some of them were worried about the present prodigal expenditures for entertainment; when he told her that the Conde-Duque said there was no cause for alarm, because France, as well as England, might have an interest in the Palatinate, that was the end of the matter, as far as he was concerned. Isabel did not feel it wise to make inquiries on these points unless Philip gave her an opening, which he showed no signs of doing. He still came to her apartments every night, expressed his concern about María's health and his appreciation of Isabel's kindness to his sister; voiced his growing antagonism to Buckingham; and dwelt with satisfaction on the latest hunting party or the latest bullfight that had been given in honor of the Prince of Wales. Then he wanted to go to bed, though this did not mean, automatically, that he wanted to go to sleep. Isabel was wise enough not to make the information she craved the price of wifely compliance; but she resolved to find out what she wanted to know from some other source and her choice fell on her brother-in-law Fernando.

She had always been on very good terms with all the members of her husband's family, but, if anything, Fernando was her favorite. As was natural, he looked in from time to time, to help beguile the tedious hours of his sister's fever; and when she dozed off, thanks to the sedative which her physician was still administering, he and Isabel continued to sit near her bedside, chatting companionably in low-pitched voices. On one of these propitious occasions, Isabel surprised him with an unexpected question.

"I have become interested in the subject of cardinals, Fernando. What can you tell me about them?" she asked.

"Why? Do you want to appoint one?"

"Not particularly. After all, I have you handy and you suit me very well. But I do not know whether or not you are typical."

"And I do not know whether or not there is such a thing as a 'typical' cardinal. They come in all sizes, shapes and ages. For instance, Alfonso de Carrillo, the prime advocate of the great Isabel's right to the crown of Castile, was, I have always heard, a huge, hearty man. On the other hand, Jiménez de Cisneros, her confessor, who eventually became Primate of Spain, was a pale, emaciated creature. Incidentally, she maneuvered him into this See when her husband wanted it for his love child, Alfonso of Aragón, whom he had made Archbishop of Zaragoza at the age of six. That makes my appointment at the age of ten seem almost tardy, doesn't it? But then, there's the case of the Duke of Lerma, who didn't take refuge in a cardinalate until it was clear that his days as a *privado* were numbered and by that time he was quite an elderly man."

"Fernando, I'm not in the mood for jesting. . . . Don't cardinals confine themselves to ecclesiastical matters?"

"I'm afraid they don't. In the first place, little boys of six to ten don't know much about ecclesiastical matters and—"

"I told you I wasn't in the mood for jesting."

"And as *I* was about to tell you, when you interrupted me, Carrillo cut a very fine figure on the battlefield."

"But at least cardinals are always good Catholics, aren't they? They wouldn't have any traffic with heretics?"

"What are you driving at, Isabel?"

"Well . . . in the course of conversation the other night, Philip mentioned a French cardinal whose name I've forgotten and said he wouldn't do anything to offend the Huguenots."

"By any chance are you talking about Richelieu?"

"Yes, that's it. Richelieu and the Huguenots. Is this Richelieu very highly placed—a king's brother or love child or something of the sort, like you and Alfonso de Aragón? And, if he has so much power, why doesn't he simply crush the Huguenots and have done with them?"

Fernando smiled. "I'll have to answer your questions one at a time, because they're not very closely related to each other. Richelieu isn't of royal blood or even of illustrious ancestry. Quite the contrary, which makes his rise all the more remarkable. His family hasn't much of a title, so they're generally known by the name of the place they came from, which is just a small village not far from Chinon. His grandfather, a great ruffian, though he was a captain in the French army, was chiefly notorious for his blasphemies, his robberies and his fornications. He was assassinated in Paris by one of his fellow ruffians who, like himself, was in very dubious female company. The eldest son of this swashbuckler, a fairly respectable person, married a certain Françoise de Rochechouart, a girl who represented an alliance with aristocracy, but with a deplorable taste for vengeance. When her husband was murdered by one of his neighbors, she could not rest until her brother-in-law murdered the other murderer. The brother-in-law, a page of Charles IX, then fled to Poland, where he attracted the favorable attention of the Duke of Anjou who, for certain cogent reasons, was then in that country; and, when the Duke returned to France as Henry III, the page returned with him and rose rapidly to the rank of Provost Marshal of the Realm and Knight of the Holy Ghost. He was a loyal and devoted subject and, when your father succeeded to the throne as Henry IV, he was glad to keep such a faithful servant as *his* Provost Marshal. Unfortunately, this admirable character died young, leaving a widow—Suzanne de la Porte—and five children in a state of abject poverty, dependent on the charity of the vengeful Françoise, with whom Suzanne was on very bad terms."

"Fernando, you're a good storyteller, but I'm still not getting the connection among all these murders and exiles and faithful liege men and my brother's new Minister."

"I'm coming to that slowly. I told you I had to answer your questions one at a time and I also told you, previously, that there wasn't any such thing as a 'typical cardinal.' To prove the latter point, I thought I had better tell you something about the background of the one in whom you are interested. He was the youngest son of that poor widow, Suzanne de la Porte, who belonged to a good, middle-class provincial family, but not to the nobility, and who was left to the tender mercies of her aristocratic sister-in-law."

"And what happened next?"

"The little boy spent his childhood in the family chateau at Richelieu which was evidently a grim sort of place at best and which was in a very unsettled region. As you know, France is not immune to religious disturbances and these had had a disastrous effect on the region around Richelieu; it was in a state of upheaval, the scene of banditry, robberies and skirmishes. The chateau, which was strongly fortified, was not actually besieged, but its occupants realized that they would be safer within its walls than outside them. The child had practically no company except his female relatives and led a dreary life. He was delicate and particularly susceptible to intermittent fevers and, since he was ailing a good deal and could not be active physically, he made up for this by precocious mental development. He was remarkably alert and observant and could express himself well. When he was ten years old, one of his uncles sent him to the College of Navarre, in Paris, and he was a prize pupil from the very beginning. There was every indication that he would make his mark as a military man, just as his father had done; instead, he became a bishop."

"What do you mean, he *became* a bishop?"

"I mean that, thanks to the loyal services given to Henry III and continued under your father, the Bishopric of Luçon had become a perquisite of the Richelieu family. Our hero's elder brother had been regarded as the logical recipient of the crook and the mitre in his generation. But, lo and behold! he preferred to be a humble Carthusian. That left an unexpected vacancy and there was nothing humble about Armand Jean du Plessis."

Isabel suddenly leaped from her seat with a gasp of amazement, her dark eyes sparkling. "Fernando, do you mean to tell me that, all this time, you have been talking about the Bishop of Luçon?"

"Why, yes. That is, at one stage of his career, Armand Jean du Plessis—or shall we now go ahead and call him Richelieu?—was Bishop of Luçon—one of the meanest, most desolate sees in all of France. But he had the wisdom, when your father was assassinated, to offer his services immediately to your mother, the Queen Regent, in whatever capacity she would like to use them, instead of waiting to see what your brother, a child of nine, would have to offer later on. Her response was so far favorable that, in little or no time, Richelieu became Almoner, Councilor of State and next, having been named French Ambassador to Spain, he chose to become Secretary of State instead. He has not been without his ups and downs, because there has been so much friction between your brother and your mother, and he has always stood by the latter. At one time, when he followed her into her virtual exile at Blois, it looked as if his sun had set; when he himself was exiled to the papal city of Avignon, it looked as if he would have to face the dark night of the soul. But he has singular powers of recuperation from all his persistent fevers and he came back stronger than ever to rejoin your mother at Angoulême when she resumed the greater part of her regal prerogatives. I'll not say that most of his extraordinary good fortune is not due to his own uncanny ability; but he has been remarkably favored by the timeliness of several assassinations which removed persons who were in his way; not that I hold him responsible for them, but, as I say, they were certainly timely; and the sudden death of your brother's favorite, the Duke of Luynes, almost automatically meant that the last obstacle in Richelieu's path to the cardinalate had been eliminated. To be sure, he has been a cardinal for less than a year now and your brother has not yet admitted dependency upon him and obedience to his policies. But he will. He is no more capable of functioning without a *privado* than Philip is. When Louis bows to the inevitable, France will be a potential enemy.

That is what Philip meant when he said that the new Minister might have an interest in the Palatinate. It's more than probable that he will."

"You haven't asked me why I was so surprised when I found out that Armand du Plessis and Cardinal Richelieu were the same person."

"That's right, I haven't. I thought you'd probably tell me in due course."

"I know you don't like to be interrupted. But now that you have paused, I will inform you that Armand du Plessis and I are—or, rather, we were—great friends."

"You were! When, where and under what circumstances?"

"When I was on my way to Spain to marry Philip. In Poitiers. Of course then I wasn't called by a title, only *Madame,* like the daughters of all French kings, and I was still Elizabeth, not Isabel—*Madame* Elizabeth. I came down with chicken pox and the cavalcade went on without me, leaving me to recover as best I could and re-join the others when I had. In prospect, it wasn't a very cheerful experience for me. But Armand du Plessis had just been advised by my mother that he was to be appointed Almoner to the young Queen—your sister Ana—and he had come to pay her and Louis his respects. So there he stayed, to look after me—instead of being Almoner to Ana, he was Infirmarian to me! He's witty, he's urbane, he's charming—in fact, he's everything the Conde-Duque is not. I don't wonder my mother thinks the sun rises and sets on his head. She's often written me about him—only, you see, she never called him Richelieu. And I assure you he helped me pass the period of my convalescence most pleasantly. I was very grateful to him. I always shall be. Of course I was only twelve at the time I met him, but I had the feeling, and I still have it, that he and I would always understand each other. Perhaps that episode might have useful consequences."

"You're quite right. It might. I'm glad you told me about it. You'd better tell Philip, too."

"I will, but so far you have answered only one of my questions. I know you said you had to give them separate replies, but can't you answer the other one now?"

"I can try. You wanted to know why Richelieu didn't crush the Huguenots if he were so powerful. I think the main reason is because his primary purpose isn't to crush the Huguenots, but to continue your father's policy of bringing them into line and keeping them there, so that they can form a helpful part of the French hegemony. The first time this great friend of yours ever attracted public attention was when he made a speech at the closing session of the Estates General, to which he had managed to get himself elected as delegate. While not only proclaiming loyalty to the Church, but insisting that its authority must take precedence over that of the nobility, he recommended tolerance to those who 'blinded by error' nevertheless lived peacefully under established rule—in other words, those who were making no trouble. 'We should think of them in terms of desiring their conversion, and the only weapons we should use against them are our good examples, our careful instructions and our fervent prayers,' he went on. That is quite a different policy from arresting them, throwing them into prison and finally dispatching them at *autos de fé*. I think Philip told you the Church didn't operate the same way in France as it does in Spain, that, if it had, your father could never have become King of France. What is more, you never could have become Queen of Spain. Why, come to think of it, you had a narrow escape from being a Huguenot yourself!"

"Now you're joking again—aren't you? . . . Then a French hegemony is what Richelieu wants most?"

"Exactly. Just as a Spanish hegemony is what the Conde-Duque wants most and Richelieu has fewer difficulties in the way of getting one and keeping one. In the first place, as I've just tried to explain, differences in religious viewpoint don't worry him too much when they're under control, whereas Olivares is committed to the maintenance and spread of Catholicism and the suppression of anything that even smacks of heresy. In the second place, the kingdom of France is a good deal more fertile and a good deal more compact than the kingdom of Spain. It has the Atlantic at the west and the Mediterranean and the Pyrenees at the south and all these are natural barriers. So, normally, it's got only the north and the east to worry about. On the other hand, we've got Naples, Sicily, Sardinia,

Milan, Franche-Comté, Artois and the Spanish Netherlands, which are all actually part of Spain, beside Austria, which is an integral part of the Hapsburg alliance."

Fernando paused and sighed. "It's hard to reconstruct history objectively, especially when you're talking about your own family. But I can't help thinking sometimes that, when my great-grand-father Charles V abdicated as head of the Holy Roman Empire, it might have been better if he'd broken all connections with it, since he found he wasn't strong enough to secure it for his son Philip. Instead, as of course you know, he resigned in favor of his brother Fernando and this meant that two royal families and two states, widely separated geographically, still had to operate together as the Hapsburg House of Austria."

"It sounds more and more formidable to me the more you talk about it."

"And, so far, I've only been talking about Europe. I haven't mentioned everything we've got in the New World. When Richelieu worries about enemy encirclement—as he does—he's only got to think of Germany, the Valtelline and Italy. When the Conde-Duque worries about it, he's got to think of all those other places I've men-tioned and he's got to be sure of uninterrupted access to them. So that's the reason the Palatinate might come in. And the reason Richelieu might get the better of the Conde-Duque. And the reason France and Spain might go to war."

As Isabel digested this résumé about cardinals, her already fa-vorable opinion of Fernando's intelligence and scope of information increased to such a degree that she decided to sound him out on the second subject which was troubling her, namely that of finances. Like most Frenchwomen, she had a very wholesome respect for the value of money and, even though she might—and did—enjoy elegant and costly dress, she soon became uneasy in her mind when she thought she had spent too much or that she was doing it too constantly. She had been quite sincere in telling Philip that, when the ordinances against extravagances had been suspended, her first idle thoughts had turned to the dazzling figure she would cut at the entertainments for the Prince of Wales; but her sober second thoughts had taken quite a different direction. If she were not mistaken, one of the purposes—perhaps the main purpose—of the proposed economies had been to better finance the army; she began to wonder how far the expenses incurred at the "House of Seven Chimneys" would interfere with this. If Fernando himself did not have a rough idea, she was sure he had the means of finding out and, without much preamble, she put the question to him at the first opportunity.

This opportunity presented itself sooner than she had dared to hope, on an unseasonably chilly day. Isabel believed in having a fire lighted if she felt cold, whatever the time of year; and, when Fernando next stopped by to see her, after visiting the invalid, he found her ensconced beside a round, felt-covered table. He knew this cloth concealed a brazier and, while he was conscious of neither smoke nor fumes, the gentle warmth which pervaded the room betrayed the hidden fire of burning olive pits. Though, theoretically, she differed from the other members of the royal family in her appreciation of such creature comforts, she noticed that they not infrequently joined her at this vantage point when she had drawn up an extra armchair beside her own, and the armchairs were sure to be comfortable, too—big ones with leather backs and leather seats, for Isabel did not like small hard benches any better than she liked bleak rooms. She looked up with a smile as Fernando was ushered in and she was not in the least surprised when, without hesitation, he took the place she indicated and shoved his feet under the felt mantle which fell in ample folds to the floor, confining and concentrating the heat from the bed of burning olive pits.

"Do you want to ask me more questions about cardinals?" he inquired, as he settled himself.

"No. Today I want to ask you questions about expenses. Ana de Guevara says they live better at the 'House of Seven Chimneys' than we do at the palace."

"Ana de Guevara? The nursery governess my father appointed for Philip? I thought Olivares banished her when he came on the scene."

"Oh, not officially. If she keeps more or less out of sight, the Conde-Duque lets her alone. If she doesn't, she gets sent away. But she always manages to come back—very unobtrusively, of course. And he's much too busy with other things just now to worry about her."

"So—very unobtrusively, of course—she's managed to observe how they live at the 'House of Seven Chimneys' and tell you about it."

"Yes. Naturally, no one would begrudge the Prince and his retinue a good table. But in a month it's cost over forty thousand *maravedís* and a lot of that money has gone into spices and sweets and sherbets. . . . How much does it cost to maintain an army for a month?"

"How large an army?"

"Well, say an army of twenty thousand."

"With horses and cannon?"

"Yes, of course."

Fernando meditated for a few minutes and then briefly jotted down a few figures on a small tablet. He smiled rather ruefully. "I should think that forty thousand would just about do it."

"The Prince has been here almost two months already. So, at this rate—"

"At this rate, if his visit lasts much longer, there won't be a great deal left for the army—or anything else, unless we can raise more money and I don't see how. Certainly we shouldn't tamper with the value of currency any further. I've already told Philip how I feel about that. But he didn't like to discuss it because he worshiped our father and he resents any suggestion that seems like a reflection on him. You see, he was the first to debase the coinage—his predecessors on the throne never did that. But when Father was King, there was an 'easy' device. Spain began the coinage of money made out of copper without the addition of any precious metal."

"You mean *vellón*?"

"Exactly. And that presented a dual problem—inflation and counterfeiting. A *maravedí* isn't worth half what it was five years ago and it's easy for foreigners to make copper coins and smuggle them into Spain. Meanwhile, the people who have any silver are hoarding it. I'd like to see a law passed that would make it illegal to manufacture any more *vellón* for at least twenty years."

"Will you let me have a page from that tablet?"

"What are you planning to do with it?"

"I don't know yet. But something."

"Take the whole tablet. While you are making notes on the subject of *vellón,* you might make a few on the subject of taxes, too. Our trade is being killed by some of those."

"Then, if our coinage is debased and we are not getting what we should from trade, where *is* our money coming from?"

"I am sorry to say that quite a good deal of it is coming from the sale of titles and offices. You might look into that, too."

"What kind of titles? What kind of offices?"

"Oh, the higher the better! That is, the more money they bring in—especially ecclesiastical titles."

"Can't you do something to stop that?"

"And get us still closer to bankruptcy? What help would that be to our country?"

"I don't know, but I should think we could try to raise money more decently and honestly and I should think that, as a cardinal, you might know some way of getting around those religious difficulties I hear so much about."

"I'm afraid I don't. My duties as a cardinal haven't required much knowledge of Canon Law."

"At least you might try to do something. That's another thing I wanted to talk to you about. María's very unhappy."

"You think she would really be pleased to marry the Prince of Wales?"

There were very few persons whom Isabel trusted, but Fernando was one of them. She decided to tell him about the "bold stroke" at the *Casa de Campo* and the largely fictitious nature of the fever. He listened attentively and sympathetically and shook his head.

"I'm still afraid there's nothing I can do. But on the strength of what you've told me, I'll try. Poor child, poor child! If there were only a question of Charles, the whole thing would be easier. Everyone likes him, everyone would be glad to compromise, in as far as that's possible, if it would bring about a happy ending. But Buckingham undoes with one hand what Charles has accomplished with the other and the English duke and the Conde-Duque are practically at swords' points."

This was all too true. The strain between Buckingham and Olivares had reached the breaking point and now these two violent and headstrong men were quarreling openly. Buckingham, in a fury, announced his intention of severing all negotiations and returning to England at once, persuading Charles to go with him. Normally, such persuasion would have been difficult; but Charles had also become aggrieved by this time; he was in love, he wanted to marry the Infanta more than he wanted anything else in the world; but he resented what he considered pressure to do so under still unsettled conditions. The Pope had taken the unprecedented course of writing to him personally, urging immediate conversion; and he knew that, in his reply to this letter, he had gone further in compliance than was safe, as far as public opinion in England was concerned. He dared go no further on his own responsibility; and a letter to his father, dictated by Buckingham, setting forth the Spanish demands at length and begging his "Dear Dad and Gossip's" acceptance of them, was written without much hope that they would be.

The gloom which had settled over his spirit was more than reflected in his father's; Olivares had adroitly slanted the whole question toward the religious issue, on which James had personally been quite willing to compromise, but which he realized was poison as far as Parliament was concerned; and absolutely no reference to the Palatinate had been made in Charles' letter which, as far as the King of England was concerned, was what mattered most. In his despair, he wrote saying he feared the grief caused by his son's letter was so great that it would shorten his days; that he knew not how to meet his people's expectations; and that, if the Spaniards would not alter their decree, his boys were to come speedily away and "give over all treaty." He added that he repented ever having suffered them to leave him, that he cared nothing about the match if he could only have them back. He ended the letter by saying:

I protest ye shall be as heartily welcome as if ye had done all things ye went for, so that I may once more have you in my arms again, and God bless you both, my sweet son and my only best sweet servant, and let me hear from you quickly with all speed as ye love my life; and so God send you a happy, joyful meeting in the arms of your dear Dad.

By the time this letter reached Spain, Buckingham's rage had, to a certain degree, subsided and Charles' wounded feelings had been soothed. Olivares, first having made sure of approval by the ecclesiastical hierarchy, was willing that the Prince and the Infanta should be betrothed in Madrid, their marriage to be confirmed in England only after that country lived up to what was promised in relief for the oppressed native Catholics of England. Buckingham was willing and Charles was eager to believe this and, after much backing and filling on both sides, without any real concessions on either, a marriage treaty was finally drawn which Charles, taking his oath on the Gospels, faithfully swore to fulfill; Philip, on the other hand, merely agreed that, when the Pope's consent had been received, the marriage would be solemnized and that, as soon thereafter as feasible, the Infanta would set sail for England.

Even the commemorations of Corpus Christi, which had been observed with more pomp and ceremony than ever before, paled before the festivals given to celebrate the betrothal of the Prince and the Infanta.

These culminated in a cane tourney at which Charles, symbolically arrayed in white satin, occupied the seat of honor beside Isabel and Philip led his squadron to victory, using twelve lances and scoring a bull's-eye with three of them. He was especially fond of this sport, as the skill required for horsemanship was child's play for him, and he was equally accomplished in the art of directing the small cane javelins against his opponents. It was nothing new for him to win prizes and he was greatly pleased with this one—an image of the Infant Jesus, made entirely of diamonds. After the contest was over, he rode, flushed with victory, with Charles at his side, to the palace of the Countess of Miranda which—still stressing the bridal note—had been hung with white damask for the occasion. There a collation consisting of various conserves, dried suckets and rose water confections was provided for their refreshment and, as sweets were Philip's favorite fare, his mood became increasingly mellow as the evening wore on. In fact, the general atmosphere for the next few days was one of effusive cordiality on all sides and lavish gifts of many different sorts were exchanged: precious jewels, rare paintings, daggers, swords and pistols encrusted with diamonds, Arab horses, sedan chairs of tortoise shell and gold. Even Olivares was again geniality itself, as far as Buckingham was concerned, when preparations for Charles' departure were unmistakably in progress; and he raised María's hopes by telling her jocosely that, if he could have his way, he would turn her and Charles out of Spain together! As he jested even less often than Philip, she really believed that he meant it, that she would have the unspeakable joy of accompanying her beloved to England. Then her hopes were dashed again. She was summoned to her sister-in-law's apartments to receive the Prince when he was conducted there in state to take formal leave of her and the Queen.

The visit was brief and strained. María fought for self-control and achieved it. She made all the proper responses to all the proper remarks addressed to her and expressed suitable admiration for the magnificent pearl parure that was her fiancé's parting gift to her. But when Charles had departed, escorted by his retinue, after kissing her hand and the Queen's, without even a murmured endearment to accompany the empty salute, she fled to her own room and flung the parure down on the nearest table before she locked herself in. She had often heard that pearls stood for tears; now she did not need to have anyone prove this to her. The portals leading into the beautiful bright world, illumined by love, through which she had passed a few months earlier, had been closed as suddenly as they were opened; nothing was left to her but outer darkness. If she had not been taught, from earliest childhood, that self-destruction was a mortal sin leading straight to the gates of hell, she would have taken her life before anyone could force the door and prevent her. Even the threat of eternal damnation might not have stopped her if the intrusion on her desperate solitude had not come very quickly.

It was Isabel, of course, who had followed her and who ordered her to open the door and who now sat down calmly beside her and did not try to talk with her until her paroxysm of grief had worn her down through sheer exhaustion. Then, still as if her idea were quite within the normal order of things, Isabel made a quiet suggestion.

"Why don't you and I make a brief visit to the nuns at the *Descalzas Reales?* I think it would be a pleasant change from all the turmoil we've been through lately."

"I don't care where I go. I wish I were dead."

"I know. So, as long as I think the convent is a good idea, you might as well go there as anywhere else. Doña Margarita has packed your things and the coach is at the door. Incidentally, Philip approves my plan of making a retreat, so there's nothing to worry about on that score. He and Carlos and several hundred courtiers are leaving at dawn tomorrow to escort the Prince to the Escorial. They've mapped out quite an elaborate program for him, partly gloomy sightseeing and partly cheerful hunting before he goes on to Segovia and thence to Santander. But they thought the palace visit represented the end of today's activities, as far as they were concerned, and turned Charles over to Fernando for this evening. He suggested a farewell visit to *Sor* Juana de la Cruz and Charles agreed that was an excellent idea. Probably they've already reached the convent. So we'd better hurry. I don't think we've any time to lose."

When Isabel and María were ushered into the lofty drawing room with its famous frieze of Moorish plasterwork and its priceless paintings and its superb mirrors which was the one set apart for royal visitors, Fernando and Charles were already awaiting them and they greeted each other as kinfolk and friends and not as royalty. Then Fernando said quietly that he was going to the oratory to read his Office and Isabel said she would go with him to say the prayers that were proper preparatory to a retreat. They gave no sign of thinking that, as soon as they had left, Charles and María would be in each other's arms; and when they returned, an hour later, they gave no sign that they knew their expectations had been fulfilled. They had never seen María look so happy and, though the beautiful new diamond ornament she was wearing might account, in part, for her rapturous expression, the source of the gift and not its value was unquestionably what counted. The giver was her true love, her affianced husband, and in a few short months she would join him, voyaging in the fleet that was already standing by to take her to the island realm where she would be his wife and his queen. She would use the period of their separation to prepare a trousseau worthy of her new role and the days would fly past. Never, in the whole history of mankind, had a girl been given more cause for rejoicing.

Charles stood by, holding her hand, and saying little, but smiling complaisantly and nodding consent as she poured out her paean of rapture. He was affable and engaging to the last and, even after he had gone, the charm of his personality still pervaded the austere room like a living presence and María chatted on as contentedly as if he were still there. She did not need comments from her brother and sister-in-law on what she was saying. Indeed, to their great relief, she did not notice how few they made. They were thankful that they were not required to put into words their sad conviction that María would never see Charles again.

Chapter 8

AT FIRST, this conviction had no sounder basis than intuition. From Charles' behavior, Fernando and Isabel had every reason to suppose he was in love with María and none to suppose that he would deliberately deceive her. Besides, they both saw the letter he wrote to Philip from Segovia, in which he reiterated his desire and intention to marry her; they did not see the one he wrote at the same time to Bristol, in which he revoked the full powers he had given the English Ambassador to conclude the espousals when the Pope's consent arrived, on the ground that there was nothing in its provisions to prevent the Infanta from embracing a conventual life after the marriage. If they had, they would have spared the poor girl months of hopeless anticipation of a marriage which they would have known to be doomed. It was not until Buckingham and Olivares embarked on a series of recriminations so vituperative that they led with tragic inevitability to estrangement, where there should have been rapprochement, that an alliance between England and France instead of an alliance between England and Spain was consummated.

Meanwhile, María's faith in Charles remained unshaken; it was actually only when she faced the terrible truth of his betrothal to Henriette Marie, the youngest sister of Louis XIII, that she was forced to believe in his desertion and that Isabel could find no words to assuage her futile grief.

"He loved me. I know he loved me," she wailed over and over again.

"Yes, I think he did. But he didn't love you enough."

"Enough for what?"

"Enough to stand firm against the English Parliament and Buckingham. Enough to compromise with Olivares on his own responsibility. Enough to go straight to the Pope with promises that he intended to keep. Enough to risk his throne and, if need be, to give it up. As far as I know, there's never been a king who loved a woman enough to do that."

"But Charles might have been the first!"

"Yes, he might have been, but he wasn't. As a matter of fact, I'm afraid he didn't see any reason why he should."

"I'd have gladly given up everything I have or hope to have for him."

"Yes, but that's different. You're not the heir to a throne with all the responsibilities that go with that position."

"Oh! I suppose you'd be glad to find excuses for him. After all, Henriette Marie is *your* sister as well as Louis'. It's natural you should have her happiness at heart more than you have mine. I'm only your sister-in-law."

"Darling, I haven't seen Henriette Marie since I married Philip and she was only six years old at that time—the youngest in our family of six children. As a matter of fact, I didn't see much of her before my marriage. We each had our own nursery governess and own apartments. You seem much more like my sister than she ever did or ever will. Besides, I don't feel at all sure she's very happy about marrying Charles. I've heard that she's been in love, ever since she was a child, with our cousin, the Duke of Soissons, and that he's been in love with her. They grew up in the belief that they would marry as soon as they were old enough. Now it seems just as necessary for Richelieu to strengthen relations with England as it did for Olivares to neglect them. I'm afraid Richelieu is right and that Olivares was wrong—you know, I think he's wrong about a good many things. Anyway, Henriette Marie is being sacrificed to a policy and, instead of envying her, you ought to feel sorry for her. And you'll also feel better if you try to think that Charles was mindful of his responsibilities, that he felt he must weigh them against his love for you, if he couldn't convince his best advisers that it would be feasible for you to become his wife."

"Isn't Henriette Marie a Catholic?"

"Yes, of course."

"And hasn't England agreed to all the concessions the Pope wanted for me? A confessor of my own nationality, a chapel of my own and freedom to worship in it, control of my children until they were ten years old and so on?"

"I—I think so."

"Then why couldn't it have made the same concessions for me? I should think Fernando could have arranged for them. He's a cardinal."

"Darling, Fernando did everything in his power to help you. But he isn't a prime minister as well as a cardinal. Richelieu is."

"Well, if Fernando didn't have enough power to make the English accept me as Charles' wife then I could have been his *querida*. I didn't care so much about being his queen as I did about being his beloved."

"You don't know what you're saying. And whatever else you do, don't say that to anyone else but me. It will get you into all sorts of trouble—perhaps land you in a convent."

"I'm perfectly willing to go to a convent. I know I'll never love any man except Charles."

Isabel began to fear she had said too much. Although no other alliance had recently been mentioned, she knew it would be only a matter of time before Philip, mindful of his dying father's injunction that María should marry the heir of the German Emperor, would bring up the subject again and that María would be expected to regard this arrangement with complacence. She was Spain's only Infanta, and seemed likely to remain so, Isabel reflected sadly; none of her own infant daughters had survived more than a short time and at the moment there was no prospect of another baby. To be sure, she could not see that international marriages inevitably made for peace between nations; France had a Spanish-born queen and Spain a French-born queen and neither had, so far, been able to lessen the growing strain between the two countries. But she knew that, theoretically, that was what international marriages were supposed to do. As she had reminded María, the latter was not heir to a throne and this was true enough—at least, for the time being. But she might become one and she would certainly be called upon to provide one. She did have responsibilities, too. . . .

Isabel looked up from her brown study to see that María was standing near the door, as if already preparing to take a shortcut to a convent. She rose, too, and put her arm around the girl.

"Well, we'd better talk that over with Fernando," she said easily. "You know that, since you're a member of the royal family, the only convent you'd be allowed to enter would be the *Descalzas Reales*. It isn't as if you could pick and choose among them and find out which one had the Rule most acceptable to you, so I hope you won't decide hurriedly to take the veil. I would miss you very much if you left and, besides, I've been hoping that perhaps you'd help me with some investigations I've decided to make. You see, we spent a good deal of money while Charles was here—money that was meant to be used to equip the army and relieve the suffering among the poorer people we don't see at Court."

"Yes, I keep hearing about that, as if it were my fault. I didn't ask Charles to come here. Nobody asked him to come. He did it of his own accord because he wanted so much to marry me. And he didn't need bullfights and banquets and cane tourneys to persuade him that he loved me. They were just a waste of time as well as a waste of money, as far as he was concerned. He thinks bullfights are cruel and cane tourneys are silly and he doesn't like Spanish food. Those best advisers of his that you're talking about aren't the only ones that prevented him from doing what he came for. The Conde-Duque was just as much to blame as any Englishman, even that horrible Buckingham. The Conde-Duque *is* what the English call the prime minister here, isn't he?"

"Yes."

"And it was he who drew up that schedule for economical reforms, so we could equip the army and help the poor and then he was the one who insisted on all those festivities. It doesn't make sense to me. It all seems futile. If he wasn't going to let the marriage take place, why couldn't he say so sooner and save money for our country? Not to mention, saving me from heartbreak?"

"I don't know, María. It doesn't make much sense to me, either. Of course, we had to be hospitable, and we wouldn't have met Spanish standards if we hadn't entertained Charles with bullfights and cane tourneys and banquets. And you must confess that you enjoyed those; I know I did. But you're right. We shouldn't have had so many and they shouldn't have been so sumptuous when we were short of money. Fernando and I have already discussed that. You're right to be aggrieved about the Conde-Duque, too. He could have shown his hand sooner, without being nearly as discourteous as he was later on when, between them, he and that horrible Buckingham, as you so rightly call him, succeeded in making England our enemy. It's unfortunate that he isn't always as successful in perfecting policies as he is in devising them. He didn't cling to the purpose of achieving economic reform until he'd fulfilled it. He abandoned it for no better reason than the determination to show England how prodigal we could afford to be. So I want to see if I can't do something myself to help solve our financial problems."

"Is that what you meant when you spoke of making investigations?" María asked, without much show of interest.

"Yes. I've offered to sell my jewels if we can't raise what we need in any other way; and I know of Court ladies and members of the clergy who would help, too, if I asked them. So would the Cortes in the different provinces, at least, most of them—it's always hard to get anything out of Aragón and Cataluña, though it isn't impossible. But, after all, measures like that would be just a stopgap. I want to find out what Spain's real resources are and see if they can't be used to better advantage than they are now."

"How?"

"Well, we've got to face the fact that France has double our population and that we can't compete with her in fertility of soil. On the other hand, there's our wool. I understand that sheep farming requires less land than arable farming and the extra man power available makes it easier to raise armies and colonize the New World. I've always been fascinated by the sheep walks of the *mesta,* the routes the flocks take from the north to the south and back again every year, so they'll always be where the climate is best for them. I've been told that, at one time, there were more than three million of these sheep and the demand for their wool was enormous, especially in Flanders. And wool isn't by any means the only natural source of riches—there are olives and vines. There's a great demand for manufactured goods, too. Silk and leather, ceramics and steelwork. Of course, I haven't any idea how to get statistics about all this, but I'm determined to find a way and, also, to find out just what Fernando meant when he said our trade was being killed by taxes. Of course, I understand that people haven't any incentive to work hard in order to earn money and then have it all taken away from them again. I'm going to make up lists, the same way I did when I was planning our new clothes. And I'm going to consult experts."

María would have been more interested in visiting convents under Fernando's guidance, which at least would have offered an excuse for getting out of the dreary old palace, than she would have been in making up lists and consulting experts with Isabel. However, having discovered that she was limited to one convent, she decided that the Rule of the *Descalzas Reales*, as outlined to her by *Sor* Juana de la Cruz, was too rigid for her to follow in comfort and that she preferred, after all, to stay where she was, at least for the present. Meanwhile, her main preoccupation seemed to be in gleaning news about the impending marriage, by which she was morbidly fascinated, from the French Court. And she developed what seemed to Isabel an uncanny faculty for finding sources of information and then putting tidbits of gossip together. The hated Buckingham had been sent to the Louvre as special ambassador in charge of negotiations and, far from creating the same bad impression there that he had in Madrid, was cutting a dashing figure. Didn't Isabel remember how terribly uncouth she had thought him? Isabel remembered only too vividly. Well, it seemed that Ana thought certain aspects of this characteristic amusing. For instance, he had a habit of covering his clothing with pearls, very loosely tacked on, and purposely letting a few fall every so often. Then the Court ladies would scramble to pick these up and everyone would go into gales of laughter. Ana thought this was delightful. Afterward, she made Buckingham even more welcome to her presence whenever he wanted to see her.

"But she managed very badly," María said smugly. "After she had succeeded in persuading her ladies-in-waiting to withdraw, so that she could receive him alone in a sheltered corner of the garden, she screamed when he embraced her and, of course, her attendants came hurrying back. It wasn't that she was offended by the embrace—she had invited it. But Buckingham had come to his rendezvous in full regalia, Order of the Garter and all, and when she felt the sharp projections of that great golden chain pressing against her bodice she was startled. As you know, I didn't scream when I was embraced in the garden at the *Casa de Campo,* though I was taken completely by surprise, instead of having everything carefully planned. But then, of course, Charles had more sense than to wear such trappings. It wasn't necessary for him to try to impress me or anyone else with his importance by wearing a lot of decorations. We knew he was important even when he arrived looking like a ragamuffin. It will serve Ana right if she never gets another chance for a *solitude à deux* and if her ladies tattle, as they will. But I'm sure she'll try again. And if the Queen of France, who was an Infanta of Spain, can have a *querido,* why shouldn't the King of England have a *querida* who is an Infanta of Spain?"

This time, Isabel was even more aghast than she had been over the threat of a religious vocation. If María had heard this gossip about Ana, the person who had whispered it to her would whisper it elsewhere; and though she herself did not for a minute believe that the Queen of France had been guilty of anything more than a trifling indiscretion, that was serious enough. She had not forgotten the tragic consequences of the one trifling indiscretion in which she had become involved, through no wish or initiative on her part. If Ana were voluntarily playing with fire, and her associate was the Duke of Buckingham, what would be the repercussions in the present chaotic condition of things?

She need not have worried, as far as that aspect of the situation was concerned. She busied herself to find her own sources of information, some of which were nearer the Alcázar than she would have imagined. Her brother Louis was more interested in their sister's marriage than he had ever been in his own, and he was not likely to stage the drama of a jealous husband and thereby upset an advantageous political alliance, when there was a possibility that any such action on his part might bring to light secrets which he would naturally prefer to have kept dark, regarding his own lack of virility. Isabel found that her sympathy for María must now be comprehensive enough to include Ana and, with a degree of satisfaction which she had never believed she would experience, she dwelt on Philip's insatiable sexuality, unresentful that he had strayed from her side in attempting to assuage this since, in the end, he had always returned to her. Whatever her disappointments and disillusions had been, she still had led a rich and rewarding life as a king's consort, in every sense of the word; and, if she had not yet given birth to a son, she had proved her powers of fecundity over and over again. She could continue to do so, mingling her ready response to her husband's desire with compassionate thoughts of his sister's sterile existence as a queen who was not really a wife.

Chapter 9

LITTLE by little, María adjusted herself to a future in which Charles had no part, but in which she herself must play one with dignity and self-control as she advanced toward womanhood; and her admiration for Isabel inspired her to follow the Queen's example in giving national problems precedence over personal troubles. There were cogent reasons for doing this: Europe had once more divided itself into rival camps, one to assert and the other to dispute the hegemony of Spain, which was still determined to preserve this at all costs, however devastating these costs might be; and it looked as if these would be ruinous. France, Savoy and the Protestant powers were all united against the Hapsburgs; and their only allies were certain Italian principalities, whose rulers were connected with them by marriage. However, Richelieu did not want a declaration of war just then; he had only recently come into supreme power and he preferred to go forward cautiously. He knew that Spain was in a state of exhaustion and bankruptcy; possibly he could gain his ends without openly hostile measures. He would see. By holding out to King Charles of England the old bait—restoration of the Palatinate—he attracted England into an alliance with France and, shortly thereafter, Cádiz was attacked by the English fleet. He next directed French and Swiss troops, amply supplemented by forces from Venice and Savoy, to invade the Valtelline, which had been held by the Spaniards since the revolt of 1618, when the Duke of Feria had established fortifications there. Richelieu greatly coveted this valley, as it represented both the Spaniards' means of passage from Milan to Vienna and the threat of encirclement to France. At first, his maneuver seemed successful; everything was going according to plan. Then, to his great surprise, Spain rallied. The Duke of Feria, General Spínola and Admiral de

Santa Cruz showed such unexpected energy in so many different directions that Richelieu was obliged to begin relaxing his hold on the disputed territory. At this juncture, he received two letters which gave him food for thought.

The first was from Pope Urban VIII. How did it happen, His Holiness demanded, that a cardinal of the Church was making common cause with heretics against an orthodox Catholic power? That was something he would have to look into and, if necessary, act against. The communication was no mild reproof; it was a definite threat and it was backed with power, both in the present and for the future. A pope who had hitherto shown himself especially friendly to France, now supporting Olivares against Richelieu with all this implied? No, that would never do. . . .

The second letter was brought to him by a quiet elderly woman with a pleasant face, whom the young monsignor who was his secretary had at first declined to admit to the great presence. However, though respectful and soft voiced, she persisted that her mission was important and, somehow, the secretary was eventually persuaded that it might be and that she was right in saying the message she carried must be delivered by her into the Cardinal's own hand. The young monsignor left her, well watched, in the antechamber and consulted His Eminence, who asked a few questions.

"Is this woman French?"

"Obviously not. She speaks French, but with a decided accent. And she is not dressed like a Frenchwoman, nor does she move like one. She holds her elbows close to her body and glides, rather than walks."

"Then did it cross your mind that she might be Spanish?"

"Yes, Your Eminence. But she in no way resembles in manner the type of Spaniard we have occasionally seen around Paris of late."

"You mean the spies?"

"Well—yes. However, she did not give the impression that she was trying to find out something, by circuitous or dubious means; on the contrary, she insisted that she had a message for you which she hoped and believed would please you. She said the writer was an old friend of yours."

"Oh—and what was the scene and time of this friendship?"

"If I understood her correctly, she said it was Poitiers, several years ago. And she murmured something about an attack of chicken pox and your talents as an infirmarian."

The Cardinal smiled slightly. "By all means, bring this lady in to me," he said. "And when she leaves here, see that she is offered suitable lodging and refreshment."

The young monsignor bowed and withdrew, stifling his curiosity and bewilderment. The pleasant-faced elderly woman came calmly into the Cardinal's study and knelt to kiss his ring. She did not seem in the least overpowered by his magnificent surroundings or his voluminous scarlet robes. As a matter of fact, she was making a swift mental comparison between him and the Conde-Duque and it was all in the Cardinal's favor: delicate features in an ascetic face, instead of bold eyes, a big nose and rubicund coloring; slim white hands on which glittered a single great ring, instead of pudgy fingers overloaded with heavy jewels; quiet grace of movement, instead of blustering haste; dignified presence, instead of swaggering importunity. Her appraisal of him was no more favorable than his of her; His Eminence looked at her with unqualified approval.

"May I ask you to tell me your name, *señora?*" he said in Spanish.

"It is Ana de Guevara, Your Eminence."

"Of course, I should have guessed. . . . And you have been good enough to bring me a letter from an old friend, whom I remember as Madame Elizabeth with great affection?"

"As she does Your Eminence."

Ana produced the letter from her person and remained standing. The Cardinal courteously told her to be seated and broke the seal:

YOUR EMINENCE—

A short time ago, I asked my brother-in-law, who is very dear to me, to describe a typical cardinal. He is a cardinal himself, so I thought he would be able to do so. But he told me there was no such thing as a typical cardinal and went on to talk a lot of nonsense about little boys who had been appointed cardinals, and had no idea

· 77 ·

what it was all about, and old men who became cardinals when there was nothing else left for them to do. And so on and so on. But when I said that at least one thing about them must be certain, and this was that cardinals were always good Catholics, that they never would have any traffic with heretics, my brother still would not give me a definite answer. But by-and-by in the course of conversation, he surprised me by telling me that my old friend, the Bishop of Luçon, was now a cardinal; and when I said I was sure this cardinal and I would always understand each other, as well as we had when I was just a sick lonely little girl and he did not have much of a diocese, my brother said he thought I was probably right. I am sending you this letter because I hope he was right, that we will still understand each other as well as we did in Poitiers.

My brother also suggested that I should tell my husband how I felt about this, but somehow the right time never came. I am sorry, for I feel he does not always have the best advice from his chief counselor, whom I do not like very well; and though it is bold for me to suppose so, I cannot help feeling that sometimes I might make a helpful suggestion. As I haven't had a chance to make this one to my husband, I hope you won't mind because I am making it to you instead. My suggestion is that it would not be very hard to compromise about the valley if the people who live there had the guarantees about their religion, just as a different group has in France. A good Catholic who was, incidentally, a cardinal would not be trafficking with heretics, would he, if he could bring that about? Just acting consistently. Of course, if that plan didn't work, he could try something else after a year or two, but in the meantime, why couldn't he try this one?

I am sending you this letter by someone you can trust with a message. She does not like my husband's chief counselor any better than I do; but she is devoted to my husband's interests and to mine and I am sure these will best be served if you and I can go on understanding each other.

YOUR OLD FRIEND, ELIZABETH.

The Cardinal read the letter through twice very carefully and the expression on his face remained pleasant throughout the reading. Afterward, he took the letter over to the fireplace and watched it burn. Then he turned to Ana. There was a soft rustle of silk from his scarlet draperies as he moved.

"Please tell my old friend that she and I still understand each other," he said. "I cannot promise that we always will, but certainly we do now. You may add, if you like, that her letter came very shortly after one from His Holiness, expressing very much the same views that she has, but less graciously. At any rate, her opinion is shared in this very high quarter, and I predict that some day her husband will wish that he had listened to her sooner, instead of to the chief counselor whom she does not like. Let me give you my blessing before you leave. I am afraid proper provision for your comfort in Paris and on your journey through France has not hitherto been made. You will find it better now."

The treaty regarding the Valtelline, signed in 1626 at Monzón, provided that the Valtelline Catholic inhabitants should no longer be harassed by the Protestants of Grisons; they should practice their religion unmolested and, though paying a tribute to the Swiss canton, they should otherwise be virtually independent of it; and Spain should continue to use it as a pass and thereby have free access to Flanders and Austria. For her, the treaty represented solid success.

Olivares boastfully announced that he had put Richelieu in his place and, of course, no one contradicted him. Meanwhile, the surprising show of Spanish energy continued and brought about increasingly happy results: Don Enrique de Toledo destroyed the Dutch fleet off Gibraltar and Spínola, in dramatic response to an order from Philip, famous for its brevity—*Tomad a* Breda—Take Breda—captured that city after a siege of ten months. To complete the picture of Spain's unwonted success, the Dutch were expelled from Bahia in South America and from Puerto Rico in the West Indies; and the Moorish pirates who had harried the Mediterranean and even the Spanish coast for years, were crushed by Philip's galleys. Spain, in a fever of pride and jubilation, hailed the young King, who had never left Madrid, as Philip the Great and the Planet King and Olivares caused these titles to be officially accorded his young master. And Philip himself, in a review of the situation, made before the Council of Castile, spoke in words of proud satisfaction:

Our prestige has been immensely improved. We have had all Europe against us, but we have not been defeated, nor have our allies lost, while our enemies have sued me for peace. Last year, 1625, we had nearly 300,000 infantry and cavalry in our pay, and over 500,000 men of the militia under arms, while the fortresses of Spain are being put into a thorough state of defence. The fleet, which consisted of only seven vessels on my accession, rose at one time in 1625 to 108 ships of war at sea, without counting the vessels at Flanders, and the crews are the most skillful mariners this realm ever possessed. Thank God, our enemies have never captured one of my ships, except a solitary hulk. So it may truly be said that we have recovered our prestige at sea; and fortunately so, for, lacking our sea power, we should lose not only all the realms we possess, but religion even in Madrid itself would be ruined, and this is the principal point to be considered. This very year of 1626 we have had two royal armies in Flanders and one in the Palatinate, and yet all the power of France, England, Sweden, Venice, Savoy, Denmark, Holland, Brandenburg, Saxony and Weimar could not save Breda from our victorious arms.

We have held our own against England, both with regard to the marriage and at Cádiz; and yet, with all this universal conspiracy against us, I have not depleted my patrimony by 50,000 ducats. It would be impossible to believe this if I did not see it with my own eyes, and that my own realms are all quiet and religious. I have written this paper to you to show you that I have done my part, and have put my own shoulder to the wheel without sparing sacrifice. I have spent nothing unnecessary upon myself, and I have made Spain and myself respected by my enemies.

But though Philip and his Castilian subjects were blinded to political expediency by what they proudly considered their religious privilege and duty, the subjects of his eastern realms, hard-headed men of other racial origins and political traditions, had no notion of allowing themselves to be ruined for a sentimental idea, however grandiose. When the King had asked the Aragonese Cortes for the usual grant in 1624, he was told that he must first present himself before the parliaments of Aragón, Cataluña and Valencia to take the usual oath to respect their constitutions, before they would make a grant; and, as they stiffly held to the principle, which the Castilian Parliament had lost, of "redress before supply," they could vote nothing until their legislative demands were satisfied. With as good a grace as he might, Philip promised to visit his eastern subjects, perfectly well aware that his progress was not likely to be a mere voyage of pleasure, as his trip to Andalucía had been a year previously.

And there was the further question of direction during his absence. He not only enjoyed Madrid; it was his capital, the seat of his Court and the Castilian Cortes and, as such, his essential responsibility. Of this he was not unmindful, however much he might delegate his authority to his *Privado*. Besides, when he left, the Conde-Duque would leave, too, for, though he regarded it as his perquisite to dictate to all branches of the government, he was less concerned about the Cortes of Castile, always the most tractable, than he was about the refractory eastern Cortes. Moreover, keeping in close personal touch with his sovereign was his chief concern. Someone must be empowered to act for both of them.

For several days, Philip turned the matter over in his mind, without speaking of it to anyone. Then, as he wandered rather aimlessly into Isabel's apartments, somewhat earlier than was his habit, he found her comfortably seated in her favorite place beside the covered *brasero* with several sheets of paper, in which she seemed to be completely engrossed, spread out before her. In fact, she was so absorbed in the notations on these that she did not even hear his approach. And when he leaned over her, putting his arm around her shoulders, she jumped up, scattering the papers as she did so. He bent over to help her retrieve them, though she tried to forestall him, and saw that they were covered with figures and brief scribbled memoranda.

"Is it indiscreet to ask what you are doing?" he queried, with unaccustomed lightness. "From all appearances, you do not seem to be writing tender messages to anyone. Yet, you were certainly very intent on your penmanship and you seemed in a great hurry to pick up these pages before I could get a good look at them."

"Only because I was afraid you would make fun of me. I'm trying to find ways of improving our financial situation, which doesn't seem to be very good, and I realize I'm very inexperienced. I probably haven't added correctly, much less put figures where they belong, in connection with receipts and expenditures."

She handed the papers to him and reseated herself, looking away from Philip, as if there were nothing more she needed or wanted to say to him. He straightened the sheets and, instead of giving them a brief cursory glance, began to examine them with interest. She had made a careful list of the crown revenues from the Church and from the gold of the Indies, together with one of Spain's various products, with the normal revenue derived from each and the sales tax—the famous *alcabala*—on each. These items were labeled, "Taxed too high" . . . "Production lagging" . . . and, in one or two cases, "Reasonable." She had further made an equally careful listing of the amounts supposedly at the command of numerous high-ranking nobles who were exempt from taxation, whether the title was inherited or purchased, and the estimated disbursements of these individuals, which were generally far in excess of their estimated incomes. Queries concerning the source of the money to cover these discrepancies were bracketed with the sums they represented—"Extortion, Graft, Blackmail"—as well as estimates of the amounts they must have secured from usurers. It was obvious that she had reached two conclusions: first, that there should be a better balance between production and taxes; and, secondly, that a great deal of private money was being wasted or improperly come by and that much of this waste and misuse could and should be prevented.

"So you thought it might be a good idea, while I was in the eastern provinces trying to raise money, if you tried to salvage some."

"Yes, I did and I do," she answered, speaking far more earnestly than he had. "Especially as far as the nobles are concerned. I've been hoping that I'd come across another note like the one the Duke of Lerma wrote you when Olivares forced his retirement, but, so far, I haven't."

She walked over to the tall metal lectern which stood on the other side of the room and, taking from it a document she had not given him with those she had been working on, passed it over to him. It was dated April 13, 1621—a fortnight after his accession to the throne—and it read:

I am very rich and content that Your Majesty has inherited the crown. I give you thanks for the honor of canceling the income of 7,000 ducats allotted me by the King, my Lord, from the treasury of Sicily, because all that is the pleasure of Your Majesty can only be my pleasure as well.

"Where did you get this?" Philip asked in amazement.

"I am not without friends on the Council of Finance," Isabel said demurely. "One of them brought it to me, thinking perhaps I might show it to you at some opportune moment. He was afraid it might have escaped your attention."

"Escaped my attention! I never saw it before—the letter or the 7,000 ducats paid into the treasury annually—that would amount to 35,000 ducats by now. They must have been diverted in ways with which I am not familiar."

"I think maybe I had better familiarize myself with those ways. I'm afraid if I don't do it, no one else will."

"And I'm sorry to say you are probably right, but I think this letter and your tax figures are extremely interesting. Would you feel like making me a copy?"

"Of course. I'd be glad to. Shall I do it now?"

The rare smile which she so loved to see brightened his face. "Oh, there isn't that much hurry. Tomorrow morning would do just as well. It happens that I came here, still wondering if I should ask you to do something for me. Now I'm not wondering any longer. I'm going to tell you that I hope you will."

"You know that whatever it is—"

"I want you to act as Regent for me while I'm gone. I'm convinced you'd be a very good one. And—to quote your own words

—if you don't do it, I don't know who would. So now that I've offered you the position and you've accepted it, suppose we devote the rest of the evening to pleasure?"

The King and his brother Carlos left Madrid early in September, attended by the Conde-Duque, the Admiral of Castile and several other nobles, but with much less state than usual and a smaller attendance, the plan being to travel rapidly, and hurry the Cortes into voting what was needed. He found the parliaments of Aragón, Cataluña and Valencia in no very flexible mood. Each one of them stood upon the letter of its ancient charters and resisted pressure of the sort that had reduced the Cortes of Castile to impotence. Olivares, bitterly resentful of any institution that dared to stand in the way of his will, was haughty and peremptory, and began by inducing the King, on a show of opposition from the Cortes of Valencia, to abolish by a stroke of the pen its power to refuse the supply demanded. The Cortes of Cataluña were more stubborn and refused the great and unconstitutional demands made upon them. Their refusal, indeed, was so emphatic that Olivares, in real or pretended alarm for the safety of the King, precipitately withdrew him from Barcelona, leaving behind him the seeds of trouble which were in due time to bring forth a plentiful crop.

From Madrid, Philip tried to appease the Aragonese by voluntarily reducing the contribution they had at length voted; but the result of his journey left not only resentment in the hearts of his non-Castilian subjects, but led to outrageous raids of angry Castilian soldiery into Aragón, and aroused in the King himself a bitter feeling toward the peoples who had been the first to challenge the despotic supremacy which he felt was his divine birthright. Like his immediate predecessors on the throne, Philip was obsessed with the idea of divinely delegated authority. To oppose his will was not disloyalty alone, but impiety, and it was naturally difficult for him to understand that this view, which was generally held by his Castilian subjects, whose kingly traditions were sacerdotal, could not be shared by peoples whose institutions were based upon a purely elective military monarchy, and feudalism modified by a representative democracy. How the anger rankled in his breast was seen in the long exculpatory which, on his return to Madrid, he addressed to the Council of Castile:

Anything is better than to burden more heavily these poor unhappy vassals of Castile, who, by their love, their efforts and their sufferings have made us masters of the rest of what we possess, and still preserve it for us, as the head and part principal of our commonwealth. I would far rather take burdens from these poor people than impose further sacrifices upon them, and when I think of what they have to pay, and also the trouble and annoyance they have to submit to in the collection of it, in good truth I would rather beg for charity from door to door, if I could, to provide for the funds necessary for the national defence, than deal so harshly with such vassals as these. . . . I grieve in my very soul to see such good subjects suffer so much from the faults of my ministers. If my own lifeblood would remedy it I would cheerfully give it. And yet, though you know how this cuts me to the heart, and though I reproach you, you propose no remedy. . . . I tried the Cortes of Aragón, running, as you well know, serious risk, and incurring great trouble and inconvenience, solely for the purpose of alleviating the pressure upon these Castilian subjects, and I am directing my efforts in the same way with my other realms, so that some day I hope we may be able to lighten the taxes in Castile. God knows, I yearn for the coming of that day more than to conquer Constantinople.

As time went on this attitude was the one natural to Philip through all the troubles which gathered blacker and blacker, while the evil seed sown by him and Olivares grew and ripened. He himself, acting conscientiously and—as he was convinced—under divine inspiration, never believed himself wrong in the measures he adopted. If suffering and adversity came, they always came either from the wiles of the evil one, or for some wise inscrutable purpose of God. They were never at this time a consequence of any want of wisdom or prescience of his. His heart bled for the misery of his subjects, but it never occurred to him that the way to remedy it might be to alter an untenable position in his foreign relations, and devote his energies to the concentration of national resources for the promotion of productive industry and interior economy.

During Philip's five months' absence in Aragón, the party against Olivares had taken courage in Madrid. More and more clearly it was apparent that the spirited young Queen chafed under the complete subjection in which the King was held and the tutelage which the Countess of Olivares endeavored to exercise over her; and that the Infantes, Carlos and Fernando, were also in a state of rebellion against the restraint which the Conde-Duque tried to impose on them. It was evident to the favorite, on his return to Madrid, that the atmosphere was more hostile to him than before and this was not only because the Queen and the Infantes were increasingly antagonistic. The nobles, priests and ladies-in-waiting had been able to speak more boldly while they were relieved of his alarming presence; and though Isabel, as a devoted wife, was glad to have her husband home again, as Regent she had discovered the advantages of freer action for herself and a voice in directing the actions of others. The discovery was to prove portentous.

PART TWO

The

Actress

1627-1629

The Balcony of Marizápalos

For each month of the year
Madrid has prepared
A holiday to divert her people
In their leisure moments.
The echoes of merry Christmas
Reach as far as January;
February has its dances,
Its masks and its harlequins;
March celebrates the holiday
Of the glorious Patriarch. . . .
But, why go on
If in Madrid it is an established fact
That no week is without a fiesta?
Nor one month without a festival?
What the point is, and it matters,
Is that in July
There is a splendid festival.
It is the feast of Saint Anne and everyone knows
That this is one of three days
In the capital of Spain
When there are bulls in the Plaza.
A gathering throng
Hovers happily and noisily
On the recently built platforms
And in the balconies and windows.

The House of *Panadería*
Is gorgeous with glittering adornment
For according to custom its balcony
Awaits the King and Queen.
In front of the Portal of *Pañeros*
Rise the stands
Where all the Councils
Have a reserved place.
But only the Council of Castile
Is permitted to occupy a position
Face to face with the King.
There is no standing room in the Plaza,
There's not an empty balcony
Nor a deserted window,
Except toward the street
Of Boteros, where there's a house
That has no opening
Because it has no façade,
And then suddenly appears
An improvised balcony;
The balcony is empty
But on it rises a rich dais
And looking toward that place
Someone whispers.
"What are they waiting for?" some say.
"What are they waiting for? It's
Clear that it's for the owner of the dais
To come out to look at the fiesta."
"Is it known who she is?"
"The one who lives in back
Of the balcony."
    "The Calderona?"
"The very same one
Whom everyone calls the Marizápalos."
"Impossible! So daring,
It cannot be! The *comedianta*
Must not have forgotten that

Not so long ago
She was expelled
From a balcony by the Queen."
"Because of that, the monarch
Has made certain
A private dais for his ladylove."
And when a gentleman
Occupying a small place
Of the Portal of *Pretineros*
In the higher stands said this,
A confused and muffled rumor
Rose suddenly in the Plaza,
And with surprise and astonishment
The excited crowd could see
That simultaneously were occupying
Their balcony, the monarchs
And her dais, the Calderona.

—Ángel R. Chaves. Abbreviation from
Recuerdos del Madrid Viejo.
Leyendas de los Siglos XVI y XVII
(Selected Verses).

Chapter 10

IT was good to be back in Madrid, to be able to go to the theater again, not to one of the semiprivate performances at the palace, which took place twice a week and of which the Queen was the patroness; but to a public theater, the Corral de la Cruz, which was his favorite, though why Philip should have preferred it to the Corral de la Pacheca, he did not know for, to all intents and purposes, they closely resembled each other. Of course, theoretically, he did not go publicly; he went masked, inconspicuously attired and escorted, and stepped straight from his coach into one of the small, grilled rooms, known as *aposentos,* which comprised the first floor of one of the houses which surrounded a large open courtyard. These were all exactly alike, except that the interior grille of his was gilded. Here, without being seen and without acknowledged recognition, he could overlook both the section where benches were placed for that portion of the male audience which could pay well; the space which gave standing room to the men who could not; and the enclosed gallery—the *cazuela*—where women were seated separately. Aside from the pleasure which almost any dramatic performance gave him, there was the added delight in being at ease, at being hidden and in having the feeling of satisfied secrecy.

It was some time since he had been able to enjoy such an outing. He had been absent for several months in bleak Aragón and other provinces hardly more to his taste, and Olivares had been with him throughout this period. Meanwhile, Isabel had acted as his regent in Madrid. There was no denying that she had done this very ably; for the first time she had revealed herself not only as pleasure-loving, but as quite capable of statecraft. She had continued her careful study of crown revenues and taxes and had convinced Philip that a law, forbidding the further manufacture of *vellón,* should be passed, as Fernando had recommended. Philip was more than ready to give her credit for her industry and good business sense, as well as her adroitness in handling several ticklish situations, though, personally, he felt that this aptitude impaired, rather than enhanced, her feminine charm. Besides, she had taken advantage of her increase in power and opportunity to magnify the prejudice of the nobles, priests and ladies around her against Olivares; Philip was very much afraid that this would mean more unwelcome tasks for himself and was not disposed to thank his wife, if this should prove to be the case, as indeed it did. The Conde-Duque found, on his return, that he would have to take drastic measures to recover lost ground and his first step—a bold one—was to send the King a document headed:

PAPER FROM THE CONDE-DUQUE TO HIS MAJESTY, IN WHICH HE URGES HIM TO CONSIDER AND DISPATCH CURRENT AND PRIVATE AFFAIRS HIMSELF, WITHOUT OBTAINING THE OPINIONS OF THE JUNTA AND, ABOVE ALL, THE OPINION OF THE CONDE-DUQUE, SO THAT THE KING HIMSELF MAY, BY A STEP LATER, TAKE ENTIRE CONTROL OF AFFAIRS OF STATE AND GOVERNMENT.

The text of the document read:

Your Majesty is good witness of the many times I have told you how important it was for your best interests that people should not only see the result of your own actions, but that they should also recognize them as such, and give you the full credit for them. For it is certain, Sire, that in the present state of this republic no other course will remedy our ills. Let people recognize in Your Majesty attention, resolution, a determination to be obeyed, and if this be not sufficient, let it be recognized in the orders you give, and even in your own person in insignificant acts, nay in the most private actions in your own chamber, where most of the fears which the people entertain have their origin. I have tried to show you how indispensable it is for Your Majesty's conscience, for your reputation, and for the redress of the evils of the Government, that you should work, or everything will sink to the bottom, no matter how desperate my efforts may be to keep things going. I have decided, therefore, to make a last appeal to you, because during the last few months affairs have become so urgent that there really is no other course but that Your Majesty should put your shoulder to the wheel, or commit a mortal sin.

If Your Majesty will not do as I ask you, I will go away at once without asking your leave or even letting you know I am going.

I have said all that a subject may say, clearly and boldly; I would rather risk your anger than fail in my duty. The evil is great. Reputation has been lost, the treasury has been totally exhausted, ministers have grown venal and slack. Take, I pray you, Sire, the work into your own hands. Let the very name "favorite" disappear. I urge Your Majesty to shoulder this burden that God Himself has cast upon you, to labor with it, if you will, without overworking yourself, but not without work at all.

Being interpreted, the impassioned appeal meant that, as far as possible, Olivares intended to shift the responsibility for the terrible conditions in the country to Philip's shoulders. But the latter read it as an appeal to his conscience, which was always as easily pricked as it was easily soothed, and he dashed off a reply, writing this at the bottom of the last sheet which the Conde-Duque had used:

CONDE—

I have resolved to do as you ask me, for the sake of God, of myself and of you. Nothing is boldness from you to me, knowing, as I do, your zeal and love. I will do it, Conde, and I return you this paper with this reply, so that you may make it an heirloom of your house, that your descendants may learn how to speak to kings in matters that touch their fame, and that they may know what an ancestor they had. I should like to leave it in my archives to teach my children, if God grant me any, and other kings, how they should submit to what is just and expedient.

—I THE KING

Before he could put these good resolutions into practice, he fell gravely ill and Olivares found himself with a new set of problems. The Queen had not yet borne a child who lived more than a month or so; and neither Carlos—that easygoing, gentle young man, in appearance and character so like his elder brother—nor Fernando—the young Cardinal who was so much more able and animated—was on good terms with Olivares. Fernando, at the moment, was especially resentful because the Conde-Duque had succeeded in turning him out of his bedroom, in order that Olivares might occupy it during the King's illness. Again, the Conde-Duque resorted to a ruse. He himself took to his bed, a prey to some undefined but allegedly critical illness; and, while lying seemingly isolated and seemingly helpless, he carefully organized a plot by which he and his lieutenants, in the event of the King's death, could seize the government, use whatever measures were necessary to bring the Queen and the Infantes to a state of subjection and continue a triumphant progress.

As the Conde-Duque lay reflecting on the potential advantages of these arrangements, an attendant entered his room and told him that the King was conscious again and that there was every hope of his permanent improvement. Olivares sprang up in bed.

"Who told you this?" he inquired imperiously.

"Dr. Polanco," the attendant replied, naming the Chief Physician.

"Send him to me at once."

Dr. Polanco was not as speedy in obeying this summons as Olivares might have wished and, when he did come, he gave a very guarded reply: the King did appear to be a little better; but he was still by no means out of danger; he must be kept very quiet. Olivares went on summoning physicians until one brought him the message for which he had been waiting: His Majesty desired to see his Minister. In a surprisingly short time, for a presumably prostrate invalid, Olivares was up and dressed and on his way to the King's chamber, where he was doomed to disappointment. On either side of His Majesty's bed were standing his two brothers; and though Carlos was so genuinely delighted by his brother's improvement that he received the Minister politely, Fernando did not bother to conceal his displeasure at the intrusion and his dislike and distrust of the Conde-Duque. Olivares had every reason to be worried by such open enmity; the sooner the Cardinal could be sent out of the country, or at least away from the Court, the better it would be for everybody—that is, everybody connected with Olivares. The idea was by no means a new one. He had long considered the possibility of having Fernando made Viceroy of Flanders or Grand Admiral and Prince of the Sea or, possibly, Bishop of Oran. On the whole, it would probably be better to keep him in his ecclesiastical state. Perhaps, despite his youth, he might become Inquisitor-General. . . .

For the moment, however, there was nothing to do but to bow to the King's feebly murmured request to be left unburdened by the cares of the kingdom; he was very tired, he wanted only to rest; he would have to see his Minister later, after all. Olivares retired to continue his plotting and when, at last, the King was sufficiently recovered to listen, the Conde-Duque told tall tales of treachery in the immediate family.

"The Infante Fernando, Sire, is in very bad hands!"

"Really? What about Carlos? Is he in better hands?" the King inquired languidly and changed the subject.

Obviously, all schemes for sowing seeds of dissension in the family must lie in abeyance; but Philip was easily prevailed upon to write a letter, a copy of which was sent to each of his many counselors, treating the administrative actions of his reign as a case of conscience for himself:

I. If I have caused any damage or loss of property to anybody by any act or order of mine or otherwise, I desire that redress shall be given to the sufferers.
II. If by any means or way property belonging to any person be unjustly taken or withheld by any act of ours, I command that the wrong be righted at once.
III. Consider the means that can be devised to pay all my debts, so that in this respect my conscience may be clear, and in future as far as possible let all necessary expenses be justly met and paid.

IV. Consider whether any of the contributions payable by my vassals can be abolished, and what reform is possible, both as to the amounts levied and the mode of collection.

V. If any minister of your Council does any unjust act, if he fails to administer justice righteously, or if any grievance is inflicted by him on my subjects, severe punishment must be meted out to him. Great vigilance must be exercised by you in this respect.

VI. If, in order to favor or benefit me, any injustice has been done, it must be redressed at once, regardless of every other consideration.

Consider all this maturely, and report to me.

—I THE KING.

Having seen this letter on its way, with a great lifting of spirits, the King dismissed the whole matter from his mind and decided that he was now well enough to go to the theater again. He set out, incognito, to take his place in his *aposento* with no other companion than Olivares, who had also experienced a great lifting of spirits. The new comedy opened with every indication of being a success. The setting was adequate, the lines effective, the acting creditable. But Philip, who had removed his mask when he reached the seclusion of his grilled room, knew, as soon as he glanced at Guzmán, that something about the performance was not wholly satisfactory to the Conde-Duque.

"I find this very pleasing," he said agreeably. "Is there something about it which does not meet with your approval?"

"Your Majesty's glance is too penetrating. I'm not able to hide even a minor source of disappointment. It is, indeed, a promising production. But I am beginning to wonder if it is going to live up to its promise."

"Which was—?"

"That a young actress of the troupe, which is appearing for the first time tonight in Madrid, is really as charming as one of my agents, who had them sent up from the country, is so extravagantly claiming. I had expected her on stage sooner than this. If she does not come presently, the play will be half over before she is seen. And she was supposed to be playing the lead."

"Well, let us be patient. Wait—could that be the girl you have in mind? The one who has just entered from the left?"

Guzmán followed the direction of the King's nod and nodded in his turn. But, by common consent, neither spoke, for the girl's voice was so sweet and her use of it so captivating that both wanted to listen; and, as the comedy progressed, both became more and more entranced, for her acting was as arresting as her voice. She was, moreover, extremely graceful and, as she moved across the stage, she did this so lightly and so swiftly that it was a joy to watch her. When she disappeared into the wings, though the curtain had not yet fallen, the lack of her blithe presence instantly made itself felt.

"I would say that your agent justified your confidence in him, after all," Philip said, speaking in the rather toneless way which was becoming more and more a habit with him. "Where is the girl from?"

"Where could it be, but Andalucía?"

"Oh, it might have been somewhere else, though I admire your loyalty to your native heath. What is her name?"

"Inés. María Inés Calderón."

"Inés! The little saint of purity! Is that a fitting patroness for an actress?"

"Perhaps that would depend on how she interpreted it."

"Well—it might be amusing to find out. At all events, we should congratulate her on her performance this evening. Have the goodness to send someone to bring her here, after the play is over."

"With your permission, I shall escort her here myself."

Philip was quite prepared to be disillusioned. It was one thing to look at the girl and listen to her when she was on the stage, separated from the *aposento* by the space for standing room, the benches and the *cazuela*. It might be quite another when she was brought to close quarters with him. But, if anything, her voice sounded sweeter, her manner appeared more engaging than it had at a distance. Without being actually beautiful, she was very lovely to look at. She had gentle blue eyes, a disarming smile, a dimple or two. Her red-gold hair, which the two spectators had assumed to be a theatrical wig, proved to be her own, somewhat disarranged, but becomingly so, and there were masses of it. She had removed her make-up and now that the paint and powder were gone, the soft skin and the delicate pink and white coloring that normally went with such hair were delightfully revealed. Without the slightest sign of embarrassment, she answered questions about her family—she was one of several children and their parents were living; her age—she was just sixteen; her home—a few leagues from Seville; and her new career—which was very exciting; she thanked the gentlemen for the compliment of their praise. Perhaps she would take supper with them, the King suggested. She appeared to hesitate, still without embarrassment, though Philip felt sure that Guzmán had already revealed his companion's identity and, even if he had not, that she might well have heard the only *aposento* with a gilded grille was the one reserved for His Majesty. Without insistence, Philip suggested that, possibly, she would prefer the next evening. She thanked him and said that she would, though only because she had already accepted another invitation for tonight. It did not seem to occur to her that her sovereign's invitation should take precedence in any case. On the other hand, she obviously realized that she should not, a second time, decline to do his bidding.

"Shall I come again to this *aposento*?" she asked, speaking without timidity or eagerness, and dropping a curtsy.

"No. I shall be waiting for you in a pleasanter place," the King replied. "One of my gentlemen will come to bring you to me."

Chapter 11

THE room into which she was shown the following evening was a large one, softly lighted, partly from the candles which stood in tall silver candelabra and partly from the flames which gleamed in the great stone fireplace. In the middle of the apartment, set with glistening silver and fine crystal and a big bowl of glowing fruit, stood a table; and in one corner, where only a vigil light burned under a crucifix, was a great curtained bed on a raised platform. The walls were adorned with portraits of the King's brothers, the Infantes Fernando and Carlos, and of the Conde-Duque, and Inés gazed at them with rapt interest.

"Were these portraits painted by Don Diego de Velázquez?" she asked excitedly.

"Yes. How did you guess?"

"The night after my arrival in Madrid, some of my companions at the theater invited me to stroll along the Liars' Walk beside San Felipe; and from there we saw Don Diego's portrait of Your Majesty on horseback, displayed against the wall of the Oñate palace. It was the most wonderful picture I had ever seen. Of course, everyone is very proud of Don Diego in Andalucía and I was disappointed that, before I left Seville, I did not see his picture of the Adoration of the Magi which hangs in the home of his father-in-law Maestro Pacheco, though I did see some of Don Diego's still lifes. I was delighted when I heard that he had come to Madrid and that he had found favor with Your Majesty. Of course, I could only view Your Majesty's portrait at a distance! And now I can see these portraits of the Infantes and the Conde-Duque in the very room to which Your Majesty has brought me!"

"You may also see the equestrian portrait at close range whenever you like," the King told her. "It has been brought to the Alcázar and it can easily be placed in this room or any other room where you may come to visit me. It is quite true that Velázquez has found favor with me—in fact, I may put it a little more strongly than that. I like him immensely as a man and I consider him more than capable of fulfilling the functions of Court Painter. So I have provided him with a studio and living quarters for his family here at the palace in order that he may have space for his work and facilities for doing it. Furthermore, I have just made him a Gentleman Usher of the Privy Chamber with a regular allowance as such—the same stipend that the barbers' assistants receive—so that he may have ready access to me at any time. I will arrange to have you meet him if you like. I am always gratified that a guest's taste in pictures appears to be much the same as mine and especially so in your case. I hope that the same will be true of the dishes I have chosen for our supper. Shall we sit down and see if they are?"

The girl showed no nervousness over being at table alone with the King. She served herself moderately but not sparingly from each of the rich dishes passed to her and ate with healthy appetite. She suffered her cup to be refilled when she had emptied it of wine and held it up to the light to admire the color of its contents. And while she ate and drank, she chatted, easily and pleasantly, as she had in the *aposento,* of her home and her family, her role in the current play, the future for which she hoped on the stage. The King found increasing satisfaction in listening to her musical voice and watching her artless manner. When the last dish had been cleared away and the lackeys had left the room, she waited for some signal which would tell her what she was supposed to do next; and, as none came, unmindful of protocol, she asked a question without first having been addressed.

"Is it Your Majesty's wish that I should leave him now so that he may rest? Or can I contribute to his pleasure in some way by staying a little longer?"

"My rest will come with you and through you," he said slowly. "And you will contribute to my pleasure by staying. But I hope this will not be merely a little longer. I hope it may be a good deal longer."

"I am at Your Majesty's service. But I am afraid I do not wholly understand."

"I will explain to you."

It seemed impossible that she should be as completely lacking in experience as her words would indicate. Nevertheless, her guilelessness had the stamp of sincerity. He rose and came to her place at table, slipping an arm around her waist. She made no effort to withdraw from the caress, which at first was gentle, almost casual in character, even when the King drew her more closely to him and tightened his hold a little. She had immediately risen also and, though she looked at him questioningly, she smiled as she did so. She was a tall girl and he hardly needed to bend at all to bring his face close to hers. He kissed her gravely on the brow and then lightly on both cheeks before his lips strayed to her mouth. Even then, there had still been no insistence to their pressure when he asked her if what he did was offensive to her.

"Your Majesty, how could it be?" she asked.

From the way she spoke, it was impossible to doubt that the question was one of complete simplicity, as it was one of complete candor. "Then may I proceed?" he asked.

"But, Sire, you must know the answer is yes."

At his request, she had come to the palace straight from the theater, still wearing the peasant costume in which she had appeared on the stage, and there was no pointed lace-edged ruff around her graceful neck, above a rigid bodice tightly fastened with jeweled buttons, no vast farthingale secured around her waist. His kisses easily reached the breast he had bared by untying the single ribbon that fastened her loose white blouse and, as his hands strayed still further, he undid her full skirt with equal ease. Clad only in her shift, she was even lovelier than he had guessed. She stood very still, but if she felt either surprise or shame, she did not show it. Philip blew out the candles, leaving only the vigil light under the crucifix, and lifted her off her feet. She lay quietly in his arms as he crossed the narrow strip of carpet between the table and the bed.

"The kisses were very sweet, but I find they do not suffice," he said as he put her down on it.

He had never thought they would and, surely, this girl could not have thought so, either. She must have known, from the beginning, what he meant to do to her, but she still showed no signs of either fright or revulsion, and lay, silent and quiescent, where he had placed her, as if waiting, without anxiety, whatever he might next require of her. After all, she was a public entertainer, a girl of the people, who had come willingly enough from a small provincial village to become an actress in Madrid; to all intents and purposes, that meant becoming a courtesan as well. His conscience did not disturb him with its still small voice, as it sometimes did when he was preparing to seduce a lady of quality, presumably virtuous; he had never been so quickly kindled to urgency and he was conscious of no compulsion to repress this. Yet, he had hardly begun his eager trespass when he was halted by a strange misgiving.

"Surely, you are not a virgin!" he said, almost harshly.

"I believe Your Majesty has just realized that I am," she whispered. And then, bewildered by his unexpected restraint, she asked, "Does that make any difference, Sire?"

"Of course," he said, more harshly. "It makes you doubly desirable and should make you doubly invulnerable . . . not that it will," he added vehemently after a moment. "You are everything that I have long sought in vain and I would be less than human if I renounced you now. Then, afterward, I shall reproach myself."

"Your Majesty will reproach himself! For deigning to accept the only gift at my disposal?"

Suddenly he understood. She was trying to tell him not only that she believed he had a royal right to her maidenhood, but that she was joyous in being able to offer it to him. He was infinitely moved, but at the same time that his heart was touched, his senses were spurred; and, though he meant to be gentle, desire had become a driving force, consummation a crying need. Even so, with possession came tenderness and concern.

"I did not mean to hasten or hurt you. I did not want to. And I know I have. But you yielded so quickly and so completely—"

"Was it not meet that I should, Sire, since you are my king?"

"I would rather it had been because you knew me for your true love."

"Then let me dare to say it was for that reason, too. I have loved Your Majesty from the first moment I saw him."

"As I have you, dear heart."

He drew her to him again, this time with gentleness and, after he had embraced her once more, she went to sleep in his arms. He lay awake for a long time, delighting in her and cherishing her. Then he, too, fell asleep and his slumber was peaceful and profound.

Chapter 12

IF he could have had his way with her in everything, as he could and did in their lovemaking, he would have insisted on her retirement from the stage. But on that point, she was firm. She was an actress, just as he was a king; they must both do their appointed work; and she was so insistent about it that he actually attended to his royal duties with more industry and energy than ever before, and spent more time in the open air, so that he might be physically fit to meet his mental obligations. He had always been a superb horseman, but he had insisted that, since the Conde-Duque was rightly regarded as the greatest in the kingdom, he had not been inclined to dispute this title; now it intrigued him to do so, at the same moment that he took over more of his Minister's work. This gave only tempered satisfaction to Olivares, who was afraid that, at this rate, control of the kingdom might slip from his own grasp; in providing a new attraction, his purpose had been entirely different. The Queen, too, fretted because the King did not join her in more of the pastimes devised for them; she pouted a little. It seemed he was spending more and more time with Velázquez; hardly a day passed that Philip was not in Diego's studio at the palace, taking his ease in a great leather armchair and watching the process of covering huge bare canvases with color. If the King had time for that, the Queen insisted, he should also have more time for balls, for torchlight parades, for equestrian shows. Even the theater did not seem to interest him as much as it once had.

The latest complaint was certainly made tongue in cheek. What the Queen really meant was that her husband did not frequent the private performances at the palace and that he seldom went to the

Corral de la Pacheca any more. On the other hand, he never failed to be in his *aposento* at the Corral de la Cruz when la Calderona was playing there. If the Queen did not mention the further fact that la Calderona nearly always came to the palace to sup with the King after a performance, it was not because she ignored this. It was partly because, like everyone else, she viewed the King's new liaison with comparative tolerance, since it had had the effect of weaning him away from more questionable associations; and it was partly because, on the one occasion when she had given public evidence of her resentment, her impetuous action had proved a boomerang:

Inés had taken her place on a balcony to view a spectacle in the Plaza Mayor, given to celebrate the feast day of St. Peter and St. Paul, at almost the same moment that the Queen had taken hers on her own balcony and the attention of the populace had immediately been diverted from the royal family to the royal favorite. This was the first time la Calderona had appeared in public, except when she herself was acting, since the King's attentions to her had become common knowledge and she was the object of tremendous friendly curiosity to the people who considered the product of a small village as one of their own and had taken pride in her achievements as an actress. Isabel, piqued by the enthusiastic demonstration of the populace, rashly decided that this should be the last time, as well as the first, that the limelight would be stolen from the Queen and ordered that the opposite balcony should be vacated. This was promptly and quietly done and she felt she had scored a triumph—after suffering such a public rebuke, la Calderona would certainly not risk a second one. But Isabel had reckoned without her host.

Fiestas came frequently on the calendar and the next, in honor of Santa Ana's feast day, was one of exceptionally great gala. The Plaza Mayor was as sumptuously adorned as it had been in honor of the Prince of Wales, its hundreds of balconies hung with crimson and gold. All the stands, erected especially for the occasion, were filled with spectators in merrymaking mood and all the balconies crowded with more privileged onlookers; a latecomer would have found it impossible to get space anywhere, though there were more than six hundred available windows in the tall buildings that framed the plaza and fifty thousand persons could be crowded into its open

area. For the occupation of the royal family, the plaza's most imposing structure had been prepared and suitably decorated. This was
the *Casa Panadería,* a four-story, red brick building with twin towers at either end, arcades on the ground floor and row after row of
railed balconies above these. On the opposite side of the plaza, before
the Portal of the Pañeros, had been prepared the dais for the Council
of Castile—the only group entitled to be seated face to face with His
Majesty. This was also according to custom and caused no surprise.
But the gaze of the multitude was soon diverted from Royalty and
Council to a house on the corner of the Calle de los Boteros, which
had a uniquely blank façade. As far as anyone could remember, this
house was the only one on the plaza which had never had a balcony.
What could have happened to it? Certainly it had one now and,
moreover, this balcony was the most richly adorned of all. It was
empty and the people, almost with one accord, stared at it in fascina-
tion, waiting to see who would occupy it. When la Calderona, magnificently dressed in gold brocade, stepped out on it and graciously
acknowledged the plaudits with which she was greeted, the enthusiasm of the crowd became uproarious. This time, it was the Queen
who left the plaza before the spectacle had begun.

That night, she did something she had not done since they were
still children, playing at love; she came on her own initiative to the
King's apartments and, finding them empty, as she expected, save
for the Gentlemen of the Bedchamber in the anteroom, awaited his
return and confronted him with fury: he had insulted her publicly
and all for a cheap little actress who did not even have the decency
to refuse herself to other lovers. If he would go to la Calderona's
house, unannounced, instead of always having her brought to the
palace. . . .

"I have just come from her house," Philip answered, interrupt-
ing the outburst. He spoke with his usual calmness, but it was evident to Isabel that he, too, was very angry. "It may interest you to
know that I did so at her request—to receive an ultimatum. She did
not accept my invitation to supper tonight, not because she wanted
to receive another lover, but because she wanted to tell me that she
would never again consent to appear at a public spectacle, except on
the stage when she herself was playing a part. She told me she was

very much ashamed because of the balcony scene this evening. I reminded her that there would have been no such scene had it not been for the one that occurred on the feast of St. Peter and St. Paul, for which *you* were responsible—indeed, there would not have been a balcony hastily constructed on a blank façade. She insisted that was entirely different, that you were quite justified in asking her to leave the Plaza Mayor, if her presence there were displeasing to you, though she had not thought it would be, when she went there in a wholly private capacity, so to speak. She had not realized that the people already recognized her as my mistress and that they had become attached to her on her own account. Now she does realize it and, unless I consent to her conditions, she will decline to visit me in the future."

"You may be very sure that if she does that, it will not be because she is ashamed of what happened today, but because she is looking for a pretext to have more free time for another lover."

The King shrugged his shoulders. "If you are talking about Medina de las Torres," he said, this time speaking coldly as well as calmly, "it may interest you to know that I threw him out of her house, very early in my association with her—apparently with her entire approval. As it happens, the first time I invited her to have supper with me—which was also the first night I saw her—she asked to be excused on account of a previous engagement. It was, of course, a very naïve thing to do—she did not realize an actress does not properly decline an invitation from a king because of 'a previous engagement.' But I found this naïveté rather refreshing—it is certainly rare. She did not mention the name of her prospective host, but of course I took prompt steps to find out who it was and, yes, you are quite right, it was Medina de las Torres. Unquestionably, he made advances to her that night, but also, unquestionably, they were unsuccessful."

"What makes you so sure?"

"Because the next night she came to me and—I confess, to my great surprise—I found that she was still a virgin. I assume you do not need to have me explain to you, in detail, how I know this."

"No," Isabel said contemptuously. "I realize that you are an expert in such matters. And I admit that she played her cards very well on that occasion. But this was four months ago. Since then—"

"Since then, she has visited me almost every evening. And on the few evenings when she has asked to be excused from doing so, I have missed her so much that I have usually gone to her house, and always without telling her beforehand whether or not I intended to do so. It was on one of these occasions that I threw out Medina de las Torres. Although I did not actually injure him, much as I was tempted to do so, I acted with such force that I do not think he will be tempted to repeat the experiment, even if he were in a position to try. As it is, he is not, for I have given him formal permission to leave Madrid for an indefinite period. Moreover, I have now installed my old nurse, Ana de Guevara, in the house on the Calle de los Boteros and I feel reasonably sure that in the future Inés will be free from intrusion."

"I am surprised that the Conde-Duque permits such an appointment. After all, it was he who was responsible for poor Ana's banishment from the palace."

"I will explain to him, just as he used to explain such matters to me when I was a child, that I feel the time has now come for her quiet reinstatement in a new capacity. This is not an official appointment, but a wholly domestic arrangement. And, since his son-in-law is responsible for its necessity, I do not believe he will feel inclined to find much fault with it. After all, he is a reasonable man. I wish I could say as much for you as a woman."

The King had remained standing throughout his conversation with his wife. Now he glanced casually at the clock and bowed.

"It is rather late," he remarked. "Will you permit me to escort you back to your own apartments? I am afraid you must be very tired. You are not usually so ill tempered or so lacking in dignity. Tomorrow the scene at the Plaza Mayor will be almost the sole subject of gossip on all the Liars' Walks and every pamphleteer and ballad-monger will be hard at work. You have injured your position and mine by inviting an actress to outface a queen. That was most unbecoming. Can you imagine, for a moment, that under similar circumstances your mother would have retreated before Gabrielle d'Estrée? Of course not! Perhaps you are not only exhausted but ill. I hope that you will feel better after a good night's rest. If not, I shall insist on summoning a physician."

Inés was as good as her word: she never again appeared in public except as an actress; and, viewed by the standards of the day, she was a model of decorum. She went regularly to rehearsals, she was courteous to her fellow players and did not give them the impression that she thought royal favor had taken her out of their milieu. She filled every theatrical part for which she was cast with ease and grace and occasionally invited other members of the company to her house and accepted invitations from them for the early evening. But at the end of each performance, she slipped quietly away to the room where she knew the King would be waiting for her.

The servants did not come to serve supper until he summoned them; he liked to be alone when he greeted Inés and this he always did with tenderness and affection. In leisurely companionship, they told each other everything that had happened since they had last parted. It was not until he rang that anyone intruded on their happy *solitude à deux;* and though the service given them was perfect in all its details, it was not prolonged. Then, after supper was finished, by common consent and with no discussion of something that should be taken for granted, they made love and went to sleep in each other's arms.

Philip had wanted to install Inés in an elegant apartment with attendants and furnishings of her own; and she had declined to consider this, just as she had declined to give up acting and to receive costly presents. The room which the King had chosen for their first assignation was the one to which she wanted to return, night after night, the only one she wanted set aside for her use. And what would she do with a retinue, a country girl who had always waited on herself? It was fitting, of course, for his safety, that the King should be escorted when he came to her and when he left her for the state apartments of the Alcázar; nor did it disturb her to know that his attendants on these occasions were well aware of what was happening beyond the doors that were closed to them. It was also fitting that the King should have his cupbearer at his side while he supped, that everything about his table should be in accordance with his rank. But these accouterments were for him and not for her. She wanted from him nothing that he could give her except himself. And, as far as it was in him to give to anyone, he gave to her.

As a solemn and lonely boy, he had wholeheartedly welcomed the gay companionship of a lively, attractive young girl; his life had been immeasurably brightened by Isabel's vivacity and, as far as it was possible for him to fall in love at such an early age, he had done so. But it was attraction based primarily on adolescent impulse heightened by propinquity; he did not miss her greatly when he was separated from her, as on his recent sojourn in the provinces. His feeling for her had not always been strong enough to sublimate jealousy and anger. Though it had never occurred to him or anyone else, including the Queen, that he would be faithful to his marriage vows, while he exacted such faithfulness from her, the affairs in which he had so far indulged had been only passing fancies, the subject of tittle-tattle, but not really troublesome in any way, least of all to the King's peace of mind. Now, for the first time, as a grown man, he loved deeply and passionately; and the knowledge that his love was returned in full measure, without self-interest or self-seeking, intensified his ardor and his devotion. If Inés had been willing to accept a half of his kingdom, he would have joyfully given it to her. But she had spoken the truth: it was the man, not the monarch, whom she loved.

In their first raptures, they were heedless of the probability that their passion would be productive; and when a year had passed without such results, though they no longer ignored it as an eventuality, it did not trouble them. If, during all these months when the King had come to her night after night, Inés had not conceived, surely she would never do so! Then one evening she fainted dead away in the middle of a performance and, though she revived quickly and insisted on going on to the end, receiving tremendous applause for her courage, malicious whispers were mingled with the expressions of sympathy and admiration. The King who, as usual, was present at the theater when she acted, was deeply concerned; but she succeeded in soothing him before he left her at dawn the next morning. It was nothing, she insisted, except the unseasonable heat, bad enough everywhere in the city, almost insufferable in the wings of the theater. However, when she swooned again, this time while she was quietly preparing for bed in the great airy room which they shared and the King himself was the one who restored her to consciousness, his anxiety was not so easily assuaged. As he laid his hand over her heart, to assure himself of its steady beating, he noticed a change in her bosom. Her breasts were beautifully formed and very soft, but they had been small; after all, she was still very young. Now, unless the flickering candlelight and his own sense of touch were playing tricks, they had become larger and firmer. He had not forgotten the first time he had noticed a similar change in the Queen, when he was only a boy of fifteen. He and Isabel had jested about it, as they did about everything at the beginning of that unfortunate pregnancy, which had ended with the premature birth of their first daughter. They had thought that the first change in her person and those that followed it were all very amusing. But Philip was not amused now.

"My darling, is there something you haven't told me?"

"I would have told you—presently. It was too soon for me to be sure."

"Too soon?" He looked at her questioningly and put his hand over her heart again. She took it in both of hers and raised it to her lips.

"We can still have some months of happiness together if that is my true love's wish. And then I shall go back to my own pueblo and the public here will forget me."

"I doubt if the public will ever forget you. Certainly your true love will not. But then there will be no chance to forget, for I shall not permit you to leave me. The stage, yes, that you must do at once. But you will leave it for the palace. So far, I have bowed to your wish that you should have no attendants, that this one room should serve as your bower. You shall keep this, because you have become attached to it—as I have because it was here I first took you for my own and because of the many times since then that we have been rapturously together. But there are other rooms leading out of it which must be made into a suite for your greater ease and comfort; you will now spend all your time here. And, of course, there must

*Philip, Prince of Asturias, afterward Philip IV, at the time
of his marriage to Isabel de Bourbon.*

Isabel de Bourbon at the time of her marriage to the Prince of Asturias, later Philip IV.

Conde-Duque de Olivares.

Velázquez — self-portrait.

Philip IV as a young king of Spain.

Isabel de Bourbon as a young queen of Spain.

be suitable attendants to wait on you—women of mature years, kindly and competent. When do you think this child of ours will be born?"

"Not before mid-April, Sire. And I could well continue to act until after the New Year."

"As far as your figure is concerned, very likely. But I cannot have you taking chances with your health. It is too precious to me."

"Will you not make a bargain with me, Sire, and agree that if there is no more swooning, I may act through the festivals of the *Navidad*? I have heard that often these fainting fits come only early in this period of expectancy, as does sometimes a distaste for food and other unpleasant symptoms which I have not had at all. If Your Majesty will agree to what I ask, I will agree to come to the palace and stay—until after the child is born. Is that not a fair bargain?"

He hesitated, but she now had her arms around his neck and was drawing him down closer to her. The candlelight was not so flickering that it failed to disclose her loveliness as she lay there— the loveliness which had seemed to increase, night by night, and which had never been as irresistible as it was now. When his lips met hers, he consented to do what she asked.

Chapter 13

FROM that time on, her health remained radiant and her farewell performance was a triumph. There was a gala banquet after it, attended by numerous grandees; toasts were drunk, gifts exchanged and many laudatory references made to la Calderona's great talents as an actress, and to the loss which the theater would sustain in her "temporary" absence, because she had given so much to her art that her physicians were enjoining a period of rest. ("So much to her *art!* Rather so much to the King!" ran some of the whispers. "And it is to be hoped that *he* will now let her rest—or there will be another stillborn premature child, or one that is malformed and diseased." . . . "No, no!" came the vehement answer. "This child will not be born before term, whenever that is, nor will it be malformed or diseased. Granted that it was conceived in sin; it was not conceived within the bonds of consanguinity, forbidden except by special dispensation. And its mother is not a delicate princess, but a healthy girl of the people, albeit, she can put most Court beauties to shame by her looks. She will bear her child easily and it will have her health and her looks and it will be a boy. The King will have a son at last." . . . "But not, alas! an heir." . . . "Perhaps not. The Emperor Charles V could not make Don Juan of Austria his heir. But he made him the greatest prince in the world and that prince made himself the greatest hero of the age at Lepanto!")

The gossips who whispered, first at the banquet and later on the Liars' Walks, continued to dispute and to prophesy and the King and his love knew of this, but it did not disturb them overmuch. Their affair had attained an idyllic quality. Heavy doors had been opened out on either side of the great room which had been their first trysting place and where stood the curtained bed to which the King still came as often as ever, though now it was with passion restrained by tenderness, for never would he let his sweetheart feel that he had failed her in this when she most needed it. On one side of this room was the one where now slept the two women whom the King had chosen to care for Inés—a room less sumptuous than hers, but still with everything needed for comfort; it had seemed natural for Ana de Guevara to accompany the girl to the palace and Philip had left the selection of his old nurse's companion to her discretion; on the other side was the room where Philip and Inés now sat to dine and which he had caused to be richly adorned. Its floor was covered with rare rugs and its windows were hung with rich draperies. Among the tapestries on the walls were great mirrors and a new painting by another young aspiring artist named Alonso Cano, which the King had prevailed upon Inés to accept as a gift because it was such a gentle and touching representation of her patron saint. There was always a fire burning on the great hearthstone through the winter evenings, and its glancing light fell on the tapestries and the picture and the polychrome statues that the King had brought there for the room's greater embellishment, as well as on the King and his love as they sat at meat, or at chess, or side by side while one sang to the other and the one who was not singing strummed some instrument. The King himself was an accomplished musician, as well as an accomplished ballad maker and sonneteer; and after he had first composed the verses, he then sang songs to his own accompaniment on a guitar or a lute. And la Calderona learned all the words he wrote, so that sometimes she sang to him, instead of he to her, and sometimes they sang together in a harmonious duet.

She encouraged him to develop his obvious but neglected talents, to take them more seriously. At first, he laughed at her. Since he knew he could not write satires like Quevedo, sonnets like Góngora or plays like Calderón de la Barca and Lope de Vega, to mention only a few of those he had gathered around him, what was the use of trying?

It was not primarily competition she was urging, Inés said; it was creation—though, as far as that went, certainly there was no reason why he should not match his wit against others in the Literary Academies and the Floral Games then so greatly in vogue. At all events, it would please her very much if he would try to do so. He needed no other spur after this simple statement; and the ballads which he brought her, before offering them to select groups, won prizes, not because he was the King, but because she had inspired him to write real poetry.

As they spoke more and more of his talents, they spoke less and less of hers, for Inés did not refer, of her own accord, to a resumption of her theatrical career; and though she made her former companions welcome when they came to see her, she was not the one to suggest that they should do this. So, gradually, they came less and less, for they understood that she was content to be alone, except when the King could be with her, and that her heart was so wholly his that she could no longer share it easily with anyone else. When she walked abroad, as she did every day at dusk, for air and exercise, enveloped in a great fur-lined velvet cloak, which shielded her from the cold and from the gaze of the curious, one or both of her tire-women went with her and she kept either to the secluded gardens in the palace grounds or to one of the less frequented walks near by. Even in a city where assault and robbery were matters of such common occurrence that they caused little or no comment, she was safe; she was known by sight to everyone and beloved by all, except those who were jealous of her; and the few who did not wish her well would not have dared to lay a finger on the prospective mother of the King's child.

The baby, as she had expected, was born at mid-April—"the most beautiful and perfect child that ever was seen"—and taken, richly robed, when he was four days old, to the parochial Church of San Justo y Pastor for his baptism. His godfather was Don Melchor de Vera, Gentleman of the Bedchamber to the King, who had been the first to escort Inés to the palace and who had been her firm and faithful friend ever since. And when the ceremony was over, the baby was brought back to his mother's room by the King himself. It would have been contrary to etiquette for him to appear at the baptism, even of a legal heir; but he had managed to flout protocol by observing everything from a closely curtained pew, which he reached from an adjoining house. And now, holding the child in his arms, he described its exemplary behavior in glowing terms and acknowledged that he had insisted on giving it the name of his great-uncle.

"The second Don Juan of Austria will become even more famous than the first," he told Inés. "Everyone already recognizes him as my son, but this recognition will be formalized in due course of time. He shall be brought up in royal state, which he will adorn." The King looked fondly down at the beautiful baby, who was beginning to show signs of restlessness and then, handling him with the inexpertness typical of all males, brought him to the bed and laid him down beside his mother. "As you will," he said, bending over to kiss her and to fasten in place a magnificent necklace.

"Sire, it was agreed that I should accept no gifts," she said quietly. She did not try to remove the necklace, as both hands were occupied with the baby; but something in her tone told the King that, as soon as she could release herself, she would undo the diamond clasp and let the jeweled chain fall in a glittering heap on her bedside table. There was the same finality about her tone that had been there when he had first tried to persuade her to give up acting and live entirely on his bounty and for their joint pleasure.

"Yes, but didn't that agreement come to an end when I gave you this?" he asked, pointing to the baby, who was now nursing greedily.

"Because you gave me this, there is all the more reason why our agreement should hold. It is enough for me to have borne the child of the greatest monarch on earth."

"Dear love, I am not the greatest monarch on earth. You are confusing generations. That was the father of the other Don Juan."

"You are perhaps not as great as he in some respects," she said calmly, as if quite willing to concede the point. "But you are still the greatest one on earth today. You are not only a patron of the arts which have so flourished under your leadership that Spain has attained a preeminent place in the world of culture. You are yourself a painter, a poet and a musician of impeccable taste and exceptional talent. Of what other king can you say as much? Louis of

France? Charles of England? Sire, you are pleased to jest. And this is no moment for jesting. It is a moment for sober speech. When you spoke of bringing up our child in royal state, just what did you mean by that? Where is this royal state to be kept?"

"Why here! With you at its head."

"Sire, you know that cannot be. You have a wife—a Queen."

"She will lose nothing by what I give to you. She will only resemble more closely the queens of her own country who accept, without question, the *maîtresses en titre* of their husbands. I am planning that the same arrangement, the same recognition shall take place here. Why should the King of Spain relegate his true love to the place of light-o'-love while the King of France glorifies his?"

"Is it real glory, Sire? Or does it have the glitter of false gold? My glory is that I have been your love, your true love, as you have been mine. But it has been a sinful love, for you are the husband of another woman and I am not your wife, but your mistress."

"More dearly loved than any wife could ever be. Will you not grant that, since kings are not free to choose their wives, they should at least be free to choose their loves and that, without remorse?"

"I wish that I could say yes, Sire."

Looking at her more closely, he saw that her eyes were filled with tears and, when he would have kissed them away, she turned her head so that he could not do so.

"It has been a joyous love, but a sinful one, as I said before," she repeated. "And now that it has been crowned by this gift of a fair son, it must end. As soon as provision can be made for our child, so that he will not miss his mother too much, I must beg your leave to go."

"*To go!* To go where?"

"I had thought of the Badiel Valley. In it there is a little village called Valfermoso da las Monjas and near by a convent of the same name, where I would be made welcome. My mother has a kinswoman in the Community."

"Valfermoso de las Monjas! A hamlet in a deep valley of the Alcarria Range! A region of moor and of scrub and of little else besides! You would leave a royal lover and a royal palace for a cloistered life in a place like that!"

"Yes, Sire, I not only would, I shall."

Before he could move swiftly enough to stop her, she had put down the baby, now peacefully sleeping, removed the necklace and slipped from the bed to her knees before him.

"Sire, permit the mother of your son to go and sin no more. Let her devote the remainder of her life to cloistered sanctity. Is this too great a boon for her to ask of her King? That she should spend her days in prayer for divine pardon—for herself, but most of all for him?"

"I will not suffer you to kneel to me, Inés. Neither will I suffer you to leave me."

For the first time, he spoke to her sternly. But she was strongly built and, though childbirth was still but a few days behind her, she was able to resist him when he tried to raise her to her feet. She put her arms around his knees and clung to him.

"Sire, I have heard it said that the Queen again has hopes of a child. You have not been with me so constantly that you have forgotten your duty toward her and to the kingdom. I believe the rumors are true and that, this time, if she receives the same loving care that I have had, she may bring forth a healthy child. And I pray that it may be a son—a son truly entitled to every prerogative of the throne. And when this happens, I, in my quiet convent, will lead the prayers of thanksgiving."

For a full hour, they strove against each other in both speech and action. Then the child began to whimper and both knew that the strife between them must end so that she could suckle him again. There was something about her, as she lay down again, with the baby at her breast, that reminded the King of the first time he had seen her lying in that same bed, when he had been struck with the strange and sudden knowledge that he was not about to claim a courtesan, but to ravish a virgin. He had been halted then, though not to the extent of leaving her inviolate, at least to the extent of trying to treat her, however unsuccessfully, with the same tenderness, the same effort toward gentleness, that he would have shown a lawful bride. Now he was halted further still. Though he had been astonished at her vigor, the fact remained that it was only a few days since her travail; he could not take her, when she was hardly past parturition, when she had not yet been churched—decency, as well as compassion, forbade it. And yet he knew, as he looked down on her, that if he did not possess her then, she would never be at his mercy again. She would first evade him and then escape him; she would go to her lonely convent in its desolate valley, to lead a life of poverty, chastity and obedience, in remission of sins.

In the fullness of this knowledge, he bent over and kissed her once—Inés and the child asleep beside her. Then he left her, gathering up the spurned necklace as he did so.

PART THREE

The Queen Regent

1629-1642

A restless figure, never fully at ease either with others or with himself, Olivares was less one personality than a whole succession of personalities, co-existing, competing and conflicting within a single frame. By turns ebullient and dejected, humble and arrogant, shrewd and gullible, impetuous and cautious, he dazzled contemporaries with the versatility of his performance and bewildered them with his chameleon changes of mood. Somehow he always seemed larger than lifesize, bestriding the Court like a colossus, with state papers stuck in his hat and bulging in his pockets, always in a flurry of activity, surrounded by scurrying secretaries, ordering, hectoring, cajoling, his voice booming down the corridors of the palace. No man worked harder, or slept less.

— U. H. Elliott. *Imperial Spain* 1469–1716.

In Philip II, shrewdness, prudence, reserve, and severity were qualities overemphasized to defend himself from inner weakness. Lack of will power was already evident in Philip III, who also lacked the resources with which to disguise it, and for that reason sought refuge in religious fanaticism and in the self-reliance of his *Privado*, the Duke of Lerma. The degeneration of will power appeared still more clearly in the sons of the devout king. However, in Philip IV and the Cardinal-Infante, the two whose lives are of historical importance, the paralysis of initiative and decision was balanced by other excellent qualities and by the intrinsic goodness common to all the dynasty, especially to Philip IV. Actually, this king was intelligent, spiritual and full of courtly grace. It is difficult to define the influence of heredity in his case. His brother, the Cardinal-

Infante, was gifted with great personal prestige, as was evident from his career in Flanders; he was a military leader in the best traditions of the golden age. This quality harks back through two generations of kings who were neither ecclesiastics nor soldiers—his father and grandfather—to his glorious great-grandfather, Charles V. If it were possible for the historian to play the game—prohibited because it is fundamentally immoral—of enlarging upon what might have happened if things had been different, one of the most agreeable aspects of the game would be to dream about the potential future of Spain if the throne of Philip III had been inherited by Don Fernando, the general, and not by Don Philip, the philanderer.

—G. Marañón. *El Conde-Duque de Olivares*
(La Pasión de Mandar).

Chapter 14

THE birth of her only son, Baltasar Carlos, nine years after the consummation of her marriage and after the loss, almost every year, of a baby girl, completely changed the tenor of Isabel de Bourbon's life.

The sarcasms of the Conde-Duque, regarding the sole usefulness of women, were stilled forever, as far as she was concerned; if she had been less successful in dealing with the Condesa's persistently arrogant attitude, she could afford to disregard it; she also could afford to dismiss from her mind all resentment of the other baby boy, six months older than her own, now entrusted to the watchful care of reliable but alien guardians at Ocaña, while his mother served her sacrificial novitiate in a remote convent of the Badiel Valley. Since la Calderona's insistent withdrawal, Philip had treated Isabel with the greatest tenderness and consideration; and though she was well aware that the lack of ardor in his attitude toward her was not due entirely to her condition, she felt equally sure that there had been no successor to the actress in his affections and she doubted if there ever would be. For the time being, the King, who had sustained a severe shock in the loss of his "true love," was still stunned by it; and though, later on, there would be transient affairs again, these were inevitable, given his temperament and training; and Isabel could accept those philosophically, as long as no deep abiding emotion was involved. Actually, Inés had unsuspectingly imposed a new restraint on the King by her willful retirement; this had been so highly regarded as showing delicate feeling that it was now tacitly understood a convent must be the proper and logical sequel after a liaison with the King, that

· 129 ·

he must never have a successor in a subject's affections; and more than one young lady had taken to locking her door on the mere suspicion that Philip was casting amorous glances in her direction. One rebel had actually cried out, "No, no, Sire! I don't want to be a nun!" and, as she was overheard, there had been some unseemly jests on the subject. Philip's sense of humor, never very keen, had not been strong enough to dismiss these jests lightly. Isabel was amused as well as gratified by them.

Even though the secondary purpose of her marriage—a guarantee of friendship between her native country and her adopted country—had not been fulfilled, her failure in Spain had been no greater than her sister-in-law's in France and this was a source of some consolation: the Infanta Ana's marriage to Louis XIII had been expected to achieve the same results as Isabel de Bourbon's to Philip IV and these had been circumvented by Richelieu just as successfully as hers by Olivares. Besides, her French origin had long since been forgiven and, indeed, by many almost forgotten, since she had proved herself, in so many ways, essentially a Spaniard. She had been popular from the beginning, beloved since she had sacrificed her jewels to help finance the wars which the Hapsburgs were almost incessantly waging against their numerous enemies. Now that she had provided an heir to the throne, she was acclaimed. Her birthday, which marked her first public appearance after her confinement, was made the occasion of unprecedented celebrations in her honor; and an open area, which had just been transformed, seemingly almost by magic, into a royal seat and given the name of the Buen Retiro, made an ideal setting for these.

Olivares was responsible for this remarkable transformation and was justly proud of the ingenuity and speed with which his project had been carried out. Always on the alert, as far as the King's temperament and tastes were concerned, he had long been aware that the grim old Alcázar, on the cliff overlooking the Manzanares, had never appealed to Philip as the setting for his frivolities; though his idyll with la Calderona had marked a happy interlude, he was more and more inclined, as time went on, to regard this royal palace as a place where his beloved father had died, in a tragic way, and where he had been obliged to take over the heavy burden of government at the age of sixteen, quite unprepared to deal with such a hive of intrigue, hate and jealousy. The Escorial was equally distasteful to him; as far as he was concerned, it was primarily a mausoleum, not a pleasance. Aranjuez, he enjoyed, but that had been pronounced insalubrious, except in the springtime; and though the reason for this was not clear to him, he accepted it, as he did other vague pronouncements, rather than taking the trouble of investigating or denying them. He enjoyed the Pardo, where he had merrily begun his wedded life, and the *Casa de Campo,* sometimes the scene of less legitimate pleasures; but, after all, those were hardly more pretentious than hunting lodges and were intended to be used chiefly as such.

Conscious of all this, Olivares decided that the situation warranted a fifth royal residence in the Madrid area; and, fortunately, the extensive and beautiful grounds, attached to the Royal Monastery of San Jerónimo, were available for his purposes, as was the monastery's suite of apartments which was set aside for occupancy by the royal family during periods of retreat or mourning. There was no reason why this suite should not be enlarged and redecorated for more permanent residence—why, indeed, a separate building should not be provided for the King's accommodation—why a few fountains and summerhouses should not be added to the general decor. And, presently, there was another palace, this one bright, elegant and airy, and a series of groves and gardens, all in a setting of lakes and cascades. For a surprisingly long time, Olivares had managed to keep his vast plan a secret from the King by seeing that His Majesty was diverted elsewhere; and when the final results of his project were revealed, in all their imaginative taste and magnitude, the King was unstinted in his praise of his chamberlain's achievements. A ceremonious inaugural took place, at which Olivares—the self-constituted Honorary Constable of the palace —knelt to hand its golden keys to the King on a silver salver and the King returned them with an affectionate salute. Thereafter, came a series of gorgeous entertainments—cane tourneys, bullfights, balls, masques—which delighted the Queen as much as they did the King. Therefore, the celebration of her birthday furnished a welcome pretext to prolong and repeat these.

The baptism of the heir to the throne was an event of even greater seasonal importance; and the new Queen of Hungary acted as sponsor for Baltasar Carlos at his christening, which was even more splendid than those of his poor little short-lived sisters. She welcomed this opportunity to shine in reflected glory. Earlier that year, when she was still only the Infanta María, she had been married, by proxy, to the Emperor's heir, Ferdinand Ernest, and, as Philip was ill at the time, the wedding had taken place in his apartments, with the Queen and the Infantes Carlos and Fernando as almost the only other witnesses. Throughout the ceremony, the King had reclined on his bed, clad in a dressing gown, and the sole decorations, even suggestive of proper preparations for a bridal, were the flowered carpets which had been laid, the silken curtains which had been hung and a couple of new mirrors. María was aggrieved and complained to Isabel, who was still her best-beloved confidante; they agreed that the Conde-Duque was probably to blame, though it was not apparent that they had any sound reason for this; and a further source of grievance was provided by the delay in arranging for a suitable escort to take the new queen to her husband's home. However, just before the birth of Baltasar Carlos, a special envoy from the Emperor arrived in the person of Prince Guastalla, who brought with him gifts for the bride, valued at more than three hundred thousand ducats, and an urgent summons for her to start on her way at once.

Five years had now elapsed since she took a fond farewell of the Prince of Wales and he had already married Henriette Marie of France, the sister of Louis XIII. She had been sure for a long while that her heart was broken; now she was ready to admit that it had only been badly wounded and she was not yet wise enough to know that she could not escape the common lot of carrying the scars made by a wound from first love to her grave. She had been "docile" when the new match was proposed to her, though she was, not unnaturally, inclined to regard her second suitor as a laggard in love, when she contrasted his wooing with the first's, and to feel the lack of tender messages and small keepsakes; but she was placated with the prospect of a royal progress in the immediate future and her eventual position as Empress of the Holy Roman Empire, which would carry with it far more glamour and prestige than the position of Queen Consort of England. Moreover, the company of her three brothers, who all went with her as far as Zaragoza, leaving Isabel to act as Regent again, served as a very effective solace for the time being. The rest of her journey, made under the supervision of the Duke of Alba, was tedious and uncomfortable; winter soon set in and there was a long delay before she could proceed any further than Italy. Isabel, reading the homesick letters that came to her by courier, was sincerely sorry for her sister-in-law; but the days when she could do anything to help María were gone forever. Nothing united their lives any longer and hers was rewarding and complete, now that she had borne a son and he was hale and hearty. She might well have said of him, as was said of One much greater, that he "increased in wisdom and stature and in favor with God and man."

When Baltasar Carlos was two years old, he was taken to the Church of San Jerónimo, where a magnificent staging had been erected before the high altar, to receive, as heir to the throne, the oaths of the Castilian Cortes. Clad in crimson and gold and equipped with a miniature sword and dagger, both diamond studded, he was escorted to the staging by his two uncles, whose leading strings he did not require, except for direction. He strutted proudly along by himself and the assembled grandees, who had been quarreling among themselves about precedence only a few minutes earlier, were silenced with pride and pleasure, as they watched his smiling and sturdy progress.

Tragically, this proved to be the last time that the two attractive young Infantes appeared at a public function with their promising little nephew. Shortly thereafter, they accompanied the King to Barcelona, where he went to convoke the Cortes of Cataluña, while Isabel once more assumed the role of Regent. The childhood devotion between them and Philip had never lessened, but neither had ever shared his faith in Olivares. As in the case of the Queen, the Conde-Duque would have been wiser to allow them at least a nominal voice in public affairs; denied this, their idleness was an invitation to dissipation, and they made powerful friends among his antagonists, including the Admiral of Castile and his kinsman, Don Alfonso de Moscoso. Olivares, in turn, resented both the family solidarity and the intimacies elsewhere; all were a menace to his own power. For some years, he had dwelt on the possibility of sending Fernando to Flanders as the King's representative; their aunt, the Infanta Clara Eugenia, who had been appointed its governor by Philip II, was now a very old lady, and it was advisable to provide for the contingency of her death at any time. By continuing the policy of Philip III and allowing their nominal subjects, the Dutch Protestants, to live independently from the rest of Flanders, she and her husband, the Archduke Albert, had managed to enjoy peace for a long while; but now the normally stolid Dutch, in a fighting mood, opposed the renewal of their former allegiance, which the Conde-Duque was trying to enforce. Everyone agreed that Brussels, the Flemish capital, must have a member of the royal Hapsburg family in residence, but the choice of the youthful cardinal for this important post was less logical, and his departure had been postponed for one reason after another, lack of funds among them.

Much as Fernando wanted to go, he was willing to bide his time, especially since Carlos had plucked up courage to object. There was no jealousy between the brothers, but he was the elder of the two; moreover, he was a "man of arms," while Fernando was a "churchman"; the latter pleasantly agreed to step aside in favor of primogeniture and profession. This did not solve the problem for Olivares, however. Carlos was next in line as heir to the throne, after Baltasar, the Conde-Duque reminded him smoothly, and the child did not seem as well as usual. It was not fitting that the Infante should go far away just then for any length of time, especially as they were also trying to find a suitable princess for him to marry. Later on, he would be given the command in Portugal, which was much more important than command in Flanders. Or, possibly, in Cataluña. Therefore, such a trip as the King was about to make would be just the thing to prepare him for his future responsibilities. Carlos took very little stock in these promises—as far as he could see, Baltasar Carlos was in robust health; and he and everyone else had abandoned hope of finding exactly the right princess for his own bride. But he was both too amiable and too indolent for further argument and, as long as his seniority was at least theoretically recognized, he was willing to let matters drift. So was Olivares; he knew that Carlos would cease to present a problem in Madrid if Fernando were elsewhere and, for the time being, why not dispose of the troublemaker by keeping him in Barcelona? It would not cost much to get him there, in the King's retinue, and the wealthy Cataláns could well afford to support a viceroy. The appointment in Flanders could still be dangled before Carlos.

Fernando was, indeed, less amenable to unquestioning control than his elder brother and, when he learned that his personal household had been ordered to precede him to Barcelona, he went raging to the Queen, in whom he knew he would find a willing listener to his grievances. The convocation of the Cortes, which did not require his presence, since he would be allowed no voice in what happened, was just a ruse to get him out of Madrid and sidetrack him from the governorship of Flanders, despite the fact that, for six years, he had been led to believe the Conde-Duque, who had now apparently changed his mind, had destined him for that post. He had been glad to defer to Carlos, as long as there was any chance that the latter might have the coveted position; but it was now clear that the Conde-Duque did not intend to let him get it and, evidently, he was not being considered seriously for Cataluña, either, for, if so, why these preparations to keep him, Fernando, there?

Isabel listened with rapt attention. "I'm very much afraid you are right," she said. "I have seen a letter that Olivares wrote Philip, in which he made some very grave accusations against all the nobles who are your friends—a revival of that old story that you had fallen into very bad hands. And then, he went on to accuse you, personally, of all sorts of schemes."

"How did you happen to see this letter?"

"Philip brought it with him when he came to see me last night. He had not even opened it then, but he finally read it and tossed it aside. I do not need to tell you that is another old story—permitting Olivares to make accusations, but not taking them seriously enough to be much influenced by them. I do not know about Carlos, because he does not always take the trouble to stand up for himself; but I feel sure you will get the governorship of Flanders before very long.

Poor old Aunt Clara is failing fast and now that Olivares has plainly said he will not let Carlos succeed her, you certainly would be next in line. No one can say you are too young any more and you have apparently managed to raise the necessary funds on your own responsibility."

"How did you find that out?"

"I gathered it from something in the letter. Isn't it true?"

"Yes. I have arranged to borrow 240,000 ducats from some *Fúcars*. What has become of the letter?" Fernando asked, disregarding the subject of Aunt Clara for the moment.

"Why, I've just told you! Philip tossed it aside! So, after he left this morning, I picked it up and made two copies of it. Then I sent the original back to him, so that if he wanted to say anything about it, in the course of his conferences with the Conde-Duque today, he could do so. But I have the copies right here, one for you and one for me. I felt reasonably sure you would come to see me privately before you left."

Isabel walked over to the beautiful inlaid *bargueño*, which was one of the room's chief ornaments, as well as one of its most useful pieces of furniture, and, after pulling out several drawers which were in plain sight, reached into one which was skillfully hidden behind them. From this, she extracted two pieces of thin paper, covered with minute handwriting and, after returning one to its hiding place, handed the other to Fernando. He read it with a darkening face:

The Infantes must both be separated from all their friends and this voyage to Barcelona will offer a good opportunity for doing it without attracting public notice. Fernando is already kicking over the traces and assuming airs on the strength of his going to Flanders; and the money at his command is making him dangerous. He and Carlos are close friends and their secret communications indicate an evil bent. Under the pretext of these Cortes in Barcelona Your Majesty might get Fernando and his servants out of Madrid, saying that you wanted him to look after ecclesiastical affairs there and the noble and university members of the Cortes, leaving him there when you return to deal with and close the assembly. Moscoso, who has a wife in Madrid and does not like traveling, would stay here and, if he were bold enough to disobey orders and try to join the Infante, we would soon find means to upset his projects. As for Don Carlos, when the Admiral is away from him and the Prince absent, his household will assume a very different aspect. Seeing the musters of enemies on our frontiers and the dangers threatening us on every hand, it will be a good plan to send the Catalán nobles to their own estates, to see what troops they can raise, giving out that Fernando is to be their leader, surrounding him with grayheads to keep him more enclosed, and even imprisoned, for it is a grave crime for him to show annoyance, as he does at Your Majesty's orders.

So, Sire, if we get the Admiral away from here there will be a way to prevent him from returning, and the Infante Fernando may remain in Barcelona better occupied than he is now, while Carlos, quieter and in better frame of mind, may stay by Your Majesty's side.

Fernando looked up from the letter and flung it down on the nearest table, almost incoherent with anger. "And you advise me to take this lying down?" he asked between clenched teeth.

"Yes, for the time being. Your turn will come later. Besides, don't forget that while you are gone, Philip will be gone, too, at least the first part of the time and I shall be Regent again. Your friends and mine are the same. You may be very sure that we shall be faithfully looking after your interests."

The royal progress lasted more than two months, the Infantes riding throughout it with loaded pistols at their saddle bows. The first stop of any length was made at Valencia, where the Cortes were convoked and allegiance sworn to Baltasar Carlos. Then the whole Court moved on to Barcelona where, as had been foreseen, there was a long and bitter struggle to get the funds which had been the primary purpose of the trip. Moreover, the Cortes of Cataluña objected violently, not only to voting more money than usual, but to accepting the King's brother as viceroy. If His Majesty expected the same support from this body as from the Cortes of Castile, he should divide his time between Barcelona and Madrid more evenly; for the moment, they would be satisfied if he stayed four months. This Philip had no idea of doing and the wrangling went on and on, until the Cortes compromised by consenting to give him the usual supply, without the increase he had demanded, and accepting Fernando as viceroy.

After an outburst of temper, which did nothing to improve the status quo, he somewhat sulkily watched his brothers depart for Madrid without him and betrayed his dissatisfaction with his position by harping on all sorts of minor details, to which, in a more amiable frame of mind, he would have paid no attention: he objected to having the Deputies appear before him with covered heads; they insisted this was their prerogative. He forbade them to repair and strengthen the city walls; they at once trebled the force of men working there. The bickering went on and on. Then he was subjected to an insult which, though indirect, was nonetheless intolerable: contrary to Olivares' expectations, Moscoso had overcome his dislike for travel and his reluctance to leave his wife; within a few days after the King's party had left Barcelona, it was met by Don Antonio who, with an imposing retinue, was on his way to join Fernando. He was summarily ordered to return whence he came and, smarting under this humiliation, complained bitterly to Fernando who, in turn, complained bitterly to Philip. The letter, setting forth his resentment, was sent under cover to Isabel, so it was to her and not to Olivares that was entrusted the task of bringing it to the attention of the King, an infringement on his prerogatives which the Conde-Duque deeply resented. The Regent was rapidly supplanting the *Privado* in official responsibilities. Too late, he began to recognize her power as an antagonist. He had not yet begun to recognize it as an enemy.

The King's return to Madrid was made the occasion of a great *auto de fé* in the Plaza Mayor and the King and Queen, with Don Carlos, occupied their balcony on the *Casa Panadería* from early in the morning until late in the afternoon, while watching the long, gruesome spectacle provided by the indictment and execution of the victims suspected of heresy by the Inquisition. Though such rites were taken as a matter of course and occurred fairly frequently in the Spanish Empire, where they were regarded as an integral part of religious observances, they were not considered joyous occasions, even by the most hardened, and Philip and Isabel were essentially kindhearted. The presentation was something of an ordeal for them and, as the day wore on, they were troubled to see that Carlos appeared depressed and more listless than usual. The long trip had been an exhausting one and summer heat had come earlier and been more intense than was normal. He admitted that he was weary, that he felt feverish; he begged leave to retire.

The royal scion whose health should have been a matter of concern to Olivares was not Baltasar Carlos, but the elder of his two uncles. In a few days the Infante was dead.

The suddenness and untimeliness of the tragedy came as a severe shock and the overwhelming grief of his family was shared by great and humble alike. Though there were the usual whisperings about poison, as in the case of every sudden death in royal circles, and innuendos to the effect that indiscriminate dissipation had resulted in a disgraceful disease, these were quickly stilled as slanderous.

Sir Arthur Hopton, the new English Ambassador, in reporting the tragedy, wrote:

The mourning could not be more hearty for the King and they have good reason, for he was a prince who never offended any man willingly, but did good offices for all, being bred upp amonge them to as much perfection as they could expect.

And, for once, an official expression of profound regret was quite sincere; even Olivares could afford to join, without hypocrisy, in the tribute paid to the young Infante's memory. He had not been ambitious and aggressive enough to cause trouble, except in connection with Fernando, and the latter quickly became less of a problem. The mourning for Carlos was hardly over when the long-awaited death of the Infanta Isabel Clara Eugenia finally took place and Fernando's appointment as Governor of Flanders could no longer be delayed.

Chapter 15

FROM ISABEL DE BOURBON, QUEEN OF SPAIN, TO THE
CARDINAL-INFANTE FERNANDO, GOVERNOR OF FLANDERS.

MY DEAR BROTHER—

You see, I was right; you had only to bide your time. It was a
bitter disappointment to me that I could not see you again before
you started on your long journey; but of course I realized it was logical that you should take the most direct route from Barcelona to
Italy, so you could make connections in Milan with the Spanish infantry which you were to lead to Flanders. Our latest news, however, is that you are not going direct to your new post, as the Emperor has appealed to you for help, which may delay you consider-
ably. We had hoped that, after the death of King Gustavus Adolphus
at the Battle of Lützen last year, the allies would no longer have
the purpose or strength to oppose us. But it seems we lost so heavily
in man power—is it possible that the number was twelve thousand?—that we have not been able to make any effective headway
in Germany since then. Therefore, as I understand it, Philip and the
Conde-Duque are determined to strike an indirect blow at France
by checking the progress of the Swedes and Germans, in order to re-
establish imperial power in north Germany and thus ensure the encirclement of France, besides proving a standing menace to the
Dutch. Of course, I may not have everything straight, as it seems
very complicated to me, but I am sure that, now you are in charge
of our forces, victory is only a matter of time.

YOUR AFFECTIONATE SISTER, ISABEL. Madrid, 8 January, 1634.

*   *   *

MY DEAR BROTHER—

The glorious news from Nördlingen has just reached us and is
being celebrated with a *Te Deum* at San Jerónimo's and, also, with
bullfights and bonfires. Philip and I are going to church and,
of course, to the bullfights and displays of fireworks as well. I am
jubilant over the consciousness that I was right again—only your
command and your example as a leader were needed to assure our
victory. I am not forgetting that the Spanish infantry is incompara-
ble and that this should mean it is invincible. But I am sure it is the
sight of you riding before your men that spurs them on and on
until the enemy is no more. I found it hard to believe, as you know,
that we had lost twelve thousand brave soldiers at Lützen. But now
I find it easy to believe that there are eight thousand of the enemy
dead on the field and that four thousand are our prisoners. What a
blow to the policy and prestige of Richelieu! I hope it does not mean
that he will strike back by taking a direct part in this war, instead
of operating through the Swedes and Germans. But if it does, I
know that he will again meet his match in you.

Philip and I are both greatly pleased with all the beautiful ob-
jets d'art—obviously spoils of war—that you have sent for the adornment of the Buen Retiro, especially as we know that, in your case,
these were a free will offering made with much affection, whereas
I am afraid this has not always been true. Indeed, some of the nobles
have gone so far as to have copies made of their most valuable paintings and have sent these to the Buen Retiro, secretly keeping the
originals themselves. But in the instances where this ruse has been
discovered, the Conde-Duque has been furious and the crafty courtiers are out of favor. When Olivares tried to persuade his nephew, the
Marqués of Leganés, to turn over the pictures and articles of vertu
he had acquired in Italy, his wife stepped in and claimed that the
whole collection was her dowry, so the Conde-Duque was thwarted
that time! However, his brother-in-law, the Count of Monterrey, has
had to surrender the vast store of pictures he secured in Naples; and
all the painters in Madrid are busy copying and designing canvases

under the direction of Diego de Velázquez, who has at last returned from Rome, bringing with him some wonderful landscapes of the Villa de Medici. Of course, Philip is delighted to have him back and has resumed his frequent visits to the studio in the Alcázar, where Velázquez is hard at work.

YOUR AFFECTIONATE SISTER, ISABEL. Madrid, 12 September, 1634.

*   *   *

FROM ISABEL DE BOURBON, QUEEN OF SPAIN, TO THE CARDINAL-INFANTE FERNANDO, GOVERNOR OF FLANDERS.

MY DEAR BROTHER—

We have just had a state visit from your cousin Margarita, the widowed Duchess of Mantua, who is on her way to Lisbon, where she will be invested with viceregal honors. Of course, there has been the usual round of festivities to celebrate her stay here and Philip and I have been glad to give her a place of honor beside us whenever we have all appeared in public together, though a few of the *madrileños,* who always find fault with something, think that is exaggerating the importance of her position. If they are going to murmur, in my opinion, there are sounder reasons for doing so than that. It seems that in 1580, when the crowns of Spain and Portugal were united, because the Portuguese King, Sebastian, had died childless, the latter country was promised by your grandfather, Philip II, that, if he could not be in Portugal himself, a member of the Portuguese nobility or a member of the Spanish royal family should act as viceroy. Since Margarita's mother was your great-aunt, the Infanta Catherine of Spain, perhaps that takes care of the situation. But I can't help wondering how the Duke of Braganza feels about it—after all, his great-grandfather was Edward, the youngest son of King Manuel and his second wife María, who, like his first wife, was a daughter of Fernando and Isabel. By rights, the throne should have gone to Catherine, the Duke's grandmother, but her sex disqualified her for the crown. Your grandfather claimed that he had a prior right, in any case, because of the fact that his mother, Isabel, had been the *eldest* daughter of Manuel and María.

At present, I think the main idea is that, since Margarita is a woman and virtually a foreigner, she can be more easily managed by the Conde-Duque than the Duke of Braganza, but I can't help feeling that Olivares has made another mistake, which may be even more costly to Spain than the one he made about the Prince of Wales and that the Duke, who is tremendously rich and powerful, may make trouble.

YOUR AFFECTIONATE SISTER, ISABEL. Madrid, 10 November, 1634.

✻   ✻   ✻

ORDERS FOR THE VICEREINE OF PORTUGAL
FROM THE KING OF SPAIN.

MY LADY COUSIN—

It had been my hope and plan that my beloved brother, the Infante Carlos, might become the Viceroy of Portugal. Owing to his untimely death, my choice has now fallen upon you as Vicereine and I herewith submit a set of rules for your careful observation.

Watch out for the Church—favor the Inquisition. I recommend inspection visits of prelates. Have a special care to punish public sin.

In administration of justice, be there brevity and equity. . . . See to it that your administrators of justice be paid their salaries promptly.

See to the observance of all my laws.

Having convened a tribunal, have the justices come to you with pertinent matter for you to decide on. Thus you do not have to go yourself to tribunal after tribunal.

Let them all know that I love them: the Prelates, the Grandees, the Nobles and the People.

According to their merits—and on your recommendation—my vassals will receive my favor.

Let special pardons be few and far between so as not to detract from the proper functioning of justice.

Matters of State: You will treat every Monday afternoon with my Council of State.

Most especially I charge you with the important duty of seeing

· 144 ·

to proper and prompt departure of my fleets for the Indies. On arrival of any ship from the Indies, I charge you to send me, under seal, a copy of its manifest. You still have one copy of the manifest for inspection of the cargo.

Tuesdays and Thursdays, in the morning, you will hold public audience for any and all. You will then have around you the officers of your household guards, as you would for going out to Mass, or out to dine.

In order to have time to attend all who seek audience, you will generally go to Mass in your own chapel. Whenever you wish, go out to Mass, but at different places, in order to visit one by one all the churches and monasteries.

At ordinary audiences, you do not receive hidalgos. They can be received standing, as suits your convenience. Should some of them come on My business, you will receive them in private, telling them to be seated and to keep on their hats.

You will bid the following to put on their hats: archbishops and bishops, grandees and titled men whom I have honored.

Lisbon being the best and most convenient seat of government, you should be there at all times, with minor exceptions.

From my treasury for your annual expenses—table and almsgiving and personal expenses—you may count on 25,000 *cruzados*.

Documents sent to me with a council decision should have all signatures of the councilmen and, outside on the margin, your own opinion.

In any Royal Tribunal and upon the death of a judge (or other grave impediment) you should go ahead and name a substitute to avoid delays.

Expedite royal favor for Worthy Subjects in the Indies. You will get annual news of the Indies and if you make up lists of Worthy Subjects residing there and send these quickly to me, I can provide the favors called for in time for the boat mail of the next year's fleet from Lisbon. Thus, a Worthy Subject in, say Brazil, can get royal favor without ever leaving Brazil.

As a precaution against spying, smuggling, etcetera, let no foreigners establish themselves on the waterfront, but in the middle of the city.

To no Minister of the Kingdom of Portugal will you give permission to come visit this Court.

The Porter of the Chamber will keep the keys of your apartments, and of the offices, including the audience room.

As soon as you reach Lisbon, you will convene the Council of State and, before it, cause to be read this set of rules.

YOUR COUSIN, I THE KING. Madrid, 20 November, 1634.

*　　*　　*

MY LADY COUSIN—

I have your letter of the 29th of December past in which you tell me of your safe arrival in Lisbon on the 20th of the same month.

I was pleased to learn that you summoned the Council of State on the 25th and that the orders which I outlined to you, under which work is to be carried on, were proclaimed to the government of this kingdom.

I was further pleased to read that you arrived in the best of health. It is my hope that the good results of your zeal and vigilance will be evidenced daily, that I may depend on your assistance in governing and that conditions in the kingdom will greatly improve.

Blessed be the name of Our Lord.

YOUR COUSIN, I THE KING. Madrid, 24 January, 1635.

*　　*　　*

MY DEAR BROTHER—

I firmly believe that your first defeat may be a blessing in disguise. This is partly because it revealed how greatly you are beloved by the Spanish people. You cannot imagine how much tenderness and concern were shown for you on every side. There was not a word anywhere to indicate they felt you had failed them; on the contrary, the clamor was they were afraid they had been prevented from helping you enough. And when they found out, as they did all too soon—for, as you know, there are always plenty of spies around —that you had written for further resources after you lost the battle at Tirlemont and that the Conde-Duque had concealed the letter from Philip, their fury knew no bounds. Neither did Philip's. As far as I know, this is the first time that he has flown into a violent rage with Olivares, but, believe me, it will not be the last. What is more, he has not only acted in defiance of the Conde-Duque's advice this time, he is determined that, from now on, he will not allow anyone else to make up his mind for him. I do not need to tell you he has never lacked courage and that, though he is indolent by preference about business matters, under normal circumstances he shows remarkable endurance when hunting, riding and cane throwing and he is quite capable of prolonged exertion in other directions when circumstances that are not normal call for it. Now, inspired by your example, he is eager to distinguish himself in the same way that you have, at the head of his armies. He wants to be off to the Catalán frontier, where the French are threatening it, as was to be expected, since Richelieu at last has formally declared war. (I am afraid the days when he and I could reach an understanding are gone for good!) But, apparently, the situation is not really serious there as yet; even so, the Conde-Duque is opposing Philip's departure on the ground that the King of Spain must not risk his life, and he may be sincere about this—I do give him credit for being sincere about a few things! But I am convinced that the main reason he does not want to let Philip go is because that would be the end of the strangle hold on the King's policies, as well as his person. I don't know yet what the outcome of all this will be for, though Philip's first rage has abated somewhat by now, daily squabbles are still going on. It may be that, as far as Philip's departure for the front is concerned, the Conde-Duque will win out this time, unless some serious new development arises. But, if he'll only look at it, the handwriting on the wall is already there; his days of power are numbered.

YOUR AFFECTIONATE SISTER, ISABEL. Madrid, 19 July, 1635.

* * *

French negotiators are everywhere. Be on the lookout about what the French may be offering to the Emperor. Do not trust any Frenchman.

I THE KING. Madrid, 26 January, 1636.

*　　　*　　　*

FROM ISABEL DE BOURBON, QUEEN OF SPAIN, TO THE
CARDINAL-INFANTE FERNANDO, GOVERNOR OF FLANDERS.

MY DEAR BROTHER—

All the news from you continues to be good. Of course, it was to be expected that Richelieu would finally come out in the open and declare war on both Houses of Hapsburg; the wonder was that he did not do so until last year. But that he should also encourage the Dutch to attack you from the rear was an unwelcome surprise. And now the fighting has spread from Flanders and Germany to Italy and part of the time the enemy seems to have the advantage of us. Still, what does that matter when you have advanced so far into Picardy and Champagne and succeeded in pushing your forces beyond the Oise as far as the Somme and actually threatened Paris itself?

When the news of your victories in Picardy reached Madrid, the rejoicings were frantic. Philip and I, accompanied by all the Court, rode to the shrine of Our Lady of Atocha to give thanks; and when we returned to the palace, after nightfall, the streets were illuminated by thousands of torches. All the Councils were ordered to celebrate the occasion with feasts and they are doing this with great sumptuousness. I am told that those which have already taken place have cost no less than two thousand ducats apiece and others are yet to come which may cost even more. I do not by any means feel sure that this part of the celebration will please you as much as the thanksgiving, because I know you share my anxiety about expenses that are incurred needlessly or greatly in excess of actual needs. But I am afraid there will be no way of limiting them as long as the Conde-Duque is at the helm.

Of course, the great display of Spanish vigor which your troops have shown has resulted in freeing the Catalán frontier from fears of imminent French invasion. I recognize that this is of great national advantage to us. On the other hand, it means that Philip has been forced to desist from his importunities about going to the front and I am not sure this is a good thing, because the Conde-Duque feels he has won his argument that it is best for the King to remain far from the scene of danger.

YOUR AFFECTIONATE SISTER, ISABEL. Madrid, 1 October, 1636.

P.S. We have also had good news from Lisbon: the fleet has come in from Brazil with a cargo of *100* cases of sugar, as well as gold and pearls. *Te Deum Laudamus* was sung in celebration of the safe passage and escape from the clutches of pirates.

✳   ✳   ✳

FROM ISABEL DE BOURBON, QUEEN OF SPAIN, TO THE
CARDINAL-INFANTE FERNANDO, GOVERNOR OF FLANDERS.

MY DEAR BROTHER—

I am glad that the news from the North continues to be so good, because I am a little troubled by the letters Margarita is sending us from Portugal.

She claims that two Portuguese of dubious background, Miguel Vasconcellos and Diego Suarez, who are not only traitors to their own country, but in the pay of the Conde-Duque, have so usurped her authority that she is but a mere figurehead. When Philip sent her to Lisbon, he told her it would be necessary to introduce new taxes, so that these, combined with existing ones, would ensure a fixed assessment of *500,000 cruzados* a year. Even though the Portuguese were told these additional taxes were to be spent in an effort to recover their lost overseas possessions, they were not placated —you know how they have always resented the union with Castile. They believed—and, I am afraid, rightly—that this was just another ruse of the Conde-Duque's to obtain funds for our use and, consequently, the people in Évora, the capital of Alemtejo, as well as those in the adjoining Province of Algarve, revolted.

A rumor spread that Philip would go to Portugal, to restore order, and I am inclined to think it might have been a good thing if he had. But like so many rumors, this one had little foundation in truth. He did send a Spanish force, under the Duke of Medina-Sidonia, straight from Andalucía into Algarve, while another army threatened the north of Portugal. As a result, the Portuguese seem to be cowed and the uprisings have gradually subsided, but Margarita feels this may not be for long and I fear she is right.

In this general connection, you may be interested to know—if you haven't already heard it—that a certain Francisco de Melo, a man of letters who has served as Portugal's Crown Minister, has been sent here by the Duke of Braganza to acquaint Philip and the Conde-Duque with the tax situation from the Duke's point of view. I don't think Melo is going to accomplish much, but he seems to be a rather interesting type of man. He was educated for an intellectual career and proved very precocious; when he was still in his teens he wrote an epic, after the manner of his fellow Portuguese, Camoëns, in honor of the recapture of Bahia and, also, a mathematical treatise and a novel! But when his father died, leaving him in straitened circumstances, he had to drop his pen and reach for a sword, in order to make a living; so he signed up in a Portuguese regiment of infantry, destined for Flanders. But he never reached there, because of a terrible storm at sea, which resulted in a total wreck. After the storm subsided, Melo supervised the recovery of 2,000 cadavers from the Bay of Biscay and saw to it that they were given proper burial. He greatly admires the commanding officer of this ill-fated expedition and proudly relates how he dressed in his finest regalia to face certain death and, while awaiting it, took from his papers a new sonnet by Lope de Vega and read it to Melo, asking for his opinion!

Of course, he never got to Flanders that time, but I gather he would still like to if occasion arose. He's lived partly in Madrid and partly in Lisbon for several years now and I suppose I must have seen him around before this, but previously he never made much impression on me. Now he has, as an original. Also, I understand he is more or less responsible for the Conde-Duque's decision to take the punitive action of sending those two armies into Portugal.

But here I go, gossiping about Melo, instead of congratulating you for preventing Cardinal de la Valette from succeeding in his campaign against you. All in all, this does not seem to be a very good year for France. She has been defeated all along the line in Germany and, worst of all for her, has lost Alsace—or, perhaps, that isn't worst of all, perhaps her internal troubles are more serious than her foreign ones. I thought, with the suppression of the Huguenots at La Rochelle, Richelieu would have no obstacles to overcome at home; but evidently my brother Gaston and our cousin, the Duke of Soissons, are far from being on good terms with my former friend the Cardinal and are doing their best to make trouble for him. So is the Duke's sister, the Princess of Carignano, from whom we recently had a visit, as well as from her friend (and their enemy!) the Duchess of Chevreuse. These ladies have had every possible delicate attention paid them here at Court. A strange situation. I'd be delighted to have some comment from you on it.

YOUR AFFECTIONATE SISTER, ISABEL. Madrid, 5 February, 1637.

*   *   *

FROM ISABEL DE BOURBON, QUEEN OF SPAIN, TO THE
CARDINAL-INFANTE FERNANDO, GOVERNOR OF FLANDERS.

MY DEAR BROTHER—

I have let a longer time than usual go by without writing you for two reasons. The first, as you probably guessed, is because of the trouble in the Basque Country. When the French army crossed the Bidasoa River and captured Irún, the situation already looked serious. When the enemy began to besiege Fuenterrabía and the harbor of Pasages, by both sea and land, of course, it looked worse. But even the Prince of Condé on land and the Bishop of Bordeaux at sea couldn't prevail against the Marqués de Vélez and the Admiral of Castile and their splendid forces. A dashing charge threw panic into the French camp and the besiegers fled. Rejoicing and a sense of elation have, naturally, taken the place of consternation throughout the land. In Madrid, we celebrated the victory with a triumphal procession. Philip and I rode in a gilded amber cart, drawn by six horses and preceded by twenty-five coaches, the most magnificent I have seen here, all decked out in silks and velvets and metal ware.

The second reason I have not written sooner is because I've been so enthralled with my new baby, a beautiful little girl, who has been christened María Teresa, that I've hardly paid any attention to anything or anyone else. She is strong and healthy and though, in some ways, we are disappointed because she is not a boy, for we would like to have a second one, on the other hand, thank God, Baltasar Carlos is also so strong and healthy that all anxieties about a male heir to the throne have long since been stilled. Philip and the Conde-Duque are already talking about the alliance with France this birth might facilitate now that, at last, there is also a Dauphin, born at practically the same time as the Infanta. I suppose some Court gossip from the Louvre reaches you and that you already know my brother Louis got caught in a thunderstorm and unexpectedly had to take refuge for the night in poor Ana's apartments, where, somehow, he made the tardy discovery that he is a man, as well as a king. In Ana's place, I certainly would not feel very much flattered that, after twenty-two years of nominal marriage, an accident brought about its consummation. On the other hand, I know what it is like to despair of giving an heir to the throne and I am thankful that Ana's worries on that score are over, though I confess I think she has acted like a fool, both in not finding any way to get the better of my weakling brother, long before this, and also in not handling her affair with Buckingham to her greater advantage.

I was very much interested to learn, rather tardily, that, as a result of the uprisings in Portugal, Francisco de Melo—the interesting Portuguese about whom I wrote you last year—was later required to raise two new regiments of volunteer infantry and that he was put in charge of one. (This was his first command.) He couldn't find enough volunteers in Portugal and completed one regiment with Castilian volunteers. So he should soon be the one to respond to your call for more forces and, before leaving Spain, he gave a good account of himself when the French fleet attacked Coruña. He fought them off, then effected the embarkation of ten thousand Spanish and Portuguese troops in two days. I feel sure you'll find him useful to you.

YOUR AFFECTIONATE SISTER, ISABEL. Madrid, 3 November, 1638.

*   *   *

MY LADY COUSIN—

Give him all consideration. He is working on special assignment of the Governor General of the Frontiers of the Realm of Portugal. He will visit Lisbon and will inspect castles and military posts. And all the cavalry and infantry is to be under his orders, just beneath your command.

I have sent to Portugal 30 sergeant majors and captains for the coastal defense.

YOUR COUSIN, I THE KING. Madrid, 23 March, 1639.

*   *   *

FROM ISABEL DE BOURBON, QUEEN OF SPAIN, TO THE
CARDINAL-INFANTE FERNANDO, GOVERNOR OF FLANDERS.

MY DEAR BROTHER—

Of course the principal topic of conversation and the principal cause for concern in Madrid are the invasion of Roussillon and the capture of Salses by the Prince of Condé. The Cataláns' call for help from Madrid has gone unheeded, as far as I can make out because Olivares is determined to make them see how helpless they are without Castile and bring them to heel in that way. However, they have managed to raise an army of 10,000 themselves and, though they lack leaders, they are at least preventing the invasion from spreading. I suppose that is the best we can hope for at present.

To turn to a more cheerful subject, I think perhaps it will interest and amuse you to hear how Philip's birthday—it does not seem possible that he is actually thirty-four!—was commemorated in Lisbon last April. Before the usual review of troops, there was a parade, which included an empty "coach of respect" decked out in velvet of blue and black and drawn by six chestnut horses from Denmark.

Margarita, with the usual regalia of hat and staff of office, was prepared to review the troops on horseback, but her courtiers advised against this—they were worried lest the "vigorous" sun of Portugal smite her. Though she did not agree with them, she graciously acceded, saying that "her palfrey was not essential to her on such an occasion, as long as she had it to mount the day it were a matter of facing some foreign enemy." Consequently, she went by litter instead, being protected from the "vigorous" sun by black damask draperies.

In a more serious vein, Margarita has expressed concern over rumors she has been hearing about the Duchess of Braganza. I'm sure you have heard that in March Philip made the Duke second in command to Margarita, with all the cavalry and infantry under his supervision. Anyhow, according to these rumors, the Duchess aspires to a more lofty position for her husband—that of King of Portugal, no less! Philip pooh-poohs the idea and says he knows the rumors must be unfounded, since the Duchess, who belongs to the senior branch of the Guzmán family, is a cousin of the Conde-Duque's and if anything were a-foot, Olivares would be sure to know about it. But I wonder. . . . Incidentally, she's also the sister of the Duke of Medina-Sidonia and neither brother nor cousin would mind having a queen in the family, even if that meant disloyalty to Spain. I wonder how the Portuguese feel about her. You know their old saying, "From Spain blows neither a good wind nor a good marriage."

We are all well and I wish you could have a glimpse of your young niece, María Teresa—she is the delight of all who see her and Baltasar Carlos adores her.

YOUR AFFECTIONATE SISTER, ISABEL. Madrid, 30 July, 1639.

*   *   *

FROM ISABEL DE BOURBON, QUEEN OF SPAIN, TO THE
CARDINAL-INFANTE FERNANDO, GOVERNOR OF FLANDERS.

MY DEAR BROTHER—

I do not know if you remember the fears I expressed in writing you several years ago, as to whether or not the Conde-Duque would be able to manage the Duke of Braganza as easily as he would the Duchess of Mantua. Perhaps he could have if the Duke had been a bachelor, because he is naturally unambitious and indolent and cares more about hunting and banqueting than he does about doing anything that involves effort or responsibility. He was perfectly happy with the title of Military Governor, which Philip had given him, together with funds to repair fortifications—funds he used for something else, though he is tremendously wealthy, owning estates which cover about two-thirds of the country, so he has all he wants to do looking after those. But there is no doubt whatsoever that his wife, the *Conde-Duque's cousin,* is aiming higher and that they have a little daughter Catherine for whom they probably already envision a royal marriage.

At any rate, yesterday, while Philip was playing cards with several courtiers, the Conde-Duque rushed into the room, saying he brought great news and Philip casually asked what it was.

"Without making the slightest effort, you have won a great dukedom and vast wealth!" shouted the Conde-Duque.

Philip looked up with more interest and the Conde-Duque bellowed, still more loudly, "The Duke of Braganza has gone mad and proclaimed himself King of Portugal, so it will be necessary for you to confiscate all his possessions."

It was a terrible moment, for of course Philip and the courtiers knew what this meant: that there had been a revolution which could not be quickly suppressed and that union between Spain and Portugal might well be threatened. I do not need to tell you that Philip dislikes a jest, especially one that is ill timed; however, outwardly, he was quite calm. He said, "Then let a remedy be found," and picked up his cards, which the Conde-Duque knew was a signal for dismissal. Afterward, the game was finished in silence. None of Philip's companions dared say anything and he had no intention of making some comment which could be repeated and misinterpreted. But, when he came to my room last night, he sat for a long time with his head bowed in his hands and kept repeating dully, "We have lost Portugal! We have lost Portugal!" The next morning, he was ready to face the world with the pretense that the insurrection was bound to be short-lived and in no time this wishful thinking became the conviction that Portugal, like Cataluña, must be brought to heel. But you know, as I do, that Portugal really is lost to us and that Cataluña will never be "brought to heel." If it can't get help from Castile, it will fight the French by itself and we can only hope that it will continue to be as successful as it was when Condé, after his first defeat, returned with a stronger army, to meet defeat again, at the beginning of this year. But if the wild disorders of Corpus Christi Day are an indication of lasting resentment against Castile, I think we may very soon expect news from Barcelona as bad as the news from Lisbon.

YOUR AFFECTIONATE SISTER, ISABEL. Madrid, 19 December, 1639.

*   *   *

FROM ISABEL DE BOURBON, QUEEN OF SPAIN, TO THE
CARDINAL-INFANTE FERNANDO, GOVERNOR OF FLANDERS.

MY DEAR BROTHER—

Alas! My fears in regard to Cataluña were all too well founded. I am writing this while more and more dreadful details about the royal army, too late assembled, under the Marqués de Vélez, continue to come in. It seems that the Cataláns actually combined their forces with those of the French against the Castilians and a battle took place on the hill of Montjuich, outside the walls of Barcelona. When the Marqués gave the order to retreat, the last chance of bringing the revolt of Cataluña to a speedy end was lost. Barcelona has declared itself a French city, more and more French government troops have poured into the country and the remnants of our army have retreated to Tarragona. The situation certainly looks extremely grim, but I still hope and believe that Cataluña isn't lost to us forever like Portugal.

Of course, we have been deeply concerned about the safety of poor Margarita, especially after the news reached us that all the Castilians in Lisbon had been interned in the Fortress of St. George. But shortly after I last wrote you, we learned that she was never in danger and, in fact, she was never even treated with disrespect by the rebels. She showed herself very brave, declining to hide even when the mob was at the very gates of the palace, and was restrained with difficulty by Don Carlos Noronha from going out into the courtyard and making a personal appeal for loyalty to Philip. But it was too late. The crowd was shouting, "Long live our new king!" and even her promise that the insurgents should be pardoned, if they disbanded then and there, went unheeded. However, though she was asked to leave the palace, so that it might be put in readiness for the new king, this request was made courteously and she was then conducted to a convent outside the walls of Lisbon, accompanied by all her ladies-in-waiting and the Archbishop of Braga. After she had spent a few days there, she was escorted, still with perfect politeness, to the frontier and is now in Badajoz. Unfortunately, she has been very ill, which is not surprising considering the strain she has been under; but she does not blame the Portuguese at all; in fact, she insists it is evident that, even when they are angry, they still remain attentive and gallant toward ladies. She maintains that all the trouble might have been avoided with a different policy on the part of the Conde-Duque and believes Philip will feel the same when she has had a chance to tell him the inside story. There is no doubt whatsoever that, though the Duke of Braganza, as I thought, was perfectly willing to let things drift, at least for the present, the Duchess shocked him into rebellious action. She kept nagging him, admitting that he might be penalized if the rebellion were unsuccessful, and then going on to say, "Which is better—to die with a crown on or to live in a backwater and under chains? Death awaits you in Madrid—perhaps in Lisbon, too. But in the Castilian Court you would die wretchedly, while in Portugal you could die in glory and as a king. Stop being a coward, stop hesitating. Go ahead and act!" So, finally, he did and I am afraid Philip is right—that we have lost Portugal or that, if we haven't yet, we are going to. But there is one good thing about it: from now on, he'll never trust Olivares implicitly again and, if I'm not very much mistaken, the Conde-Duque has made one mistake too many and this is the beginning of the end *for him.*

After telling us about her journey to Badajoz, Margarita went on to express some anxiety lest her letter might not reach us, as there has been much tampering with her correspondence and communications that have reached her, allegedly from Philip, were obviously forgeries. Philip is very concerned about her and has sent one of our own physicians to her; he has been most successful in treating her and she is now better. As soon as she is pronounced able to travel, she will go first with her ladies to Mérida and then by easy stages to Ocaña, where Philip is putting suitable apartments in the palace at her disposal. (As you know, part of it is already occupied by his love child, Juan of Austria, and his entourage, but there is still plenty of room for another retinue.)

YOUR AFFECTIONATE SISTER, ISABEL. Madrid, 12 February, 1641.

＊　　　＊　　　＊

YOUR MAJESTY—

It is my sad duty to inform you concerning the manner of the illness contracted by the Cardinal-Infante Don Fernando, which culminated in his death here yesterday.

After losing Herc, the Cardinal-Infante fell ill with fevers and ague. He had been incapacitated for 88 days when he felt the end was at hand and sought religious consolation. An image of Our Lady of Bois de Duc—much venerated in Flanders—was brought into the sick room and the Cardinal-Infante greeted this with the hymn, *Maria, Mater Gratiae*. He had gone only as far as the words, *Mater Misericordiae,* when he gave up his spirit.

Among others with me at the death bed were the Marqués of Velada; the Count of Fontana, Don Andrés de Cantelmo and the Archbishop of Malinas, all of whom have requested that I convey their most respectful condolences to Your Majesties with mine on this great loss to the Royal Family, Spain and her people.

I remain, Your Majesty's Most Humble Servant,

FRANCISCO DE MELO, FIELD MARSHAL.

Brussels, 9 November, 1641.

Chapter 16

T HE death of Carlos had been the occasion of sincere and widespread sorrow; the death of Fernando was not only the cause of even more profound grief, it was a threatening blow to Spanish prestige. Philip now had no relative with whom to replace the Cardinal-Infante in Flanders, a patrimony of the Hapsburgs through their Burgundian inheritance. Field Marshal Francisco de Melo, who had been with the Cardinal-Infante at the time of his death and who had served Spain so well, was the obvious choice. However, despite the outstanding record of the Portuguese scholar-soldier, as far as Philip was concerned, no one would have seemed adequate to fill the post in comparison with his beloved brother; and his lack of faith in the wisdom of the appointment added to his deep and prolonged depression.

He kept reiterating that Fernando would have made a much better king than he was—which, unfortunately, was true!—and that it would have been much better for Spain if he had been the one to die. He took to spending long hours at the Escorial, reciting prayers for the dead and perfecting the design of the royal mausoleum. After vainly trying to console him, Isabel decided to experiment with teasing him by saying that now she was eligible, as the mother of Baltasar Carlos, for burial in the mausoleum, Philip was showing exaggerated interest in its adequacies. He replied with cold fury that her accusation was not only in very poor taste, but completely untrue; she knew perfectly well that it was those who had already died, especially the one dearest to him, on whom he dwelt in his sad petitions and reflections.

She had not seen him so angry since he had berated her for retreating from the Plaza Mayor when la Calderona had been installed on her own balcony; and Isabel did not again make the mistake of trying to lighten his grief in a way that only deepened it. But, as usual, Olivares sought for means to direct the King's thoughts, when these were gloomy, into more cheerful channels. It was harder to do this than formerly, partly because the King was no longer as easy to direct as he once had been, and partly because the Conde-Duque was no longer in the most vigorous health, and every extra task represented a real effort. He was having trouble with a shoulder that had been dislocated and unskillfully set; and he was also troubled with gout which made him increasingly dependent on a stout cane or crutch. There were not a few who believed that he really did not need this crutch, as far as his gout was concerned, that it was a clever device, possessed of magical powers, rather like the hair of the Biblical Samson, in which lay much of the Conde-Duque's strength. He was wise enough not to disabuse the public of this conviction; but actually, as he became more handicapped physically, his mental processes also became more labored. After careful consideration, he decided that he had hit upon a plan which might logically dispel Philip's gloom, besides serving a dual purpose by furthering certain interests of his own. These had been seriously undermined in several ways. Reluctantly and belatedly recognizing the tragic results of his policies in both Portugal and Cataluña, he had made superhuman efforts to raise money and armies; but Castile's resources were now totally depleted and a series of defeats had disheartened the royal troops, while giving fresh impetus to their enemies. Olivares had long been hated as a tyrant by the people and now his own kinsmen were beginning to turn against him: his agents had unearthed a conspiracy of Andalucian nobles, led by the Duke of Medina-Sidonia (the brother of Portugal's new queen and the Conde-Duque's own cousin!) and the Marqués of Ayamonte; and its purpose reached the dizzy heights, not only of supplanting the Conde-Duque in power by the nobles of Castile, but of making Andalucía, like Portugal and Cataluña, an independent state!

To be sure, the conspiracy had failed, but the Conde-Duque knew that the nobles continued to plot and things were still going badly in Cataluña. The French had completed the conquest of Roussillon by capturing Perpignan and the army commanded by the Conde-Duque's cousin and close friend, the Marqués of Leganés, was defeated in its attempt to recapture Lérida. Something must be done to bolster the *Privado's* tottering prestige and, incidentally, to make his private life, as well as his public life, more satisfactory. He hoped to do both together and, choosing a moment which seemed to him propitious, almost without preamble, posed a leading question.

"I have been meaning for some while to ask Your Majesty whether he did not think the time was ripe for the acknowledgment of Don Juan?"

"What do you mean by 'acknowledgment'?" the King asked abruptly, almost harshly. "I have acknowledged him from the day of his birth."

"Naturally, all the world recognizes him as the son of Your Majesty and knows of Your Majesty's pride and delight in him," Olivares said smoothly. But he did not look at Philip as he spoke. He could not risk the chance that the King might guess what was in his thoughts—in the King's thoughts, too, if he were not mistaken. Philip's first-born son, whose people were gentlefolk, had been taken, shortly after his birth on the estate of his grandfather, the Conde de Chiral, and his baptism with the name of Francisco Fernando, to the house of Don Baltasar de Alamos, Councilor of the Treasury, and had remained there four years. Then, at the suggestion of the Conde-Duque, he had been secretly removed to Salamanca and placed in the charge of Don Juan de Isasi Ydiaquez, who was a friend of Olivares. Philip had approved this plan and the child had been most tenderly treated, as frequent detailed reports to headquarters showed; and certainly there must have been every cause for satisfaction or the King would not later have appointed Don Juan de Isasi Ydiaquez governor and tutor of his legitimate son and heir, Don Baltasar Carlos, who was safeguarded at every turn. But, though Philip had sent one of his boon companions, the Count of Humanes, with a midwife to ensure the child's safe delivery, an action which in itself was a tacit admission of paternity, he had not otherwise acknowledged the little boy until the futility of his guardian's solicitude was revealed through a letter written by Don Jerónimo de Villanueva, the King's Protonotary, to Isasi Ydiaquez to the effect that, "His Majesty had received with the deepest grief the news of the death of Don Francisco Fernando, who showed such bright promise for his tender years. His Majesty highly appreciated all the care that had been taken with him." This letter was followed with arrangements, made by Villanueva, for the transportation of the poor little corpse, elaborately clothed in red and gold and enclosed in a black velvet coffin, to the Escorial; and there "the body of Don Francisco Fernando, son of His Catholic Majesty Philip IV," was entrusted to the Bishop of Ávila for burial.

Olivares had, indeed, used the wrong word in referring to Don Juan, he told himself ruefully, fearful that his well-laid plans might go astray. If burial in the Escorial were not "acknowledgment," then he did not know what would be. And, of course, this was not the whole story. There were several other little boys who, the King admitted, were undoubtedly his sons, and whose mothers had been provided for financially, but who, with their mothers, had been consigned to oblivion. There were others about whom the King merely shrugged his shoulders, saying that they might very well be his, but that there was nothing to prove it and that, considering the characters of the women who had borne them, their existence did not burden his conscience. Olivares, who had introduced Philip to a life of licentiousness when the Prince was a mere boy, and had actually encouraged his earlier excesses, now had moments of regret for having done so, not because of any moral scruples, but because the almost unbelievable potency of the King complicated the Minister's life. . . .

"I asked you, some moments ago, just what you meant by 'acknowledgment,'" the King repeated, more harshly than the first time. "Surely, it does not require such deep thought as that in which you seem to be engulfed to give me an answer."

"I beg Your Majesty's pardon. His question diverted my thoughts to others which were correlative." This time, Olivares did not avert his gaze, but looked boldly at the King, almost as if challenging him to ask what these correlative thoughts might be; the Conde-Duque was never discomfited for long. "I meant," he went on, "that, if such a plan met with Your Majesty's approval, I should be in favor of bringing Don Juan from seclusion at Ocaña for presentation at Court and, by decree, giving him the same semi-royal honors that were bestowed by your grandfather upon his famous half brother for whom this beautiful and promising child was named." Again, Olivares paused. The King could, of course, have given semi-royal honors to poor little Francisco Fernando, had he been so minded, and he had not done so. In a way, it would have been more logical than in the present case, for Francisco's mother was a gentlewoman, while Juan's had been only an actress; and such a gesture on Philip's part would have assuaged, at least to some slight degree, the outraged dignity of a family which, hitherto, had no blot on its escutcheon. On the other hand, obviously the erring gentlewoman, though she herself must have been deeply in love—how else to explain her lack of resistance?—had failed to inspire the King with anything stronger than passing attraction, remorse which was easily allayed and a sense of impersonal responsibility; whereas la Calderona. . . . Besides, as far as Olivares knew, Philip had never once visited Francisco Fernando in Salamanca, though he always managed to make frequent excursions to Ocaña. The gentlewoman's child had meant nothing to him; the actress' child was his best beloved. . . .

"The celebration could and should be made the occasion of numerous festivities to mark the event," Olivares continued. "I am sure the Papal Nuncio would take a prominent part in such an affair. It is even possible that His Holiness might send the Apostolic Blessing to the young Prince."

"Urban? Despite his well-known animosity toward Spain, which Richelieu is doing his best to foster?"

"Despite any disadvantages which might occur to Your Majesty. If one stops to think of those, instead of favorable circumstances, very little is accomplished in this world."

"And what are the favorable circumstances in this instance, as you see them?"

"The temper of the populace, eager for a show of some sort. There have not been too many lately and, as Your Majesty knows, it is well to give constant and careful thought to this aspect of his reign. Besides, there is real eagerness to see Don Juan, of whose gallantry and good looks so much has been heard and so little visualized. It is time to reverse that order of things. Most of all, I am thinking of the satisfaction it would give Your Majesty to witness this ceremony. I am right, am I not, in believing it would make Your Majesty's heart glad?"

Philip did not have sufficient will power to deny this, though he was well aware that Olivares had an ulterior motive which he had not mentioned: public recognition of the King's illegitimate son would facilitate that of a young man, the Conde-Duque's offspring, whom he was trying, somewhat belatedly, to force on his family and on the Court. The person in question, now introduced as Enrique Felípez de Guzmán, had previously gone by another name and passed as the son of a minor government official in Madrid. He was without any special attainments and he was not personally attractive; the entire Guzmán family, with the exception of the Conde-Duque, were violently opposed to his acceptance as one of them. But the *Privado* was infatuated with him and realized that much of the opposition would be stilled if the King would recognize him. Philip was equally aware of this and had already gone as far as he felt was wise, if he were not to risk offending a powerful clan, in showing favors to the newcomer. But he could likewise visualize just how his own love child would look as he received the plaudits of the multitude and closed his consciousness to the correlative effects which Olivares had in mind. Though Juan otherwise strongly resembled his mother, he was as dark as she had been fair; and not the least factor in his appeal to the public was his coloring—that of a typical Spaniard and not of a typical Hapsburg. If he had been sandy-haired, blue-eyed and lantern-jawed, he would never have become their idol. . . .

Philip also closed his mind, though with more difficulty, to the consciousness that, though the Queen would not refuse to grace the ceremony with her presence, *her* heart would not be glad to see her son's half-brother occupying the preeminent place which should have rightly been that of Baltasar Carlos on any grand occasion. The heir to the throne, so tardily born, was a sturdy, attractive little boy, popular in Madrid. His smile was winning, his manner frank and friendly. He rode his plump pony well, he was already interested in hunting, he was much in evidence at all times, his name was given to fresh regiments as these were raised. But he could not compare with Juan in either brilliance or beauty, nor had he captured the imagination of the people to the same dazzling degree. He was the symbol of heritage and hereafter, rather than romantic present, and his royal state raised him above the populace, who felt that la Calderona had been one of them and that, therefore, they were closer to her son than they ever could be to the Queen's. They would wildly rejoice at the prospect of welcoming Don Juan to their midst.

Neither Philip nor Olivares had miscalculated the varied effects of Don Juan's presentation in Madrid. The formal declaration of the boy's semi-royal state was followed by a series of great festivals and triumphant processionals, in the course of which the King received the official congratulations of the Papal Nuncio, the princes of the blood and the grandees of the realm; meanwhile, the public became tumultuous in its joy. After the great ceremonials were over, Juan was conducted to the palace to kiss the hands of the King and Queen and the heir to the throne; and, though Isabel received him with quiet dignity, the warmth which was one of her most charming characteristics was totally lacking in her manner. She failed to address Juan as *mi hijo*—my son—a favor Philip had requested of her and Baltasar Carlos was equally cool in his greeting, omitting the *mi hermano*—my brother—which Philip had also requested. Undoubtedly prompted by his mother, he addressed his half-brother as *"Vos"*—"You"—the term used in speaking to nobles, but not to royalty; and, cutting short Juan's petition for affection, he said, "I shall love you in as far as I see you are properly serving His Majesty, my father."

The Queen and the Crown Prince were not alone in their qualified enthusiasm for the series of festivities celebrating the acknowledgment of Don Juan. As had been foreseen, the formal legitimation of the Conde-Duque's protégé, now officially know as Enrique Felípez de Guzmán, was among these gala events and he forthwith summoned a family council and required his sisters and all their children to address the newcomer as "Excellency" and recognize him as their relative. Not only those nearest the Conde-Duque, but

Castilian nobility in general, regarded this demand as an insult; and the indignation became even more widespread when Enrique's marriage to Leonora de Unzueta, a girl of unblemished reputation and good family, whose father, Don Leonardo de Unzueta, had been one of the King's secretaries, was annulled. There was no question of coercion, a lacking baptism, previous marriage in the case of either one, impotence on the part of the bridegroom or the refusal to cohabit on the part of the bride; but the marriage had been privately performed in the home of the bride's widowed mother, instead of in a church, and the Conde-Duque, whose vaulting ambition visualized a much more brilliant alliance for his protégé, seized on this as a technicality. The Governor of the Archbishopric of Toledo was permitted a free hand by Rome in dealing with the case and the newly married couple, who were deeply in love, were forcibly separated, the groom being sent to the home of his tutor, Jerónimo Legarda, and the bride to the Convent of the Piedad in Guadalajara. The poor girl pleaded against the sentence, appealing tearfully to convents, *confesionarios,* courts of justice, doctors of jurisprudence and theologians; and the great Jesuit, González Galindo, Lector of Theology at the *Compañía's* college in Madrid (who had declared that the Conde-Duque was not entitled to absolution after confession) in a public paper pronounced the annulment a mortal sin against religion, justice and charity.

But all this, of course, was of no avail when the Conde-Duque had decided otherwise. As soon as the decree of annulment was signed, he ordered the Constable of Castile to authorize an alliance between his daughter and the Conde-Duque's son. A vicious couplet, satirizing this second marriage, was soon circulating through the streets of Madrid and the great satirist, Quevedo, lashed out at the *Privado* in a searing memorial. Almost immediately thereafter, Quevedo was arrested at the home of his friend, the Duke of Medinaceli—who himself was exiled—and secretly conveyed to prison in distant León.

The circumstances surrounding this arrest and imprisonment were veiled in mystery and the reasons attributed to these were vague; but it seemed unlikely to his friends that the timing was wholly coincidental and that the Conde-Duque was not at least partially responsible for it. For several years, Quevedo had been living quietly in his house at Torre Abad, a small isolated village in the province of Ciudad Real, and his great tortoise-shelled spectacles and sober black garb had seldom been seen on the Liars' Walks. He had been less vituperative than formerly in his satires deriding and denouncing the follies and vices of the Court; on the other hand, there had been murmurs about his association with the Papal Nuncio and the French Ambassador which were not to his credit as a loyal Spaniard and, in the pathetic letters he wrote from his foul cell to the Conde-Duque and others, he referred to "false friends" who were responsible for his misery, as if there were several such enemies. It even seemed possible that the King, if not directly responsible for his incarceration—any more than he had been directly responsible for the murder of Villamediana—had done nothing to prevent the imprisonment in the beginning and had tolerated it after it was a fait accompli. Philip had sometimes been an appreciative listener to Quevedo's biting verse and malicious prose and the play, *Who Lies Most Thrives Most,* of which he and Mendoza were joint authors, was performed at an entertainment given in the King's honor by the Countess of Olivares and "the smart sayings and courtly gallantry of Quevedo with which it was crammed delighted the Monarch." But at other times these risky meters had irritated him and the poet was in exile almost as often as he was in favor. Prison was not an infrequent aftermath of exile.

As far as the King was concerned, he did not allow the Queen's annoyance, the resentment of the Guzmáns or Quevedo's unhappy fate to interfere with the pleasure he found in the companionship of his elder son. Juan's "ardor of spirit," which so far surpassed that of Baltasar Carlos as to be a constant source of jealousy to Isabel, was a constant source of joy to Philip. The boy was already a fine horseman and a good shot and he excelled not only in sports, but in his studies. He spoke Latin as fluently as he spoke Spanish and his aptitude for mathematics astounded his Jesuit tutor, Father Ricardi. Laughingly, Philip told Juan that he would have to start studying again himself if he did not want to be outdistanced in the classics and the sciences. He hoped he could still hold his own in forest and field.

After semi-royal honors had been bestowed on the boy, his residence was changed from the old walled city of Ocaña to the regal country seat of the Zarzuela on the Manzanares River, near the suburban palace of the Pardo, where Philip had spent his honeymoon and which served him as a glorified hunting lodge. The name was derived from the *zarzas*, whose bristly growth covered the fields all around the house, which had originally been built for Philip's beloved brother, the Infante Fernando, whose tragic death in Flanders had been a source of such deep grief to the King. He found a source of solace in seeing it put to new usefulness again for another dearly beloved, appointing the Count of Fontanar as its governor and providing a staff which included three noblemen, three chief clerks, three doctors, a surgeon, twenty-eight royal pages, five servants of lower degree, many stewards and equerries, besides beaters, coachmen, lackeys and muleteers. The mansion house was of the type known as a *palacete,* a structure not sufficiently large and imposing to be called a *palacio,* but still with palatial attributes. It was a beautifully proportioned, one-story, rectangular building with a high-pitched, dormered roof and a high perron, its granite columns interposed at regular intervals between the rosy bricks of its walls; and from it could be seen the rooftops, towers and churches of Madrid rising beyond its rolling terrain. Fountains sparkled and flowers bloomed brightly in the gardens with which it was surrounded and they, in turn, formed terraces above a series of porticoed galleries; and these gardens provided a charming mise en scène both for the light operas which were a favorite form of diversion at the Zarzuela and which, in turn, took their name from the estate, and for the alfresco suppers which were prepared in a great pot buried in the ground and surmounted with coals. Veal, mutton, pigeons, hare, pigs' feet, pigs' tongues, poultry, hams and sausages were all cooked in this way. Sometimes as many as four thousand guests feasted on them at a sitting; and there was always food left over to send back to Madrid.

Beyond the flowering terraces lay the farmery or "physic garden," plentifully supplied with everything on the so-called Charlemagne list—"plants and trees to be planted in the royal domaines," including pennyroyal, catmint, mallow and lavender; and beyond this lay kitchen gardens, orchards and nurseries and beyond these the woodlands deepening into forests, where many kinds of game abounded. Considering his predilection for both theatricals and hunting, no one expressed surprise at the frequency of the King's visits to the Zarzuela and no one felt any because Juan was admittedly a further and very special attraction. Any man might well be proud of such a son.

PART FOUR

The

Novice

1642

The terrible depravity of the religious orders in Spain was un-covered in the scandals of the nunnery of San Plácido, which caused no small stir in Madrid and even in distant England. The nunnery had been founded in 1623 under the name of *La Encarnación de San Plácido* with funds furnished by Gerónimo de Villanueva, Marquis of Villalba, *Protonotario* (Secretary of State) of Aragón, and by the family of Doña Teresa de Silva (also called Valle de la Cerda), who was elected abbess. She had been for some years under the spiritual direction of Fray Francisco García Calderón, a Bene-dictine of high reputation, who was inclined to mysticism. Villa-nueva had an agreement with the superiors of the Order giving him the appointment of spiritual directors, and he naturally placed Calderón in charge. Before the year was out one of the nuns be-came demoniacally possessed; the contagiousness of the disorder is well known from experience in many parts of Europe, and soon twenty-two out of thirty were similarly affected, including Teresa herself. Calderón was reckoned a skilful exorcist, as was likewise the Abbot of Ripoll, who was called in. At the suggestion of the latter, the wild utterances of the demoniacs were written down and a mass accumulated for some six hundred pages, for it was a cur-rent belief that demons were often compelled by God to utter truths concealed from man. . . .

For three years this went on, to the despair of the exorcists, and Fray Alonso de León, who had been associated in the direction, hav-ing quarrelled with Calderón, denounced the whole state of affairs to the Inquisition (1628). A long enquiry uncovered an appalling story of sacrilege, black magic and immorality combined, for which all persons concerned were severely punished. Calderón, who had attempted to escape to France, endured without confessing three rigorous tortures. He was, nevertheless, condemned as an *alumbrado,* guilty of teaching impeccability and other heresies ascribed to Illuminism. Doña Teresa was relegated to another nunnery for four years and the nuns were scattered in various houses.

In all this Villanueva was compromised. His house adjoined the nunnery and he was much there, especially at night, after his official duties were over. The conventual discipline had become inevitably relaxed. . . . He had taken much interest in the demonic prophecies, especially those which foretold his importance in the Church. He had taken part in interrogating the demons and writing what they said, and he had kept the writings in his house. . . .

To demonolatry was again added the terrific offence of sacrilege, also in connexion with the nunnery of San Plácido. After the scandal of 1628 the matter was condoned—probably with justice—and in 1638 the nuns went into residence again.

—R. Trevor Davies, *Spain in Decline, 1621-1700.*

Everyone says that his [Villanueva's] connection with the convent of the Encarnación Benita, commonly called San Plácido, which has been the occasion of such a commotion, was the cause of his arrest. [This is easy to believe] since he was responsible for the foundation of San Plácido and had built himself a large house nearby. Many add that Doña Teresa Valle de la Cerda, who had become abbess for life, and three other nuns were removed from the convent at the same time, and that inquisitors from Valladolid came to take other prisoners as well. But this is not certain. The Holy Office proceeds in such cases with so much secrecy and unanimity that if it does not actually make a public statement, I remain unconvinced. It is true that the possessions of the protonotary have not been seized and that on the very day of his arrest and the following day he received official papers of great importance from His Majesty, and his Chief Clerk, Josef Navarro de Echarren, opened them in his official capacity.

—José de Pellicer (A contemporary pamphleteer), *Avisos Históricos.*

Chapter 17

GASPAR de Guzmán, Count of Olivares, Duke of Sanlúcar and Principal Chamberlain to His Majesty, was taking his ease in the quiet of the evening with his friend, Jerónimo de Villanueva, Marqués de Villalba, His Majesty's State Secretary, Confidential Agent and Protonotary. Olivares' lame leg rested comfortably on a stool and both men were richly but informally dressed for, now that the *golilla*—a spreading collar covered with white material on its inner surface and on the outer with dark cloth to match the doublet—had superseded the wide cylinder of the great ruff, known as the lettuce frill, they were not half throttled any more. Doublets were correspondingly easy of fit; stiffness was no longer a sign of elegance and a sheltered garden, like this one, offered an excuse for latitude which the palace grounds could not have afforded. The day had been one of unseasonable heat and both men were half reclining on divans; the trickle of the three fountains, which were a special feature of the garden, and the chirping of the small birds, confined in the golden cages that hung along the wall of the house, were the only sounds that penetrated the restful stillness. For some time there had been companionable silence between the two men. Then Olivares, fingering a half-empty glass, asked a casual question.

"Has it occurred to you, my friend, that the King is showing signs of restiveness?"

"It has crossed my mind. Of course, he worries a great deal about Portugal and Cataluña, but I had thought that the Zarzuela would provide all the necessary distractions. It seems I was mistaken. Have you any suggestions for a remedy?"

"It had been my hope that the Buen Retiro might do so. But, if I have failed there, another avenue of approach to excitement can certainly be opened by you."

Gaspar de Guzmán, while referring openly to his own contributions to the King's diversions, deemed it wiser to permit his boon companion to discover for himself "the avenue of approach" which the Conde-Duque had in mind. After all, though he was given to bold measures, it was sometimes convenient to be able to claim that an actual suggestion had come from someone else, that he had only been helpful in carrying it out and, in this case, that happened to be true. When the King was in residence at the Buen Retiro, so was the Queen; when he went to a ball, so did she; when he took part in a cane tourney or a masque, she was in a place of honor among the spectators; when there was a bullfight, she shared his place of honor. The Queen was still a beautiful woman, a regal figure; she had an appreciation of drama, of music and of art as keen as the King's and she could share his enjoyment of these intelligently. But, after all, Philip had now been married to Isabel for more than twenty years and, after many disappointments, they had at last achieved two charming children, Baltasar Carlos, the heir to the throne, and María Teresa, already envisioned as a future Queen of France. Isabel no longer represented to the King a temptation, a novelty, a mystery, a challenge or a danger; and Philip needed at least one of these ingredients to still his restlessness.

So that was why Gaspar de Guzmán hoped that Jerónimo de Villanueva might be helpful and, at the same time, felt it wiser not to define temptation, novelty, mystery, challenge or danger. The situation was extremely delicate, not to say tricky. Some years earlier, Villanueva had founded a convent for Benedictine Nuns, which had been given the name of San Plácido, and which was located next door to his own residence. At that time, he was betrothed to a very beautiful girl, Doña Teresa Valle de la Cerda who, "suddenly smitten with Divine Grace," had given her dowry to her *novio's* convent and entered it as a novice. Eventually, she had become its abbess and, shortly thereafter, it had become involved in such scandals—largely as the result of the tales circulated by its chaplain, Fray Francisco García Calderón—that it had been ordered closed by the Holy

Inquisition and the unfortunate abbess had been confined elsewhere. The scandals had finally been hushed up—there were always plenty of new ones to arrest public attention; the convent had reopened; and Doña Teresa, her name completely cleared, again ruled as abbess and—according to reliable report—had induced some very promising and attractive young ladies to present themselves as postulants to the Order.

Just why Doña Teresa had retreated from such an auspicious match as marriage with Jerónimo de Villanueva would have represented, in order to lead a life at least nominally dedicated to chastity, poverty and obedience, no one, not even Olivares, had been able to figure out. The only reason given had not been a convincing one: Divine Grace did not often seem to smite that hard in Court circles. The fact that the erstwhile lovers became and remained friends and collaborators would have been equally puzzling if, meanwhile, Jerónimo had not become Teresa's brother-in-law. As it was, there seemed to be no resentment on his side for having been jilted, no disappointment on hers for having—theoretically—renounced the world, the flesh and the devil. (Though the world came freely to the locutories at San Plácido and some of it was very fleshly; while the devil figured largely in those stories which Fray García had spread and which had been responsible for the temporary closing of the convent!) Villanueva seemed quite as pleased to have Doña Teresa as the head of the convent he had founded as he would have been to have her his wife; and she seemed quite as pleased to welcome him to the locutory as she would have been to preside at his table. What else or what more, if anything, there was in the relationship that provided them mutual satisfaction no one knew, and those who hazarded guesses did so secretly. . . . But now Olivares was not hesitating to say that, perhaps, Villanueva could suggest a new avenue of approach to the King's enjoyment.

"I understand that, when he is not at the Zarzuela, he spends more and more of his leisure with Diego de Velázquez," Villanueva said idly—so idly that Olivares had the impression he was playing for time: the Aragonese knew perfectly well it was not pastimes like this that the Conde-Duque had in mind.

"True. He has his own special armchair in the studio and drifts in, whenever the mood suits him, to watch Velázquez at work. He is immensely pleased with his choice of a Court Painter—his offer of a salary of twenty ducats a month, with extra payment for each picture, was a sound investment. The portrait of Baltasar Carlos on horseback, placed over a doorway, and the whole series of battle scenes, including the Surrender at Breda, which encircle a large important apartment, are a source of constant pleasure to him and of admiration to everyone who sees them, as I do not need to tell you. Very often, the Queen goes to the studio with His Majesty. The painter's children are well behaved, his wife comely and cordial—in fact, the visits are taking quite the tone of family affairs," Olivares concluded, adroitly putting into words his hitherto unspoken thought that, possibly, the Queen might be almost too constant a companion.

"And you thought he might welcome a change?"

"Only by way of contrast."

"Did you have something special in mind?"

Well, so the definite suggestion would have to come from Olivares, after all. Villanueva was too shrewd to make it himself and risk having this brought home to him later on.

"Only something for which there is excellent precedent. It is said that in the early days of the great St. Teresa the best society of Ávila was to be found in the locutory of the Encarnación. It is now said that, in the days of San Plácido's renascence, the best society of Madrid is to be found in the locutory of this convent."

"On which side of the grille?"

"Naturally on both, considering its patron—and its abbess."

"Its patron and its abbess will, of course, be greatly honored to receive the King and any friend of his whenever they choose to present their compliments."

"Thank you. And, now that you have assured me of this," Olivares added, speaking idly in his turn, "perhaps I may venture to say I have heard that some of the novices are so pleasing, it is almost a pity their charms should be wholly concealed in a cloister, and that one of them is quite exceptionally beautiful. Of course, they do go out into their garden for air and recreation, which makes a little change for them. Have you, by any chance, been able to see anything of them by glancing over the wall of your own garden?"

"I get an occasional glimpse, that is all. Hardly enough to pick out one girl as exceptionally beautiful."

"Not even if you had been looking for such a paragon? It seems there was one whose profession was marked by celebrations of extraordinary elegance, both at her family home and at the convent, and all those who attended were delighted with them. You must certainly have heard about this, even if you were not actually present at the occasions in question—and I must confess that your absence, if indeed you were absent, seems very strange. After all, San Plácido is your convent and Doña Teresa your abbess." Then, as Villanueva made only a noncommittal gesture, Olivares continued, "Under ordinary circumstances, the abbess would naturally choose one of the older nuns among those who hold office in the Community to accompany her when she came to the locutory. But, under the circumstances which we have now mentioned, possibly the presentation of this charming child would be appropriate."

"I see that, as so frequently happens, there has been a meeting of minds between us," Villanueva said suavely.

Chapter 18

JUST as no chain is any stronger than its weakest link, no plan is successful beyond the point where it falters. Doña Teresa, as her friends continued to call her, raised no objections when her former fiancé said that two friends of his with unexpected leisure on their hands had asked to have her receive them in the locutory. She still raised no objections when their very inconsequential disguise had been penetrated, and she recognized her visitors as the Conde-Duque and the King. And, since royalty must be permitted to choose its own visiting hours and to designate its preferences among those available to receive the visits, she accepted, without question, the statement that the gentlemen would find it more convenient to come to San Plácido in the evening and that they would enjoy conversing with some of the young ladies who, like Doña Teresa herself, had been led by Divine Grace to embrace the conventual life. Several girls consequently succeeded the Prioress, the Cellarer, the Treasurer and the Infirmarian as the Abbess' companion when she received her callers. Three of these novices, *Sor* Benita, *Sor* Carlota, *Sor* María Beatriz, were comely; one, *Sor* Margarita, was exceptionally beautiful.

For more than a week, all the young girls, including *Sor* Margarita, kept their hands modestly clasped under their scapulars and their eyes cast down, as they quietly listened to the conversation of their elders or answered meekly and briefly when they were directly addressed. Then, without warning, at the question, "*Sor* Margarita, how did it happen you felt sure of a vocation?" the girl raised her head and looked the King full in the face as she answered boldly, "It was my parents who felt sure of it."

The words in themselves would have been shocking enough, but her glance was as brazen as her words. *Sor* Margarita had the most extraordinary eyes that Doña Teresa had ever seen: a pure deep emerald, clear as crystal and fringed with long thick black lashes. Her skin was as white as a lily, without the slightest tinge of color in her cheeks; and the contrast which her green eyes and black lashes made to this pallor was startling and stimulating in its effect. After this outburst and this glance, Doña Teresa felt no surprise when she learned her callers hoped it might usually be *Sor* Margarita who would be chosen to accompany her; and one night when she was suddenly called away to minister to an elderly nun who had been smitten with some mysterious illness, she hesitated to leave the locutory even for a few minutes, though *Sor* Margarita was entrenched on one side of the grille and the two gentlemen on the other. On her return, only one gentleman remained and the impression persisted that he and Margarita had changed the subject of their conversation rather abruptly on her arrival. But, after all, it was merely an impression; she tried to dismiss it from her mind.

The sick nun required a great deal of attention in the course of the next few days and Doña Teresa was called to her bedside at frequent intervals. Since some of these summons came during the nocturnal visiting hours, it occurred to the Abbess that it might be better if one of her close subordinates in rank, possibly the Prioress, accompanied *Sor* Margarita to the locutory. But then, Doña Teresa was never gone long at a time and, though her sandals permitted her to come and go so silently that she could easily have surprised a scene which was in any way an offense to decorum, she neither saw nor heard anything to trouble her. The sick nun recovered, there were no more impressions of interrupted conversations and the visits, which at first had been almost nightly, decreased in frequency. Then another impression, a different one, began to trouble her. She thought *Sor* Margarita looked even paler than usual, if that were possible, and that her manner, usually so controlled, had lost some of its composure. At last, she decided to question the girl. Perhaps she had another invalid on her hands. And the thought crossed her mind that, if *Sor* Margarita were not well enough to go to the locutory for a few nights, it might be a very good thing. Villanueva's friends with unexpected leisure on their hands might find a new interest.

Having decided to question her, she sent for *Sor* Margarita that same day after Vespers and invited her to sit down, instead of keeping her standing after she reached the Superior's office, and asked her kindly if she were not feeling well. At first, *Sor* Margarita simply sat staring at the Abbess with her disconcerting green eyes; then she began twisting her hands and shaking her head to emphasize the words which denied any physical discomfort. At length, seeing that she was getting nowhere with the girl, the Abbess dismissed her and went back to her interrupted desk work. Shortly thereafter, there was a knock at the door and, even before the Abbess could respond, it was pushed open and *Sor* Margarita reentered.

"I'm not sick. But I'm beginning to be frightened," she whispered. "I don't think I can see it through."

The abrupt change in her voice and manner were not only surprising, they were disturbing. "My dear child, why should you be frightened?" Doña Teresa asked soothingly. "What is there that you cannot see through? Sit down again and tell me what has alarmed you."

The girl resumed her seat and began twisting her hands again. Doña Teresa waited for her to compose herself and at last *Sor* Margarita spoke hysterically.

"He's coming here," she said. "He's coming into the cloister. To visit me when I'm alone. At night."

"*Sor* Margarita, you must compose yourself. You are not well, you are permitting yourself to have fantastic thoughts. No one is coming into the cloister. You must know as well as I do that, even if anyone desired to commit such a sacrilege, it would be impossible for him to do so. The doors leading into the cloisters are heavily barred and bolted."

"Yes. The doors in front."

"And the arcade which surrounds the courtyard in the rear is high and has no outer opening. You must have been troubled by some false nightmare, inspired by the devil, to imagine what you have just told me."

"It may have been inspired by the devil, but it is not a false one. They are digging a tunnel."

"*Who* are digging a tunnel?"

"The workmen employed by the gentleman who lives next door —your friend, Don Jerónimo de Villanueva."

If she had not used those two words, "your friend," Doña Teresa might have found a readier and more casual answer. As it was, *Sor* Margarita spoke again before she could frame one.

"It is not for himself that he is digging the tunnel. It is for one of the friends who comes here. It was the other friend who suggested it. He had learned that the third gentleman wishes to visit me alone at night and said that, since this was the case, something must of course be arranged, for every wish that this gentleman expressed had to be granted. The third gentleman—it is the King, is it not?"

"Hush, *Sor* Margarita, you must not ask that! The gentleman of whom you speak does not wish his identity known."

"But is there anyone else of whom the other gentleman would say that if he wishes to come to a nun at night, the way must be made easy for him to do so?"

The Abbess gave no direct answer. Instead, she rose and put her hand on the girl's shoulder.

"How long have you known of this plan?" she asked, forcing herself to speak quietly.

"The first time you left me alone with the gentlemen, in order to visit *Sor* Brígida, who was so suddenly taken ill, the one whom you say I must not name put his face very close to the grille and whispered that he wanted to look more closely into my beautiful green eyes, but before I could answer him, you returned, so nothing more was said about it that evening. However, the next time—"

"Do you mean the next time the gentlemen made us a visit or the next time I was called away?"

"Both. You were called away the next time they visited us. Don't you remember? As you have been several times since!"

"Yes, that is true. So then—"

"Then it was the Conde-Duque who whispered to me. Surely I do not need to pretend about knowing him, for your friend Don

Jerónimo de Villanueva calls him by name all the time. He said everything was arranged and that, as soon as the tunnel was finished, he would let me know. Night before last, he said it was nearing completion and told me to hold myself in readiness for a visit. Your friend Don Jerónimo had already told him which room would be available—the one at the end of the corridor nearest the stairs, which is vacant just now, owing to the reduced number of novices. Unless I receive a message to the contrary, I am to go there tomorrow night after Compline."

Until she spoke the words, "hold myself in readiness for a visit," she had been fairly composed. As she said, "I am to go there tomorrow night after Compline," she was almost incoherent with excitement. The Abbess had continued to lean over her and now she put her arm around the girl's shoulders and spoke firmly.

"My child, you must control yourself. Go to your cell and stay there quietly tonight. Tomorrow, continue your daily tasks as usual and put this disturbing episode out of your mind. Of course, you will not come to the locutory at any time in the foreseeable future. I will send a message to Don Jerónimo, asking for the privilege of a private interview. I do not think he will decline to grant me one and he will certainly listen to me. When I talk with him, I shall be able to make him understand that this sacrilegious plan must be abandoned."

Chapter 19

DON Jerónimo de Villanueva did not decline to grant the Abbess the privilege of a private interview. He arrived promptly at the hour she had set and was shown into the locutory, which had been closed to all other visitors. He had hardly taken his seat in the armchair beside the grille when the curtains parted and the Abbess confronted him, her face unveiled.

"Don Jerónimo—" she began sternly. But, before she could continue, he raised his hand as if in protest and interrupted her with a smile.

"My dear Teresa," he said pleasantly, "since this is a private interview, why not be natural with each other? I gather that you have something quite confidential to say to me and confidences always come more easily if they are not hedged about with formalities."

"What I have to say to you is indeed confidential, but it is not to be treated like small talk, as you seem to think possible. It concerns an outrage."

"Really? In this convent which I had the honor to found and over which you have done me the honor to preside? A convent which has managed to surmount calumnies and triumphantly resume the even tenor of its ways? You surprise me, Teresa, you do indeed."

"Not as much as you have surprised me. If anyone had told me that you would lend yourself to such a nefarious scheme as has been revealed to me, I would have told my informer I knew he was lying."

"Should the man who was merely doing his poor best to please

· 187 ·

his sovereign, which is his bounden duty, be accused of nefarious schemes?"

"Yes, if his *poor* best, as you rightly call it, leads him to sacrilege."

Villanueva sighed. "I can see, my dear Teresa, that you are very much disturbed and this I regret. I know the heavy burden of your cares and would not willingly add to them. I am sorry if a silly girl, who has not the intelligence to match her undeniably good looks, has done so. She had only to keep her mouth shut and, in a short time, what you are pleased, with exaggeration unworthy of you, to call an outrage would have been a fait accompli. A king's passion would have been assuaged and a novice would have had a pleasantly exciting memory of a royal lover to cherish during the long years of chastity, poverty and obedience which lie ahead of her. And no one would have been the wiser or sadder for this little infringement of your rules. Now, I will admit that the situation is somewhat altered. The seduction will not be as much of a secret as I had hoped. You are upset. The girl, instead of being discreet, as we had every reason to expect, is a chatterbox. She told us herself, looking us boldly in the face with those green eyes of hers, that her vocation was of her parents' doing, not of hers. I do not feel in the least sure that she had not already been indiscreet and that this former indiscretion had something to do with her being hurried into a convent. I thought she would be secretly pleased at our plan. I still do not feel too sure that she is not. Be all that as it may, none of it alters the fact that the King will come here tomorrow night, as arranged, and that *Sor* Margarita must be prepared to receive him."

"My friend, you cannot ask me to connive in such a crime!"

"And since when, Teresa, have you considered the act of love a crime?"

He looked at her steadily as he asked the question and she met his sardonic gaze without faltering. But when she answered, her tone, though clear, was sad.

"You know that I do not consider the act of love a crime when it is the joyous union between two persons dear to each other, whose mutual devotion has deepened to mutual passion and when this has the approval of our Holy Mother the Church—or its condonation for some special reason," she added. "But rape is a crime, even when it is not committed in a cloister, against a prospective nun, and this would be rape. *Sor* Margarita is very young. She is unready in every way for the experience to which you would subject her."

"Come, Teresa, how many girls have you known who do not claim to be terrified at the mere mention of such a thing as seduction? Some sincerely enough, no doubt. Others only because they think it seemly. And the more they protest, the more often they have no reason to fear it, because, actually, they are already deflowered. They are only afraid of being found out or of still more dire consequences. Do what you can to calm this silly girl since she has seen fit to go running to you, instead of keeping her fears to herself, as any girl worth her salt, frightened or not, would have done."

"May I confess to you that *Sor* Margarita is not the only one who is frightened?"

Villanueva laughed easily. "Surely, my dear, you will not admit that the slight uneasiness caused you by our little brush with the Holy Inquisition some years ago has developed into timidity? Especially when the Inquisitor General is the King's own confessor, as well as the boon companion of the Conde-Duque. There is naught to fear from that quarter, I assure you. Nothing is more pleasing to the good Friar Archbishop than the knowledge that commands given by His Majesty and His Majesty's Chamberlain have been respected. Please believe me, there is far more danger in disobeying their orders than in following them. So see to it that *Sor* Margarita is ready for the King tomorrow night. For he will be here."

The passage from the basement of Villanueva's house on the Calle de la Madera to the basement of the San Plácido Convent was neither long nor difficult. In fact, it deserved a more complimentary designation than the word tunnel, Philip told his host, as they went through it together, lighted by the lantern which Villanueva carried. It was wide enough for them to walk abreast and high enough to clear their heads, though both were tall men; and, underfoot, it was smooth. The King lauded his protonotary on having achieved so finished a piece of digging in so short a time.

"One would almost think," he said, "that there might have been a passage of sorts here before and that it had simply been enlarged and improved. This, of course, would have been before your occupancy of your present palace or the San Plácido nuns of their present convent. How fortunate for me that you discovered it!"

"I am delighted that it is so satisfactory to Your Majesty," Villanueva replied gravely.

He opened a door, revealing a dimly lighted stone stairway. "The first flight will take you only to the ground floor," he said. "You must continue for two more flights. Then walk straight ahead of you and enter the first door on your right."

The stairs were steep and winding, engulfed in silence except for the King's echoing footsteps; and little lamps, set in niches along the ascent, gave enough light to clarify the way. The King mounted without haste and with increasing anticipation. Everything was going smoothly. There were no impediments to his progress and he was satisfied that there were no spying glances watching it. He reached the long corridor lined with cells and excitedly unlatched the door of the first one on his right. Then he recoiled in horror.

Sor Margarita was, indeed, waiting for him. The Abbess had not been able to prevent the assignation. But the young novice, clad in the purest white, lay on a bier, her eyes closed, a crucifix on her breast, tapers burning at her head and feet. If she herself had not preferred death to dishonor, then the Abbess must have chosen it for her.

The King closed the door as hastily as he had opened it and rushed toward the stairs. Then, almost as hastily, he turned back and reentered the room. If the girl were dead, that was the end of the matter, a hideous and evil end. But was she? Suddenly, he doubted the authenticity of this *capilla ardiente*.

He walked over to the bier and stood close to it. At first, he could detect no sign of life. Then, watching carefully, he saw a slight flicker of the eyelids. He leaned closer still and listened. The girl's breath was suppressed, but it had not ceased. He drew back with a sharp utterance that was edged with mockery, rather than horror.

"A clever ruse, *Sor* Margarita, on the part of your Abbess," he said. "But not quite clever enough. She counted, with reason, on my fright, but failed to consider that scepticism and ardor might overcome revulsion. I should have thought her more resourceful as to ways and means, particularly as I believe she is not without experience in such matters. But let that pass. It is not the Abbess with whom I am concerned, but with the loveliest of her novices. Is it possible that I misread the invitation which seemed so unmistakable when we were separated by the grille? If I did, you have only to say so. But I shall not believe it until I meet the gaze of your green eyes again. Open them and look upon your King."

the …… per……ar…… …… …… …… …… ……
…… …… …… …… …… ……
preferred …… …… …… …… …… ……
to exceed …… …… …… …… ……
…… …… …… ……
…… …… …… …… …… …… ……
…… …… …… …… …… …… ……
…… …… …… …… …… …… ……
…… …… …… …… …… …… ……

Chapter 20

UNEXPECTEDLY to all concerned, the person placed in the most perilous position as a result of the King's escapade was neither the Abbess nor *Sor* Margarita, but Jerónimo de Villanueva.

That the spies of the Holy Office would ferret out the facts concerning the devil-may-care intrusion had, naturally, been a recognized risk from the beginning. But that Antonio de Sotomayor who, as Villanueva himself had reminded Teresa, was the King's confessor, as well as the Inquisitor General, would take active steps to punish an intimate of Philip's for catering to a king's fancy had entered no one's calculations. His very closeness to the King, who was of course sacrosanct, whatever his offenses, was in itself so powerful a safeguard that it seemed inviolable. However, Sotomayor, after rebuking the King more severely than he had ever done before, declined to let the matter rest there; he pronounced Villanueva guilty of sacrilege and demanded his arrest.

When it came to a showdown, however, the King still held the strongest hand. Besides, though it was not in his easy-going nature to harbor a grudge, he felt that Sotomayor had exceeded his prerogatives by the manner of his rebuke. For a respectful reprimand, Philip would not only have felt no resentment, but would have been respectful in his turn; he would have promised to amend his ways and, at the moment he did so, he would have meant what he said, though probably he would soon have erred again. But Sotomayor's reproof had begun like a scolding and mounted in fury until it became a veritable tongue-lashing, and it had been repeated on several occasions. Philip did not need Olivares' subtle suggestion that such language was unbecoming a cleric of high degree at all times and especially so when he was addressing his sovereign. The day came when the Conde-Duque went to the Inquisitor General with two documents, bearing the signature, I THE KING, and presented them to the functionary in question with cold politeness: one was a decree of banishment; the other was an order granting a pension of twelve thousand ducats a year, provided the beneficiary resigned from his present position and retired to his native city of Córdoba. Very naturally, he chose to do the latter.

The new Inquisitor General, Diego de Arce, was a Benedictine friar who had long been a confidant of the Queen, and who was naturally less disposed to view the conduct of the King with tolerance than his predecessor had done, even in the latter's most lenient moments. He ordered that all papers in the case against Villanueva should be secured in a casket and sent to Rome in the charge of Alfonso de Paredes, one of the Council's most trusted messengers. There was, of course, no easy way to prevent the fulfillment of this order; on the other hand, it was a simple matter to delay its execution for a few days and Paredes was invited to present himself at Velázquez' studio, so that sketches could be made of him.

"Diego wishes to use you as a model," the Conde-Duque told Paredes smoothly. "He has been much struck by both your face and figure. He intends to give them a prominent place in one of the huge canvases on which he is presently working. You will be shown in the guise of a victorious warrior. And, since it is always necessary for Diego to make several sketches of a model when he is engaged in a major undertaking of this sort, we will send two or three of them posthaste to Italy. In this way, we shall be able to make sure that our ambassadors in Genoa and Rome and our viceroy in Naples will have no difficulty in recognizing you instantly and thus speeding your mission."

Velázquez and Paredes were both immensely pleased with the plan. The former had been casting about for just such a model as was now so felicitously provided to use in the painting on which he had recently embarked. Paredes was flattered to be chosen for this role and still more flattered by the recognition of his mission as one of such importance. He was delighted when he landed at

Genoa to find a delegation from the Spanish Embassy on hand to welcome him. These officials had been eagerly awaiting him, they assured him, for several days. After a convivial evening, he sank into a heavy sleep and, when he woke the next morning, the casket had disappeared from his bedside. He had no cause for concern, he was told soothingly; it was already on its way to its destination by a messenger no less trusted than he was; the latest orders received were that it should be thus dispatched. Meanwhile, he was to be the guest of those who had first received him until he reached the castle which had been designated as his headquarters during his stay in Italy.

Philip and Olivares opened the casket in the King's privy chamber. It had been received, safe and intact, that very morning; the kidnapers of Paredes had spoken truly when they said it had been put in the care of a messenger no less trustworthy than he was. The day was cool and a fire was burning brightly on the deep hearth under a tall marble mantel. Without even pausing to look at the papers, Philip tossed them onto the flames with his own hands and watched them blacken and curl and crumble into ashes. Then he turned to his Minister with one of his rare smiles.

"If, as you assure me, Paredes has now been conveyed to Naples and confined in the stronghold of Ovo, where measures have been taken to make sure he is inaccessible, the case would seem to be closed," the King said. "Oh, no doubt Diego de Arce and the Council will continue to importune His Holiness for a time. But to what avail? The minutes of the trial, which declared our poor friend guilty of sacrilege, have mysteriously disappeared. There is no proof against him. His detractors should be satisfied in having him remain indefinitely under painless interdiction. And he is living quietly, but most comfortably, in his own convenient house. I do not think he is in the least discontented."

"There is no reason why he should be. And, as you say, there is no reason why we should not now consider the case closed and turn to other matters."

The other matters proved so pressing that, temporarily, Philip almost forgot the fact that Villanueva had never been cleared of the charges brought against him. These were abruptly recalled by the bad news that Villanueva had been formally arrested by the Inquisition and taken to Toledo, where he was summoned before the judges *in penitenciae;* though he was accused of no specific charges, he was told that he had sinned greatly by sacrilege and irreligion and thus merited severe punishment. In its mercy, however, the Holy Office would exact only the following penalties: for as long as he lived, he must fast on Fridays; he must never enter a convent or speak to a nun; and he must give two thousand ducats to the Prior of Atocha to be used for charitable purposes.

Chagrined that other preoccupations had made him neglectful at a time when Villanueva most needed his help, Philip gave orders that Don Jerónimo was to be released immediately and brought to him under suitable guard; he himself would vouch that full satisfaction should be given the judges and that the prisoner should not be freed unconditionally until Philip was confident of this.

"I am sure, my dear friend, that you feel you got off very easily," he said when the guards had been dismissed and, after a cordial greeting, he had asked Villanueva to be seated.

"You are *sure,* Sire?" Villanueva asked quietly, turning on the King the same sardonic gaze that had upset the Abbess during the course of their most memorable interview.

"Why yes. I have restored you to your post, which is one I believe you have always enjoyed. There is no particular hardship in limiting your main course to fish on Friday, considering the variety there is to choose from. And, certainly, you will never miss the two thousand ducats you are to give the Prior of Atocha, a most excellent man, for his pet charity, whatever that may be."

"All this is true, Sire. But you have neglected to mention two items in the list of penalties imposed."

"That you should never again enter a convent? That you should never again converse with a nun?"

"May I be so bold, Sire, to first answer your question with one of my own?"

"Of course."

"If those two penalties were imposed upon Your Majesty, would that represent no hardship to him?"

The King appeared to meditate, but briefly. "If the only convent in question were San Plácido, as I imagine it is in your case, the answer for me would be no," he said. "The attraction there was of short duration. In fact, it has already caused me a great deal more trouble than it was worth. And there are also any number of convents which I must visit, as a matter of courtesy, in the course of my tedious travels to Valladolid, Valencia and elsewhere. These represent only one more tiresome duty which must be fulfilled. I would gladly eliminate those from my schedule, but I know that would not be consistent with my obligations. There is, indeed, one convent which I, too, should like to visit, one nun with whom I, too, should like to speak. But the convent in question is difficult of access and does not lie within the radius of any journey which I am compelled to make. Moreover, even if I should go there, I doubt very much if the nun with whom I should like to speak would come to the locutory. In fact, I am almost certain that she would not. There is very little resemblance between her and our green-eyed novice who, I have heard indirectly, has now taken her final vows and become a very model of austerity. . . . Well, have I answered your question?"

"Yes, but in doing so Your Majesty seems to have dismissed the two he himself asked. I have not answered them and neither has Your Majesty."

"And you prefer that I should answer them for you?"

"Very definitely, Your Majesty."

"Then I will say that I do not think you can compare my case with yours and I am surprised that you should have done so. I assure you that no further prying inquiries will be made into your private life. As for the nun in question, I should recommend that she exercise the greatest discretion. If she does that, I am sure she has nothing to fear."

PART FIVE

The Queen, the Duchess and the Nurse

1642-1643

For many years, Isabel de Borbón had suffered in silence. But in 1642 she felt the psychological moment had come to wage war on the *Privado* and she became the prime mover in a conspiracy against him which centered in the palace. Undoubtedly there were French secret agents who were very active in Spain and certainly Cardinal Richelieu himself had entered into negotiations with Isabel. [She had lent herself to these] not because she wished to benefit France at the expense of Spain, for she dearly loved her adopted country; but because she longed for the cessation of hostilities and she believed that if Olivares were dismissed, the motivating force of the war would be gone. In his prologue to the second edition of Cánovas' book about the Spanish decadence, Pérez de Guzmán affirms that the scheme to destroy Olivares was devised in the marriage bed of Philip's French bride.

—José Deleito y Piñuela. *El Declinar de la Monarquía Española.*

When Philip—who hardly went beyond Zaragoza while his troops were being defeated at Lérida—returned to Madrid, he found his *Privado* the target of combined attack from several quarters. Arrayed against him, on Isabel's side, were some persons whom the monarch held in high esteem. In this tacit intrigue several women were involved, and consequently the plot to overthrow Gaspar de Guzmán has become known as "the conspiracy of women." As a general thing, he was far from being a favorite with the weaker sex, for his youthful escapades and the devotion of his wife hardly counted; and his frequent declaration that nuns were for praying and women for child bearing certainly did not help him. . . . According to a contemporary writer, many of the most important of the court ladies, who were intimates of the Queen, entered with great efficiency into this conspiracy, which was the more successful because it came unexpectedly and secretly.

Among the Queen's accomplices were women of various positions. The Duchess of Mantua, deposed vice-regent of Portugal, had a personal grudge against the favorite and was moreover the mouthpiece of feudal aristocracy. The King's sister, the Infanta María [now Empress of Austria], had probably not forgotten that Olivares had thwarted her romance with Charles, Prince of Wales, with whom she was deeply in love, and thus prevented her from becoming queen of England. Doña Ana de Guevara, a woman of substance and station, who had been Philip's nursery governess and a protégée of the Duke of Lerma, and who had been his instrument against Don Gaspar de Guzmán before the latter had been appointed *Privado,* had been summarily dismissed by Olivares and she had never forgiven him. In the present crisis, availing herself of the King's faithful friendship, she saw her chance for revenge.

According to tradition, it was the simultaneous and combined activities of three women—the Queen, the Duchess and the nurse—which influenced the King to dismiss Olivares on the night of January 17. . . . The conspiracy of women was, in effect, more than the concerted action of only these three. It was the expression of an underlying feeling of feminine opposition to the famous minister.
—José DELEITO Y PIÑUELA. *El Declinar de la Monarquía Española.*

Chapter 21

THE news that the latest reinforcements sent to Cataluña had been defeated and that it was now completely overrun by the French struck Madrid like a thunderbolt. Furiously, the panic-stricken people clamored for a counter attack, unable to comprehend that Castile was now so drained of its resources that it could not finance another campaign. The nobles and gentlefolk of means were in almost open revolt against Olivares; large demands were made upon those who were suspected of having hoarded silver and in the capital alone more than one hundred persons were cast into dungeons because of their inability or unwillingness to meet these demands; and, despite the passage of a law against the further manufacture and devaluation of copper currency, it was tampered with until it was reduced to a fraction of its previous value. "Yesterday, Monday, the 15th of September, the feast of St. Nicomedes the Presbyter, notice was published in Madrid and in all the realm of the devaluation of the *vellón*," Pellicer, the pamphleteer, wrote in his current *aviso* for distribution on the Liars' Walks. "It is therefore necessary to face the fact that coins formerly worth eight *maravedís* are now worth only three or four and those formerly worth six are worth only one. Yesterday there was great confusion and today we are hard put to find anything to eat."

Rightly or wrongly, this wretched state of affairs was laid to the door of Olivares and his personal arrogance, which had always been a source of annoyance to his peers and hatred to the populace, now began to tell heavily against him. The Queen and the grandees, recognizing that a desperate situation called for desperate measures, urged the King to set an example of personal bravery by taking command of his scattered troops, with or without reinforcements; otherwise, Cataluña would be lost forever. The satirists and pamphleteers gibed at Philip as never before, first accusing him of weakness and vacillation and then openly of cowardice. The second accusation was unjust. Philip was not without a sense of obligation, neither was he without courage, when it came to a question of physical danger; it was self-assertion that he lacked, when Olivares was determined to restrain him and, for a time, he heeded the specious arguments marshaled against the bold step that he knew in his heart of hearts he ought to take, if he were to redeem himself before his wife, his nobles, his critics and his people. The arrival of Louis XIII on Spanish soil finally spurred him to tardy action; never should it be said that a French king should act the invader with impunity while a Spanish king lacked the initiative and the courage to defend his heritage. Philip tore up the Memorial that the Council, directed by Olivares, had drafted to oppose his departure, and announced that he was off to the front. If the Conde-Duque did not join him at Aranjuez, where he would make his first stop, he would proceed without his *Privado;* and, having made this declaration, he galloped, fully armed, out of the palace courtyard.

The immediate result of this dramatic departure was one of widespread enthusiasm and some of the murmurings against Olivares were stilled when his tardily acknowledged son organized a corps of young nobles which made a brilliant showing and set an example for other gilded youth. Money and men, which Castile could not supply, were almost miraculously forthcoming from Andalucía; meanwhile, the Court and Clergy responded to appeals from the Queen and a new force was somehow put together to accompany the King on his way to Aragón.

Unfortunately, Olivares did not fail to join him at Aranjuez, with many new pretexts for delay. Widespread murmuring soon supplanted widespread acclaim; the King's bold ride had come to an early end; had it been only a ruse to raise money and men? It was the Queen who succeeded in silencing these murmurs by speeding the King on his way again, this time with an unwieldy but practical entourage. His next stop was to be at Ocaña and he was making this stage of his journey by coach. His cousin Margarita, Duchess of Mantua, the deposed vicereine of Portugal, had been visiting him and the Queen at Aranjuez and he suggested that she should keep him company on her return to the palace, which was now at her complete disposal since Don Juan had moved to the Zarzuela. She accepted the invitation for the drive with alacrity; she had been longing for a chance to get Philip's ear when she would not be overheard; Olivares had always managed to advance reasons why she should not be entertained again at Madrid and there had been no opportunity for a tête-à-tête in Aranjuez. Now her pent-up indignation over the reasons for the revolt in Portugal, which she had hitherto not been able to voice, was all the more vehement because it had been so long suppressed. She poured out a story of mismanagement, duress and cruelty that came to Philip as a great shock. If Margarita had not exaggerated, it might well be too late for him to regain control of Portugal; but he firmly resolved that, if conditions such as she had disclosed should also exist in Cataluña, he would not permit them to be hidden from him until it was too late to remedy them.

As usual, his intentions were excellent and his fulfillment of them negligent. His progress was a leisurely one, via Cuenca to Molina and various other places which were not on the most direct route, but which afforded opportunities for pleasant visits. By the time he finally reached Zaragoza, Aragón was infested by French raiders from Cataluña and, though he occasionally reviewed troops before they left for the front, he neither saw his own army as a whole nor approached the enemy during the entire course of his stay there. His presence in the Aragonese capital should have at least afforded an opportunity for the grandees to confer with him on the calamitous state of the country and to take counsel as to what might be done to improve it. But, when they presented themselves in a body, Olivares, who still exercised his prerogatives, refused them access to Philip and they departed in anger, proclaiming that they would yet have their revenge on the insolent upstart who, in their opinion, had made their king virtually a prisoner. As a matter of fact, it was all too true that Philip was kept almost completely isolated on the ground that he would risk his life if he left his quarters.

Richelieu had died and this might represent at least a reprieve in the strain of relations with France; otherwise, the news brought to him in his seclusion went from bad to worse; and, at last, he decided to return to Madrid in the desperate hope of raising another army.

During the King's absence, Isabel had acted as Regent with her usual success, presiding at Council meetings, raising money, gathering troops, reviewing soldiers, capitalizing on the people's pride in Baltasar Carlos and all the time further undermining the prestige of Olivares by proving herself capable of meeting situations with which he had failed to cope. This, of course, was not because she was actually more efficient than the experienced and hard-working *Privado;* it was largely because she was increasingly beloved and he was increasingly hated. Nor was this hatred confined any longer to the people who felt he had despoiled them. The legitimation of his son Enrique had been a boomerang, offending his own most influential kinsmen, who had regarded themselves as his rightful heirs; and these, together with other former friends, who were nursing grievances, joined the Queen's faction. While Olivares was doing the King no good and much potential harm on the latter's journey to Zaragoza, he was involuntarily playing into Isabel's hand as he had never done before. "My efforts and my boy's innocence must serve the King for eyes," she announced to a willing audience, as she stood with Baltasar Carlos ensconced at her side. "If he use those of the Conde-Duque's much longer, my son will be reduced to a poor King of Castile, instead of a great King of Spain."

She was even more striking in maturity than she had been in youth. Her large black eyes were expressive as well as sparkling, her countenance was alive with intelligence. Her bearing had glamour, as well as distinction, and she had become a past mistress of dramatic appeal. Her every appearance weakened the Conde-Duque's cause. On the King's return to Madrid, she came out to meet him, magnificently dressed, and as they passed in their state coach from the Buen Retiro to the Alcázar, it seemed all too obvious to him that the blessings and cheers which rang out from every side were directed to her and not to him. He knew that he had failed. He had signed decrees drafted by Olivares, imposing upon Castile new and crushing burdens, with which to raise a fresh army. An-

other "voluntary" levy of money was ordered, a new loan authorized, the seizure of all church and domestic plate enjoined and a
tax of seven percent on all real property demanded. No one
knew where the actual money to meet these assessments was to come
from. And what was worse, Philip had not returned as a conquering
hero, but as a defeated weakling, while throughout the people's days
of bitter disillusionment she had comforted them, she had cheered
them, she had sustained them. They were confident that, somehow,
she would continue to do so and they were voicing their trust in her.
Philip was never ungenerous and, moreover, he recognized that the
tribute to his wife was well deserved; but the realization was not
without bitterness.

When they reached the palace, he begged Isabel to excuse him
for a little while; he was exhausted by his journey and he was deeply
troubled. She would understand, he knew, that he needed to rest
and to pray; as soon as he was refreshed, he would rejoin her. She
assured him that she understood perfectly and took affectionate
leave of him. It would have been better for Olivares if he had followed an equally tactful course. But the Conde-Duque, after vainly
seeking reconciliation with his brother-in-law—whose son, the
Count of Haro, was Olivares' heir apparent—came stumping to the
King's private apartments with a complaint against the Gentlemen
of the Chamber: in his absence they had all become his enemies; perhaps he had really better retire, as he had so often told the King that
he had long wanted to do. It was an old threat which, hitherto, had
always worked to his advantage. The impassivity of Philip's expression and the inconclusiveness of his brief response betrayed the fact
that, this time, it had failed to do so and, too late, the Conde-Duque
realized that he could not have chosen a less propitious moment to
intrude on the King's weariness of both body and spirit. Olivares
clumsily withdrew, hoping that when Philip, of his own accord, left
his apartments, someone else might plead his cause better than he
had done himself. His hopes were without foundation. The first person whom Philip met on his way to rejoin Isabel was the Conde-
Duque's wife, who practically waylaid him with a eulogy of her
husband's services and a detailed description of his plans for a successful campaign in the spring. Though Philip, with his usual cour-

tesy, had permitted her to detain him, he was by this time too tired to make even a brief reply; he bowed to her gravely and continued on his way. But, before he reached Isabel's apartments, he was stopped again, this time by a messenger from his brother-in-law Emperor Ferdinand III, bringing more bad news and bitterly attacking Olivares.

Philip dismissed the messenger, still without giving any sign of disturbance, and went on his way. When he found that Baltasar Carlos was with the Queen, his spirits momentarily lifted; the sight of his stalwart young heir was always a source of joy. But he had hardly entered the room when Isabel, instead of giving him the cheery welcome to which he had looked forward, cast herself at his feet, bringing Baltasar Carlos to his knees beside her.

"Sire," she cried desperately. "For the sake of our child's inheritance, if for no other reason, cast out the evil counselor who is dragging us all to ruin!"

Philip bent over, putting one arm around her and the other around their son, raising them both to their feet. "Isabel," he said, speaking with great gentleness and a supreme attempt at restraint. "Please don't call me Sire. Please don't kneel to me. Surely, you don't need to appeal to me as if you were some poor miscreant, begging for mercy, or as if you were playing a scene in a drama. Don't let our son do it, either."

He kissed the boy, dismissed him with a smile and the reminder that it was past the time when he should have been in Velázquez' studio. "I know you mistrust Olivares," Philip went on, as the boy bounded happily out of the room. "I've known it for a long time and I've also known that you hated him as an interloper between you and me before you had any reason to distrust him as a minister. I've known that both my brothers shared your feeling. At first, I didn't agree with you. I thought he was a wise counselor, as well as a great administrator. I knew he was much more capable of outlining and enforcing policies and making decisions for the good of the country than I was. He's a much more powerful man. But, lately, I've had my doubts about him, too. I've learned that his capacity for conceiving large-scale projects is much greater than his capacity for seeing them through. I've also learned that some of his counseling has been unwise and that some of his deeds have been evil, that he was willing to sacrifice almost everything to his passion for power, even justice and mercy. Moreover, I've come to have a very high opinion of your judgment."

"Then you'll dismiss him?"

Philip sighed. "I've been considering it very seriously, but I keep putting it off. Partly because I can't help feeling sorry for him."

"Sorry for him!"

"Yes. He isn't well. I mean, quite aside from his lameness. His shoulders are burly as ever, but haven't you noticed his eyes? They used to be his dominating feature. Now they're still observant, but they're lackluster. And his cheeks are sunken. I suppose he's lost his teeth, as well as his hair, and that's why he wears a great sweeping mustache and a shaggy wig."

"None of this makes me feel sorry for him. It only makes me feel he's more repulsive than ever."

Philip sighed again. "Well, there's another reason why I hesitate to dismiss him. If I do, who'll take his place? Oh, I know you will say that we do not want anyone to take his place and, in a sense, that is true. But in another . . . I am not capable of governing this kingdom single-handed, you know that, Isabel, as well as I do. Just now, as I told you a few hours ago, I am so tired and discouraged that I am not sure of thinking very clearly. That was why I asked you to excuse me while I rested and prayed. Well, I have prayed and I have tried to rest—not very successfully. So I thought I would give up trying to make important decisions for tonight and spend the rest of the evening pleasantly with you. But perhaps, after all, it would be better if I retired to pray some more."

Isabel did not try to detain him, as he had half-hoped she would; but he was apparently fated to have his passage through the corridors of the Alcázar interrupted, if not by a countess, then by an imperial messenger and, if not by an imperial messenger, then by someone else whom he could not gainsay. This time it was by Ana de Guevara, whom he had not seen in a long while, for though Olivares had raised no objection to her temporary attendance on Inés on the occasion of Don Juan's birth, he had later taken steps to ensure her permanent removal from Court. She had been buxom and comely as a young matron; now she was a mere wisp of a woman and Philip was so startled when he came upon her in the semi-obscurity that he did not recognize her instantly. It took him a moment to collect himself and he did not even have a chance to ask her how she had managed to return, surreptitiously, to the palace when, like the Queen, she cast herself on her knees before him.

"Sire," she cried, with even greater vehemence than Isabel. "I implore you to listen to me!"

"Of course, I will listen to you, Ana," he said patiently. "What is it you want to tell me?"

"What you do not seem to know: that the looms are idle, the fields untilled, the pasturage uncropped, and why? Because one wicked man is bent on destroying the nation. The people have long endured their misery without complaint, but now they are starving. Much as they love you, they can bear no more. They will rise against you and your wife and your children, unless you free them from this evil monster's oppression."

Philip knew she was exaggerating, but he had reached the breaking point. He raised Ana to her feet, as he had Isabel, but he did not remonstrate with her for kneeling to him, as he had with his wife. Neither did he try to reason with her or explain anything to her or give any sign of the affection he had always felt for her. Instead, he said, abruptly, "I'm afraid you are right," and, turning on his heel, left her and hurried down the long corridor, obsessed with the fear that he might again be detained and importuned.

After a sleepless night, in which prayer had not played a very prominent part, he decided that probably the most effective way to prevent any more scenes would be to leave the Alcázar altogether and, at dawn, he called for a horse and galloped rapidly out to the Pardo, his favorite hunting lodge, and quickly arranged for a day in the woods. Before he picked up his gun, however, he seized a scrap of paper and wrote hurriedly:

CONDE-DUQUE—

You have often asked for permission to retire and I have not chosen to grant your request. Now I do. You may go wherever you wish with due regard for your health and need of repose.

—I THE KING.

Chapter 22

EVERYTHING that happened within the next few days had a quality not only of anticlimax, but of unreality to Philip.

When he returned to the Alcázar, he found awaiting him an urgent request from Isabel: would he please come to her as soon as he conveniently could? After a long day in the open and a good night's sleep, he felt infinitely better; without any sense of strain or dread, he hastened to her apartments and, to his surprise, found that she had already finished her morning chocolate and begun to busy herself with accounts. She looked up with a smile and motioned to a seat beside her.

"Margarita is here," she said. "She's eager to see you."

"Margarita?" For a moment, he was puzzled. It often seemed to him that every girl baby who was not christened Isabel or María must be christened Margarita, there were so many women by that name.

"Yes. Your cousin. The Duchess of Mantua."

"Really? I had no idea she was planning to make us a visit. Is anything wrong at Ocaña?"

"No, I don't think so. Of course, she is perpetually short of money. And she would much rather live in Madrid."

"Well, she is not the only person who is short of money. And I suppose, if she is really discontented in Ocaña, we can provide suitable accommodations here. Is that all?"

"She has some very important documents she wants to show you."

Philip made a gesture of impatience. "Why, just now?"

"Because she couldn't very well do it while you were in Aragón and you've been home only two days."

"Exactly. So I have plenty of other things to do at the moment. I'll look at her documents later on. I suppose she has some more disclosures about irregularities in Portugal, for which she blames Olivares."

"Yes. As I said, she claims they're very important, that if you could only see them—"

Again, Philip made a gesture of impatience. "Have her hand them over to you. I'll look at them when I have time. Just now, I have all I can do without reading old documents. I expect to be rather busy these next few days. You will be glad to know that, before I went into the woods yesterday, I wrote a brief note to the Conde-Duque, giving him leave to retire."

"Philip, are you serious?"

"I never was more so. I might have given a little more thought to the matter and stood out against you a little longer if Ana de Guevara hadn't made an appeal, quite as dramatic as yours, when I was trying to go and get some rest. Also, if the Condesa herself, as well as the Conde-Duque, hadn't stopped me in the corridor, with all sorts of explanations and complaints. I began to think I couldn't walk around my own palace without being waylaid. That's what finally drove me out to the Pardo. But now I'm feeling better—enough better to face most things, but not another wailing woman. . . . There," he added hastily, "I didn't mean to speak unkindly."

"I didn't think you meant to be unkind. And you won't have to worry about being waylaid by the Countess, today anyhow. She's gone to Loeches."

"Oh! Then perhaps that's why Olivares is still here—because his palace isn't ready for them to live in and he's sent her to see that it was put in order. He did waylay me again early this morning, repeating everything he said day before yesterday. Not that it did him any good. . . . Well, let's not talk about it any more. The next thing I must do is to prepare a statement for the Council. I'll draft it right now. Perhaps you can help me with it."

He selected a blank sheet from the stack Isabel had in readiness and wrote rapidly. Once the statement was prepared, he began to feel better, though he did not intend to use it until the Conde-Duque had actually left for Loeches. Philip decided to spend the day more or less in seclusion, recovering from strain; and Isabel's assurance that the Condesa had gone to Loeches led him to believe that the "wailing woman" whom he most dreaded to see was out of the way. Under the circumstances, it should be safe for him to pay his usual afternoon visit to his children, which he was accustomed to do unattended, and he moved quickly along the corridor which led to their rooms. Unfortunately, his cool reception of the Conde-Duque early that morning had already brought about unwelcome results: Olivares had sent off a message, posthaste, to his wife, urging her return; he had failed to recover lost ground, but perhaps she would be more successful. Considering her previous experience, two days earlier, his credulity would have been amazing were it not so plainly permeated with desperation; but she showed no more discernment than he had. Leaving her dinner untouched, she hurried back to Madrid and rushed to the Alcázar, where she again accosted the King before he could take refuge in the schoolroom. This time, had it not been for a supreme effort of will on his part, he would have bade her be gone in no uncertain terms. As it was, with cutting politeness, he asked her to excuse him and went on his way. But she still would not, or could not, recognize defeat. With persistent ineptitude, she rushed to the Queen's apartments on the chance that Isabel might not yet have joined her husband, though why she should have thought for a moment that Isabel would be in a forgiving mood, the latter was at a loss to understand; she had suffered too long under the meddling tyranny of the Condesa, when she herself was an inexperienced girl, a stranger in a strange land, to feel any pity for her now. The Queen's cold reply, overheard by Ana de Guevara, became a byword, "What God, the people and evil happenings have done, Condesa, neither the King nor I can undo."

Directly and indirectly, the discredited couple pursued their tactless and insistent course, refusing to be persuaded that, by so doing, they were laying themselves open to harsher measures against them than had so far been used or even contemplated. Convinced at last that his wife would never succeed as an intermediary, the Conde-Duque next decided to try his luck with his nephew, Don

Luis de Haro, whom he had dispossessed as his lawful heir in favor of his tardily recognized illegitimate son. Quite as if he were still in a position to give orders, Olivares summoned Don Luis to the Buen Retiro, which he had not yet left himself; and when the young man obediently appeared, his uncle reminded him that, though in some ways he might have been deprived of his rights, much had been done for him by bringing him to Court from his father's remote country seat and thereby opening the way to riches and power. Now it was his turn to grant favors. Don Luis was stunned; it would no more have occurred to him that he might have more influence with the King than his ruthless and powerful kinsman than it would have occurred to him that he might profitably covet the crown itself. Cautiously, he replied that he did not know if the King would be disposed to receive him; apparently, His Majesty was very tired after his long journey and preferred to be spared as many audiences as possible; but he, Luis, would make inquiries and, if the reply were favorable, he would do what he could. This was typical of the attributes which had won for him the nickname of *el Discreto,* that was to say, the average man, neither too refined nor too coarse, too bold nor too timid.

It so happened that Philip was perfectly willing to see Don Luis, whose "average" qualities he appreciated; he was beginning to think that the Conde-Duque's insistence actually had amusing aspects. He listened with unfeigned interest to the long list of expensive gifts and pensions which Olivares wanted the King to bestow on Olivares' servants, and said he would be glad to authorize them, though he was well aware that the *Privado* had long been enjoying an income of half a million a year and could well afford to make such provisions himself. Don Luis was also so aware of this that he suddenly found himself tongue-tied; he could not go on to the extent of asking personal favors for his uncle. Instead, he permitted himself to give answers to a few direct questions in regard to several secret political points closely affecting the fallen Minister.

While Olivares and his wife continued to besiege the palace, word that their fall was imminent gradually seeped through its walls to the Liars' Walks. But, at first, the news was received incredulously; it was simply too good to be true. The people's disbelief was not without basis, for Olivares still stubbornly refused to leave the capital. According to him, transportation represented difficulties; so did the state of his health; so did the necessity of seeing all his servitors well provided for (though Don Luis had taken care of that). The Conde-Duque did not surrender his keys until they were demanded and humbled himself by going to a public audience. There, rather than create a scene, the King conversed with him briefly; but even those who were not within earshot knew that nothing had been gained by this final attempt at an interview. When Olivares left the audience chamber, leaning heavily on the crutch which was no longer credited with magic powers, tears of chagrin were running down his cheeks.

Meanwhile, pamphleteers and satirists had begun to compose a fresh crop of squibs and lampoons which were passed from hand to hand and posted in public places and the boldest one of all was actually pinned on the palace gate. Great crowds gathered in the square before the Alcázar, shouting, "We have a king again, we have a king again!" and when the King and Queen, with the Duchess of Mantua, went abroad in the royal coach, the people surged around them with joyous cries, "Our King at last! God save the King!" And still the Conde-Duque lingered.

Philip had no wish to humiliate his Minister by a public display of irritation, but his patience was very sorely tried. At last he decided that it would, perhaps, be better for him to go hunting again, this time at the Escorial. Isabel, who recognized his need for release, refrained from sending him word that the Condesa had again managed to reach her with a tearful complaint, so he was not disturbed on that score. Two days in the open air did wonders for him and then, as he left San Lorenzo, he was met by a delegation of nobles, headed by Melchor Borja, who told him they had come to put themselves and all their worldly possessions at his disposal. They had long stood aloof; now that he was once more their king, they would be his until death.

He returned to Madrid a much happier man than he had left it and was relieved to find that, though Olivares was still at the Buen Retiro, it was at last evident that he was making preparations for departure. The Conde-Duque left the palace secretly, by means of a service stairway, and drove off in a coach with drawn curtains, attended by only four persons. It was an ignominious ending to a grandiose career.

When the news came that he had actually gone, Philip called a meeting of his Council and read them the statement which he had prepared a few days earlier:

For a long while, the Conde-Duque has been asking permission to retire, as he has been in poor health and considers himself incapable of performing his functions. I have delayed as long as possible because of the affection in which I hold him, and because of my great confidence in him, the result of proven zeal, love, purity and dedication over many years. Yet, taking into account the insistence with which he has lately repeated his request, I have chosen to grant it. . . . He has already departed. . . . I still hope that, with peace and quiet, he may recover his strength and return to my service. On this occasion, it behooves me to inform the Council that, for the lack of so good a minister, no one will replace him but myself. . . . May Our Lord enlighten me and guide me. . . .

Though this statement was, of course, courteously received by the Council, the courtesy was, inevitably, permeated with scepticism, on several counts. Almost nobody considered that the Conde-Duque's role had been one of "zeal, love, purity and dedication" and almost nobody believed that the King would act as his own minister. With this disbelief was coupled the fear that Olivares would indeed be permitted to return to the service of the King or that the new *privado,* whoever that might be, would represent a change for the worse. The continued presence of the Condesa at Court remained a source of irritation, for she managed to cling to her position as Mistress of the Robes and, though Isabel deeply resented this, Philip was now inclined to let matters slide. It was the Duchess of Mantua who finally brought them to a head when a dispute arose regarding precedence. The Condesa had never relinquished her claim to a place in the royal coach and she might have kept it had it not been that she and Margarita were not of the same opinion as to which place this should be. Isabel managed to placate the warring ladies and the outing continued with a compromise; but a few days later, when the coach was surrounded by a crowd that shouted, "Long live the Queen and down with the Condesa!" the King decided that he could not let matters slide any longer, after all. The Condesa was instructed to follow her husband into retirement.

Philip was trying very hard to do his best. He faithfully attended all meetings of the Council and dispatched urgent business promptly and efficiently. He wrote decrees and other state papers with his own hand. He rose early and began to give audiences by seven in the morning. Gradually, the scepticism of the nobles abated; perhaps this was, after all, "their king at last" and none of them questioned that Isabel was their queen; misgivings on that score had ceased long before. But a general feeling persisted that the King did not realize how much he, as well as the people, owed her. On this point, also, came a welcome surprise.

Regular visits to the Convent of the *Descalzas Reales* were still a habit with the King and Queen and both were accustomed, in the course of these visits, to ask the Community for special prayers. However, in view of Philip's positive statement that no one was to replace Olivares, there was a subdued murmur of bewilderment when Philip closed some informal remarks to the nuns with the request that they would commend the new *privado* to God, "in order that His light might shine on the government." The Sisters silently exchanged glances; then one of them, bolder than the others, ventured to ask His Majesty for whom this special prayer was intended.

"My new *privado* is the Queen," he replied. And, dropping on one knee, he kissed her hand.

PART SIX

The

Lady

in Blue

1643-1649

With the knowledge that disaster was pursuing him on all sides, for the Portuguese were raiding far into Castile and the French were threatening the capital of Aragón, Philip left Madrid, his heart wellnigh breaking, early in June, 1643. . . .

This time Philip was accompanied by a modest train, and by little of the ceremonial state that Olivares had deemed needful for his previous voyage. He traveled slowly, nevertheless, and on the 10th July, as he approached the Aragonese frontier city of Tarazona, he halted at the humble Convent of the Immaculate Conception at Ágreda, which in the previous few years had been founded by a lady whose fame for sanctity and wisdom had already become wide, though she was but forty years of age yet. María Coronel had written several mystically religious books, and the convent under her rule was known for its rigidity in an age when most cloisters had grown lax. Philip probably visited the house and its abbess as a usual compliment and duty; but the visit, whatever its motive, set its mark upon him for the rest of his life.

The abbess, *Sor* María, as she was called, must have been a woman of worldly wisdom as deep as was her piety. She must have impressed the King, moreover, powerfully as being absolutely disinterested and free from mundane temptation. He was, as we have seen, almost in despair at the magnitude of the tasks before him; the strong spirit upon which he had leant since he was a boy had passed out of his life, and he knew not whither to turn for unselfish counsel. *Sor* María, saintly, but keen, with her sad yet half humorous face, and her shrewd, kindly eyes, seemed to him a very rock of refuge, and in the long talk he had with her she spoke so wisely, yet so fearlessly, of the oppressive governance and ungodly methods of Olivares, she urged the King so powerfully to trust to God and himself alone, to work and pray and make his people cleanly, that he went forth from Ágreda refreshed in faith and hope, leaving with *Sor* María his command that she was to write to him her private counsel when she listed, and to pray for him and his unceasingly with all her saintly soul.

Thenceforward until death snapped the spiritual link that joined them, the heart of Philip was bared in all its sorrow, its weakness, and its sin to *Sor* María alone. The haughty face with the pathetic eyes and great projecting jaw remained unmoved before the world, only the deepening furrows in it showing the storm that raged within. Men thought that he was callous and cold; for he suffered silently behind his mask. But *Sor* María knew, and none but she under heaven, the true secret of the King's gilded misery. His cry of agony, of remorse, of pity thenceforward came to the cloistered nun as a surer way to reach the throne of grace than to all the cardinals, confessors, and bishops who waited upon his smile, and gently hinted disapproval of kindly vice.

—Martin Hume. *The Court of Philip IV.*

Chapter 23

" AND now, how much further to Ágreda?"
"Not more than a league or so, Sire."
"There have been days when we have gone no further than that
from sunrise to sunset. And it is my hope that we may cross the provincial frontier from Castile into Aragón before nightfall. However,
if we are late in reaching Ágreda or if we are detained there longer
than I expect, that will be impossible."

"We shall not be late in reaching Ágreda, Sire. And we need be
detained there no longer than Your Majesty desires."

"The traditional courtesies must be observed."

"True, but they may be kept to the minimum."

The King sighed, without answering, and the second speaker,
Don Luis de Haro, true to his role of *el Discreto,* saw no point in
pursuing the question, though word had already reached them that
town and gown were preparing special festivities in honor of the
royal visit. By his own fatigue, he could easily gauge the King's and
the latter's longing to reach the end of their travels. It was more
than five weeks since they had left Madrid for Zaragoza and the journey, over rough roads, even though it had been made in a superb
state coach, lined in crimson brocade and provided with a couch on
which the King could recline, instead of having been made on horseback, had been a hard one. Indeed, Don Luis was disposed to think
that the other method would have been easier as well as quicker; unfortunately, that was contrary to the rules of etiquette, not easily suspended. Royal progresses were traditionally made by coach, with
equerries and outriders and a suitable suite, though in this instance

the size of the suite had been greatly reduced. Simplicity, like economy, according to Philip, was now to be the order of the day.

Don Luis would have been perfectly content if the retrenchment were such that he need not be included among those chosen to accompany the King, especially as there had never previously been such prolonged stops at all the convents, monasteries and churches along the way: Alcalá de Henares—Guadalajara—Sigüenza—Medinaceli—Almazán—Tajahuerce del Campo—Villar del Campo; pompous bishops—drowsy priors—garrulous abbesses—it seemed the prayers of all these were needed for the remission of His Majesty's sins and the redemption of prostrate Spain! Luis de Haro shrugged his shoulders. If every time the King committed adultery —and, despite his pallor and his languor, he must be possessed of extraordinary virility—the prayers of the faithful were to be elicited, they would have time for nothing else. If the defenders of the fortress at Oran and the infantry on the field at Rocroy—those world famous *tercios*—were not powerful enough to end the long siege of the one and prevent the crushing defeat of the other, how could it be hoped that the mumbling patter of cloistered monks would have more effect?

And then there had been that inexplicable change of plan after leaving Guadalajara. Don Luis knew that the King had intended to make the Convent of Valfermoso de las Monjas, near Utande, one of his stops; and there had been much speculation among his attendants as to what this might portend, and a good many whispered opinions and surreptitious winks, not to mention wagers, had been exchanged. Although fourteen years had passed since la Calderona had insisted on the rupture of her relations with the King, despite his vehement and brokenhearted protests, and had entered a convent in the remote Badiel Valley, none of them had forgotten her charm, her grace, her gentleness. She was only a little past thirty now—in short, she should barely have reached the zenith of feminine allure; and it was hard for Don Luis and the others to believe that, in seeking her out, the King intended to ask only for her prayers. Oh, doubtless, the visit would begin correctly enough! As Philip himself put it, the traditional courtesies must be observed. The nun—two nuns—would be on one side of the grille and the King, with an attendant nobleman, on the other. But Philip would soon find a pretext for dismissing both her companion and his; then he would give her news of their son, the namesake of the King's famous great-uncle, Don Juan of Austria: such a promising boy, so handsome, so intelligent, so manly that everyone in the palace of the Zarzuela, where he was established in princely fashion, was loud in his praises. After assuring her of the boy's welfare and progress, the King would go on to describe the ceremony which had taken place when *their* Don Juan, at the age of twelve, was brought to Madrid and, by decree, given the same semi-royal honors that had been bestowed on the son of Charles V. *Sor* Dolores—was that what she called herself now? —could not help but be moved by such a recital; and, when His Majesty told her that he would require lodging for the night, for himself and his attendants, could she refuse to give it to him? To be sure, she was not another *Sor* Margarita, who must have been a hussy at heart or she would have found a way, with the help of her abbess, to make herself inaccessible to the King, despite the tunnel leading from Villanueva's basement to the cloister of San Plácido. There had never been anything of the hussy about la Calderona. The King had been her one and only love, as Don Luis himself and a number of others who had tried in vain to prevail against her chastity could testify; and she had loved the King as a man and not as a monarch. But had she ever ceased to love him, despite her flight and her vows and the blameless cloistered life she had led ever since receiving her habit at the hands of Giovanni Battista Pamfili, the Papal Nuncio? Had the King ever ceased to love her, despite his weakness and his profligacy and his futility? Don Luis did not think so and neither did any of the others. And, when the King and *Sor* Dolores came face to face again, after those years of separation when they had continued to yearn for each other, who could blame them if the exchange of glances were followed by an exchange of embraces? Certainly not Don Luis. He awaited the stop at Utande with eager anticipation; there, at least, would be a change and a break in the monotony of this cursed progress.

And then, what had happened? They had passed Trijueque, where the King had insisted on stopping long enough to inspect the fortifications and had begun the descent into the deep Badiel Valley on a late June day so beautiful that it seemed impossible to think of this region as one that was stark and grim. All the foothills of the Alcarria Range were clothed in soft greens and the fields below were richly verdant, too, except where they were already golden with wheat which would soon be ripe for harvesting; and hills and valleys alike were bathed in the resplendency of a sun which hung like a great ball in a sky as blue as lapis lazuli. This sky was cloudless and the soft air, fragrant with the scent of lavender, was crystal clear. Suddenly, far beneath them, the little village toward which they were headed came into sight as the King's *carroza* swung around a bend in the curving road—a little village which, in its essential attributes, was no different from hundreds of other Castilian villages, with small clustering houses, red roofed, low built, brown walled; but which, somehow, seemed to have a quality all its own, because it was so enfolded by its hills and so glorified by the light which shone on it. It seemed permeated with a peace that was not of this world, almost as if it were an inviolable sanctuary. And when the *carroza* came to a halt, because the bend had been difficult to maneuver, and it now stood too close to the precipitous edge for safety, the King alighted and, for some moments, stood silently looking down at the village below them with his courtiers respectfully grouped around him, silent also. Then, without any word to explain his action, the King commanded that the *carroza* should go forward no further than to the first place where it would be safe to turn it around and, after that, they were to regain the high road and to go on to Sigüenza, where they were to be the guests at the Episcopal palace. They were not to pause long enough even to feast on the famous honey of the region.

That was several days ago and the King had made no reference since to his change of plan, nor had any of the others in his hearing, though plenty had been said when he was out of earshot. It was never easy to guess the King's thoughts; ever since his father's death, his face had had no more change of expression than a mask, when he chose to keep it that way and, increasingly, he was a man of few words. But it was not hard to guess that la Calderona—or *Sor* Dolores, if that was what she called herself now—had won again, as she had when she had flung herself at Philip's feet, after the birth of their son, and begged his leave to let her go, so that she who had the honor of bearing the King's son might henceforth lead a blameless life. He had tried to break her will then, for he not only still desired her greatly, he loved her, if not as truly as she loved him, then at least as truly as it was in him to love any woman; and he had been powerless to do so. Now something had told him that he would again be powerless, that his sojourn at Utande would be one of defeat and sorrow and unappeased yearning. Or had something else happened? When he alighted from the crimson-lined *carroza* and stood apart from his men, a somber figure with a waxen face, had that glimpse he had had of a sheltered spot, which his love believed a safe sanctuary, moved him so deeply that he found he could not go on?

The others were never to know. Sigüenza and the most tedious visit of any were behind them now and so were Medinaceli and Almazán, where they had stayed at seignorial houses for a change. After Ágreda there was only Tarazona, where they would cross into Aragón and Borja, the ancestral house of Aragón's viceroy, whose family had a way of producing saintly figures as well as shrewd statesmen; and then, at last, they would be in Zaragoza, able to enjoy urban delights with the King's own palace as their headquarters. If only Ágreda could have been omitted, there was no doubt that they could have passed over the boundary line that evening; but, if it were true that the populace were turning out in full force, that a special service were to be held at the Church of the Immaculate Conception, there was not much chance of that.

Even before they were in sight of Ágreda, Don Luis knew that his last hope was gone. The bells of all the churches were ringing and sounds of jubilation rose from the streets. The people, whose acquaintance with the King had hitherto been limited to a profile on the coin of the realm and the seals used on documents associated with tax collecting and conscription for military service, could hardly believe that he was actually in their midst, not only as the Lord's Anointed, but as a man of flesh and blood. They had formed processions, they were waving olive branches, they were singing in chorus and shouting huzzahs. Their excitement was understandable. Ágreda had not previously been chosen as a halting place for a royal cortege. It was not a cathedral town and the Convent of the *Concepcionistas* was not one established by royal grant; it was merely the outgrowth of a pious neighborly unit which had, at first, been quartered in the ancestral home of the Coronel family and gradually expanded to achieve monastic status, largely through the efforts of Francisca Coronel's daughter María, who was the present abbess. And, now that he thought of it, Don Luis wondered if there were not something he had heard about this woman which might have been a determining factor in the King's decision to stop at Ágreda.

To all intents and purposes, the visit was one of routine and the King, with characteristic taciturnity, had not given the slightest indication that it might be otherwise. But, tardily, Don Luis began to remember rumors he had heard concerning this abbess: about the rigidity with which she ruled; about the books she had written, some of which had met with disfavor from the Holy Inquisition; about her great learning and mystic powers, including that of bilocation, with which she was credited, and which could not be explained through natural laws. Now that all this came to mind, Don Luis thought he remembered that his uncle, the Conde-Duque, who had fallen from favor only a few months before, after enjoying years of supreme authority, had previously dissuaded Philip from including Ágreda on his itinerary—in fact, had gone so far as to insist on a change after it was actually planned. Whether this was because such a visit might intensify Philip's interest in mysticism—an interest which he had inherited from his father, to whom it had become an obsession; or whether it might mean another tangle with the Inquisition, when the one precipitated by the scandal at San Plácido had been quite enough; or whether it was merely an aversion to the unnecessary delay caused by a superfluous visit at an unimportant center, Luis did not know. But he thought very possibly Philip was now seizing an occasion—as he had done several times already—to show that he was no longer king only in name, that he was his own master. And perhaps the very fact that he had refrained from stopping at Utande had increased his determination to find what support and solace were available elsewhere.

The *carroza* lumbered through the streets and came to a stop before the Church of the Immaculate Conception, which also served as the convent chapel. Ever since the first rumors of a royal visit had reached the nuns, they had been busily at work; they had practiced songs, they had polished ornaments, they had prepared candles, they had gathered flowers. Now, in the lighted church where the fragrance of the roses mingled with the aroma of the incense, they peered through the grille as they reverently began to sing the *Te Deum,* resentful that it obscured their view of the King's black-clad figure as he knelt, his pale face resting on his clasped hands. Only his reverence and his absorption were fully revealed. Like the people in the streets, who had acclaimed him with olive branches, the nuns wanted to see the man as a human figure—not because they associated him with coins and tax collectors, but because they associated him with *Sor* Margarita, whose story had, of course, been the more widely spread the greater the attempt to suppress it. Would any of them be admitted to the locutory when the King paid his respects to the Abbess? If so, would he look on her with favor? And then, what next? Considering *Sor* María's severity, there was not much to hope for—or much to fear. The nuns bowed their heads and accepted virginity with mingled regret and thanksgiving.

The same dignitaries of Church and State who had awaited the King at the portal of the church on his arrival, now waited to escort him to the locutory after the service was over. He was to enter it alone, for the Abbess was not to receive him with the grille between them, but as any great lady would have welcomed a distinguished visitor; and only a king could have this privilege in a cloistered convent. As the latch was lifted, the door opened quietly from within and he heard the murmured greeting, "*Ave Maria Purissima,*" with which visitors were automatically welcomed, and made the standardized answer, "*Sin peccavi conceptiva,*" even before he saw a graceful figure, enveloped in a blue cloak, and veiled with black. He took a step forward and bowed.

"I am honored by your reception of me, *Sor* María."

"As I am honored by your visit, Sire."

"Will you not be seated?"

"I feel it would not be seemly to sit in my sovereign's presence."

"Then I can only say that I shall remain standing as long as you do."

"In that case, Sire, you give me no choice."

Drawing the folds of her cloak around her, she seated herself on a stool, at the same time indicating that the King should take the chair which had been her father's favorite, the one in which she had often seen him seated at ease, in the quiet of the evening, reading from his Book of Devotions. She had brought it with her when she moved from his family house, the only other one she had ever known, to the convent; and she had seen it used, hundreds of times now, by visitors to the locutory. But, hitherto, when that had happened, she had been on one side of the grille and her visitor on the other. There were no bars to separate her from this one. In fact, there was not even distance; the locutory was small, as well as bare; either, by stretching out a hand, could have touched the other.

"And now, *Sor* María, if you would further honor me by raising your veil."

It had not occurred to her that he would ask her to do this and she hesitated, for no man had seen her face these many years now; even in the confessional, she was hidden. But this was the King, and she must obey him, as long as no order that he gave her did violence to her vows. Thoughtfully, she reviewed these and could remember nothing that forbade her to do as he asked. Meanwhile, he waited without any show of impatience, for her to reveal the countenance which, even without seeing it, he felt sure would promise so much.

Slowly she raised both hands and lifted her long black veil, holding it lightly on either side. Beneath it was another, black also, but sheer and shorter than the first and, until she raised this, too, he could not see her features clearly. Then he looked on a face of almost perfect oval, the chin firmly but delicately molded, the beautifully shaped lips meeting each other without pressure. The skin was exquisite, its pallor tinged with a faint rose that seemed to come from some inner glow that illumined both spirit and body, rather than from mere natural coloring. But dominating every other feature were the eyes: large, dark, wise, compassionate, all-seeing. They met the King's gaze steadily and, as they did so, they softened more and more and yet, at the same time, it was strength, not weakness, that they showed him—the strength of which he was so desperately in need. The mask fell from his own face, revealing it in all its anguish, all its remorse—and all its weakness.

"I have come to you, *Sor* María, in desperate need," he said brokenly. "Without your help I shall be lost and, with me, my kingdom."

Chapter 24

AS the King spoke, he leaned forward in his chair, twisting his clasped hands in anguish. *Sor María*, whose hands were folded calmly in her lap, under her scapular, resisted the impulse to tighten them and spoke quietly.

"Help must come from the Omnipotent, Sire, as you know. I could only be His instrument, if such were His Will. What leads you to think that I might be?"

"Everything about you."

"But 'everything' could be compassed in such a small space! What have I done to justify such confidence?"

"It is not what you have done or left undone. It is what you are."

"And what am I? The foundress of a small secluded convent in a provincial town. Your Majesty has been in close touch, all his life, with the sumptuous Convent of the *Descalzas Reales* in Madrid, whose foundress was the daughter of an emperor, the wife and sister of kings. The fourth Duke of Gandía, husband of Leonor de Castro, who entered Holy Orders after her death, became confessor at the *Descalzas Reales*; and three of his relatives have been its abbesses; his great-grandson is your friend, Don Fernando Manuel de Borja y Aragón, Viceroy of Aragón. Is not the Superior of this convent Your Majesty's logical spiritual adviser if you seek for some abbess to supplement the counsel of your eminent confessor?"

"No. The Convent of the *Descalzas Reales* means nothing to me except the place where I was taken by a drab churchman, when I was a little boy, to attend dull ceremonies, the only respite offered me from prayers and lessons, and the place to which I am now required, by etiquette, to make royal visits."

"But, if I'm not mistaken, Your Majesty did perform in masques with courtiers of your own age, in which you took delight and showed great talent, as you did in the declamation of verses before the elders in your father's court."

"I see that you are well informed, *Sor* María. If such details as these are known to you, there must be many others of greater weight on which you could pass judgment. Let me say that, as a rule, the masques and recitations were few and far between and that there were no other outings with boys of my own age—no games, no contests, no healthful sports."

"Your Majesty was married very young to a most charming princess. It is my understanding that she was a gay playfellow for you and that, since then, she has shared your tastes for pleasure, besides showing herself a wise regent in those periods like the present one when Your Majesty himself is, perforce, absent from Court."

"That also is true. Spain is more blessed in her queen than in her king. And, as I said before, you are very well informed. So doubtless you know that the Conde-Duque stimulated those pleasures by giving the Queen and myself the Buen Retiro as the gala setting for them."

"Yes, Sire."

"And that he is now in retirement?"

"Yes, Sire."

"And that this retirement was not entirely voluntary?"

"Again, I must say yes, Sire."

"Did you form an opinion as to whether or not this retirement was well or ill advised?"

"I believe it was well advised. The Conde-Duque had once been a pillar of great strength to Your Majesty. But, gradually, he had become a crushing weight both to Your Majesty and to your people."

"And since he has ceased to give me support, have you felt that any other has given it to me, except my wife?"

"No, Your Majesty."

"Then why should you be surprised that I ask your help and ask it desperately?"

"Because again I must inquire of you, Sire, what moves you to believe I can give you help? By my prayers, yes, but those you have without the asking, as you have those of every loyal subject in your realm."

"It is not only your prayers which I am beseeching. It is also your counsel. I have often heard it said that, if a man wishes to know what is happening in the world, he should go to a convent. I have sometimes doubted the truth of that old saw. I shall do so no longer. You know my story and, doubtless, that of my father and my grandfather, not to mention that of my present family, my advisers, my loves, my people. And, knowing them, you have given thought to them and formed opinions about them. You are a thoughtful woman."

"For the sake of argument, let us assume that is so. But that does not prove that these thoughts and opinions would be of constructive help. I know your story, yes, and the story of those who surround you and those who preceded you, but that does not mean I am qualified to comment on them in a way that would be of service. I have no acquaintance with a world like yours. In all my life I have not left Ágreda. Even my girlhood dream of becoming a Carmelite, of taking the habit in the Convent of Santa Ana of Tarazona which, as Your Worship knows, is only a few leagues from here, came to nothing. For my mother also had a dream—a vision: I was not to leave my home. My father and my brothers would leave it, to become Franciscan friars; but she and I would remain there and, joined by friends, form our own Community. It was only some years later that this was formalized, by papal decree, and that we raised the wherewithal to build this convent, in which we have had the honor to receive Your Majesty. I left my first home for this, my second one. I have never been anywhere else, not even to Tarazona."

"*Sor* María, are you sure?"

For the first time, the King, who was watching her intently, saw the translucent eyelids flutter, ever so slightly, before they veiled the great luminous eyes; and the glow in the pale cheeks became deeper when she spoke. Moreover, she did not answer with the same immediacy that had marked her speech whenever he paused before.

"I asked you, *Sor* María, if you were sure?" he repeated, more impellingly. "I am awaiting your answer."

"Since you require it of me, Sire, I must tell you that I am not—altogether sure."

"Ah! And, in that case, where is it that you have been?"

"To the New World."

"*To the New World!* And still you were almost sure that you had never been as far away as Tarazona! You could hardly have crossed seas and continents without knowing it."

Again she made no immediate answer.

"Could you?" he insisted.

"No," she murmured at last. "But I did not go to the New World as I would have gone to Tarazona."

"And how did you go?"

"It was Our Lord Who transported me," she said, still almost in a whisper. "After I had eaten the Bread of Angels, I felt myself gently lifted above the pavement where I knelt and wafted away, with the softness of a breeze and the swiftness of light. I was transported over cities, mountains, seas, deserts. I heard sounds which seemed, at first, only those of confusion, a babel of tongues; and then I knew that Arabic, Greek, the dialects of Africa were coming to my ears. I saw the heathen of China, men whose faces were the color of ivory and whose silken garments were embroidered with birds and flowers. I saw Mohammedans with dark skins, burning eyes and sensual lips, who dwell on the false promise of celestial delights in the form of fleshly pleasures. I saw the naked idolators of the Indies, their copper-colored foreheads adorned with feathers. I had eagerly read many books about the conquest of the Indies. I knew that a mere handful of hidalgos and peasants had succeeded in adding the jewels of the Aztecs and the Incas to the crown of Spain and that, since then, the dream of El Dorado has been realized. Also, that the same galleons which have brought back gold to us have taken the truth which is the treasure of the Church to the lands which have yielded us their treasures. But a century has not been enough to change idolatry into Christianity; though on every voyage our priests have accompanied our military and many missions have been founded, still there have not been enough to do the Lord's work. So I petitioned that I might have some small part in this, through my prayers. And then one day the golden cloud in which I had traveled came to rest on the earth and I saw that I was in an Indian village."

"Can you tell me about this village, *Sor* María?" the King asked gently.

"Yes." Now that she had begun, now that she had taken him into her confidence, she seemed to have no hesitation in going on. "It was not like our villages. There were no houses made of stone or brick, no roofs of dark blue slate or bright red tile. There were no belfries where a stork could build its nest, no latticed balconies. There were only round huts made of verdant reeds and roofed with yellow straw and the entrances to these were draped with bright-colored cotton blankets, woven in complicated designs. And, overhead, the sky was bluer and clearer than ours and seemed nearer to the earth than it is at Ágreda; and the air was stiller and softer and perfumed with the scent of fruits and flowers unknown to me."

"You certainly saw this village very clearly, *Sor* María. What about its people?"

"A small shabby child, whose bare shoulders shone in the sun like copper, and who was preparing bird lime, was apparently the first who saw my descent and my emergence from the golden cloud. He cried out and ran, straight as an arrow, to take refuge with his mother, showing as much fright as if he thought he had reason to believe that he was about to be bitten by a poisonous snake or snatched up and carried away by a condor. The Indian woman, half naked and disheveled, came through the small door of her hut and approached me slowly. Then she fell on her knees before me, as if she had been dazzled by something in my appearance. The child meanwhile had rushed off toward a great bronze gong decorated with crude designs that stood near by and had struck it frantically with a wooden hammer. Instantly, all the men in the village came dashing to the spot, shouting in the strange guttural tongue which is their language."

"Did they threaten you?"

"No, never."

"Never? So you went to this village more than once?"

Again she hesitated, but this time it seemed to be less because she was unwilling to inform him than because she feared she might not do so correctly.

"As nearly as I can reckon, Your Majesty, I went there more than a hundred times," she said at last. "And it was always in the same way that I have described to you. I was transported by Our Lord."

"And you were always made welcome?"

"Always. In their language, the Indians asked me who I was and I told them, speaking in ours, and we always understood each other. Then they asked me why I had come and I told them—to tell them the story of Our Lord. For I knew that my prayers had been answered, though not in the way I expected, but that is often the way with prayers. My apostleship was not to find fulfillment in my cell, but in the Indians' village."

"You say they understood you and you them?"

"Always. That is, I always understood them and they always understood my words. It was not so easy for them to grasp the meaning of salvation's story. How could they, these poor untutored savages? But our Franciscan missionaries were already in that territory, though not in the village where Our Lord sent me. So the chief of the village and the medicine men of the tribe went to the Mission and asked them to send them a friar, so that they would understand better. Your Majesty will remember that there was much ground to cover and few workers in the field; so the Superior was not instantly able to do as the Indians asked and they went again. When they persisted, he asked them why they were so importunate and they said it was because of what the lady in blue had told them."

The King's eyes traveled slowly from the Abbess' face to her habit and lingered there. "The lady in blue, of course, was you, *Sor María*," he said quietly.

"I do not see how I can doubt it. They even drew a picture, a very lifelike picture of me, from memory, and showed it to the Superior. It was correct in all its details. I do not need to tell you that the habit of very few Orders is blue. At the moment, I can think of only one other, that of the Desamparadoras, and the cut of their garments is very different from ours."

Suddenly, there was silence in the room. Protocol prevented the Abbess from speaking again until the King addressed her and he seemed content to sit as they were, facing each other but not speaking, and this though shadows were beginning to fall and soon they would be engulfed in darkness as well as silence. The King would not be able to cross the frontier into Aragón before nightfall, unless he left at once and yet he seemed to have no disposition to leave. At last, he lifted his head, which had been bent over his breast while the stillness lasted, and looked at the lady in blue, not with anguish, as he had at first or with grave eagerness, as he had later, but with a thoughtful smile.

"You have set me to wondering, *Sor* María."

"How so, Sire? Because you do not believe my story?"

"Of course, I believe it. I have heard it before, or fragments of it. Indeed, one of those same missionaries to whom the tribesmen of your village went, has written a very remarkable report, in which he devotes some space to this story. But reading it or hearing it from others is not like hearing it from your own lips. Every word of it has the ring of reality as you tell it. How could you describe the robes of the Chinese—the sensual lips of the Arab—the huts of an Indian village if you had never seen them? The sound of different languages and the clang of a great bronze gong if you had never heard them? The air of a clime different from ours if you had never felt it? But I am wondering why a woman who has been so favored of the Almighty that He has sent her on these mystical missions, and who has been so far successful in them that she is credited with no less than five hundred conversions among the Indians, should doubt that she can give solace and support to one lonely man in his extremity?"

Chapter 25

AS HE SPOKE the last words, the King rose and stretched out the hands which had been so tightly clenched, as if in appeal. The gesture was involuntary; it did not for an instant occur to him that the Abbess might take them, nor did it seem to him necessary that she should, in order that he might be sure of her sympathy and support. The tie between them, which he had recognized the moment he looked into her eyes, was so strong that it was independent of touch; but, instead of agonized repression, here was confident approach, as if his hands, as well as his lips, must show her how he felt.

She rose at the same moment that he did and stood very still. But so long as she did not draw back or avert her gaze, the King knew that she did not intend to retreat from him mentally and spiritually any more than she did physically. However, when she spoke, her words did not constitute a direct answer and the form they took came as a surprise.

"It is now more than ten years, Sire, since I have been to my Indian village. The power which Our Lord gave to me then has left me."

"You mean that it has taken other forms than mystic journeys. For one thing, you became the Abbess of this convent; because of your humility, you shrank from assuming the office, but you could not withstand the papal bull which bestowed the well-deserved honor upon you. His Holiness was aware that your intelligence, your judgment, your executive abilities and your integrity, not to mention your piety, more than qualified you for the position, despite your tender age—just as I am well aware that you are also qualified for other tasks."

"I believe that Your Majesty overestimates the intelligence and the executive ability required to govern a small convent like this one. Besides, I never could have done it without the assistance of my guardian angels."

"You speak in the plural. I know that each of us is supposed to have one, though I have often doubted that this was so in my case. Do you mean to tell me that you have several?"

"Yes, Sire, I have six. One rules over his companions and all have their special tasks, which they fulfill with great fidelity. And they are accompanied by two glorious virgins, no doubt saints, whose identity I do not recognize, who stand watch on either side of them."

"You tell me all this, obviously aware of these guardians and these glorious virgins and, at the same time, expect me to believe that your mystic powers are at an end. You must permit me to differ with you, *Sor* María. And, in any case, to return to the natural qualities which fit you to govern this convent, the degree of integrity, judgment and piety requisite must be the same, whether the field of action be large or small."

"I am as incapable of matching Your Majesty in argument as I should be in chess."

"Then let us leave argument aside, at least as far as your fitness to govern a convent is affected. After all, it is not that aspect of your abilities with which I am most concerned."

"And, without presumption, may I inquire what does most concern Your Majesty?"

"Your talent as a writer."

It was her turn to repeat the words which the other had spoken. "My talent as a writer!" she exclaimed, with greater vehemence than at any moment before. "Why, it cannot be unknown to Your Majesty that my writings have not been viewed with favor, either by the Holy Inquisition or by my own confessor."

"They are viewed with favor by me," the King said calmly. "I read your Life of the Virgin Mary and came to know her and venerate her as I never have before. When I heard—as I did—that *Fray*

Baltasar Carlos, heir to the throne of Philip IV.

Spanish
Empire in
Europe
during the
reign of
Philip IV

Dublin

IRELAND

Cherbou

Brest

Nantes

Atlantic
Ocean

Bayonne

Santander

Pamplona

Oporto

Burgos · Ágreda

Valladolid Zarag

Madrid Lér

KINGDOM OF SPAIN

Lisbon · Amegial · Toledo

· Badajoz

Évora · Villaviciosa Córdoba Valencia

Seville Granada

Spanish Empire

Sanlucar

Cádiz

Tangier · Gibraltar

CANARY ISLANDS

100

La Palma Lanzarote

Tenerife

Gomera Fuerteventura

Hierro Gran Canaria

Melilla

KINGDOM OF PORTUGAL

UNITED
NETHERLANDS

Dunkirk

lon

Dover

is

NDS

• Amsterdam

•Breda

Antwerp

•Brussels

THE

EMPIRE

Berlin •

Leipsig

Lützen

KINGDOM
OF
POLAND

Luxemburg

Nuremberg

• Praque

Rocroy

• Paris

Orleans

NGDOM

OF

RANCE

Strasbourg

Nördlingen

Innsbruck

FRANCHE-
COMTE

SWITZERLAND

TYROL

BOHEMIA

Vienna •

AUSTRIA

KINGDOM OF HUNGARY

Budapest

Lyon

SAVOY

• Geneva

PIEDMONT

Milan

VENICE

Venice

OTTOMAN
EMPIRE

use

Avignon

SSILLON

• Nice

Genoa

• Florence

Marseille

Perpignan

rcelona

CORSICA

Rome •

PAPAL
STATES

KINGDOM

Naples

OF

NAPLES

ARIC IS.

SARDINIA

e d i t e r r a n e a n

S e a

Palermo

SICILY

iers

Bugia

Goletta

Tunis

barbara long

Sor *María de Agreda.*

Don Juan at the time of his victory in Naples.

Philip IV as an older king.

Mariana of Austria, second wife of Philip IV.

The Infanta Margarita.

Francisco Andrés had ordered you to destroy this work, my anger against him knew no bounds."

"Would it be tempered if Your Majesty knew that this work has now been rewritten?"

"What do you mean, rewritten?"

"I mean exactly that. I wrote it under obedience—or so I believed—to Divine command. I destroyed it under obedience to Christ's representative—my confessor. But this representative gave no instructions to the effect that I should not rewrite it. For five years, I have devoted myself to this task, in such hours as I could spare from other duties. It is now finished. If Your Majesty will accept a copy from my hand, I shall be much honored."

The King, who had continued to smile at her from the moment that he asked how she could doubt that she was fitted to be his counselor, now laughed—a laugh of such amused appreciation that the Abbess realized she, too, was very close to laughing. Then he shook his head.

"No, I shall keep the copy I already have—the one which I hid and which *Fray* Francisco did not succeed in adding to his bonfire. But when I spoke of your talent as an author, I was not referring to this or any of your other previous efforts. I hoped I could persuade you to use it in another direction."

"And that was—"

"As a correspondent. Mine. I want you to write to me. Regularly, freely, confidentially. Your oral prayers I will take for granted. But I also need to see with my own eyes your words of counsel and support."

"Sire—"

"I could, as your king, command this, could I not?"

"Your Majesty knows this."

"And you would, perforce, obey?"

"Your Majesty knows this also."

"But since, instead of commanding as a monarch, I ask it as a favor for a friend in need, you will refuse me?"

There was another long silence while they looked into each other's eyes. Then, if he had not quickly moved to prevent it, she would have knelt to kiss his hand. But he stretched this out and took the crucifix which hung from the long rosary at her belt and pressed his lips against it.

"You shall not kneel to me and I shall not kneel to you," he said. "We shall meet and talk and part without ceremony, after the manner of friends and equals; and, when we are absent from each other, we shall write freely and fully. *For now we see through a glass, darkly; but then face to face: now I know in part; but then shall I know even as also I am known.*" He recited the Scripture as if it were natural for him to do so and without feeling that there might be irreverence in adapting the apostle's words to his own thoughts. Then he released the crucifix and stepped backward.

"Farewell, *Sor* María. You will hear from me. May God be always at your side."

"And may He guide you, Sire, on the way that leads to the greatest welfare and happiness for you and for the realm. Go with the angels."

She lowered the veil over her face before she drew back the bolts and bars of the great door leading into the *zaguán* and moved behind it as it swung open, creaking on its hinges. It was not fitting that Don Luis and the others, who had been waiting there more than two hours, should see her thus unveiled. The King stepped over the threshold and she closed the door behind him. At the same moment, Don Luis threw open the one giving onto the outer courtyard and the shouts of the people, who were still waiting in the streets for another glimpse of their sovereign, reverberated through the vestibule and beyond it. Darkness had fallen, but it was the true limpid darkness of Castile. The King ascended the steps of the *carroza,* bowing to the right and left as he did so; the grandees followed and took their places beside him. The outriders cracked their whips and the equerries mounted their horses, spurring them on. Despite the lateness of the hour, the cortege took the road to Tarazona.

In the locutory, *Sor* María fell on her knees. Much later, her Prioress found her there, still kneeling.

Chapter 26

$\mathcal{S}$OR María, Abbess of the Convent of the *Concepcionistas* in Ágreda, was an exceptionally skillful needlewoman, even during the period when accomplishments in the fine art of embroidery were considered a necessary part of every gentlewoman's education. Not only were the chasubles, worn by the priests in the convent chapel, and the altar cloths and frontals used there elaborate and exquisite, as to both design and stitchery; but likewise were every corporal and every veil for the chalice, as a result of her talent, her taste and her industry. Considering the vigilance of her rule, the attention which she gave every detail in the management of the convent and the hours which she devoted to prayer, not only in the chapel and the chapter house, but when she was alone in her cell, it was a mystery how she could achieve so much as a result of manual labor. At least, it would have been a mystery, were it not for the fact that there were so many aspects of *Sor* María's life which were a source of wonder that this seemed no more remarkable than many others. Besides, during Recreation, she never went twittering from one group to another or sat with her hands folded idly, like some of the nuns. There was always a length of linen or silk in her lap, a basket full of bright-colored skeins at her side and a gaily-threaded needle between her fingers. Her nuns were used to seeing the outline of a design develop into a pattern of fruits and flowers before their very eyes. In addition, the Abbess' own eyes were very strong, not only all-seeing, as the nuns knew when it came to their actions, but able to function hour after hour, when the rest of the convent was sunk in slumber. The Abbess was not obliged to put out her lamp at a specified hour as the rest of them were. She could burn it all night if she chose and many in the

Community felt sure that she very often did. Otherwise, how could those lengths of linen and silk be so quickly transformed into vestments and frontals, where not a single inch of material remained unadorned?

She was working on the most elaborate frontal she had so far attempted when the ringing of a bell presaged a visitor and a message was brought by the portress to the *torno* and, in turn, conveyed to the Abbess by the Prioress that a courier from the King was in the *zaguán* and requested that the Lady Abbess would receive him in the locutory. *Sor* María folded the frontal and laid her work aside as calmly as if she had received a message that the milk had soured or a broom had been broken; then she went unhurriedly to the locutory, taking the Prioress with her. She took her customary seat behind the grille and did not draw away the curtain until the royal courier said, very respectfully, that His Majesty had hoped she would permit him to address her directly. When the curtain was withdrawn, he placed the scroll in the *torno* and told her his instructions were to remain in the convent until she had read the letter and written her reply. As soon as the communication was in the Abbess' hands, she thanked the courier for bringing it and asked for his assurance that His Majesty was in good health. Having received this welcome news, she told him that, if he would return to the *zaguán,* suitable refreshment would be given him and he would be provided with a place to rest; provision would also be made for his horse. She then retired to her cell to read the King's letter.

It seemed as if the words rushed forward to meet her.

Sor María:
I write to you leaving a half margin, so that your reply may come on the same paper, and I enjoin and command you not to allow the contents of this to be communicated to anybody. Since the day that I was with you, I have felt much encouraged by your promise to pray to God for me, and for success to my realm; for the earnest attachment toward my well being that I then recognized in you gave me great confidence and encouragement. As I told you, I left Madrid lacking all human resources, and trusting only to Di-

vine help, which is the sole way to obtain what we desire. Our Lord has already begun to work in my favor, bringing in the silver fleet, and relieving Oran when we least expected it; whereby I have been able, though with infinite trouble and tardiness for want of money, to dispose my forces here so that we shall, I hope, start work with them this week. Although I beseech God and His most holy Mother to succor and aid us, I trust very little in myself; for I have offended, and still offend very much, and I justly deserve the punishments and afflictions which I suffer. And so I appeal to you to fulfill your promise to me, to clamor to God to guide my actions and my arms, to the end that the quietude of these realms may be secured, and peace reign throughout Christendom.

The silver fleet was the collective name given to the galleons, united under a single command, which brought in bullion from the New World; it had been long overdue and some anxiety had been felt, not only about the loss of its greatly needed treasure, but of the ships themselves. So now they had come safely into harbor, as she had prayed that they might! The relief of Oran was also one of the blessings for which she had most earnestly besieged the Throne of Grace; and at last the Duke of Arcos, Governor of Valencia, had managed to run the blockade and the fortress, which the Moors were beleaguering by both land and sea, was rescued! She murmured a brief and fervent prayer, this time one of thanksgiving, as she read on.

The Portuguese rebels still raid the frontiers of Portugal, acting against God and their natural sovereign. Affairs in Flanders are in great extremity, and there is risk of a rising unless God will intervene in my favor; and though affairs in Aragón have somewhat improved with my presence, I fear that unless we can gain some successes to encourage people here they are liable to lose heart and to take a course very injurious to the monarchy.

It was the Portuguese who were back of the Moors' assaults at Oran; true, it was bad enough to have them making trouble on the frontier, but at least it was not as bad as having them make trouble in Africa as well. The situation in Flanders was more serious; that would, indeed, take time and prayer to mend. The defeat at Rocroy, in which General Melo had been captured and the Count de Fuentes killed, had been a shattering blow to the Spanish forces; but the tragedy back of it—the loss of the Cardinal-Infante Fernando—was one from which it would be even harder to recover. He had been the King's best-loved brother, greatly beloved by the people as well and, in the opinion of many, the most brilliant of the three, a prince of great promise and a military commander of distinction. Yes, the King could not be blamed for his depression, as far as Flanders was concerned; if only Fernando had recovered, to take the field again, just once more! But evidently that had not been God's Will. Affairs in Aragón, however, were indeed improved by Philip's presence. The Aragonese were delighted because he had come to them without a great retinue; the Castilian grandees, in their opinion, were a disturbing influence in their homes and in their government. Moreover, Philip had promptly ordered the release of his best general, Felipe de Silva, whom Olivares had consigned to a prison, and the armed forces, under Silva's direction, were moving toward the French with great energy.

The necessities, of course, are numerous and great; but I must confess that it is not that which distresses me most, but the certain conviction that they all arise from my having offended Our Lord. As He knows, I earnestly wish to please Him and to fulfill my duty in all things; and I desire that, if by any means you arrive at a knowledge of what it is His holy will that I should do to placate Him, write to me here, for I am very anxious to do right, and I do not know in what I err. Some religious people give me to understand that they have revelations; and that God commands that I should punish certain persons, and that I should dismiss others from my service. But you know full well that in this matter of revelations one must be very careful, and particularly when these religious persons speak against those who are not really bad, and against whom I have never discovered anything injurious to me; whilst others are approved whose proceedings are not usually thought well of. The general opinion about these persons is that they love turning things over, and that their truth cannot be depended upon.

So he had cause to mistrust revelations! All the more reason then why she should be touched because he had such implicit faith in her mystical powers and that if *she* told him God had recommended he should punish certain persons and dismiss others from his service, he would believe she spoke the truth and know that her motives were disinterested. Names had been freely mentioned during their long interview and, though the King's present reference to certain persons was without identification, she knew he was again alluding to the Conde-Duque, his wife and their adopted son. Well, the Conde-Duque was already banished from Court and his wife had tardily followed him in his exile; but the son was still in evidence and there had been nothing harsh or conclusive connected with the absence of the others, who were comfortably ensconced at their country seat. She would try to make it clear to the King when she wrote that they were "really bad," that they had injured him and not only him, but all of Spain.

She would have liked to sit quietly for a long time, dwelling on the passages she had just read. But the bell was ringing for Vespers. She must go and take her customary seat in the choir beneath the statue of the Blessed Mother, which represented the Virgin as seated on a throne, with the Rule and Seal of the convent—the ensigns of its dignity—at Her feet. It was becoming to represent Her thus, for She had appeared to *Sor* María, when the young nun hesitated to assume the responsibilities of the convent's direction, with the assurance that She Herself would be the Divine Directress and that *Sor* María would be Her deputy. And, heretofore, the Abbess had taken her place beneath this symbolic image with calmness. Now she found it hard to do so, though she knew there must be no outward and visible signs of the emotion which the King's letter had aroused. Her bearing and deportment should always be an example to the Community. . . .

It must, of course, have been imagination that Vespers lasted longer than usual; but it seemed as if the end thereof would never come and, when it finally did, *Sor* María was still not free to return to her cell and finish reading the King's letter. One of the novices, a girl whom she had hesitated to accept as a postulant and who was always having aches and pains, apparently was suffering from some kind of a nervous seizure. The Mother Infirmarian had failed to soothe her. She was insisting that the Abbess must come to her bedside and, even when *Sor* María was far down the corridor that led to the girl's cell, her shrieks could be heard.

"The King! The King has returned to us! Why am I not allowed to see him?"

It was seldom that the Abbess pressed her lips together in a hard line, but she did so now, and kept them thus for some moments before she spoke to the distraught novice. When she trusted herself to speak, it must be firmly, but gently, not with severity, or the girl's hysteria would increase. "His Majesty is not here," she finally said, sitting down beside the tumbled cot. "He is in Zaragoza, where he is working for our welfare, as we must pray for his. But he has sent a trusted messenger with a letter to me, which I have not yet had time to finish reading, much less to answer. I will go and bring it here and do both, if you will promise me to be quiet and, before I reseal the scroll, you may feel it. In that way, your fingers may touch the same place as those of the Lord's Anointed."

The novice had stopped screaming almost as soon as the Abbess entered the infirmary and now she lay still, staring at her Superior. "I am going to fetch the letter," *Sor* María said. "And do you be quiet until I come back, else you shall not touch the place where His Majesty's fingers have rested." The girl had not answered, but the Abbess knew that now there would be no more trouble, so she went for the letter which she had locked away before going to Vespers. Next, seating herself beside the novice, she read on to the end of it:

I do hope that you will keep your word to me, and will speak with all frankness as to a confessor, for we kings have much of the confessor in us. Do not let yourself be influenced by what the world says, for that is little to be depended upon, seeing the aims of those who move such discourse; but be guided solely by the inspiration of God, before Whom I protest (and I have just partaken of Him, in the Sacrament) that I desire in all things, and for all things, to fulfill His sacred law and the obligation which He has laid upon me as a king. And I hope in His mercy that He will take pity on our pains and help us out of these afflictions. The greatest favor that I can receive from His holy hands is that the punishment He lays upon these realms may be laid upon me; for it is I, and not they, who really deserve the punishment, for they have always been true and firm Catholics. I do hope you will console me with your reply, and that I may have in you a true intercessor with Our Lord, that He may guide and enlighten me, and extricate me from the troubles in which I am now immersed.

—I THE KING. Zaragoza, 4 October, 1644.

The abbess glanced from the letter to the bed. The novice lay quite still, apparently half asleep, certainly at peace. *Sor* María spread the letter out on a tablet and, calling to the Mother Infirmarian to bring her an inkpot and a quill, she began to write, as she had been directed to do, on the left-hand margin of the page, where Philip had written on the right-hand side:

Your Majesty's scrupulous self-examination, resulting in a lack of self-confidence, reveals his awareness of sad human frailties, but should in nowise prevent him from trusting in the wonderful power of the Lord. He should remember what happened in the case of King David, who also recognized his failings and suffered severe remorse.

Yes, the comparison was a happy one. She was glad she had thought of it. As a youth, David had comforted a mad king by the sweet music of his harp. As a shepherd, he had composed the Psalms, which had survived as noble literature and become an integral part of Christian liturgy. Philip also had great gifts as a musician and a poet; he must be encouraged to cultivate them and not to squander them. David had slain a bloodthirsty giant, when he had no weapon but a sling, and he had become a mighty warrior; surely, with such an example, Philip could find a way to defeat his powerful enemies. David had given way to evil passions, robbing Uriah of his one ewe lamb and sending the husband of a beautiful woman to the front, so that he would be killed and David could marry his widow; certainly, Philip's sins of the flesh had been no worse than that. And David's name had come down through the ages as that of a great king and a great man; Bethlehem, the birthplace of Christ, was called the City of David in the Scriptures and Christ Himself was sometimes called Great David's Greater Son.

I offered to pray for Your Majesty and this offer I repeat. I shall do penance and I shall entreat Our Merciful Father, mindful of your good intentions, to take pity on your contrite heart, for my heart is troubled by Your Majesty's great distress. I admit that your realms are in peril. But this peril has a purpose. It comes to you as a punishment because you, a great monarch, the heir to many obligations, are at war with other Catholic kings, thereby opposing the Divine Will and, for this, you must atone. But this very chastisement is a sign of God's love.

She paused again as other passages from the Scriptures came to her mind, appropriate for the moment. There was Paul, writing to the Hebrews and saying, *My son, despise not thou the chastening of the Lord, nor faint when thou art rebuked of him: For whom the Lord loveth he chasteneth, and scourgeth every son whom he receiveth.* And there was St. John the Divine, writing in his Revelations: *As many as I love, I rebuke and chasten: be zealous therefore, and repent;* and adding the wonderful promise: *To him that overcometh will I grant to sit with me in my throne.* Yes, that would be the next point to stress.

But this is not because God does not look with loving kindness on a great monarch, the holder of a great heritage, and the lands over which he rules. It is because this great monarch has striven against other kings of his faith and waged war with them. This and other offenses to the Divine purposes have been committed. But, as soon as the old habits are overcome, there will be a renewal of blessings from the Most High. He will help Your Majesty to hold firm in new ways which are good ways.

She put down her quill, this time not because she was dwelling on Scriptural passages, but because she herself felt impelled to speak frankly and she wondered whether or not she should mention names in doing this. To be sure, both she and the King had done so in the course of their long conversation; but that was safer in the spoken than in the written word. The King would have no trouble in knowing to whom she was referring, any more than she had had trouble in guessing to whom he was referring. She would follow his example and use no names. She picked up her pen again.

As soon as Your Majesty has abandoned the old evil ways and been delivered from sin by the Lord's redemption, you will have cause to rejoice in the change from chastisement to approbation. I trust in the clemency of the Most High. He will help Your Majesty to persevere in good and holy ways and to follow the right path, punishing evil and administering justice without respect to persons; but taking care that the poor be not abused; rather for their humility that they be exalted. (Remember that God Himself became a poor man in this world for our sins.) On the other hand, the rich and the proud must be humbled when they do not govern themselves according to God's law and the worthy must be rewarded for, in the sight of God, mercy and kindness and justice are all attributes of equal merit. When all this has been done, events will take a happier course.

I cannot approve or endorse the discredit of one man for the advancement of another. It is sometimes necessary to speak candidly, but this can be done without injuring the reputation of a fellow man. Certain persons, who have Your Majesty's ear, contend that others, who are close to him, while meddlesome, are of no help in affairs of state, since private virtues are not necessarily of value when it comes to the science of governing. The argument is that there are others possessing a greater talent and capacity for statecraft. This government covers a monarchy of vast proportions; therefore, it is needful that the resources be great and varied and, just as God distributed talents unequally—to one man more, to another less—merits are likewise unequal.

She halted for a moment, Our Lord's story of the talents dominating her thoughts. But she must not take time to dwell on this now or to enlarge on it in her letter. She must finish what she had started to say.

The gravest danger lies in the fact that, instead of looking out for the common welfare and that of their prince and king, there are those who seek private advantage and personal gain.

My Lord: this happens both in peace and in war and, as a result, Your Majesty's realms are impoverished. There are still men who prosper and grow rich, who crowd to see which one can come nearest to the fire and warm himself with worldly treasures and, therefore, who feel envy toward others and a need to compete with them. At a time like the present, it would be better to reduce all such persons to a single rank. Let audiences be given equally to one after another, so that each may feel he is enjoying special favor, whereas no one would receive more than another, unless the royal will should so deign. The Creator arranged that the heart should be the center of the body, in order to vivify and animate all its parts and the sun lightens everyone without distinction. So Your Majesty must vivify, animate and enlighten all parts of his kingdom.

There is a general feeling that all of today's calamities stem from the errors of the late administration. Since success is not easily and quickly achieved, those persons who spoke of dismissal and punishment judge hastily and jump to the conclusion that the one who governed before this still governs, because those who remain close to Your Majesty must, perforce, favor the ones who brought them to his attention; and kinship is a powerful bond. And it would be prudent to give consideration among the worldly for, after all, Your Majesty has to rely on the world.

These thoughts lose much when confided to a pen, for Your Majesty's needs cannot be adequately satisfied through the written word. I trust, however, that if Your Majesty acts according to the

*desires of Our Lord, He will give solace and grant prosperity to
your monarchy. His Divine clemency desires that we seek His
Mercy and, in turn, use it for the benefit of others and, also, that
we repent and mend our ways, so that we may not be unworthy of
it.*

There was more that she might have said, that she would have
liked to say, but she had used up all the space on the left-hand side
of the paper and, according to the King's instructions, that was the
place she was to use for her reply. She rang the bell that summoned
the Sister Secretary and, when the young woman entered the infirmary, the Abbess asked a single question.

"Has the King's messenger received suitable refreshment?"

"Yes, Reverend Mother, and has expressed great appreciation."

"Then give him this letter and bid him Godspeed."

The Sister Secretary took the folded sheet, bowed and retired.
The Abbess glanced at the bed where the sick novice lay; she
was peacefully sleeping now. María de Ágreda rose and silently left
the infirmary, quite unaware that the letter she had just dispatched
was the first in a series that was to continue for twenty years.

Three months later, that is to say in November, Olivares' illegitimate son, Don Enrique Felípez de Guzmán, Marqués de Mai-
rena, who still lingered futilely at Court, received orders to leave
there with his wife and mother-in-law and retire, either to the
Conde-Duque's nearby country seat at Loeches, where the latter
had been living undisturbed until June, or to Toro, the more distant seat of his sister, the Marquesa de Alcañices, where he had then
been ordered to retreat. The exile of the Condesa, who had managed
to find one pretext or another for remaining nominally in the service of the Queen and Baltasar Carlos for some time, had begun a
month earlier than that of her stepson; she was already with her
husband at Toro. One last effort was made to render possible the
resumption of her post. But it failed, as all others in behalf of her
and her husband had failed.

From the moment that she wrote her first letter, the Lady in
Blue had prevailed.

Chapter 27

FOR six months after his meeting with *Sor* María the King, fortified by her letters and her prayers, remained with his little army, which did well in both Cataluña and Aragón; and, when the important city of Monzón was captured from the French by General de Silva early in December, Philip felt justified in returning to Madrid to spend Christmas with his wife and children. But his inclination was for solemn thanksgiving rather than for merrymaking; he was not in the mood for the frivolities of the Buen Retiro and actually preferred to live at the grim Alcázar. He went to pray, not only at the Shrine of Atocha, but at the Convent of the *Descalzas Reales,* even though the Queen, for reasons of etiquette, could not conveniently accompany him on the latter pilgrimage: his cousin Margarita was occupying the royal apartments and though, as a widowed duchess and a deposed vicereine, her rank did not entitle her to special consideration, when it came to questions of precedence, it was easier all around not to raise these.

"Since I'm the queen, I can't very well let her act as my hostess in my own quarters, can I?" Isabel asked, quite without rancor, but as if stating an inescapable rule of protocol. "On the other hand, I'm certainly not going to ask her to leave and let me take over. She seems to be quite satisfied to live at the convent and I'm very thankful. She wasn't satisfied at Badajoz or Mérida and she was definitely dissatisfied at Ocaña and the Encarnación. Let's not invite further dissatisfaction."

Philip agreed that it was better to leave well enough alone, as far as Margarita was concerned, though he regretted even this short separation from Isabel, when he knew that he should so soon be on his way to rejoin his army. But, with her at his side again, he took time to attend the rather staid celebrations which, at his request, had supplanted more sumptuous entertainments and to write a long letter to *Sor María*. She had written him a few days earlier, urging him to make himself "thoroughly versed" in everything touching him. "This admonition is very important," she had added, "and in order to adopt it with the full knowledge of the facts, Your Majesty should choose, guided by your own sound judgment, someone on whom you can depend and listen to him." Philip wanted to assure her, without delay, that he appreciated her advice and would try to act upon it; also, that he was counting on her prayers for the safe arrival of the silver fleet from the Indies, in the same measure that he had relied on them for the victory at Monzón. He wrote:

The promise you gave me when I was with you, that your prayers should not fail me, delighted me much, and I remind you of it in the greatest necessities. We are expecting hourly, by God's help, the arrival of the galleons, and you may imagine what depends upon it for us; and although I hope that, in His Mercy, He will bring them safely, I want to urge you to help me by supplicating His Divine Majesty to do me this favor. It is true, I do not deserve it, but rather great punishment; but I have full confidence that He will not permit the total loss of this monarchy, and that He will continue the successes that He has begun to give us. I should very much like to succeed in carrying out the advice you give me in your letter of the 6th instant. I can assure you I will try to do so; and for my part, I will use every effort to comply with the will of God, both personally and in official matters. May He give me grace to do it. I cannot help telling you of the joy it gave me to come hither and see the Queen and my children, for my absence had seemed to me very long. They are, thank God, very well; and although I shall feel keenly leaving such company, I am preparing to return; for the welfare of my realms must be placed before all things, even before the pleasure of being with such treasures as these. God send me the time when I may enjoy them with more tranquility.

—I THE KING.

· 258 ·

Even Twelfth Night passed without the usual revels. Instead of distributing numerous honors on that day, as had been his custom, Philip limited himself to one: he promoted Diego de Velázquez to the post of Chamberlain and presented him with the golden key which was the insignia of that office. This was Velázquez' first advancement since he had joined the King's household twenty years before and the pamphleteers praised it with enthusiasm.

Early in February, with a small and unpretentious suite, Philip returned to Aragón. It had been a wrench for him to tear himself away from his family; but the lack of his personal leadership had already made itself felt. His officers were quarreling among themselves over style and precedence; this was annoying, but it was not disastrous. A much more serious difficulty arose when a deputation of Aragonese nobles confronted him with a demand for the dismissal of his commander-in-chief, Felipe de Silva, the victor of Monzón and the ablest general available. Only jealousy could account for such a bold requirement; Silva was a Portuguese and his pre-eminence was a thorn in the flesh of Zaragoza. Philip tried to temporize with the haughty Aragonese; he was in desperate need of Silva's continued services. But the question was settled out of hand by the general's abrupt resignation; he had had enough of this petty and unjustified opposition. Philip was still trying to reason with him and persuade him to remain at his post, at least for the present, when even worse news was brought to him by a courier: the Queen, who had conceived again at Christmastime, had suffered a miscarriage and was critically ill.

Passing years had had the effect of increasing rather than lessening Philip's devotion to his wife. She had never failed to respond to his passionate demands upon her, not as if it were her wifely duty, but as if it were her wifely privilege and pleasure; and her own splendid vitality, inherited from her father, had enabled her to meet desire with desire, to take almost perennial childbirth in her stride and to welcome him back to her bed, when one ordeal was barely behind her, without dread of the one which was almost inevitably ahead of her. She had never reproached him because, despite her glad compliance and her inexhaustible fecundity, he had persistently sought satiation elsewhere. Indeed, only once in their long married life—when he had built the balcony for Inés—had she given way to jealous anger, and that very briefly. He derived comfort from the conviction that Isabel believed his feeling for la Calderona was the only one which had really rivaled his feeling for her, that all his other transitory attachments had had very little to do with love, and that they had never seriously affected his tenderness for her as his wife or his respect for her as his queen. If Isabel were thus convinced, she was right; in addition to finding her a brilliant and charming companion, and a delightfully accessible bed fellow, he had become increasingly conscious of her tireless industry, her remarkable executive ability, her perseverance in ferreting out useful facts and her patriotic loyalty to his country. But it was only recently that he had begun to evaluate the true worth and great variety of all these qualities, combined in one and the same person. Because he had not done so sooner, he naturally had failed to tell her that he did. Now, as he sat in his lonely study, far away from her, and reflected on the omission, he felt he could not wait to make amends for it. He turned and motioned to the Gentleman of the Bedchamber who was posted at the door and who promptly came forward and respectfully awaited orders.

"Do you happen to know whether or not the Marqués de Aytona is in his apartment?" Philip inquired.

"Yes, Sire. He dined at the Archbishopric. But he returned about an hour ago."

"Tell him I wish to speak with him at once."

Philip could not have explained why the Marqués de Aytona had come so quickly to mind. The nobleman in question had been in Flanders when the Archduchess Clara Eugenia died and, until the arrival of the Cardinal-Infante, had provisionally taken command of both the military and the civilian branches of the government. He had proved an able and conscientious administrator and, in recognition of his signal service, he was one of the few kinsmen of the Conde-Duque who had not been definitely dismissed and long since absent from the King's entourage; on the other hand, he had never been closely connected in any way with his sovereign. The Conde de Haro would, perhaps, have been the more logical choice. But for some inexplicable reason it was the Marqués that the King had summoned and who, in prompt response to these summons, entered the royal presence.

"I am going to Madrid," Philip said tersely. "Please prepare to accompany me. As it is now nearly eleven, I assume it will not be feasible to leave before dawn, but I propose to do so then—on horseback. We will each need two extra horses for relays. So equipped, we should have no difficulty in covering the eighteen leagues to Calatayud before night. There will stay with the Knights of Jerusalem. You will send off a courier at once to advise them of our coming."

"Yes, Sire."

"We will leave the first horses there and get others. Then we will make a longer day—covering the twenty-one leagues between Calatayud and Sigüenza. In Sigüenza, we will, of course, stay with the Bishop."

"Yes, Sire."

"The third day, we should do better still. We can change horses at Guadalajara and then push on to Alcalá—nineteen leagues. There we will be the guests of the Cardinal. By then, we are practically on the doorstep of Madrid."

Philip leaned forward in his chair, his head resting in his hands. There was a short silence. Aytona waited, uncertain whether or not he was to consider himself dismissed. Philip sighed and looked up again.

"The Queen is very ill," he said. "I am going to her. Whatever requires my attention here will have to await my return. You may so advise the proper authorities."

The sky was still gray as they rode away from the palace, but by the time they reached the bridge, the first streaks of pink appeared close to the horizon and were reflected in the waters of the Ebro. The trees along the way were just coming into bud and, though there was a chill in the air, it was only the chill of dawn. In the river valley, spring was already beginning; the real cold would come later when they began to climb.

The clatter of hooves ceased as they left the outskirts of the city, because, beyond that, there were no cobblestones; the road was very rough and every now and then the impact of a horseshoe on a loose rock made a sharp, sudden sound. The sky did not grow any brighter because there were rain clouds ahead and, presently, a slight drizzle began. If this gets any worse, it will slow us up, because then the road will be not only rough but slippery, Philip said to himself; but he did not say it aloud. He did not want to admit to Aytona that anything might slow them up.

The drizzle continued and the real cold began. There were no buds on the trees now; these were as stark and as bare as if it had been late January instead of late March. Philip had drunk a cup of chocolate before leaving the palace, but he had done it hastily, not taking time to have a second one, as he usually did; he was beginning to realize that his stomach was very empty and that when it became too empty he might feel faint. He had not slackened his pace once since leaving Zaragoza, but had gone ahead at a swift, steady gallop. Now he reined in his horse and turned to Aytona.

"It is time we changed horses, so we might as well stop long enough for a little food as well. I'd planned to halt just a few minutes by the road, but I think we'd be more comfortable under cover." He glanced toward a nearby hillside and then looked back at Aytona. "There are several seignorial houses at La Almunia de Doña Godina where they'd make us more than welcome," he said. "But then we'd have to stop for the usual exchange of courtesies and we've no time for that. I think one of those hillside caves at Ricla would be a better choice. We may be lucky enough to find one empty. If not, we can ask a cave dweller for hospitality."

"As Your Majesty wishes. . . . If we are not lucky enough to find an empty cave, does Your Majesty desire that his identity be made known?"

"Under no circumstances."

They turned their horses toward the slope, just beyond the village of Ricla, which was lined with caves, and drew up at the first one they reached. The path leading upward had been very steep and even rougher than the highway and they were glad to stop. Aytona dismounted and, as the cave had no door, he could look toward its interior. This was in semi-darkness, except at the rear, where a glow indicated the existence of a fire. Two or three persons were huddled close to it and a savory smell suggested the preparation of food. He stepped inside the opening and called out a greeting. An answering call came from within, as one of the figures detached itself from the others, and an elderly, bearded man in ragged clothing limped forward. Though he regarded the riders with puzzlement, there was no animosity in his gaze and he mumbled, *"Buenos días,"* even before the King and his companion had voiced the same words.

"Would you let us take shelter with you for a few minutes?" Philip asked. "We are cold and hungry and have already come a long way and have much further to go."

"Esta es su casa," the ragged man answered instantly, his expression changing from one of bewilderment to one of welcome. "There is not much food, but we will gladly share what we have. And at least the fire will warm you. It is a bitter day to be traveling. Before night, there may well be snow. Are you wise to go on?"

Philip had now dismounted and, as Aytona started to change the saddles, the King took a packet from his saddlebag and entered the cave.

"It is a case of urgency. If possible, we must reach Calatayud before dark. . . . We have food with us," he went on, as the old man stood aside to let him pass. "It would please us if you would accept some of ours and, in turn, we will, of course, accept some of yours. In that way, there will be no loss, but gain on both sides." While he spoke, he looked toward the fire and saw that the other figures which had been gathered close to it were a young woman with a baby at her breast and two small children, very ragged and thin, but all, except the baby, who was asleep, looking at him with friendly eyes. There was an iron pot bubbling over the fire and, when she had invited her guests to be seated, the young woman began to ladle out generous portions of the thick soup known as *puchero*. There were only two earthenware bowls to receive this, but she handed one to Philip and stood holding the other until Aytona could sit down beside him.

"We will have ours afterward," she said. "I do not know why my father told you we did not have much to eat. There is plenty for everybody."

Of course, Philip could not see the inside of the iron pot, but he doubted this. However, he was well aware that he must not voice his doubts and began to eat the soup with a large wooden spoon. "This tastes very good to me," he told his hostess. "In fact, I have seldom eaten so good a *puchero*."

The woman smiled. "It would be better if there were more meat with the chickpeas," she said. "But when my husband is gone with the *mesta,* it is not so easy to get game. My father is too old to do much hunting. However, we have some cheese and a little of last year's honey is still left. You could spread those on your bread."

"Yes, I will do that. And you must eat some of our chicken. I hope you will find it as good as I find your soup. And perhaps the children would like a *dulce*." He knew better than to say *mazapán*. He was sure they had never had any and that the name of the famous Toledo sweetmeat would confuse them; then they would hang back, hesitating to chance it. As it was, they fell on the candy almost wolfishly, without waiting for their mother to serve them any of the chicken, the ham or the white bread that also came out of the packet. When Philip set his soup bowl aside, the old man handed him a goatskin of wine and watched with interest to see if his guest would know how to handle it. These travelers were gentry, there was no doubt of that, and mostly such gentry as he had seen were very awkward with goatskins. But this hidalgo held it high and let the wine flow easily into his mouth, not spilling a drop. The old man's respect for his guests, great already, grew greater still.

"It would be pleasant to linger for another drink," Philip said, as he lowered the goatskin. "That is very good wine. But, as I told you when we arrived, it is urgent that we get to Calatayud. I have been to Zaragoza on business and there I learned that my wife is very ill, so I am hurrying to her side. There has been a mishap and we will not have the baby we expected." He turned to the young woman. "Has your baby been baptized yet?" he asked.

"No, Your Worship."

"Is it a boy or a girl?"

"A boy, Your Worship."

"Unless you have other plans, I would be very pleased if you would name him for me. My name is Philip. If you agree, I would also be pleased if you would let me give my namesake a little present."

The woman nodded and smiled and he took one of the baby's hands in his, very gently, and spread the tiny fingers out. Then he watched them curl so tightly around the coin that he had placed there that the mother would not know, until after he was gone, that it was gold.

"Forgive me if I say you should not delay the baptism too long," he said pensively, remembering how short-lived had been all of Isabel's children except two, remembering also their great baptismal feasts, when so much money had been wasted. This baby looked very frail to him, yet the other children, though thin, seemed healthy enough. He sighed and looked away. When he reached the opening of the cave, he saw that Aytona was already there, waiting for him to mount. Philip noticed that it was a large bay horse this time—the one he had ridden that morning had been black. *"Adiós,"* he said. "And thank you again for your hospitality. I shall remember it."

He and Aytona were halfway down the steep incline when they heard the cave dweller shouting after them and saw him trying to hurry toward them. He caught up with them, panting.

"Your Worship forgot your packet," he said holding it up.

Philip shook his head. "No, I left it on purpose. I hoped that you would be willing to accept the little that was left in it as a present. My namesake's mother should be having plenty of delicacies just now, you know."

The old man still seemed to hesitate. "We have what we need," he said proudly, "and we will have more next month—when my son-in-law returns from the south with the sheep. We were happy to have you and the other hidalgo as our guests and to share with you what we had."

"I know," Philip said. "But we also want to share."

The old man appeared to consider doubtfully; then his face cleared and he smiled. "Since Your Worship puts it that way and since it is true that the mother of your namesake needs extra food just now, I will accept your gift as coming from one friend to another," he said, still proudly. "Go with the angels."

It continued to grow colder. The wind had risen, blowing their cloaks open, so that these billowed around them, no longer providing protection. The rain had turned to sleet, there was snow on the hills and the River Jiloca was swollen and gray and angry. Instead of being slippery, the road had furrows in it that were already half frozen. It was impossible to make good time; the sleet was blinding, the furrows full of pitfalls. Darkness had already fallen when the travelers entered Calatayud and made their way to the hospice maintained by the Knights of St. John of Jerusalem. They were unexpected for, slow as their progress had seemed to them, they had outstripped the courier, and the Knights were appalled at the sight of their sovereign drenched to the skin and shivering with cold. They led him at once to a room where he could shed his wet garments, wrap himself in a blanket and, seated beside a *brasero,* warm the legs that were freed from their high boots, while a bed was hastily prepared for him. The Knights had no proper meal for him, they said with distress; they had long since eaten their own frugal supper and fed their pensioners; as he had not been expected, nothing worthy of him had been prepared. It did not matter in the least, Philip assured them; he had dined very heartily about midday; all he wanted now was a hot posset. Then, as soon as he felt warm to the very marrow of his bones, he would tumble into bed and sleep like a child. Meanwhile, Aytona would confer with them about horses. It had been their plan to leave those they had brought from Zaragoza at Calatayud and start out with fresh ones in the morning. Since their courier had obviously been delayed in some way, undoubtedly no arrangements had been made for this. If the Knights would help them to keep to their schedule. . . .

Aytona had known that the King intended to go to the Knights' Mass in the morning, but he could not bear to wake the tired man for such an early service and it was broad daylight before Philip roused on his own initiative, to see the sun streaming in the narrow window of his cell-like room. He was annoyed with himself for missing Mass, but not with Aytona because the Marqués had failed to call him; he understood the kindly impulse to see that he had the rest he needed, and this morning he drank two full cups of chocolate and ate some of the Knights' good bread before he started on his way. They supplied him with another packet of provisions, even more abundant, though less choice, than the one he had left with the cave dwellers and, this time, they were able to break their fast by the roadside without delay.

Again they followed a river, but it was the Jalón today, for they had left the angry Jiloca where it met the Jalón at Calatayud, and now the stream was smooth flowing and the countryside increasingly lovely. There were fruit trees and waterfalls and a little green in the grass here and there in sheltered spots. Aytona said it reminded him of some of the pleasant places he had seen in the Valtelline on his way to and from Flanders; Philip, who had not been there, could not make this comparison; but at least he recognized the change from the arid lands through which they had passed the day before.

They changed horses at Alhama de Aragón and, dismissing the consideration of even a brief stopover at the Monastery of Piedra or Medinaceli, pushed on toward Sigüenza. Philip would write to the monks, he told his companion, asking them to pray for their King and Queen; but it would take him a little out of his way if he went to see them and there was no time for that. He also asked Aytona to remind him, as soon as possible after they reached Madrid, to find out whether or not the Duke of Medinaceli had been authorized to return from the exile which had been imposed on him, for some reason Philip had now forgotten, at the same time that Quevedo, who was then Medinaceli's guest, had been cast into prison at León. Of course, Medinaceli had rather peculiar literary tastes and loved to dabble in strange languages. But there was really no great harm in that. And, by the way, it was high time that Quevedo should be released.

At Medinaceli they crossed the watershed marking the division between the rivers that flowed east from those that flowed west and from now on they would be following the Henares almost into Madrid and feel they were on the home stretch, even though the capital was still a long way off. They reached Sigüenza in time to see a glorious sunset beyond the high hill crowned by the Bishop's palace and, while they were still ahead of their courier, the Bishop was a man who lived extremely well at all times and no apologies were in order for the repast he could set before his sovereign. He had heard of the Queen's illness and special prayers were already being offered for her in the cathedral; he was relieved to know that the King was going to her. Was it possible that the travelers had left Zaragoza only the previous morning, that they had covered so much ground in a mere thirty-six hours?

"After all, the journey's simpler than it used to be," Philip replied. He did not want to take any credit for going to see Isabel or for the speed with which he had managed to travel. "It's no more complicated nowadays to go to Aragón from Castile than it is to go from Calatayud to Sigüenza; all the formalities that used to attend crossing the frontier between the two kingdoms are a thing of the past. Any law-abiding citizen can go from one to the other whenever he likes, though an escaping criminal can't claim sanctuary because he's over the border. Remember the case of my grandfather's secretary, the traitorous Antonio Pérez."

"I remember all too vividly," the Bishop replied, comfortably sipping his excellent wine from a golden goblet. It crossed Philip's mind to wonder how well His Excellency would have managed with a goatskin. It also crossed his mind that a golden goblet would make a very suitable present for María de Ágreda. This was another thing he would see to as soon as he reached Madrid—that is, as soon as he was sure all was well with Isabel.

"Of course, my grandfather was the greatest monarch in the world," Philip went on. This was not only a fact, it was one in which he could properly take pride. "But it took patience—and force—to consolidate the peninsula. Now it is an entity. Oh, we have rebellions here and there—the one in Portugal is the worst. Cataluña doesn't worry me so much. The Cataláns are finding out that they like the French even less than they like the Castilians. I'm giving a good deal of thought as to the best way to hold Spain's component parts together. That's what the Queen feels is so important. She's all the time seeking means to develop its resources and reduce its expenditures in such a way as to bring that about. I'm beginning to think I should have listened to her sooner, instead of listening to Olivares and his arguments in favor of having Spain play a dominant military role all over Europe."

The Bishop sighed. "May I venture to say it is perhaps a pity that Your Majesty did not begin thinking of that a little sooner?"

"Certainly, you may venture to say it and I shall agree with Your Excellency. Moreover, with your permission, I shall tell Isabel exactly what you have said."

The evening closed on a pleasant and cheerful note and the next morning Philip was up for early Mass and on the road at daylight. The going was smoother now, in every way—no more sleet and rain, no more mountain ranges. The Henares was a placid stream. At Guadalajara, where they again changed horses, they were so close to Alcalá that the shift would have seemed almost superfluous if one of their mounts had not gone lame. But Philip was no longer thinking of the old university city as a stopping place for the night—why, with another change of horses, should he not ride straight through to Madrid? It was only a few leagues farther on. Often, when he was on hunting parties at the Pardo, he had amazed his companions by his ability to go without sleep. Why not amaze Aytona in the same way now? Perhaps the Marqués could not manage so well without sleep. In fact, for the last hour or so—ever since they had forded the river because the old Roman bridge, just recently a ruin, had not yet been replaced—he had seemed less alert than usual, less quickly responsive when Philip spoke to him. Perhaps it was only a figment of Philip's imagination that, despite Aytona's efforts to remain wide awake, he was getting drowsy. But the impression persisted. Possibly it would be better if the Marqués stopped at Alcalá. Philip would suggest this. In fact, he would urge this. It would really suit him better to do the last lap alone, just as he had once started out alone to lead his troops to war. That time, he had been thwarted and held back. This time, no one should thwart him, no one should hold him back.

Most of the way, the riders had been practically abreast; now the Marqués was lagging a little behind and his extra mounts were not keeping up with his lead horse. Darkness was descending and the road was unexpectedly rough again; inevitably, they were having difficulty in picking their way and this might well explain the lack of uniformity in their gait. But, somehow, Philip had a sense of impending trouble; without slackening his own rapid pace or failing to keep a sharp watch for possible pitfalls, he called out an anxious question.

"Aytona! Is anything wrong? Has another horse gone lame?"

The answer did not come in words. His companion managed to gain on him, but at the same moment the tired horse he had spurred stumbled and pitched forward on its knees. The Marqués, abruptly unseated, slid sideways from the saddle, one foot still in a stirrup and his hands still clutching the reins. As he fell heavily to the ground, he lost hold of these and the extra mounts, badly frightened by the sudden lack of control, tore wildly off into the darkness. The fallen horse struggled frantically to regain its footing and, in so doing, dragged forward the prostrate Marqués, who still had one foot in the stirrup. Then the animal collapsed again, groaning and snorting.

Philip had already swung himself off his horse and, keeping a firm grip on his two sets of reins, bent over his companion, released the imprisoned foot and spoke impellingly. There was no answer. They must be fairly close to Alcalá, Philp thought, but there were no houses near at hand and the few, dimly and distantly within sight, did not indicate a settlement of any size or activity. He shouted, but the echo of his own voice was his only answer. It occurred to him that he might fire a shot, but he dismissed the idea as unwise; it would be more likely to frighten off potential help than to bring it; with the roads notoriously unsafe, no one would voluntarily risk a possible encounter with armed brigands. Neither could he leave Aytona, certainly unconscious and perhaps badly injured, alone by the roadside while he went off in search of help. Somehow, he must manage to hoist Aytona onto his own horse and, supporting his unconscious companion as best he could, get him to the nearest haven available. This would be all the more difficult because the panic of Aytona's horses had proved contagious; Philip's own were trembling and rearing and making strange sounds. He would have to quiet them before they would be manageable and it would be impossible to do this as long as the vociferous suffering of the fallen horse continued to upset them. It must have stepped into a hole and broken its leg. Feeling his way cautiously, because it was too dark to see clearly, Philip made reasonably sure that this was what had happened. Well then, he would have to fire a shot after all; he would have to put the injured horse out of its misery. When it had ceased to thrash helplessly around, bellowing with pain, he would be able to quiet the others.

From earliest childhood, his horses had always been his friends; there was a bond between him and them, closer than most of the bonds between him and other human beings. Kings did not have friends, in the sense that most men did, only courtiers, confessors, *privados*. But horses made up for much of that lack. They could not talk to him, but he often talked to them, and felt that they understood him and, in their own way, answered him. He spoke now to the horse that he was about to shoot, gently explaining why this was necessary, while he loosened his pistol from its holster and, gradually, the injured animal lessened its struggles. Then the shot rang out and the struggles ceased altogether. The other horses were not frightened by a sound to which they were accustomed through many hunting parties and, after that, they were quiet, too.

A rising moon and a few stars now shed a little light on the forlorn group by the roadside and Philip saw the gleam of a lantern and figures coming toward him, not on the road still ahead of him, where he had dimly glimpsed the houses, but from the opposite direction, whence he had already come. He shouted and an answering shout came promptly—an answering shout and words which were indistinct, because of distance, but which were friendly, even reassuring in tone and, presently, he was able to see that not only two men, but two horses which they were leading, were coming toward him. Then he recognized the horses—Aytona's spare mounts which had bolted! Somewhere along the line they had been stopped; somewhere along the line strangers had sensed or suspected a mishap of sorts; and, instead of stealing the horses, had started out blindly, in the gathering dusk, hopeful of finding their owners and lending a helping hand if it were needed! As the men came nearer, Philip could see that, while they were not actually in rags, like his host in the cave, they were shabbily clad and scantily, also, considering the chill in the air. The money the horses would have brought might well have represented livelihood to them for months. But, if they had even thought of stealing, the thought must have been quickly dismissed. Otherwise, they never would have been on the road so soon.

"Is Your Worship in trouble? Wait, we will be there presently."

The strangers' words were coming through clearly now, so his should do the same. "Yes, there has been an accident. I'll be very thankful for your help."

It had been easy enough, in the cave, to remain anonymous; this time, it might be more difficult. Philip often went to Alcalá de Henares in person; he had been seen there repeatedly, not only in the *paraninfo* of the university and in the Cardinal's palace, but at the great public festivals attended by the populace. Besides, his likeness appeared on nearly all the coins in current use—that unmistakable Hapsburg jaw! But the moonlight was not very strong yet and the lantern gave only a flickering radiance, so perhaps recognition would not be immediate. He could only hope so. The severe black garments which were now his customary garb, rather than the brown velvet he had formerly favored, might be a help; but Aytona was in uniform—the King's uniform. Philip would try to cut his greetings to his saviours as short as possible and be quickly on his way. The urgency of Aytona's need would be self-evident. And mention of Isabel's illness would explain further need for haste.

"You can see for yourselves that I am greatly your debtor," he said as the men came close to him. "The horse which my friend was riding threw him when it stepped into a hole and broke its leg. I have had to shoot it. My friend hit his head in falling and has not regained consciousness. He was riding with me to Madrid, where my wife is dangerously ill. Our relays have helped to increase our speed. But now, of course, I must see that my friend is in good hands for whatever treatment he needs before I continue on my way. If you will help me get him to the university—"

While he was speaking, one of the men had lowered the lantern to have a closer look at the fallen rider and the dead horse. Now he straightened up and spoke respectfully, "We are Your Worship's servants. We can lift your friend, with much care, on whichever horse Your Worship believes to be the most tractable and then, with his permission, we could ride the other two horses. Thus one of us would be on either side of him and very close and we could support him. But we should have to go very slowly. If Your Worship should prefer to ride on ahead at top speed and ask that a litter and a physician be sent out on the Guadalajara highway, we will stay with your friend until they come. Your Worship can trust us."

"I know that I can," Philip said gravely. He was already swinging back into his saddle. "Your second plan is the better of the two. *Adiós.* I am on my way."

The Bishop of Sigüenza had sent a messenger of his own to the Cardinal at Alcalá de Henares as soon as Philip and Aytona had entered the palace on the high hill at sunset the night before. Hence the Cardinal was well advised of their impending arrival and had prepared a veritable feast. But he was understandably startled when Philip strode into his presence alone and announced that he had left Aytona unconscious by the roadside, after a fall from his horse, in the watchful care of two peasants whom he had never seen until they came to his rescue. However, His Eminence rallied quickly to the emergency: a physician would ride immediately with the King to the scene of the accident; a litter, four litter bearers and a second physician, also promptly summoned and provided with torches, would follow. All made very good time in reaching the scene of the accident. The peasants had done their best to assure Aytona's comfort, in case he should regain consciousness, by using saddlebags as pillows and covering him with a horse blanket; but if anything had roused their suspicions as to the identity of the travelers, nothing in their attitudes suggested this, even when the litter bearers arrived clothed in the livery of the Cardinalate. They were respectful, they were efficient, but they were not overawed.

After examining Aytona by torchlight, the physicians were encouraging. The unconscious man appeared to have no broken bones, only a mild concussion, as was to be expected under the circumstances. He had obviously hit his head very hard when he fell and it might be some time before he came to his senses, and he was breathing slowly; but there was no reasonable doubt that he would recover. For the time being complete rest in suitable surroundings under professional supervision was all he needed and that, of course, would be provided.

"Is there anything I can do to help by remaining with him?"

"Nothing, Your Worship."

Philip had taken the precaution of telling the physicians that they were on no account to address him as Your Majesty, but he had been afraid they would forget. Now he breathed a sigh of relief on two scores.

"Then, if you see no reason why I should not do so, I will continue on the way to see my wife, who is very ill. I will ask you to present my apologies and regrets to His Eminence."

"Clearly, Your Worship should be on his way. No explanations will be necessary."

Philip turned to the peasants. "As I told you before, I am very much in your debt," he said. "It would lessen my sense of obligation if you would accept, as a gift from me, the horses you stopped. I should also be glad if you would tell me your names and where you live, so that the next time I pass this way, I may stop and report to you how I found my wife when I reached Madrid."

The two men looked at each other and there was evidently mutual understanding in their gaze. Then the taller of the two spoke.

"My brother and I will be pleased to accept the gift of the horses," he said. "We were, of course, tempted to steal them, when we were fortunate enough to stop them. But we withstood the temptation and, now that we have had this rich reward, it will help us to withstand the next one that comes. As to our names . . . we have no importance and we should regret if, by telling them, we might be running the risk of receiving some further reward for our services, slight as these were. But, if we may have Your Worship's promise that there is no such risk and that by telling him our names we may have the hope of seeing him again, we will do so, with one other condition."

"You have only to say what it is."

"That Your Worship will also tell us his, so that we may know whom we have had the honor of serving."

For a minute, Philip looked at them searchingly, as if considering more than one aspect of their request. Then, as if he understood and approved these, he smiled.

"Somehow, I suspect that you already know it," he said. "But you have made me still further your debtor by not delaying and hampering me with the formalities which would have surrounded such knowledge. . . . My name is Philip," he added and remembered that he had used the same words two days before, in order to assure himself of a godchild. Now he wanted no assurance of anything, except the prospect of seeing these two men again. On every other score, as far as they were concerned, he had already received assurance.

He was without any sense of fatigue or depression as he continued to cover the ground. This was quick going, easy going. He was coming home, coming to his wife. His horse—a white one this time—was galloping at the same swift steady pace as the black one that had taken him from Zaragoza to Ricla. And now there was no drizzle of rain, no sleet and wind, but clear starlight and moonlight, making the road almost as bright as day and changing the horse's mane to strands of silver. And there were no holes in the road, but the sustained and cheerful sound of clattering hooves again. There were good cobblestones out of Alcalá and better ones on the outskirts of Madrid, his own city, which he was now entering. The Calle de Alcalá led directly to the Puerta del Sol and from the Puerta del Sol the way was clear along the Calle de Arenal straight to the grounds of the Alcázar. The streets were dark, for only the vigil lights, flickering under the sacred images enshrined here and there in niches, shone through the general gloom; and there were very few people in the streets; even the vendors of *olla podrida* had deserted the corners where this humble but hearty stew was publicly sold. These were the hours, the only hours, when Madrid was sleeping—the hours just before dawn. But he was not sleepy, he was not even tired. He had been in the saddle twenty-two hours, stopping only for the accident, and two long days before that, but he was as fresh as if he had just started out.

He reined in at the entrance to the courtyard and shouted an order to open the gate. The guards on duty, roused from comfortable lethargy, stepped hastily forward, raising their lanterns and demanding the password, only to recognize, the next instant, with stupefaction, that none was needed.

"The password is I the King," Philip called back as he swept through the creaking doors. Then he leaped from his horse. He was there.

Chapter 28

THE palace, like the streets, was in almost total darkness and almost deserted. After leaving the guardroom, Philip was stopped only twice before he reached Isabel's apartments. As he entered the antechamber, a small woman who seemed to have sunk into the depths of the great chair where she was sitting slowly edged forward, raised her eyes and gazed at him fixedly. Then she tottered to her feet with a wailing sound that was totally incoherent and he realized that it was Ana de Guevara. He rushed forward and caught her, to prevent her from falling on her knees.

"Are you trying to tell me that the Queen is dead?" he asked harshly.

"No—no. She is still alive or was when they last let me see her. But she had been bled again—as if she had not lost enough blood already when she lost the child. At any moment—"

"What do you mean by 'they'?"

"Her confessor—her physicians—her ladies-in-waiting. They are all at her bedside, a crowd of them, praying and pottering and sobbing. But they drove me away."

"I'm going to drive *them* away. Stay here. I'll send for you later."

He crossed the antechamber rapidly and opened the door into the Queen's private sitting room. The door leading from there into her bedroom stood ajar and, looking beyond it, he could see the "crowd" of which Ana had spoken with such grief and resentment. The lower part of the curtained bed was completely hidden by the figures around it, some standing, some kneeling, none silent. The scene reminded him poignantly of the spectacle at his father's deathbed, which had haunted him for weeks when he was a boy of six-teen; passing years had rendered it only a little less vivid. There were even the same dark images and gruesome relics that had been brought out before, in the belief that they might effect a miraculous cure. Then he had been powerless to order the images removed and to send away the interlopers who intruded to no purpose on his grief and his father's final moments of consciousness; but now it was go-ing to be different. If this were the last time he could talk to Isabel, he would do it in a way that would at least bring some shreds of comfort to them both.

"I do not think any of you were expecting me," he said quietly as he entered the room, addressing the gathering as a whole, without any other form of salutation. But even at a moment as tense as this, his innate courtesy prevented him from giving an abrupt order that the Queen's chamber should be cleared. "However, now that I am here, I am sure you will respect your King's wish to be alone with your Queen. Her confessor and her physician may remain in the next apartment, where I can call them if I deem it necessary. The others will please withdraw to the antechamber."

After the first startled exclamations, a sudden silence descended on the room. The sobbing and the murmured prayers ceased abruptly and not even the confessor or the physician ventured to voice an ob-jection to the order or delay departure, though the King had not asked if the Queen had received Extreme Unction. It was not for them to take the initiative by informing him. He stood close to the open door as everyone filed quickly past him, with low bows but without stopping to kiss his hand. And, as the crowd thinned, he could see the bed and the figure, obscured by curtains, lying on it. When the last onlooker had gone through the door, Philip closed it and, striding over to the bed, drew back the curtains.

Isabel was lying on her back with her eyes closed, her beautiful dark hair in disorder against the pillow which, like her gown, looked hardly whiter than her face. Her hands, very white also, were lying limply at her sides and there were bandages on her arms that showed where she had been bled. Philip could not tell whether she were asleep or unconscious and it did not seem to matter. The thing that mattered was that she still lived. Her uneven breath came almost imperceptibly, but it came. He knelt down and then he leaned over and kissed her cheek, taking her hand in his.

"Isabel," he said. "My darling."

He repeated the words three times before there was any sign that she had heard. Then he saw a slight flutter of the translucent eyelids. Very slowly they lifted part way and then closed again before he had been able to catch more than a glimpse of the veiled eyes—those splendid dark eyes which had been the most brilliant and beautiful in the world. He leaned over again and, this time, he kissed the drooping eyelids and felt them lift a little under his lips. Next he felt the limp hand which he held become responsive to his touch. She murmured something so softly that it was almost inaudible, but he knew it was his name. She sighed, a sigh of deep contentment, and turned her head a little, so that she would face him. After that, with her hand still in his, she fell asleep and, kneeling quietly beside her, he also slept.

When, hours later, Philip opened the door to admit the waiting priest and physician, there was not the slightest doubt that she was better. He did not need their solemn pronouncement to tell him so and he did not want them to stay on, watching the sick woman's slow improvement. As for Isabel and Philip, she wanted no one except him and he wanted no one except her. Courteously, he again asked the others to withdraw. However, when he was able to believe that all immediate danger was past, he told her he would send Ana to sponge her face and hands with cool water and give her a little broth; meanwhile, he himself would get some food and change his travel-stained garments for clean clothes.

"But you'll come back?" she asked anxiously.

"Of course. Within the hour. Sooner if you need me."

He found on his return that she had fallen asleep again, but this he knew was a good sign, and he sat beside her waiting, without impatience, for her to wake, happy to see that she looked more like herself now that her hair had been brushed and that a little color had come into her cheeks and lips. Indeed, when she opened her eyes, he saw that some of their splendor had come back. And she wanted to talk to him.

"I'm glad you sent Ana to me. She's a wonderful nurse."

"Yes, I know. She was my nurse when I was a little boy."

"And you remembered that all this time?"

"Yes, I remembered that all this time."

That was true enough. He also remembered, though of course he would not mention this, the wonderful care she had taken of Inés when Juan was born. That baby had lived. If only he could have sent Ana to Isabel a little sooner. . . .

"I'm so sorry I lost the baby, Philip. I am sure it would have been a boy this time."

"We have a boy—a beautiful boy," he said, stifling his own disappointment.

"Yes, but we ought to have another one, just to make sure. There ought to be two at least. I mean two of mine."

There it was, the old jealousy, the old resentment of Juan, who was even more beautiful than Baltasar Carlos, which had persisted long after she had ceased to feel it against his mother. She seldom voiced that resentment, that jealousy any more. She would not have done so now if she had not been ill, if she were not grieving about the reason for her illness. He must find the right words to comfort her.

"Isabel, you're the one that matters. As long as I haven't lost you—"

Yes, that had been the right thing to say. There might be a boy who was not hers, but his mother, much as Philip had loved her, had gone out of his life. She was no longer a part of it—of him. His wife was the one that mattered—the only one that mattered. If he could convince her of that. . . . And then he saw, with relief, that he had convinced her, that she believed him and that she was happy in her belief. They began to speak of other things.

"You haven't told me how you got here so quickly."

"On horseback."

"*On horseback!* All the way from Zaragoza!"

"Yes, all the way. It was quite a ride."

"Oh, Philip, tell me about it!"

She wanted an extra pillow, so that she could see him better while he told her. But he was afraid it was too soon for her to sit up straight in bed and she did not insist when, instead of taking a chair, he took a low stool, so that, as he was seated, his eyes were on a level with hers. He told her about the cave dwellers and the good dinner at the Bishop's palace, but not about the storm or Aytona's accident, for fear that, if he did, she would worry about possible future hardships. He said nothing about returning to Zaragoza, either. But the next day, when she was obviously so much better that there was no question as to whether or not she could have an extra pillow, she brought up the subject herself.

"Aren't you needed in Aragón, Philip?"

"I left Luis de Haro in command—you know, *el Discreto*. I've had one message from him already. I think he's managing very well without me."

"For a few days, perhaps. But you shouldn't be gone long, should you?"

"I should be gone as long as I can be of any help or comfort to you."

"You have been of help and comfort to me. And now I'm getting well again. I'm sure I shouldn't have, if you hadn't come. I can't explain, but somehow, I knew that you would. So I had to stay alive to welcome you. And now it's time to wish you Godspeed."

"Perhaps it will be—tomorrow or the next day."

"You're not going to start putting things off again, are you, Philip?"

There was nothing veiled about the look she turned on him now. It had the old sparkle and it was a direct challenge. He had not consciously been making her illness a pretext for lingering in Madrid, but it was true that he would have been glad to stay there, quite aside from the need she might have of him or the happiness they might have in being together. He flinched under her gaze.

"If you'd be happier to have me leave—I mean, if you feel I haven't a right to stay away from Aragón—"

"You know I feel that way."

"I'd like to have one long talk with you before I go—about the things you wanted to do and to have me do for the good of Spain. Since my ride, I've understood, better than I ever did before, how much needs doing and how worthy many people are of help. I told you about the cave dwellers—that they had very little to eat and yet they were glad to share with Aytona and me; and that the old man chased after us because he thought I'd forgotten the packet I'd left behind and wanted to restore it to me. But I haven't told you about the men I mistook at first for highway robbers after we'd had an accident. I didn't want to run the risk of worrying you before. Now I think you're well enough to hear about it, especially as everything turned out so wonderfully."

"I'd love to hear."

So he told her about the peasants and the runaway horses they brought back and the horse he'd been obliged to shoot. "And it isn't just that they didn't steal," he said. "It's—well everything, including the fact that they guessed who I was, but realized it wouldn't be suitable for them to suggest that the King should ride off for more help —if they knew they were talking to the King. That showed good sense and it also showed fine feeling. I was quite sincere in telling them that I wanted to see them again. And I want to see others like them, to get better acquainted with my people—all my people."

"Nothing you've said to me since you came here has made me as happy as that, Philip."

"Then you must let me have that one good long talk. Don't forget you're my *Privado* now. But you're not strong enough to have such a talk yet. So let me stay until you are. I promise that the very day after our talk—"

"Very well. I can see that's important."

She was soon well enough to have several pillows, so that she could sit upright in bed with a light tray on her knees, where she spread out her papers. She looked very pretty seated in that way. Her hair was parted in the middle and tied back with a red ribbon and her arms were not bandaged any more. The long full sleeves of her nightgown were gathered into wristbands made of white taffeta and fastened with diamond buttons. A loose wrap of flowered silk, blue and flesh-colored, was thrown over her shoulders and her bedspread was also of flowered silk, trimmed with deep lace. Her bedstead was of gleaming copper and the reflection in the great mirrors on the further side of the room was one of general brightness and good cheer. Isabel did not seem like a sick woman any more. She was very earnest and very happy, making out lists again and discussing them with Philip, who sat at a small table near the bed taking notes to correspond with her lists and listening attentively to her comments.

"I don't see what you gain by selling titles, Philip. Once a man has a title, he's exempt from most taxation and you lose in one way what you've gained in another. Besides, I think it's a shameful practice."

"It makes for quick money and it's been going on for a long while, Isabel."

"Money that's as quickly spent as it's secured! And, if it's been going on for a long while, that's all the more reason why it should be stopped. . . . Now about this supplementary tax on oil, to pay for Luis de Haro's new house. Of course, it's too bad that the old one was destroyed by fire—it had all sorts of treasures in it that would be difficult or impossible to replace. But he has plenty of money himself for building—something like 130,000 ducats a year, if I'm not mistaken. Don't take anything more away from somebody who's half starved, like your friends in the cave."

"I'll try not to again."

She was very tired when they finished, but quietly and contentedly tired, not nervous or overstrained, and she went peacefully to sleep when their conference was finished. But, as she kissed him good night, she said, "If I'm still better in the morning—"

"Yes, if you're still better in the morning—"

She *was* still better in the morning—so much better that she jested with him about the royal vault at the Escorial, as she had done several times before, when she had annoyed and even enraged him by doing this. But now he was so glad to see her more like her own laughing self that he was neither annoyed nor enraged.

"I've cheated that place set aside for me as the mother of an heir to the throne," she said. "I'm going to keep on cheating it of its prey."

"See to it that you do that," he answered, smiling at her and kissing her.

When he prepared to ride out of the courtyard, she insisted on getting out of bed and putting on one of the jewel-colored dressing gowns that were so becoming to her, in order to wave to him from the window. His last glimpse of her was of a bright triumphant figure. It was wonderful to think of her all summer as invincible. It strengthened his resolve to prove his own powers of rising above defeat.

On the whole, the summer was an encouraging one, as *Sor* María was quick to notice:

I have received great consolation for the preparation and defense of the cities of Tarragona and Tortosa due to your endeavor. The second letter I wrote expressed the fear that the enemy would attack the weakest sector, and for this reason I advised Your Majesty to fortify the vulnerable parts. The enemy has cruel spies searching for the weakest defenses. Therefore, when two armies face each other, one must not fight with arms alone, but with perspicacity and subtlety, anticipating the designs of the enemy. . . .

The French were not driven from Cataluña, but they were held at bay and, in Lérida and Tarragona, they were repulsed. This time, *Sor* María wrote a word of warning:

The French must be embittered and resentful because of the defeats they have recently suffered. I fear that they will try to do us as much harm as they possibly can . . . therefore, it is necessary to be prepared and, if possible, to anticipate our advantageous positions, but, above all, appeal to God to defend us and destroy the designs of our enemies.

It was increasingly evident that the Cataláns were as restless under foreign rule as they ever had been under Castilian dominion.

Luis de Haro was proving an able and agreeable aide. No temptation to stray from the straight and narrow path proved irresistible and the presence of Diego de Velázquez, whom Philip had asked to join him in camp, when the blockade at Lérida was lifted, gave him exactly the sort of companionship he most needed and most enjoyed. The letters from the Lady in Blue were not only a source of good counsel; they provided an incentive to strive against depression and procrastination. And the news from Madrid was uniformly reassuring; Isabel had made a good recovery and was again functioning as Regent with her usual efficiency.

Then, suddenly, the blow fell.

The Queen had overestimated and overtaxed her strength. She had been attacked by a strange illness—was it called erysipelas?— and she had not been able to throw it off. Instead, she had grown worse and worse and now she could hardly breathe. She had insisted that the King must not be told, that he could not be spared to come to her a second time; but the decision was taken from her.

Again, Philip put Luis de Haro in command of the army and, again, started posthaste for Madrid, covering the rough road between the two capitals with almost unbelievable speed. But, this time, the speed did not suffice. He had passed Sigüenza and stopped a few minutes at a wretched *venta* for a little food, intending to do what he had before—push on that same night to the end of the journey. But at Almadrones, he learned that he was too late, that this time he could not comfort Isabel and bring her back to him.

He hardly listened as all the details of the fatal illness were described to him. He already knew what many of its aspects would have been, that again sacred images would have been brought to her room and that this would be full of praying, pottering, sobbing people she did not wish to see or hear and that he, whom she would have been so glad to see and hear, was not there with her, to make the end a little easier. Well, the children—they, at least, would have been a source of solace. Oh, the children! She had not suffered them to be brought to her for the fear of contagion. "There are plenty of queens for Spain," she had whispered, "but princes and princesses are rare." When Philip heard that she had said this, he turned his face to the wall and asked to be left alone with his sorrow.

Plenty of queens for Spain? There had never been another like this one, there never would be again. "Isabels have always brought happiness to Spain!" the people had shouted, whenever they wanted to pay his wife a special tribute, as they did on his return to Madrid just before the dismissal of Olivares—a dismissal too long delayed and due, in no slight measure, to her. Yes, it was true. There had been the great Isabel of Castile, the one called the Catholic, whose marriage to Fernando of Aragón had united the two kingdoms and who had ruled with wisdom and righteousness. Philip would admit comparison with her. And then there was Isabel de Valois, the one called Isabel of the Peace, the third wife of his grandfather, Philip II, reputedly a great beauty and so amiable that she made a friend of everyone who saw her. To her were credited the good relations existing between France and Spain throughout her married life; but what had she done that entitled her to comparison with Isabel de Bourbon—his Isabel? She had never studied the resources of the kingdom for the purpose of improving its wretched lot; she had never acted as a wise and efficient Regent; she had not provided an heir to the throne.

Philip went from Almadrones to the Pardo and stayed there for a few days, refusing to see anyone except Baltasar Carlos and, from there, to the Royal Monastery of San Jerónimo, for the traditional period of official mourning. Meanwhile, in the dark watches of the night, Isabel's body, dressed in a Franciscan habit, had been carried from Madrid to the Escorial, accompanied by a cortege made up of hundreds of priests and nobles, while thousands of humble mourners lined the road across the bleak plain; and now she was lying in her appointed place. He did not want to think of her as she was there. He wanted to go on remembering her as she had looked when he first saw her, riding gaily to meet him on her white palfrey, and as she had looked when he last saw her, clad in her jewel-colored robe and waving a fond farewell to him from the window. That very morning she had joked with him about the jasper pantheon and told him she had cheated it of its prey, that she would go on cheating it. But, for all her courage, she had not been able to do so.

Chapter 29

AS soon as she learned of the Queen's death, *Sor María* wrote to the King, exhorting him to resignation and patience; but for the first time a letter from her gave him no comfort. He was overwhelmed by his sense of loss, and more than a month elapsed before he gathered himself together sufficiently to respond:

I find myself in the most oppressed state of sorrow possible, for I have lost in one person everything that can be lost in this world; and if I did not know, according to the faith that I profess, that the Lord disposes for us what is best, I do not know what would become of me.

If anything that happened in his public life could have been a source of encouragement, Philip's personal troubles might not have been so devastating. But his campaign was going from bad to worse. Silva had proved irreplaceable as commander in chief of the army; his angry retirement had left a void which could not be filled. A French viceroy had scattered the Spaniards at Balaguer and all of Cataluña and much of Aragón were now again overrun by the enemy; the fact that there were still elements favorable to the Spaniards in Cataluña lay largely in their growing dissatisfaction with their new rulers; the Catalóns were increasingly convinced that it would have been better to bear the ills they had than fly to others which they knew not of. And, though the Aragonese nobles were basically faithful to Philip, they drove a hard bargain when it came to voting supplies. On his return to Madrid the following spring, his report to the Castilian Cortes was centered on war and more war—in Flanders and in Italy, as well as in the eastern provinces—and on the need for more and more money. He had reached the point where he was practically asking for bread from stones. But a special tax was placed on the sadly insufficient supply of food, and leave to sell pensions, as well as titles and high ecclesiastical offices, was granted. Thus, by means foul, rather than fair, funds were secured. The ways and means he had discussed so earnestly with Isabel never came to pass. Without her, he did not have the strength to enforce them.

Throughout this desolate time, the bereaved husband and defeated warrior had two main sources of comfort. The first was in his correspondence with *Sor María* which, after the interruption caused by the depression following Isabel's death, had been resumed with greater regularity and frequency than before. In March, he wrote her:

Your letter indeed arrived at a good time; for the cares that surround me had much afflicted me, and your words have encouraged me. I now trust that God in His mercy, looking to all Christendom, and to these realms, which are so pure in their Catholic faith, will not allow us to be ruined utterly, but will shield and defend them and grant us a good peace. Short are the human resources with which I have returned hither; and what appalls me most is to see that my faults alone are sufficient to provoke the ire of Our Lord, and to bring upon me greater punishments than before. But the greater the punishment, the greater will be my appeal to faith and hope, as you say; and I will continually supplicate Our Lord to supply with His almighty hand what we need. I for my part will do all I can, trying not to displease Him, and to comply with the obligations He has placed upon me, even though in doing so I risk my own life. I have not hesitated to give up the comforts of my home, in order to attend personally to the defense of these realms: for, while I thus fulfill this duty, I trust Our Lord will not fail me; but in any extremity I submit to His holy will. I have wished for the Prince to begin to learn what will fall upon him after my days are done; and so, though alone, I have brought him with me, and have confided his health to the hands of God, trusting in His mercy to guard him and to guide all his actions to His greater service.

—I THE KING.

The second source of comfort to Philip lay in his association with his sons. The days which he managed to spend with Juan at the Zarzuela represented interludes of peace and pride between the sessions with Councils and Cortes and the grapples with the military. The atmosphere was serene. There were no longer any irritating discussions as to how the boy was to be addressed and how he was to address others. To be sure, instead of being a Royal Highness, he was a Serene Highness, but he had the royal prerogative of addressing his gentlemen-in-waiting as *"Vos."* He had been made a Grand Master of St. John, which automatically made him also Grand Knight Commander of Malta and would entitle him to wear the habit and mantle of the Grand Prior of Castile and León after he had pronounced the necessary vows; and it further placed at his disposition five thousand *escudos* of annual rent and a castle at Consuegra. He delighted the courtiers around him—as well as his father —by his boyish assumption of sovereign dignity. Philip foresaw a brilliant future for him, one that would rival that of the first Juan for whom he had been named. This assumption was only a form of promising playacting, like so many of his attributes and activities; but the time would come when the sovereign dignity would be real and when a Grand Mastership and a title of Serene Highness would be only the beginning of the honors that would be due him. Some day there would be a counterpart to the Battle of Lepanto and Juan would be its hero.

Philip had not forgotten Isabel's resentment at the part Juan played in his life. He realized that it was natural, probably inevitable; and now that she was dead, he was scrupulously careful to see that, while the rival claims of the half brothers each received their due, no invidious comparisons would be made between them. Baltasar Carlos occasionally went to the Zarzuela for the hunting or theatrical spectacles and there was no friction between the two boys; on the other hand, there was no real affection. Like the King, they both remembered how Isabel had felt and both were old enough now to share his realization that the feeling had been natural, though Juan had never quite forgiven Baltasar Carlos for referring to "*my* father," instead of "*our* father," on the occasion of their first memorable meeting and once, long after that, Juan made an oblique reference to it.

"Do you ever study history?" he asked his half brother.

"Of course. Every day."

"I meant particularly family history."

"So did I."

"Then you probably remember the rather touching account of the first meeting between our great-grandfather and the hero of Lepanto."

"I can't say that I do," Baltasar Carlos answered rather curtly.

"Our great-grandfather had just come back from the Netherlands when his half brother, who was years younger than he and whom he had never met before, was brought to kiss his hand. The King asked the first Don Juan if he knew who his father was and the boy was abashed and didn't answer, so Philip II embraced him and said, 'Take courage, my child. You are descended from a great man. The Emperor Charles V, now in glory, was your father as well as mine.' And from that time on, the boy was treated on a footing of equality by all members of the royal family. He was girded with the King's own sword and decorated with the Order of the Golden Fleece."

Baltasar Carlos looked fixedly at Juan for a moment without speaking and Juan met the gaze with one equally direct, also in silence. Then, while he still stood his ground, Baltasar Carlos turned away. The subject was never raised again and neither boy mentioned it to his father. But it resulted in a restraining influence on what might otherwise have been good companionship.

As a matter of fact, Philip really preferred to have Juan to himself when he was at the Zarzuela. Royal etiquette forbade the presence of an illegitimate son at the Alcázar, except for special events and by special invitation; and while this rule had been relaxed in favor of the Buen Retiro, and Juan was now free to go there whenever he chose, he preferred his own house and went elsewhere very seldom. Therefore it was only at the Zarzuela that Philip could enjoy a normal father and son relationship with the boy who reminded him so vividly of his mother, whose personality was so attractive and whose talents were so marked. In addition to his aptitude for languages and mathematics, he now revealed a flair for music and a passion for astronomy; his voice was pleasing, he played several instruments with ease and spent hours on end gazing through a telescope. Philip never tired of listening to his singing and playing or watching the stars with him.

The King could not get to the Zarzuela as often as he would have liked, but on the other hand there were no obstacles to his constant companionship with Baltasar Carlos and this was rapidly assuming an official as well as a private character. Two years after Isabel's death, the heir to the throne accompanied his father to Zaragoza and Valencia, so that the Cortes could swear allegiance to him. The Cortes of Navarre came next; but their stay in Pamplona, its capital, was shadowed by the severe illness of the Prince, who came down with tertian fever; and though he eventually made a good recovery, it was two months before they could continue on their way to Aragón. Meanwhile, despite the fact that Baltasar Carlos was only seventeen years old, plans for his marriage were already beginning to take shape. The chosen bride was Mariana of Austria, the daughter of Philip's sister María and the erstwhile King of Hungary, who had now succeeded his father as Emperor of the Holy Roman Empire. This consolidation of the two Hapsburg branches was paramount in Philip's mind as it had been in that of his predecessor; he was conscious of no impediment to another marriage between own cousins and the Pope offered no objections to another dispensation.

As soon as official arrangements for the alliance had been completed, Philip wrote with satisfaction to *Sor* María:

My son is very much pleased with his new state and I am also, to have chosen such a good daughter-in-law, as I hold this marriage certain to produce very beneficial effects to the Catholic religion, which is my sole aspiration.

This letter was followed, shortly thereafter, by one from Baltasar Carlos himself. By this time, Philip had taken his heir to

Ágreda, so that he, too, might come into direct contact with *Sor María* and the visit had been a pleasant one. Now the boy wrote enthusiastically about his prospects for happiness:

Mother, two or three days ago my father gave me a letter from you congratulating me on the marriage that my father has made for me with the Archduchess Mariana. I am the most pleased in the world to have taken this state, especially with my cousin, who was the one I wished for ever since I had use of my reason; and it seems impossible to me that I could have come across any other woman so much to my taste. So I hope His Divine Majesty will let us be very happily married, which is all I can hope for. I ask you to pray for this. Our Lord guard you.

—I THE PRINCE. *Zaragoza, 20 July, 1646.*

This shared satisfaction about the marriage strengthened the bond of affection between father and son and Philip began to take heart again. But his happiness was short-lived. In October, he wrote to *Sor María* with anguish:

Since yesterday my son is oppressed with very extreme fever. It began by severe pains in his body, which lasted all day; and now he is delirious, and we are in such fear that we hope it will turn to smallpox . . . of which the doctors say they see signs. I know, Sor María, that I deserve heavy punishments, and that all that may come to me in this life will be insufficient to repay my sins; but I do cry now to the divine mercy of Our Lord, and the intercession of His holy Mother; and I beseech you to help with all your strength.

Three days after this desperate letter was written, the boy was dead and *Sor María* wrote to Philip with infinite compassion:

For the consolation of all and for the good of the Monarchy, how desirable would it be to have His Highness alive! But for the good of the Prince and his salvation, the Lord has done better, for He has taken him away at such a tender age from the dangers of government and the passions of this valley of tears, in order to carry him to reign under better conditions and less suffering than in the kingdoms of this world. Don't think of your son as dead and absent forever, but transferred to that celestial fatherland where there is no weeping or clamor or anguish or pain. He's gone where Your Majesty wishes to go. . . .

But, again, Philip derived no comfort from what she had written. Baltasar Carlos' death represented not only a supreme bereavement to a stricken father; it represented the loss of the only heir to the throne. Philip had failed his country in many ways and it had forgiven him over and over again. But it would not forgive him if, at forty-two, he shirked the responsibility of begetting a legitimate son. He had very little to offer a bride; any woman he married would, inevitably, suffer by comparison with Isabel and he would not be able to conceal from her the sad fact that he was making the comparison. He had never been good at pretending either ardor or admiration which he did not honestly feel; now it was quite impossible for him to do so. If the position of Queen Consort had in itself retained its former glory, that might compensate to some women, though not to the sort of woman he could love, for the personal indifference of a royal husband. But, alas, the crown was tottering over a ravished and war-torn land. The last of its radiance had been buried with Isabel.

Philip was wretchedly lonely, since he had not only lost Isabel and Baltasar Carlos forever; he had steeled himself to parting with Juan. A serious revolt in Naples had threatened the loss of that part of the kingdom and Philip was without an experienced leader to head either his fleet or his army. With the rashness born of despair, he suggested to Juan that the latter might do both.

At first, his son thought that he was jesting. Well, halfway, Philip admitted; but it was a sorry sort of jest, for the situation was grave—so grave that, foolhardy though his suggestion might appear, it seemed to represent the last chance to make a show of power —perhaps a hollow one, but at any rate a show. He proposed to give Juan the title of Lord High Admiral and Prince of the Seas and Commander in Chief in all states the King possessed on the mainland of Italy and, also, in Sardinia and Sicily. He believed that no man had ever been given such supreme and absolute authority as he was offering. Of course, Juan did not need to accept. . . .

"Do I start today?" was the only question he asked his father.

It was not that day, but it was surprisingly soon thereafter. Far from making any objections to the appointment, the Council confirmed it immediately and *Sor* María wrote, expressing her unqualified approval of the step the King had taken:

The Almighty will undoubtedly reward your firmness in the defense of the Catholic religion, your endeavors and your risks in exposing Don Juan of Austria to the dangers of the sea and the discomforts of such long seafaring pilgrimages.

Presently, the fine flower of Spanish nobility, delighted at the prospect of serving in the retinue of the Prince, flocked to the waiting armada of six ships, a pitiable successor to the one which had so proudly—and so mistakenly—been labeled invincible sixty years earlier. Then the miracle happened. This one did prove invincible. Immature and untrained as he was, Juan's playacting at sovereign dignity had not been without its effects, and a talent for military strategy was among his many natural gifts. In a surprise attack, he recaptured Naples for his father and was acclaimed as a saviour by the populace. This was *his* Lepanto.

Desperately, Philip wondered if it might not be possible to proclaim Juan his heir. Somewhere in the history of the world, if not in the history of Spain, he believed that similar action had been taken. Indeed, he now remembered that Portugal had once been very near doing so. That was when young King Sebastian died childless and three descendants of King Manuel claimed the throne: Catherine, Duchess of Braganza, who was declared ineligible on account of her sex; Philip II, King of Spain; and Antonio, the Prior of Crato. Despite his illegitimacy, he was the choice of the popular classes, some of the nobility, the regular clergy and the Pope himself and he pushed his candidacy with great ability. But a Spanish army, under the Duke of Alba, promptly invaded Portugal, routed the forces of Antonio and secured the Portuguese crown for Philip. If Antonio had only been successful, there might be a chance for Juan now. But of course the whole picture would have been different anyway. What was the use of thinking about it? In Spain, there was no precedent for such a bold move and that for which there was no precedent was so hard to bring about that it might as well be declared impossible first as last. Juan had every kingly qualification—except legitimacy; and, lenient as was the general attitude toward the privileges of royal bastards in most respects, the rules regarding succession were made of cast iron—the mandate which prevented their residence at the Alcázar was in itself sufficient proof of this rigidity. He was a Serene Highness, but not a Royal Highness. If Philip's will power had not long since been weakened by lack of use, he might have tried to see what he could do. As it was, he was ready to accept defeat before he made a last determined stand for victory. Numbly, hopelessly, he fell back before the pressure brought upon him by both Court and people. Early in the new year he wrote to *Sor* María, telling her of his capitulation:

I have received a letter from the Emperor condoling with me for the loss of my son and, at the same time, offering my niece to be my wife. As this agrees with my own feelings, I think I may decide to accept this marriage, which is doubtless the most fitting one for me; so I hope that Our Lord will help this with His powerful hand, so that the business may tend to His service, and to that of my own country.

A few weeks later, he wrote again, saying that arrangements for the alliance had been completed. A marriage between an uncle and a niece had been substituted for a marriage between cousins. Madrid, perpetually eager to celebrate almost anything for which it could find a pretext, was favored by two simultaneous and valid causes for rejoicing. Mariana had started on her way to meet her royal bridegroom and her progress had been marked by endless festivities in Trent and the Italian cities; Madrid could never permit such places to outdo it in splendor. The announcement of the impending nuptials coincided with the triumphant return of Don Juan, whose diplomacy had saved Naples for Spain; as a boy, he had been the people's favorite. As a conquering hero, he was their idol.

PART SEVEN

The

Niece

1649-1665

Philip IV only survived the Treaty of the Pyrenees for six years, for he died in September, 1665. His letters to the nun María de Ágreda have enabled posterity to form a better estimate of his character than was possible for his contemporaries. They reveal a passionate man whose outward impassivity was but a mask. Indolent and self-indulgent, Philip was very far from being a fool, and his great failing was not a lack of ability, but a want of application. Unfortunately for Spain, Philip II had devised a system of government which imposed a life of unremitting toil upon the monarch, and neither his son nor his grandson had the will to shoulder this burden.

In spite of the decline of Spanish power during the reigns of Philip III and Philip IV, both kings were the patrons of literature and art, in which Spain continued to lead the world. . . .

In fine, the reverses suffered by the Spanish arms, and the growing poverty of the country, were entirely without influence upon its literature and art, which continued to enjoy their old supremacy, and the seventeenth century may justly be described as the golden age of Spanish civilization.

—Louis Bertrand and Sir Charles Petrie, Bt.
The History of Spain.

Chapter 30

"WHAT has become of my beautiful presents?" Mariana demanded angrily.

She had never seen such diaphanous silk stockings, such sheer chemises, such dainty petticoats as had been brought to her the day before. The stockings were in many different colors, dozens and dozens of pairs, and so fine that they could be passed through a ring; the chemises and petticoats were so deeply bordered with lace that hardly any space was left for linen, but where there was some, it was exquisitely embroidered. She had not been provided with much of a trousseau, as far as intimate apparel was concerned, for Vienna, like Madrid, scrimped and saved in places that did not show; and she had been delighted when the great chests, sent to her with the compliments of the City Fathers, had been opened to disclose all these treasures. She had amused herself for several hours by fingering them, stroking them, sorting and resorting them, arranging them in different piles and gloating over them generally, much as a child might have amused herself with a surprise assortment of new toys. It had been hard for Mariana to tear herself away from her gifts at bedtime, but she had finally been persuaded to leave them in the antechamber until they could be officially docketed. However, she had selected a set that was especially attractive to her and had planned to put it on in the morning. Now Doña Emilia de San Ricardo, the lady-in-waiting who had come to her bedside looking rather unhappy, told her that the chests had all disappeared.

"*Disappeared!*" Mariana repeated, still more angrily. "How could anything like that disappear? You speak as if those chests had been wafted away by magic."

Looking increasingly miserable, Doña Emilia murmured something that was unintelligible, but that sounded vaguely apologetic. She was one of the youngest among the thirty-two Ladies of the Wardrobe and the Bedchamber in the suite which had been sent to meet the bride at Roveredo, under the leadership of the Duke of Maqueda y Nájera, and which numbered in all nearly a hundred persons, besides the servants who waited on these functionaries: a cardinal, a bishop, two royal chaplains, three grandees of Spain, two princes of Genoa, two royal equerries, a Mistress of the Robes, an aide-de-camp, eight shield-bearers, eight pages, two doctors, a treasurer, a comptroller, a notary, a chief clerk, a head caterer, a pastry cook, several bakers, fruiterers and other victualers and a beater for hunting, all with numerous helpers; and the retinue was guarded by a detachment of soldiers. Mariana had not endeared herself to her personal attendants and, in so far as it was possible for them to do so, the seniors among them relegated their duties to their juniors. Nevertheless, the division was not always strictly impartial; the young girls who were supposed to be tractable rather than argumentative found themselves pressed into service oftener than those who stood up for their rights and privileges.

"Didn't you hear me?" Mariana repeated, as the unfortunate lady-in-waiting continued to stand by the bed, looking unhappy and murmuring incoherencies.

"Yes, Your Highness. But I am not sure what I ought to say, except that the chests have disappeared. That is all I have been told to say."

"Who told you to say that?"

"The Condesa de Medellín, the Mistress of the Robes."

"Then you had better tell the Mistress of the Robes to come here at once."

"Your Highness, I am not allowed to tell the Mistress of the Robes what she should do. She tells me what to do."

"Well, at least you can take her a message. Or can't you even do that?"

"Yes, Your Highness. I can do that. If—"

"If *what*?"

"If it is very humbly worded."

"I have not the least idea of being humble to the Mistress of the Robes. If you do not go at once and make her understand, in whatever way you can, that I want to see her immediately, I shall get out of bed and go myself."

Mariana tossed aside the bedclothes and swung her bare feet toward the floor. She had nothing on but a flimsy dressing gown, very inadequately fastened. Horrified, Doña Emilia scurried from the room. Mariana thrust her feet into her slippers and pulled a quilt around her, not because she was afraid of appearing immodest, but because the room was chilly. Then she sat on the edge of the bed and awaited developments. As she expected, she did not have to wait long. The Condesa de Medellín appeared promptly, but her curtsy was one of routine and not of reverence. She spoke icily.

"Your Highness summoned me. I assume she is ill."

"I'm perfectly well. But I'm very much annoyed. I intended to put on some of my new clothes. And that stupid girl who was assigned to me this morning said that all the chests that came yesterday had disappeared. Then she stood around making little moaning sounds and wringing her hands. She claims that she hasn't been told to say anything else and therefore she can't. She's a complete nitwit."

"I beg Your Highness' pardon. She is a very devout, correct, intelligent young lady who belongs to one of our most exalted families. In telling you that the chests had disappeared and not enlarging on the fact, she was obeying orders. It is not her place to explain them."

"Then you had better explain them."

The stiff stance of the Condesa became actually rigid, her expression grim to the point of malevolence. "The chests, with their contents intact, have been returned to their donors," she said tersely.

"Sent back!"

"Yes, Your Highness. With an appropriate message."

"Those beautiful clothes! The nicest present I've had since I left home! What kind of a message could possibly be appropriate?"

"That a Queen of Spain has no legs."

Involuntarily, as she spoke, the Mistress of the Robes lowered her eyes which, hitherto, had been riveted on Mariana's angry face and the glance fell on the legs that the girl had swung over the bed and that were completely uncovered. She was a big buxom girl and her limbs were not slender and shapely, but short and stocky. She now drew them up under the bedclothes and screamed.

"What do you mean, a Queen of Spain has no legs? What happens to her legs?"

"Your Highness must understand—"

"I understand that I want to go straight back to Vienna! And you had better understand it, too, and make everyone else understand it! *No legs!* Of course, I have legs! Of course, I'm going to keep them. If you think I'm going to let one of those barber chirurgeons you've brought along cut off my legs—"

She had become completely hysterical. The Mistress of the Robes found herself in an extremely difficult position. Even if her personal antipathy to this Austrian had not made her averse to touching the girl, the hard and fast rules of royal etiquette would have forbidden it. But the antipathy must be overcome, the etiquette disregarded. She approached the bed, seated herself beside it and, taking Mariana's hand in one of hers, placed the other gently but firmly over the girl's mouth.

"Stop screaming and listen to me," she said sternly, without bothering to use a respectful form of address. "Of course, no one is going to cut off your legs or harm you in any way. Your welfare and comfort are of the greatest concern to Spain. The chief *mayordomo* was merely trying, by a figure of speech, to give the City Fathers a lesson in delicacy—a lesson of which Italians and, evidently, Austrians as well are in great need." The Mistress of the Robes felt she had reason to speak feelingly, if not discreetly or respectfully. This was the second episode in regard to gifts which had tried her soul since she had left Spain and she could scarcely be blamed for taking it hard: a brother of Mariana, who had accompanied her on her journey, had attached all the costly presents which the Spanish delegates had made to their sovereign's bride and had returned to Vienna, taking the gifts with him; the courteous Spaniards had been put to great trouble, not to say great expense, to replace these. "The Queen of Spain is at all times discreetly, as well as elegantly, clothed," the Condesa continued with a sigh, "and what she wears beneath the beautiful dresses, which cover her from head to foot and thereby conceal her other garments, is never discussed, any more than it is ever seen. In fact, all thoughts of it are dismissed by her subjects as being a presumptuous intrusion on her privacy, her— her modesty." Involuntarily, as she had glanced in the direction of Mariana's unalluring limbs, now mercifully covered, the Condesa hesitated over the word modesty. Clearly, it was not an intrinsic attribute of this girl; it was something she would have to be taught.

The Condesa could not repress another deep sigh. She had been having her troubles from the very moment the retinue had made connections with the bride at Roveredo and she had already been obliged to speak severely on numerous occasions, to tell Mariana that a Queen of Spain did not laugh in public or otherwise disport herself in an unseemly manner. And Mariana had flouted her by laughing harder than ever. Such flouting must cease. And, obviously, the question of laughter was only a minor one in the rigorous rules the Condesa must enforce. "The greatest monarch in the world has chosen you for his bride," she went on. "It will be most displeasing to him, to his nobles and to his people, if you do not show yourself sensible of this honor in every way—by your speech, by your actions, by your appearance. For the sake of your own peace of mind and future happiness, if for no other reasons, you must allow yourself to be guided. Put aside foolish fears or, if you cannot do that, at least keep them to yourself. You cannot afford to be ridiculous. That is a failing which no Spaniard ever forgives."

As the screams abated in violence and frequency, the Condesa had removed her hand from Mariana's mouth, but she continued to sit beside her until she saw that something she said made an impression—possibly not a very favorable one, but still an impression. At least the girl realized how silly she had been in thinking her legs were endangered. Probably she would continue to sulk, because the fragile finery she coveted had been sent back to its tactless donors, but that could not be helped. She was apt to be sulky anyway, when she was not boisterous—one mood could succeed another with surprising suddenness. It was perhaps unfortunate that she must be discouraged from laughing, because it was when she was merry that she was most attractive; except for her bright red cheeks and otherwise white skin, such charm as she had lay in her vivacity. She was full breasted and wide hipped for a girl of fifteen, but that might be a good thing, considering that prompt maternity was the main object of this marriage. She should make a good brood mare even if she did not make a superlative queen. But you could not always tell. Unaccountably, it was sometimes slim delicate young women who produced babies most easily and great strapping girls like this one who had a hard time. Perhaps she would not find so much to laugh about, if she were promptly and uncomfortably pregnant, and still less, if her first childbed were agonizing yet futile, as far as an heir was concerned, and she found that she was expected, as a matter of course, to become pregnant and give birth again and again and again. It did not distress the Condesa to think that, perhaps, this was exactly what would happen to Mariana. On the contrary, the prospect was pleasing rather than otherwise.

She smoothed the bedclothes and rose. "I will send another lady-in-waiting to you," she said, "since you do not appear to appreciate the excellent qualities of Doña Emilia. She will see to it that you are supplied with whatever is suitable for you to put on and there should not be overmuch delay about your dressing. Perhaps it has slipped your mind that we are leaving for Rome later in the day. The journey will be an interesting one, through beautiful country, with many pleasant stops. And I understand that, in Rome, a great honor awaits you. His Holiness has announced his intention of giving you the Golden Rose. With that in your proud possession, you will quickly forget such trifling disappointments as that caused by the return of the insignificant gifts which were made you here. And when we leave the city of Rome, it will be to go to its port at Ostia, where the flotilla that is to take you to Spain awaits you. From all accounts, your galley is the most splendid one in history, if not also one of the largest. As you step aboard it, you will realize, better than you seem to do now, what it means to be Queen of Spain."

Chapter 31

THE Condesa de Medellín had not exaggerated the size and splendor of the royal galley or the wonderment and delight Mariana would feel in it.

It was indeed huge, with twenty-eight benches along either side, each bench seating six or seven rowers. The oars of these rowers were painted red with golden tips and the galley's ladders were gilded, as were also the helm and the corridors. Dominating the bow was the figurehead of Santiago, the patron of Spain, and the poop was adorned with gilded figures of saints and angels and lighted by three lanterns in the form of dragons. Inside, it was the epitome of elegance: the draperies were all of crimson damask; the walls were set with silver and ebony; the cabinets were gold framed; the canopied bed was white and silver; and, from the chamber where this stood, led a dressing room and a saloon similarly adorned. Besides this sumptuous enclosure, a tent of half-silk, red and gold in color, was provided to use on the poop, wind and weather permitting; and there was also a longboat aboard, for incidental or emergency use, supplied with eight gilded oars and decorated with sea gods and sea monsters. The crew wore crimson damask, the musicians brocade. The strains of horn and fife and sordelinas sounded all day and much of the night above the rhythm of the oars; and, when the flotilla stopped at Tarragona to take on water, a fine representation of Roque de Figueroa's latest comedy was performed on the quarterdeck.

If the passage had been stormy, all this magnificence and all these entertainments might well have been wasted on a seasick bride; but the weather was so exceptionally beautiful that Calderón felt it worthy of celebrating in verse and promptly wrote a poem in which he described "the waves, the winds and the monsters of the deep" as paying reverence to their future sovereign. Mariana stepped ashore at Denia in the same blooming health and in much higher spirits than she had left Ostia; if her voyage had been a sample of royal state in Spain, she was, indeed, quite ready to keep it.

Unfortunately, the trip overland was something of an anticlimax, though Philip, in a pathetic attempt to play the part of an eager bridegroom, plied Mariana with love letters and more substantial tokens of his affection, all sent by special messenger every other day. But the countryside through which they passed was, for the most part, bleak and dreary, its fields untilled, its rough roads infested with vagabonds and beggars, and the village of Navalcarnero, where the marriage was scheduled to take place, was a poverty-stricken little hamlet; far from suggesting royal state, it did not even suggest elementary comfort. When Mariana was shown to the room in the miserable *venta* where she was to spend the night before the wedding ceremony, she made no effort to conceal her contempt for such quarters—the worst of many bad ones with which she had been obliged to make do. The luckless Doña Emilia, who always seemed to be on duty when Mariana was in her most difficult moods, was stung beyond endurance by the bride's querulous questions and complaints and told the unvarnished truth about the choice of such a mise en scène.

"When a royal marriage takes place in a village, Your Highness, that is free forever after from the burden of paying tribute. Therefore, the poorer the place, the smaller the loss to the treasury."

"The wedding is taking place here so that the King can *save money?*"

"Yes, Your Highness. It is extremely important that he should."

It was on the tip of Doña Emilia's tongue to mention the *limosna al rey* (alms for the King) which was again in process of collection by gentlemen of the Court, each accompanied by a parish priest and a friar, as they made a house-to-house canvass, where the head of every family was asked to give what he could spare. Many members of the nobility, Doña Emilia among them, felt this to be not only a high-handed but a sinful way of raising money and had been thankful when it fell into such disrepute that it was abandoned. Now it was in full force again. Nor were the gentlemen and priests the only beggars; ragged and starving soldiers were also going from door to door, trying to collect their wages.

"It didn't look to me as if he were economizing on that galley," Mariana said impudently, while Doña Emilia was still trying to decide whether or not she should speak her mind. She contented herself by saying, with what she thought was admirable self-restraint, "All the more reason why he needs to do so now."

Mariana had not had the sense to connect the vagabonds on the road with the depleted state of the country. Now her annoyance flared into anger, as it was so apt to do. Fortunately, a theatrical performance had been planned for her amusement before supper and, as it was broad comedy, the type that especially appealed to her, rage was soon smothered by hearty laughter. Philip, in conformity with the traditional usage of the Spanish Court, had come to Navalcarnero that same day in what passed for disguise and, without announcing his arrival to his betrothed, watched the play—and her—from a secluded nook where he could observe without himself being seen. Unexpectedly, he was favorably impressed. This merry young girl, with her red cheeks and her buxom body and her easy laugh would put new life into him. For the first time, instead of looking on his prospective marriage as an unwelcome duty, he began to think of it as a means of rejuvenation and good cheer.

He spent the night at the neighboring village of Brunete and, early the next morning, with an imposing retinue, came galloping back to Navalcarnero. Mariana was waiting to greet him at the entrance of the inn, rosy-cheeked and wreathed in smiles. Without the slightest sign of abashment, she met his searching glance full face. Then she made a quick curtsy, without bending her body and, still looking up at him brightly, dropped to her knees. The gesture pleased Philip. If she had not knelt, her bearing might have seemed bold; since she had done so, it showed the reverence that was due her sovereign, while the rest of her behavior revealed that she was ready and glad to welcome him, that she would not be a timid or reluctant bride. Besides, since of course he must raise her instantly, he had a cogent reason for touching her and found satisfaction in so doing.

Without further preliminaries, he led her to an adjacent chapel where Mass was celebrated and the marriage ceremony performed by the Primate of Spain. Then came a public dinner, a bullfight and another comedy, during all of which Mariana sat by her bridegroom's side, smiling and self possessed; and afterward the newly-married couple entered their great lumbering coach and, attended by the Court, rode to the Escorial, where they were to spend their honeymoon.

Philip had been quite right in his estimate of the ease with which Mariana had approached the marriage state. She was, of course, without definite information about its exact nature, but what she had gleaned not only roused her curiosity to learn more, but fascinated her with its suggestion of pleasures she had not yet experienced. When she and Philip were alone in the body of the coach, she chatted gaily and, when they approached the Escorial and she saw how brilliantly the immense structure had been lighted for their reception, she clapped her hands with joy.

"How many candles did it take to make it shine so?" she asked.

"More than ten thousand," Philip replied with pride. He was charmed with the trivial question, as he had been with everything else. Mariana clapped her hands harder than ever and said she had never seen anything half so entrancing in Vienna.

On their arrival at the palace, he left her briefly to the ministrations of her ladies-in-waiting and they found her equally merry. It was unseemly, they whispered to each other, as soon as they left her; and, just as the Mistress of the Robes had not been able to suppress the cruel hope that childbearing would go hard with her, when the time came for that, so they felt they would not be sorry if her wedding night proved an unforeseen ordeal. Her blithe reception of them the next day was proof positive that the loss of her maidenhood had been exciting rather than distressing. Philip had never willingly hurt or frightened anyone and, after all, he was singularly experienced in the art of possessing a woman. It had been his intention, beforehand, to combine gentleness, which would touch his bride and give her confidence in him, with a show of intense passion which, though feigned, would make her feel that she was irresistibly desirable. To his surprise and delight, he found that Mariana neither expected nor wanted gentleness and that he did not need to simulate passion because she so quickly aroused it and responded to it. The speedy consummation of their marriage was highly satisfactory to them both and, for the next few weeks, this satisfaction remained unabated. For a time, the King's correspondence with María de Ágreda, like most of his other routine occupations, was sadly neglected; but when he finally did write it was to say:

I confess to you that I do not know how I can thank Our Lord for the favor He has shown me in giving me such a companion; for all the qualities I have seen in my niece up to the present are great and I am extremely content and desirous not to be ungrateful to Him Who has granted me so singular a boon: showing my gratitude by changing my life and executing His will in all things.

In her reply, María de Ágreda placed much stress upon the great need of the country for an heir to the throne and urged the King "to fix his whole attention and good will upon the Queen, without turning his eyes to other objects strange and curious." At the moment, Philip had no difficulty in following this advice, for he was more than pleased with Mariana and fully as anxious for a son as were his people.

Possibly it was partly because these hopes for an heir were not speedily fulfilled that the mutual satisfaction of the King and Queen was so short-lived. If Mariana had promptly become pregnant, Philip could probably have continued to keep their relationship one of intensity until her condition made this unadvisable. Since nothing happened to put a curb on his passion, it gradually wore itself down and, now that the novelty had worn off, Mariana was relieved, rather than otherwise, when he claimed her less and less frequently. He continued to treat her with kindly attention and went with her, as a matter of course, to the comedies and masques in which she took such unbounded pleasure. But his own taste for them was dulled by previous overindulgence, just as his virility had been weakened by it. He did his best to appear interested and amused, but he could not successfully disguise his weariness and apathy and Mariana soon found her stepdaughter, who was not much younger than she was, a more congenial companion at bull-fights and balls than she did her husband. Instead of resenting this congeniality, Philip was pleased with it. Except at the very beginning, he had seldom referred to Mariana as "my wife"; far more often, he had referred to her as "my niece." Now, with increasing frequency, he bracketed his references to the Queen and the Infanta by speaking affectionately and tolerantly of "the girls."

Even if this state of affairs was neither ideal nor idyllic, it was peaceful and pleasant until the instinctive dislike and antagonism between Mariana and Juan became so evident that it was impossible for the King to disregard it. She was jealous from the moment she learned that the festivities celebrating her betrothal had been coupled with those celebrating Juan's victory in Naples; and though he did not share in her triumphal entry to Madrid, except as a spectator, she could not forget that he had been the people's idol and his father's before she appeared on the scene and that he might still be a very formidable rival in their affections. All the sparkling fountains transformed into classic temples and dispensing nectar in her honor; all the balconies hung with tapestries and decorated with armorial shields; all the streets illumined with lanterns and torches; all the banquets and bullfights did not suffice to appease "the green-eyed monster." She demanded her stepson's complete removal from the scene where she occupied the center of the stage.

When this happened, Philip, to whom it had not even occurred that there would be friction between Juan and Mariana, tried to reason with her. Isabel's resentment had been natural enough, because of Baltasar Carlos; but Mariana had no son of her own and alas! no prospect of one. The King saw no reason why she should not be as friendly with Juan as she was with María Teresa and told her so.

"María Teresa is sweet and gentle," Mariana retorted. "Juan is as arrogant as if he were the heir to the throne, instead of the by-blow of an actress."

Philip winced. "Juan's mother was very dear to me," he said coldly. "I was her only love and I believe that, like the Magdalene, her sins are forgiven her because she loved much. I wish I could believe the same of mine. She had the sweetest voice of any woman I have ever known and she has now, for many years, been the greatly respected abbess of a convent established by royal grant. I would prefer that you should not speak of her or of her son in that way—

in fact, I must ask you never to do it again. I may add that Juan is himself very dear to me, as you must have guessed. I was proud and happy to acknowledge him as my son when he was still a child, because of his brilliance and beauty. Now that he has become a man, I have every reason to be proud of him because of his still more remarkable attributes. How many inexperienced young leaders could have won such a victory as he did at Naples?"

"That was probably just a happy accident. I don't believe he could do anything of the sort a second time. Why don't you send him to Cataluña and find out?"

The last thing on earth that Philip wanted was to send Juan away from him again. But Mariana gave him no rest and, unlike Isabel, she could hold a grudge against him and bargain with him for compliance. When he came to her bed, she made her acceptance of his advances contingent on her whims and it was often plain that he would not be able to possess her fully unless he used force, which it was not in him to do. And they had been married now for more than a year and there was no prospect of an heir. He himself was driven to bargaining.

"When you tell me you are pregnant—" he began and decided he must start over again. Mariana could and did lie to him. "When I know that you are pregnant, I will send Juan to Cataluña," he told her sorrowfully.

Juan had not the slightest objection to leaving for Cataluña. In fact, he was very much bored at Consuegra, which was his official residence as a Knight of Malta, and he did not enjoy the Zarzuela nearly as much as he had before the advent of Mariana. Although, with more consideration than she had shown in his case, he did not tell his father what he thought of Mariana, he regarded her as bold, hard and vulgar. He was relieved that he would no longer have to pretend to be polite to her; and that he might the sooner be relieved of this obligation, he decided to pay an unscheduled and unofficial visit while the final preparations for departure to Cataluña were being made. He went to Valfermoso de las Monjas and asked to see the Abbess.

In doing so, he obeyed a sudden impulse; such a visit had long been at the back of his mind. As a boy, he had thought repeatedly of asking permission to see his mother and more than once the words had been on the very tip of his tongue. But a certain shyness, such as he had never experienced in connection with anything else, had held him back. Since his father had never suggested a meeting of this sort, Juan decided there was some reason why Philip did not feel it would be best or, perhaps, that it would open an old wound. Then had come the triumphant interlude at Naples and the ovation on his return to Madrid, with all its attendant excitement. The first fruits of victory had been so sweet, they had sufficed to keep his thoughts from other matters. Now, idling away his days between Consuegra and the Zarzuela, he decided that the time was ripe for the long-delayed excursion to the Badiel Valley.

He left the Zarzuela without making any mention of his destination or, indeed, without any advance mention of the journey and Philip, who had become more and more dependent on his company, sent a messenger to ask why he had not been to pay his respects, as usual, at the Buen Retiro. When the messenger returned with the news that His Serene Highness was not at home and that no one seemed to know where he had gone, the King was deeply worried. It was ridiculous, of course, to suppose that any harm, either accidental or premeditated, should come to Juan; surely, he was one of those rare human beings who lead a charmed life. Nevertheless, the little forking fears persisted until Juan presented himself, unannounced, at the palace, to be soundly rebuked for his absence.

"I did not realize I had been so much missed," Juan said coolly after Philip had finished his tirade. "Mariana is certainly eager enough to get rid of me. And you are naturally eager to please her. In a few days I shall be gone to Cataluña for an indefinite period. I anticipated this by only a few days more in going elsewhere."

"What do you mean by 'elsewhere'?"

"I rather hoped you would not ask me. After all, I am twenty years old now. I supposed I was entitled to a certain liberty of movement."

"You are not entitled to speak to your father, much less to your king, in that way and you know it. Of course, if you have become involved in some sort of a liaison, you do not need to tell me the young lady's name or that of your trysting place, though it might save complications in the end if you did. If these were not the circumstances, I should like to have you give me the information for which I have already asked you."

"This was not a liaison in the generally accepted sense of the word. I think you know there was one of that kind in Naples and what the young lady's name was—or, at all events, that her father, an eminent painter, is known there as *el Españoleto*. Even if you can't boast, like your grandfather, that you can rule the world on two inches of paper, you are very well informed about what is going on. Actually, I am surprised there is anything I can tell you. This time, the place I went to was a convent in the Badiel Valley and the name of its abbess is *Sor* Dolores. Is there anything else you would like me to tell you about her?"

The countenance of the King, normally very pale, suddenly became ashen. He bowed his head, fearful that the suddenness and force of his emotion might betray him and that he would not be able to mask his expression; but Juan could see that his beautiful white hands were trembling. He made no immediate answer to the question put to him with such cruel arrogance and presently the silence between the father and son became oppressive. It was the father who finally broke it.

"No," he said in a strangled voice. "There is nothing else you need to tell me about her. You may retire." Then, as Juan bowed and turned away, still without speaking, Philip called him back before he reached the door. "Wait," he said. "There is something. Is this abbess—*Sor* Dolores—well and—happy?"

"She seemed to be well. And happy? I think perhaps contented would be the better word."

"And did you see her without a veil?"

"Yes—for a moment, at my urgent request. It had not been her intention that I should."

"And is she—lovely to look at?"

"Very lovely."

"And her voice—is that very sweet?"

"I think it is the sweetest I have ever heard."

The King drew a deep breath. "That is what I have always thought myself," he said in a low voice. "You may go now." Then, a second time, he called Juan back. "It is only fair that I should tell you I am glad you went to see this abbess," he said, still speaking almost in a whisper. "Though, if you had asked for permission beforehand, I should have declined to give it to you for fear such a visit might cause her grief. But it means a great deal to me to have news of her. I am sorry I spoke to you in anger when you first arrived. Come and kiss me as you bid me farewell."

Two days later, Juan left for Barcelona. His career in Cataluña was a fitting sequel to his victory in Naples. To be sure, it represented less of a coup d'état, for the Cataláns had long since had all they wanted of the French and they liked Juan personally from the beginning. He did not have to win them over, as he had the Neapolitans. They were quite ready to accept him as their leader and his prompt success, in ridding them of the invaders, endeared him to them still further. He might easily have remained among them indefinitely, to their advantage and very probably to his own; but it seemed to be indicated that his next command should be in Flanders.

From there, he sent Mariana a beautiful silver cradle with brocade hangings. It was one of the most sumptuous gifts provided for the Infanta Margarita María.

Chapter 32

MARGARITA María lived and throve. Her sunny presence provided almost the only light in the encircling gloom of the dreary and despondent Court.

Though there were still sporadic attempts at gaiety, the calendar, for the most part, was marked by dull routine: on a certain fixed day, the royal family moved from Madrid to Aranjuez; on another fixed day from Aranjuez to the Escorial; and, in all three places, the pre-arranged round of daily occupations was much the same. Philip continued to hunt a good deal, both wolf and boar, and to find welcome diversion in so doing until overexposure to unfriendly elements took too heavy a toll. On his way to the Escorial, the coach in which he was riding overturned in a flooded river and, though he persisted in going on, when he reached his destination drenched and chilled, the snowfall was so heavy that the wolves, more prudent than he, refused to brave it. The following day, he waited, standing chest deep in an earthen blind, still hoping for his prey, which still failed to appear. Alternating chills and fevers and a hand temporarily paralyzed by the cold were the result of this rashness and the King's physicians forbade any further hunting in winter weather.

Deprived of his favorite sport, Philip spent a great deal of time at his desk, but accomplished very little by sitting there. He no longer attended Council meetings in person, but listened to the reports of these as they were brought to the throne room once a week by secretaries. After the documents were turned over to him by Luis de Haro, he merely scribbled on their margins, *Como parece*—As it appears—or *Está bien*—It is well—meaning he was willing the measures should be passed as they were presented to him, without bothering to verify whether or not appearances were deceitful or whether all really was well. And, actually, it was not. His finances were more hopelessly involved than ever. Out of the ten million ducats voted to him the year before by the Cortes of Castile, he had received only three million; and out of a total normal revenue, including the gold from the Indies, of eighteen million, he had received only eight or nine and confessed to an uncovered debt of one hundred and twenty million. Fresh taxes of two percent were put on food and even fireplaces and windows were taxed more heavily than ever before and, meanwhile, *Sor* María was writing:

For God's sake, moderate some of the taxes the poor people pay, for I know that villages have been depopulated in consequence of them; and that the poor people only keep body and soul together on barley bread and the herbs of the fields. . . . So many changes in the coinage, too, are most injurious.

He knew that she was right, but he had reached a stage of apathy, as far as finances were concerned; and the whole situation was so far out of control that any effort to improve it seemed futile.

He was a kind and devoted father to his daughters, stifling as best he could his disappointment because he did not have a legitimate son and his longing for the illegitimate son who was so far away. He also did his best to be a kind and devoted husband, but this was harder for him. Just as Mariana's mood had formerly veered quickly from merriment to rage and from rage to sulkiness, a more marked and lasting change had now come about: her hoydenish habits had been supplanted by a taste for an observance of etiquette even more rigid than any which had hitherto existed in Spain; and far from making her husband's country her own, and his people her people, she became more and more stubbornly and aggressively Austrian in viewpoint, manner and conduct. The widespread poverty did not trouble her, except as a personal inconvenience; once when she had gone without sweets for several days, she asked her lady-in-waiting why they had not been served as usual, and was told that the confectioner had gone so long unpaid that he refused to supply them. The necessary coins were supplied by the Court Jester, Manolito de Gante, after the lady-in-waiting had also offered to make up the deficit with a ring which she then and there took from her finger. Mariana could hardly be blamed for feeling that this particular episode cast reflections on the dignity of the crown and for losing her temper, but there were other occasions when she might well have made the best of things if she had not resented the lack of luxury which she had taken for granted and complained that she was homesick for the pleasures of Vienna. As the Vienna branch of the Hapsburgs was in circumstances quite as straitened as the Madrid branch, the complaint had no very solid basis. But it troubled Philip, who felt that he was failing her in every way; it did not occur to him to excuse himself with the assertion that she was failing him. A fresh series of festivities were arranged at the Buen Retiro to solace and enliven her; the services of an ingenious Florentine were secured with the hope that his novel entertainments might divert her; and she consented to admit, rather grudgingly, that she had found him amusing.

The domestic situation was sad enough; the foreign situation was even worse. England had never forgiven Spain for the slight put on Charles, Prince of Wales, when he came courting the Infanta María; and, despite everything that had happened since then, the ancient grudge still persisted and with it the desire to feed it fat. (Spain had its grievances, too; England had accepted another Catholic princess—Henriette Marie of France—with hardly a murmur, after refusing to accept a Spanish Infanta, and she had recognized the Duke of Braganza as King of Portugal, dismissing the Hapsburg rights to that throne almost casually; but Spain was no longer in a position to feed anything fat.) To be sure, England had herself done worse than repudiate Charles when he became the king; she had permitted him to be overthrown, beheaded and supplanted by Oliver Cromwell, whose government Philip had recognized, swallowing the bitter pill this recognition cost him as a monarch who believed in the divine right of kings and antagonizing all English Royalists and Catholics. What was worse, this craven act provided him with only a few years' respite from war; the year of Margarita María's birth was marked by an exchange of courtesies between Spain and England and a formal alliance seemed to be in the offing.

But Cromwell set a high price on this. He demanded that English merchants should be allowed to buy wool in Spain, that reciprocal advantages should be given to English and Spanish trade in Europe and that freedom should be given English ships to trade in the West Indies. There were also several other conditions, but these were the major obstacles to an agreement as far as Spain was concerned and the demands were refused. Without waiting for a declaration of war, English ships set sail for the Indies, captured the silver fleet and took possession of Jamaica. The loss of this key to the Caribbean was the gravest blow Spain had yet received in the New World. Desperately, she faced the fact that she must try to fight on both sea and land and that England, as well as France, was now her enemy.

Four sterile years had now passed since the birth of Margarita María, but at last Mariana was pregnant again and with this pregnancy came a glimmer of hope; but the baby was another girl and this one lived only a fortnight; the following year still another girl was born and lived only a day. At this point, the Cortes, discouraged and disheartened, petitioned Philip to declare María Teresa his heiress. The Salic Law, which excluded females from inheritance to the French crown, did not apply in Spain, and one of its greatest rulers—Isabel the Catholic—had been a Queen Regnant. Nevertheless, the inherent conviction that it was only as a last resort an Infanta should succeed her father was so strong that Philip clung desperately to the hope it might not be necessary for him to do this. However, he was well aware that, sooner or later, he might have no choice in the matter. Indeed, he had refused to listen to a certain *Monsieur* de Lionne, a close friend of Cardinal Mazarin, who had succeeded Richelieu as Chief Minister of France, when the French emissary had come to Madrid for conciliatory discussions with Luis de Haro about the possible retrocession of Cataluña to Spain; and, noticing that Don Luis wore a medal representing María Teresa on his hat, had incidentally made a very tempting suggestion.

"If your king would give my master the original of that medal for his wife," de Lionne said suavely, "peace would soon be made."

With deep regret, though with apparent lightness, Haro dismissed the subject. Such a marriage, desirable as it would have been from every other point of view, would have meant that María Teresa would have had to renounce her right to the throne and this could not be considered. Now Philip refused the Cortes on the ground that such a declaration would distress the Queen; she was very ill and nothing should be done which could possibly upset her. After all, she had already borne three children and she was still only twenty-two years old. (He dismissed from his mind the unwelcome realization that two of the three had been so diseased at birth that they were doomed to an early death and that there was no sound reason to believe that other children, whether male or female, would be more healthy.) There was plenty of time for more. His Councilors were not disposed to share his hopefulness, but for once it was justified. Still another baby was born the next year and this time it was a seemingly healthy boy.

Mariana was very ill again and did not respond favorably, even when treated with oil of lavender, usually so efficacious in such cases; but now Philip's concern for her was engulfed in the general rejoicing. The poet Jerónimo de Barrionuevo did full justice to the event in writing to his friend, the Dean of Zaragoza:

On the day of the birth not a bench nor a table was left unbroken in the palace, nor a single pastry-cook's nor tavern that was not sacked. In the Admiral's house, too, one of his equerries and riding master to some of the greatest gentlemen in Madrid, named Chicho Cristalino, killed his groom in the stable, stabbing him for some trivial cause. . . . He has escaped. He was a Knight of Calatrava. The same night three or four other similar misfortunes happened, and in the rejoicings nobody's cape was safe. . . . Tomorrow they say that His Majesty will go on horseback to Atocha to give thanks to the Mother of God. . . . They say the Prince is a pretty little chap, and that the King wishes him to be baptized at once, before the extreme cold comes on. . . . There are to be masquerades, bullfights, and cane tourneys as soon as the Queen gets up to see them, as well as plays with machinery invented by an engineer, a servant of the Nuncio, to be represented at the theater at the Retiro, and in the saloon of the palace. . . . The municipality, following the lead of the Councils, have gone to congratulate the King

. . . and no gentleman, great or small, has failed to do the like. There have been some funny incidents. Here are two. The little Count de Haro, the Admiral's child, six years old, went and the King was much pleased with the little man, as he was so serious, and especially when he said to His Majesty, "But, Sir! those buttons of yours are against the pragmatic; they are gold!" They were really diamond buttons that the King had put on for the celebration. The favorite [Haro] accompanied him and one of the courtiers present came up to him [Haro] and said: "God bless Your Excellency for the boon you have bestowed upon Spain in sending us a Prince," as if Haro had been the artificer of the work. There was much laughter at this.

Barrionuevo's next letter was equally vivid:

On Thursday, the 13th, the corridors and courtyards of the palace were decorated with great splendor, and three canopies were erected, one in each corridor and one in the chapel. There was a very sumptuous bed adjoining the King's curtained closet, and a step away a staging, with two steps and a triangle of silver. Upon this was placed the font of St. Dominic's baptism, and six great silver braziers very full of fuel, which were replenished every now and then from the fireplaces, so that the air might be warmed, which it was until it was like an oven. There were also sconces which perfumed the air divinely. Shortly after two the ceremony commenced; the Inquisitor-General and the Bishop of Sigüenza, apparelled in pontificals, assisting the Cardinal, who awaited the arrival of the Infante near the altar, while the whole chapel was hung with the most beautiful hangings the King possesses. Don Luis Ponce, without a cape, led the way with the Spanish Guard, followed by peers, nobles, and grandees; after whom came the Nuncio and ambassadors. Then came the minister (Don Luis de Haro), dressed in a gown of cloth of gold and a red sash. (It will be recollected that this was the same costume as that which Olivares wore at the baptism of Baltasar Carlos, and which then puzzled the people. The dress, whatever it is, seems only to be worn at christenings.) Following him, the Prince, richly adorned, was borne in the arms of the Countess of Salvatierra, seated in a crystal chair; and the Infanta (María Teresa) walked behind, her train carried by the Mistress of the Robes, after whom marched the heralds and archers of the Guard, who entirely surrounded the space. The Marqués of Priego carried the sacred taper, Alba bore the custode and napkins, the Admiral carried the ewer, which was of a single emerald, very large, and set with diamonds. The marchpane [the piece of bread upon which the bishop wiped his fingers after anointing the baby] fell to the Count of Oñate, the towels to Medina de las Torres, the salt cellar to the Prince of Astillano, his son. The ladies of the Court followed the Infanta, their trains borne by pages. The presidents of the Councils, with their two senior officers on each side, were ranged around the chapel, with the grandees before them; and when the ladies entered they stood in front of the grandees. The lady-in-waiting handed the Prince to the Infanta naked, except for a very short little jacket of plush much adorned, and with false sleeves. The Infanta cried out in a very clear voice: "Why have you not put his clothes on? Why do you give him to me so undressed?" The lady replied: "That is done on purpose, Madam, that it may be seen that he is a male." The water they baptized him with was from the Jordan . . . brought lately by some friars who came from the Holy House. The Prince screamed lustily when he was baptized and, attracted by the loud resonant voice, the King, who was looking through his jalousies, exclaimed, "Ah! that does sound well; the house smells of a man now."

The birth of Philip Prosper did much more than provide for lavish celebrations in Madrid; it entirely changed the international picture. There was no longer any necessity to regard María Teresa as the heiress presumptive; hence there was no reason why she should not be used as a pawn for peace with France; and one calamity after another had shown that Spain could no longer keep up the hollow pretense of being the greatest power in Europe.

Not long after the Infante's ceremonious baptism, fresh trouble arose with Portugal. A state of hostility had existed along the border for years and the frequent forays by the Portuguese were always met with quick reprisals by the Spaniards;

but there had been no formal declaration of war. Now, taking advantage of Philip's increasingly depleted strength, the militant Queen Mother of Portugal, though a Spaniard by birth, engineered an attack on Badajoz. In retaliation, an army of eight thousand was somehow assembled by the exhausted Spaniards, but the old problem of "lacking heads" still made the question of command a difficult one. Don Juan could not be spared from Flanders and there was no adequate substitute for him; Philip finally decided on Luis de Haro as the best choice he could make and, when the news reached the invaders that a Spanish army was on the way, they retreated into Portugal. If Haro had been more skilled in the arts of war, he would have realized that his wisest move would have been entrenchment at Badajoz. Instead, he pursued the Portuguese, was ensnared in an ambush and was himself obliged to retreat with great loss of men and equipment. This was really the end as far as Portugal was concerned.

Meanwhile, Louis II de Bourbon, better known as the Prince of Condé, and the bitter enemy of Cardinal Mazarin, had for a period entered Philip's service against his own country, for which he had fought so valiantly and triumphantly at Rocroy, and he now commanded the Spanish army in Flanders, where Don Juan had succeeded Mariana's brother, the Archduke Leopold, as governor. Between them, the two brilliant young men had upheld Spanish prestige in Flanders for some time; but when an alliance between Mazarin and Cromwell was signed, Spain was outmatched. One by one the strongholds along the Flemish frontier gave way before the combined onslaught of France and England; but no defeat seemed absolutely crushing until Dunkirk, blockaded and bombarded by an English fleet and attacked on land by a French army, was forced to surrender. The rout of the *tercios* at Rocroy four years earlier had already cast the dark shadow of impending doom over the Spanish Empire. Now it had received its death blow. Flanders was lost, just as Portugal was lost. Philip could no longer hope for conquest; all he could hope for was peace. And for that he must be prepared to pay almost any price.

How high this price proved to be had been shown by his desperate answer to an English agent who, aghast at his own boldness, asked the King whether he would give an Infanta in marriage to the son of Cromwell.

"Yes," Philip answered vehemently, "I would give not only my daughter but all the blood in my veins if it meant reduction of England to the Church and to peace."

Things had changed, indeed, since he had opposed the marriage of his sister María to the Prince of Wales. He was ready, if need be, to sacrifice María Teresa to a commoner, who was not only a heretic, but a regicide. Fortunately, no such sacrifice would be necessary if it were not too late to take advantage of the suggestion de Lionne had made to Haro three years earlier. Now that the birth of Prosper had provided Philip with a male heir, the proposed alliance was no longer an impossibility, as far as Spain was concerned, but a highly desirable expedient: Louis was no commoner, no heretic and no regicide; he was a Catholic King and peace with France would now automatically mean peace with England. A Spanish emissary, Antonio Pimentel, was sent to Mazarin to refresh his memory in regard to de Lionne's suggestion; and both Ana, the Queen Mother of France, and Mazarin listened willingly and attentively.

Mariana was against the French alliance from the beginning and did everything she could to circumvent it. To her, the only suitable match for her stepdaughter—and for the Hapsburgs—was her own brother Leopold, who had recently succeeded their father as Emperor. She convinced this brother that it would not be too late to redeem Flanders if he would send his army there to defend what had not yet been lost to Spain—and if he would replace Don Juan as commander. Fortunately, before her plans matured, Philip and Louis signed a truce and elaborate plans for the royal wedding, which was to take place in San Sebastián the following year, were soon underway.

On the 15th of April, 1660, Philip set forth on his journey to the French frontier to give his daughter María Teresa to his young nephew Louis XIV as his wife and to meet his sister Ana, Queen Mother of France, whom he had not seen since their early youth forty years before. The train that accompanied him surpassed anything that had ever been previously seen in Spain. It was so long that the van of the royal convoy was entering the town of Alcalá de

Henares, eight leagues away, while the rear was just leaving Madrid. Luis de Haro himself was served by a household of two hundred persons and scores of other nobles vied with him in magnificence. Their route took them from Alcalá to Jadraque and then to Atienza, where the Bishop of Sigüenza, who had so often been Philip's host, came to pay his respects. Then they continued northward through the mountains and down to Berlanga de Duero, where they were welcomed and entertained by the Duke of Frías, and followed the river valley as far as Aranda, before turning north again. No matter what hour the daily journey began, this came to a halt at six in the afternoon and, for the most part, the huge company was warmly received at seignorial houses and at the numerous monasteries and convents along their route, though sometimes these were not large enough to accommodate them and the humbler members of the retinue were obliged to take refuge in *ventas* and *mesones*—the most wretched of inns. They reached Burgos on the 24th and remained there until the 30th, resuming their progress toward Bribiesca early in the morning in the face of a chilling wind. On and on the train wended its slow way—through a narrow valley to Pancorbo—Miranda de Ebro—Armiñón, which brought them to the Basque Country—Vitoria—Mondragón—Oñate—Villareal in time for the Feast of the Ascension—Tolosa—Hernani—and finally, they were in sight of the sea. A league more and their Majesties entered San Sebastián, where the first marriage ceremony was to be performed. Their journey had taken them just under a month and in the course of it they had stopped at twenty-one different places.

The following day, while preparations for the public interviews upon the Isle of Pheasants were being made, Philip embarked with his daughter, Haro and a very few attendants, among them Diego de Velázquez, and landed privately upon the little island in the middle of the Bidasoa River. The buildings, which had been especially erected for the peace conference of the previous year, were constructed with the jealous precision which always marked the intercourse between France and Spain. According to plan, the strictest etiquette was to be observed, even in Philip's meeting with Ana, Queen Mother of France, the sister from whom he had so long been separated. But when he landed on the Spanish part of the island and entered the Spanish House, he bade all his attendants stay behind, except Haro, Velázquez and one or two more, and strode into the conference hall which connected it with the French House, accompanied only by these chosen few. Schooled as he was in self-control, he did not want to risk the loss of it, which he knew might well happen when he came face to face with Ana, who would be standing on the other side of the dividing line.

He was thankful that he had taken this precaution. Presumably, Ana had also tried to limit the number of witnesses to their meeting for the same reason that he had. But she had no sooner looked at him than she burst into tears and, confronted with her unrestrained emotion, his own supreme effort to maintain apparent calmness became badly shaken. They could hardly have been human if their encounter had been otherwise. They had been separated not only by the years, but by the ravages of war; and they were coming together not because of the mutual affection which had been so strong when they were children and which they had been schooled to suppress, but because they were again meeting as they had parted forty years earlier, to play a predestined role in a royal pageant. Now they were too old and their hearts were too heavy to find excitement and reward in such playacting and for this reason, as well as for all others, they grieved. They tried to speak words of comfort to each other, but, as so often happens in moments of great emotion, they found themselves tongue-tied and the words that did come were trite and ineffectual.

"Philip—can it be true? After all this time. . . ."

"Thank God, it is true."

"But how can we make up for the lost years?"

"By seeing how quickly we can span them."

"Yes, yes, you are right. And not only for our own sakes—"

"Also, for our children's sakes and our countries' sakes."

The few hurried sentences were all they could manage before Don Luis and the Cardinal came quickly toward them and their moment of privacy was lost forever.

Three weeks elapsed between the Court's arrival in San Sebastián and the day when, at last, all was ready for the ceremonial meeting and delivery of the bride to her new country. In the meantime, there had been dances, masquerades and a water carnival in the nearby Bay of Pasajes, which had been the scene of such a great naval victory for the Spaniards. The King was received with a salvo from two hundred cannon and more than two thousand muskets and the sound of the shots discharged from warships and the fortress of the mole mingled with martial music and hearty cheers. The royal barge was escorted by innumerable small craft, both Spanish and foreign, all gaily decorated, as was the entire shoreline and rival crews which raced each other. This outing provided, by all odds, the brightest interlude in a long series of formal conferences and banquets.

Finally, on Sunday, the 6th of June, both monarchs stepped from their boats at the same time on a given signal, Philip in Fuenterrabía and Louis in St. Jean de Luz, followed by crowds of other boats filled with courtiers. The two kings and their suites entered the conference hall by opposite doors. After a meaningless exchange of courtesies, Philip formally handed his daughter to her new husband and the four sovereigns took their seats side by side on thrones arranged for them across the line. Then Mazarin came forward with a missal upon which Philip swore to keep the terms of peace and the Patriarch of the Indies administered a similar oath to Luis. The personal marriage took place in St. Jean de Luz the next day; and then the Spanish Court started on its weary way home.

Philip was so exhausted when he reached Madrid that he had neither the strength nor the will to cope with the complexities which faced him. His three-year-old heir, Prosper, who had been dressed in a miniature military uniform to greet him, was overcome by the excitement of the occasion; he had been spared all physical effort, for his nurse had carried him in her arms; but he was a delicate child and the next day he succumbed to a fever so high that it menaced the life on which so much depended. Philip's best-loved son Juan was impatiently awaiting troops and means for an expedition. Mariana had finally succeeded in having him replaced in Flanders by the Archduke Sigismond and he had accepted the change with fairly good grace, since it was all too evident that he was needed in Portugal. Now the requisite equipment was being withheld by Luis de Haro, who did not relish the idea of having Juan, whose path had so far been strewn with victory, succeed where he had failed. Again Juan was the victim of jealousy and this time he was chafing under it. Mariana had not even been gracious enough to invite her stepson to Madrid and his enforced inactivity at Consuegra was an added grievance. Philip knew that his resentment was justified, summoned him to the palace and promised that, somehow, an army should be scraped together; but Mariana and Don Luis both still refused to see Juan and Philip was unequal to the task of placating the conflicting parties.

He was sleeping very badly and his restless slumber was riddled with dreams. Over and over again he seemed to be sitting on his curtained throne beside the high altar in the Church of San Sebastián, a humble parish church which had been richly adorned for "the greatest wedding that ever was seen in the world." But it was not this "blaze of magnificence" that he saw so clearly, or the French prince and princesses or the Spanish grandees or the officiating Bishop or even Don Luis, who was to act as proxy for King Louis, but his daughter as she stood looking up at him with streaming eyes. When the Bishop asked her the ritual question, "Would she take His Majesty, the most Christian King, for her husband?" she sank on her knees and the Bishop was obliged to repeat his question three times before she could control herself sufficiently to answer. Philip had known she was unhappy from the moment he told her she was to be married and, though he had tried to comfort her and cheer her, he knew now that he had not succeeded, that he had not told her the right things or been as patient and painstaking about it as he should have been. Marriage, to her, did not mean wedded bliss or the glory of becoming the Queen of France; it meant exile from the only place she had ever lived, separation from the only people she knew and loved, a struggle with a language which she had not mastered, the bewilderment of customs which were alien to her habits and which, because of unfamiliarity, she might fail to observe as she was expected to do and thereby bring shame to herself, her father and her country. And there would be no one to help her over the hard places. She was not like Isabel, who had been debonair by nature, who had come to Spain as a carefree little girl, loving it from the beginning and being loved in return by the people whose queen she became only years afterward, when there was nothing strange to her about them or the diffident boy who was presented to her as her "bridegroom," but who did not really become her husband for a long while, since he was even younger than she and they were simply playmates. Neither was María Teresa like Mariana, already ripe and eager for union at fifteen, greedy for excitement, lapping up luxury. María Teresa had lost her mother when she was only five years old and, though she and her stepmother had been good friends, Mariana had no feeling of responsibility for her and no deep abiding affection for her. Indeed, Philip strongly suspected that his wife who, for selfish personal reasons, was so strangely averse to the French marriage, had painted a dark picture of the Louvre for her frightened young stepdaughter in one of the intimate talks which "the girls" had together and which, at first, had been so pleasing and reassuring to him. Whether or not this had happened, María Teresa had grown up hedged in by the implacable routine of Court life, without the saving grace of tenderness and wisdom with which Isabel would have surrounded her upbringing. As a result, she was pathetically shy, sensitive and withdrawn. What preparation had she to face the blinding light of the *roi soleil*—the Sun King? None, none whatsoever, Philip told himself bitterly, half waking from his dream. And, if Louis recognized this inadequacy, would he deal with it patiently and understandingly or would he be irritated and annoyed by it? How would it affect his conduct as a king—and as a bridegroom? Now, as clearly as Philip had seen María Teresa weeping, he saw Louis coming forward to greet her, a handsome, self-assured young man wearing a black peruke that fell in long curls over his lace collar, a bright-colored, long-skirted coat opening in front to show a decorative vest, and red shoes with high heels. Philip had the terrible feeling that his behavior would be no less different than his clothes from anything to which María Teresa was accustomed and that they were almost a symbol of the ordeal before her.

His clothes? Well, of course, clothes did not really matter too much, it was not those that made the man. And yet, it was undeniable that Philip and his suite had felt self-conscious about their clothes all through the period they had spent at San Sebastián and on the

Isle of Pheasants; and in only one case had this feeling of self-consciousness been one of pride and pleasure. Diego de Velázquez had worn a dark, close-fitting habit, brightened with silver braid, and had carried a short gala sword in a scabbard of silver. Around his neck was a heavy chain of gold enamel from which hung a shield-shaped pendant, diamond studded and set with the insignia of Santiago; the graceful cape flung over his shoulders was embroidered in scarlet with the great sword-like cross which proclaimed him a Knight of the Order of Santiago. At last he was taking the place to which his birth and breeding, as well as his genius, entitled him, among the greatest in the land. This honor had come to him tardily after he had faithfully attended the King for years in positions associated with servitude.

He should, Philip reflected sadly, have had this honor and many others long before. Peter Paul Rubens who, in Philip's opinion, could not hold a candle to Velázquez as a painter of elegance, restraint and skillful characterization, had been accorded ambassadorial honors, and this though he was really only a high-level domestic official, when he brought state documents from the Archduchess Clara Eugenia in Brussels to the King in Madrid. He had spent nine months in Philip's capital and had executed fifty paintings while he was there, meanwhile receiving the most considerate treatment; then, after his return to Brussels and the delivery of documents to the Archduchess, he had gone to London as a special envoy from the Hapsburgs—indeed, it was he who had ratified the treaty when the formal peace was made between Cromwell and Philip. To be sure, the King had twice invited Velázquez to join him during his official progresses. The wonderful portrait of him—Philip's favorite —had been painted at Fraga (in three days!) shortly after the blockade at nearby Lérida had been lifted; and both "The Bridge at Zaragoza" and "The Vista at Pamplona" were inspired by scenes in the course of that journey when Baltasar Carlos had gone to receive the fealty of the Cortes at Navarre. But, during all this time, Velázquez had been acting in a subordinate position and treated as if it were there he belonged. He, too, should have had honors comparable to those given an ambassador. . . .

Philip's thoughts had wandered in thinking of Velázquez. He

had begun by dwelling only on the painter's dress at the wedding and how the latter's had outshone that of all others. Now his reflections about ambassadorial rank had brought him back to the apparel of his courtiers. He dwelt on this as he had more than once on the dress of his soldiers. It was strange how quickly they had lost their verve after being put into regular uniforms, instead of being allowed to dress as they pleased. The cherished individuality of the Spaniard was one of his strongest national characteristics and it would be as great a mistake to suggest changes in the Court as it had been in the military. Besides, the elegance and richness in dress of his suite at the wedding had equaled, if it did not actually surpass, anything worn by the French. But there was no denying that it was different and that this difference marked a conservatism, a lack of grace and ease that was behind the times. It was, indeed, a symbol—a symbol of rival powers, one waning, the other waxing. For more than a hundred and fifty years, Spain had been the greatest power on earth; her explorers and missionaries had opened up a new world and Panama, Mexico and a dozen other countries were as much a part of her empire as Castile. Her religion, her language, her customs and traditions were theirs. The arts in which she had led all Europe had become the leading arts of the world. But now her frontiers were shrinking, as one battle after another was lost, one treaty after another spelled greater indignities. She was no longer strong enough to triumph over the English or the Dutch or the French. The French! That was hardest of all. Richelieu had not been able to prevail over Olivares, but Mazarin had prevailed over Luis de Haro. Now the Sun King had prevailed over the Planet King. The current slogan, "Now there are no more Pyrenees!" did not mean that Philip had leveled them. It meant that Louis had surmounted them.

With all his heart and soul, Philip wished that he had not lived to see it. As far ahead as he could look, in his troubled dreams, he could visualize nothing but defeat and death.

Chapter 33

AND that was the way it happened.

Philip was still striving to get money; and, as a last resort, silver was now reduced to one-half its value and all securities lodged for loans were seized. Thus, by hook or crook, another army was finally assembled for the reconquest of Portugal by Don Juan and, at first, it looked as if this might actually come to pass. He won an important victory at Évora—one of the first places that had revolted against Spain more than twenty years earlier. But shortly thereafter, he was overwhelmed at nearby Amegial, the Portuguese having been reinforced by the English. His retreat became a rout, which his personal courage did not suffice to avert, though he fought bravely, pike in hand, until he was borne away in the flight. But the day of the pikemen was over. Originally, they had taken the brunt of infantry offenses; now in a general spread of firearms they were turned into a purely defensive body for the protection of the slower-loading musketeers. For Philip, the defeat at Amegial was an even greater personal tragedy than Rocroy had been, because it came closer to home in every sense of the word. Flanders was far away; Portugal was next door. The *tercios*—those hitherto invincible infantrymen—who were defeated at Rocroy were the pride of every Spaniard, including the King; but the pikemen defeated at Amegial included the King's son.

From Badajoz, which he finally reached, Juan was recalled to Madrid, ostensibly for a series of conferences with the King and the Council. But it was soon evident that Mariana wanted to separate him from the army altogether; it had too many potentialities of further glory for him, despite this first defeat. It would be a good idea, she thought, for him to conduct the Infanta Margarita to Germany—this twelve-year-old child had been betrothed to her uncle, the Emperor. Don Juan flatly refused the commission. He hated everything about the Austrian connection and, most of all, he hated Mariana and her Jesuit confessor, Father Nithard, who increasingly had a hand in all her schemes. If he were to be kept away from his army, why could not something be found for him to do in Madrid? Since Haro had died, perhaps he could be First Minister? And, since he already had semi-royal honors, why should he not go the whole way and become an Infante of Spain?

Philip had already had the same thoughts himself and he was giving the matter careful consideration. But such an elevation had no part in Mariana's plans and she opposed it bitterly. There were already far too many people at Court who were looking hopefully toward Juan to prevent the closer alliance with Austria on which she was determined. It would be better to send him back to Badajoz, after all. Since that was what he really wanted, he went quite willingly; for the moment, he would simply bide his time. Neither he nor anyone else foresaw that, when he was next recalled, two years later, it would be to go into semi-retirement at Consuegra after declining to become either Archbishop of Toledo or Inquisitor General. Philip believed that Juan had returned more than once to the Badiel Valley, though the subject was not mentioned between them again. However, without self-consciousness, he spoke now and then of his half brothers, Don Alfonso, a Dominican who had become the Bishop of Málaga and with whom he was on terms of close friendship; and Don Fernando, who was Governor of Navarre and General of Artillery in Milan. He knew that the former, at least, Philip held in high esteem and certainly both had achieved distinction on their own merits; and finally he asked Philip why they, too, had not been acknowledged.

"They have," Philip answered, readily enough. "That is, I have never denied that they are my sons or wished to do so. As a matter of fact, there are several others, among them the Bishop of Oviedo, whom you have not mentioned, that belong in the same category. But if you mean why have I not given them semi-royal status, I will tell you—it is because I have loved only one woman enough to honor her son in that way."

Through the machinations of Mariana, the command in Portugal had been given to the Count of Caracena, who had distinguished himself in the war against the Turks on the frontiers of Hungary. The scheme proved a boomerang; Caracena was routed at Villaviciosa with terrible carnage and with this rout came the last hope of retrieving Portugal. When the news was brought to Philip, for the first time in his life he broke down in the sight of men, casting himself on the ground in a paroxysm of grief.

He was not only a defeated monarch, grieving for the loss of part of his kingdom; he was a man, grieving for what might have been. That regicide, Oliver Cromwell, was dead and gone and his son, to whom Philip had once been ready to sacrifice María Teresa in the interests of peace, was no longer the heir of a dictator but a disgraced nonentity. The monarchy had been restored in England and the new king, Charles II, son of that erstwhile Prince of Wales who had come courting Philip's sister, the Infanta María, was on the throne. If Olivares had not played false, this new king would have had María of Spain and not Henriette Marie of France for a mother and Philip would have been the uncle of the King of England as well as the uncle (and incidentally, the father-in-law!) of the King of France and at peace with both!

There was still another angle to this debacle: Catherine, the daughter of the Duke and Duchess of Braganza, was now the Queen of England and the dowry which she had taken her bridegroom was the richest in Europe—"almost double to what any king had ever received in money by any marriage." And money was only part of the numerous treasure. England had acquired free trading rights for shipping in the ports of Brazil and the Portuguese East Indies. Tangiers and Bombay were generously ceded for good measure. The moribund East India Company was revived. Ships laden with porcelain, silks, rugs, lacquers, furniture, pearls, perfume, exotic spices and a strange new drink known as *tay* were crowding the docks in England. A quarter of a century earlier Isabel had said, speaking about the Duke of Braganza, "If he had been a bachelor, the Conde-Duque could have managed him as easily as he did the Duchess of Mantua. He was perfectly happy with the title of Military Governor. Besides being naturally indolent, he cares more about hunting and banqueting than he does about anything that requires extra effort. He is tremendously rich and owns about two-thirds of the country, so he has all he wants to do just looking after his own estates. He cares nothing at all about becoming king. But his wife is aiming higher and there is a little daughter, Catherine, for whom the Duchess already envisions a royal marriage."

Well, Isabel had been right about that as she was about so many things. But if the fates had only been kinder—or state affairs better managed—Catherine might have been the bride of Juan of Austria instead of Charles II of England. The Portuguese were less sensitive about the bar sinister than the Spaniards, as had been proved when Antonio, Prior of Crato, had been the choice for king of many nobles, the regular clergy and the Pope himself. This time the Portuguese would have stood behind Juan if he were married to their princess and declared an Infante of Spain and his father's legal successor; the Spaniards would have stood behind him, too; and all those riches of the Orient would have come to impoverished Spain at the same time as the beautiful young bride. What a pair she and Juan would have made!

Ever since María Teresa's marriage, Philip had been mourning the death of others. The loss of Portugal was his own mortal blow. He lay in his bed, dwelling on those other deaths. The first had been Velázquez', who did not survive the wedding for more than a month; then had come Luis de Haro's and then poor little Prosper's. Prosper was hardly cold in his small tomb at the Escorial when another baby boy was born and with this birth came a short reprieve to Philip's overwhelming grief. He sent a pilgrim to the Holy Land, provided with a purse of ten thousand *reales,* to pray for the health of the Queen and the Prince and he wrote to *Sor* María:

> *Our Lord has deigned to send me back my son, by bringing me another; for which I am as grateful as so signal a boon and mercy demands. Help me,* Sor *María, to prostrate myself at His feet and*

beseech Him to preserve this pledge, if it be for His service, otherwise I desire it not, but to bow my head to His will. The Queen and the child are well, and I am content.

But he knew in his heart of hearts that this child, who was christened Carlos, was not well, that his only heir, like Prosper, was sickly and scrofulous, that the chances were that *he,* too, might be short-lived or that, if he lived, he would never reach normal maturity. Should this happen, Philip's death would mark the end of Hapsburg rule in Spain. María Teresa had renounced her rights to the succession of the throne and Louis had sworn to respect her vows. But such oaths had been broken before on both sides of the Pyrenees and would be again. Mariana who, this time, had made a good recovery would fight for her son, which was natural and proper; but, meanwhile, she would be plotting to bring about the downfall of Philip's other son in whom, the King was increasingly convinced, lay the only hope for the country's future. It would be easier for her to carry out her designs when her husband had breathed his last and no one could dispute her rule as Regent. He knew she was making careful plans and that she did not think she would have long to wait. She was superstitious, she believed in portents. A comet had appeared the previous December and had progressed across the sky above the moon. Then it passed under Capricorn and went toward Sirius. Comets, especially those above the moon, presaged the death of royalty. Mariana was reckoning that it would be only a short time before Philip would be dead.

He wrote to *Sor* María, but he no longer confided all his troubles to her, though he admitted he was not well. A conserve of mallow leaves had been brought to him and, as he still had not lost his taste for sweets, he ate it with a certain amount of relish; but it was not effective as a remedy. *Sor* María replied in her usual vein of encouragement and good counsel. It was her last letter. The correspondence which had been Philip's mainstay for over twenty years was ended by another death and now that he had lost *Sor* María, he turned his face to the wall, as he had when he lost Isabel. But, this time, he never faced life again.

He was again sleeping very badly, as he had after his return from San Sebastián, but he was not dreaming as much as he had then. Instead, he kept thinking of the things he had not done and that it was now too late to do. He was not without literary and artistic talents and he should have left something creative behind him besides a few light verses and comedies, a few inconsequential sketches. True, he had been a patron of the arts and his reign would be remembered as the Golden Age because of Velázquez and Murillo and Zurbarán, Calderón de la Barca, Lope de Vega and Góngora; but if he had only tried a little harder, as Inés had urged him to do, he might have produced something which would have borne comparison with the work he had encouraged in others.

He should not have spent so much time at bullfights and cane tourneys, balls and banquets that he had no strength or leisure left for anything except hunting and philandering. He had told Isabel he wanted to know his people better, all his people, with her to help him; and when she had died, he had not felt equal to making the effort without her. Besides, in mingling with his people, he should have learned more about their country, and his. He remembered how interested Isabel had been in the *mesta* and how his own interest in it had been stimulated, not only by hers, but by the woman in the cave, the mother of his godchild, who would be having more to eat for herself and her family when the sheep came north again after their winter's sojourn in the south. He wished that, once, he could have followed one of the famous sheep walks all the way from Seville to Madrid. It would have enabled him to understand their value better. And he should have sat with the Tribunal of the Waters during some of their weekly meetings at the door of the Cathedral in Valencia and learned how the rich lands of the *huerta* were governed by their own people, so that their produce would be safeguarded and increased. And then, he should have taken time to enjoy the beauty of that countryside and the beauty of Galicia and the Basque Country, so different from that of Valencia and Andalucía, but none the less verdant and refreshing. He had dwelt too much in Castile with its strangled industry and its long desert-like stretches and its gaunt mountains and the great rocks which had given part of it the name of Land of Stones and Saints—for many saints had come from that strange barren province; it was, after all, the soul of Spain, just as the other places were its sinews. And it had its own beauty. What was that line in Scriptures he had always loved? "I will lift up mine eyes unto the hills, from whence cometh my help." He should have stopped and lifted up his eyes more often, when he was galloping from place to place at top speed, in order to attend another extravagant festival. If he only had, he would not be so tired now.

He knew, all too well, what the death chamber of a Spanish king would be like in its visible attributes. These were dreadful enough, but there were other factors which disturbed him still more. He was dying, he was ready and eager for death, because he was old before his time and weary and suffering and because he could do no good for anybody by living—except that, as long as there was breath in his body, the strife between his wife and his best-loved son could not break all bonds and damage the kingdom. He tried to think of some way in which he could prevent this damage or at least lessen it. But he was too tired. Aytona finally turned the King's confessor out of the room and forbade him to return because he and another priest had quarreled so violently about administering the Last Sacrament. It was quieter after that. Mariana and her children, Margarita and Carlos, came to say good-bye. He took tender leave of them and of the numerous nobles who filed past his bed and of his gentlemen in waiting, to many of whom he granted titles and knighthood; and it occurred to him that he might have sent for his son Alfonso, the Bishop of Málaga, or his son Antonio de San Martín, the Bishop of Oviedo, to administer the Last Rites. It would have been quite fitting and he was rather sorry he had not thought of it sooner. But when the news was brought to him that Juan was in the antechamber, Philip knew that this son he could not bear to see.

Juan would understand.

Epilogue

WITH the death of Philip IV ended the golden legend of Spain as the country predestined by God to fulfill a sacred mission and through the favor of Heaven to remain ever invincible and invulnerable. Gone were the kings who governed the earth from a corner of a palace or the seclusion of a monastery. Gone were the soldiers and sailors who heroically shed their blood in every part of the vast empire. Gone were the conquerors of kingdoms and continents.

The last strains of the great epic had died away. The picaresque novela came into its own.

—José DELEITO Y PIÑUELA. *El Declinar de la Monarquía Española.*

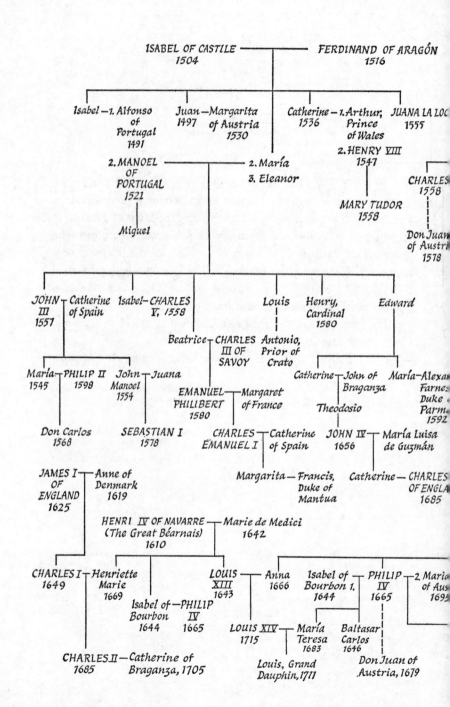

ISABEL OF CASTILE — FERDINAND OF ARAGÓN
1504   1516

Isabel — 1. Alfonso   Juan — Margarita   Catherine — 1. Arthur,   JUANA LA LOC
         of Portugal   1497   of Austria   1536   Prince   1555
         1491   1530   of Wales

       2. MANOEL   2. María   2. HENRY VIII
          OF   3. Eleanor   1547   CHARLES
       PORTUGAL   1558
         1521   MARY TUDOR
                                                                      1558   Don Juan
         Miguel   of Austri
                                                                                       1578

JOHN — Catherine   Isabel — CHARLES   Louis   Henry,   Edward
III   of Spain   V, 1558   Cardinal
1557   1580

               Beatrice — CHARLES Antonio,
                          III OF   Prior of
                          SAVOY   Crato   Catherine — John of   María — Alexar
María — PHILIP II   John — Juana   Braganza   Farnes
1545   1599   Manoel   Duke
                    1554   EMANUEL — Margaret   Theodosio   Parm
                             PHILIBERT of France   1592
Don Carlos   1580
  1568   SEBASTIAN I   CHARLES — Catherine   JOHN IV — María Luisa
                      1578   EMANUEL I of Spain   1656   de Guzmán

JAMES I — Anne of   Margarita — Francis,   Catherine — CHARLES
OF   Denmark   Duke of   OF ENGLA
ENGLAND   1619   Mantua   1685
1625
              HENRI IV OF NAVARRE — Marie de Medici
              (The Great Béarnais)   1642
                     1610

CHARLES I — Henriette   LOUIS — Anna   Isabel of   PHILIP — 2. Maria
1649   Marie   XIII   1666   Bourbon 1.   IV   of Aus
            1669   1643   1644   1665   1692
                Isabel of — PHILIP
                Bourbon   IV   LOUIS XIV — María   Baltasar
                1644   1665   1715   Teresa   Carlos
                                                  1683   1646
                                                                             Don Juan of
   CHARLES II — Catherine of   Louis, Grand   Austria, 1679
   1685   Braganza, 1705   Dauphin, 1711

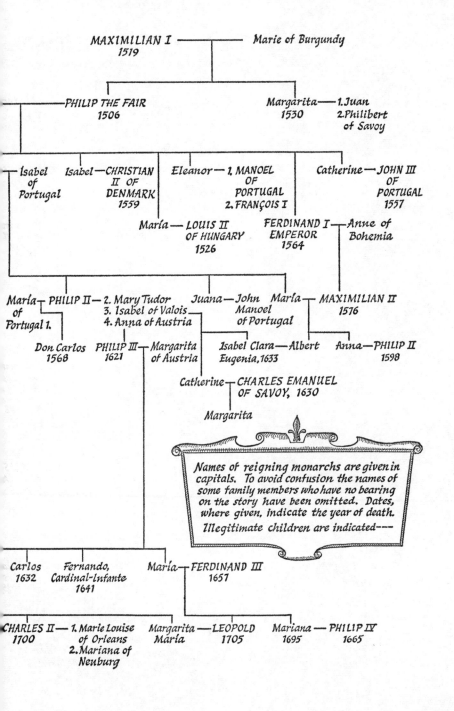

MAXIMILIAN I — Marie of Burgundy
1519

PHILIP THE FAIR   Margarita — 1. Juan
1506   1530   2. Philibert
                                              of Savoy

Isabel   Isabel — CHRISTIAN   Eleanor — 1. MANOEL   Catherine — JOHN III
of   II OF   OF   OF
Portugal   DENMARK   PORTUGAL   PORTUGAL
                    1559   2. FRANÇOIS I   1557

           María — LOUIS II   FERDINAND I — Anne of
                   OF HUNGARY   EMPEROR   Bohemia
                   1526   1564

María — PHILIP II — 2. Mary Tudor   Juana — John   María — MAXIMILIAN II
of   3. Isabel of Valois   Manoel   1576
Portugal 1.   4. Anna of Austria   of Portugal

     Don Carlos   PHILIP III — Margarita   Isabel Clara — Albert   Anna — PHILIP II
     1568   1621   of Austria   Eugenia, 1633   1598

                              Catherine — CHARLES EMANUEL
                                          OF SAVOY, 1630

                              Margarita

Names of reigning monarchs are given in
capitals. To avoid confusion the names of
some family members who have no bearing
on the story have been omitted. Dates,
where given, indicate the year of death.
    Illegitimate children are indicated ---

Carlos   Fernando,   María — FERDINAND III
1632   Cardinal-Infante   1657
         1641

CHARLES II — 1. Marie Louise   Margarita — LEOPOLD   Mariana — PHILIP IV
1700   of Orleans   María   1705   1665
             2. Mariana of
             Neuburg

Author's Note

I HAVE remarked many times before and—if I go on writing—shall probably remark frequently again that books are conceived and developed in various ways and that these are often as much of a surprise to an author as they can be to anyone else. I enlarged on this subject in my Author's Note for *The Explorer*, which was conceived in a dream and developed in localities as far apart from each other as Washington, D.C., and Lima, Peru; so I will make no more general comments on the subject now, but confine myself to the conception and development of the current book, which did not even begin with its present title.

The Washington dinner party, an object of scorn to many persons who have never been invited to one, is actually one of the most fertile fields, not only for enjoyment, but for the enlargement of limited horizons—at least, it has always been so in my case. Several years ago, I was seated at one of these functions beside the Count of Motrico who, at the time, was Ambassador of Spain to the United States; and, in the course of conversation, he asked me if I had ever thought of writing about María de Ágreda. I confessed that I had never even heard of her.

"What! The great friend and confidante of Philip IV! His wisest counselor! His correspondent over a period of more than twenty years! I thought you were a student and an admirer of our history."

I bowed my head in shame as I admitted that, though a student, I was not a scholar and, though an admirer, I was not an authority; I should be grateful for anything His Excellency might do to lighten the darkness of my mind.

"I will send you a book, entitled *Un Mundo en una Celda—A*

World in a Cell—by Felipe Ximénez de Sandoval. I am sure that, when you have read it you yourself will want to write a book about María de Ágreda."

I thanked the Ambassador and said this undoubtedly would be so. Naturally, I did not add that I saw not the slightest chance of doing it, in view of the unfulfilled commitments with which I was already burdened. In due course of time, the promised book arrived and was regretfully put aside, with several others, for future reading and reference. It was not until the late spring of 1963, when I was preparing to leave New Orleans for the summer, that I started to leaf through it and found in it the record of a great life, a remarkable friendship, and correspondence comprising letters exchanged between the gifted and sensitive but lonely monarch of the most far-flung kingdom in the world and a cloistered nun who never, in the flesh—I use that term advisedly—had left the small frontier village where she was born and raised and whose family home had become a convent.

These letters have been pronounced "unique in the history of the world" * and no wonder. They were written more than three centuries ago and they always followed the same pattern: the King wrote on the right-hand margin of a single sheet, leaving the left-hand margin blank for the nun's reply; and, as more than six hundred of the letters have been preserved, you can see, to this day, his handwriting and hers side by side: the cry of agony and remorse, the prayer for help; and the wise counsel, the quiet sympathy, the answering loving-kindness.

Because I was so thrilled with my first glimpse of this correspondence, I mentioned it casually to a clerical caller who had come to see me about a phase of my work which, as far as I knew, had nothing to do with *Sor* María de Ágreda in her cloistered convent: I was trying to prepare a comprehensive anthology on the activities of Christian Missions from the time of the Apostles to the present day—a somewhat overpowering undertaking; and I had sought help from the Academy of American Franciscan History in Washington for data about Junípero Serra and the earlier missionaries to New Mexico.

* *Un Mundo en una Celda* by Felipe Ximénez de Sandoval.

"I keep getting sidetracked," I complained. "My latest temptress is the counselor of a Spanish king."

"I assume you are referring to María de Ágreda," my caller replied in such a calm, matter-of-fact way that it was obvious he knew all—or, at least, a great deal—about her already. "But why do you say she has sidetracked you?"

"Because she never left her native village, which is so small it is shown only on the larger maps, and so close to the boundary line between Castile and Aragón that you have to look carefully to see that it is actually in Castile. And, at the moment, as you know, I shouldn't be poring over Spanish maps. I should be devoting all my energies to learning more about the early Franciscan missions in New Mexico."

"Then I strongly advise you to find out more about María de Ágreda. You had better begin by reading the Benavides Memorial of 1630. You will find in this that *Sor* María is credited with hundreds of conversions in New Mexico."

"But if she never left Ágreda—"

I thought I heard a carefully suppressed sigh. "Naturally, you have heard of bilocation?" my caller asked patiently.

I have moments of wishing that gentlemen whom I admire and respect very much did not have such a fatal faculty for revealing my lack of erudition. The tone of voice in which my present visitor spoke was sadly reminiscent of the one in which the Count of Motrico had asked me if I had never heard of María de Ágreda. And now, to make matters worse, apparently I should not only have heard about bilocation, but of this—whatever it might be —in connection with her.

"Bilocation is the gift of being in two places at the same time," my mentor went on. "St. Ignatius is among several saints credited with having possessed it. There seems to be no doubt that *Sor* María did. At all events, a settlement of Indians, which our missionaries had neither time nor man power to reach, persistently sent emissaries to our current Superior in New Mexico. These emissaries asked for instruction in the new religion and stubbornly declined to be put off. When the Superior inquired why they were so determined, they said because of the lady in blue."

"The lady in blue!"

"Yes. They insisted that she had appeared to them several times and had told them a wonderful story. They were not sure they understood it very well, but they wanted to understand it better. When the Superior asked them if they could describe this lady, they drew a picture of her. There is not the slightest doubt that it was meant to represent María de Ágreda. Not many Orders, as you probably know, wear bright blue habits. Moreover, the style of those worn by Conceptionists is distinctive. María de Ágreda is credited with at least five hundred apparitions before the Indians."

Gradually, we returned to the general subject of Franciscan missions in New Mexico, but not before my caller had convinced me that María de Ágreda was entitled to a niche in my story about them; and, increasingly, as I learned more about her, I also became convinced that, in addition to this niche, she was entitled to a story of her own. The apparitions took place many years before her correspondence with the King began. Then followed a period devoted to writing—a Life of the Virgin, a book entitled *The Mystical City of God* and other works. Acting under orders from her conscientious but unenlightened confessor, she destroyed the first version of the biography, but fortunately she later rewrote it, devoting five years to the task. It seems sad to us now that the views she expressed on the Immaculate Conception should have caused her trouble, not only with the local priest, but with the Holy Inquisition. (They are the views now embodied in the Dogma of the Church, largely thanks to the visions of Bernadette Soubirous.) And it is good to know that later *Sor* María was fully vindicated and that her earlier writings are now regarded by some Spanish authorities as "being second only to those of Teresa of Ávila in mystical importance." *

This is rating them very high, possibly no higher than they should be, though John of the Cross certainly belongs very close to the top of the list. But there is no doubt that her correspondence with the King is indeed "unique in the history of the world"; and it is around this that I soon felt her story should be centered. Its title, I decided, unquestionably should be *The Lady in Blue*. I saw it first as a biography and then as biographical fiction. And,

* *Un Mundo en una Celda* by Felipe Ximénez de Sandoval.

eventually, I persuaded a publisher to see it in the latter light and, seizing on a break in family cares and professional obligations, flew to Spain with Ágreda as my objective.

The break was not long enough to permit more than a cursory examination of the story's possibilities. But I knew before I left for home in the autumn of 1963, laden with reference material and grateful memories of a wonderful reception at the Conceptionist Convent in Ágreda that I should have to come back, at least twice, before I could hope to do my story any kind of justice. And, besides knowing that I must come back to Spain, I knew that I must study the entire reign of Philip IV (1621-1665) in order to understand, evaluate and interpret the part María de Ágreda had played in his life. Furthermore, that in order to do this, I must understand, evaluate and try to interpret the parts other women had played in his life, for these were interwoven with hers. And, among many, four stood out, crying for recognition:

First, Isabel of France, daughter of the great Henry of Navarre and Marie de Medici, Philip's child bride who became the gay companion of his pleasurable days in Madrid and the wise Regent when he was absent in the distant parts of his dominion.

Second, Inés Calderón, generally known as la Calderona, the sixteen-year-old actress from the provinces who caught the King's eye when he first glimpsed her on the stage and who became the great love of his life and the mother of his most cherished son; but who herself declined to continue the liaison and retired to an isolated valley to end her days in prayer and seclusion.

Third, *Sor* Margarita, the beautiful novice at the degenerate San Plácido Convent, who countenanced the invasion of the cloister.

Fourth, Mariana of Austria, Philip's second wife, bold and selfish, who made the last years of Philip's life even sadder than they would inevitably have been in any case.

By this time it was, of course, clear to me that I must try to persuade my publisher that we did not have a brief, more or less mystical, novella on our hands, but a full-length biographical novel, which would represent a far greater outlay of both time and money. It was also clear to me that the book must have a different title, since it was not to be solely the story of María de Ágreda, but also the story of Isabel, Inés, Margarita and Mariana and, still more accurately, the story of the King himself as reflected in his relationship to these women. So it seemed suitable that the book should take its title from the designation which Philip IV, like all kings of Spain, including the late Alfonso XIII, used for himself in his every official act and signature: *I the King*.

That great romancer, Rafael Sabatini, once said that, in order to give authority and vitality to a biographical novel, it was necessary to know its period well enough to write the history of this; and when someone who was neither a student nor a writer challenged his statement, he sat down and wrote a history of the Borgias which is the last word in reliability! I wanted to reverse the process and, having begun with the history, to write the novel!

So the summer of 1964 saw me back in Spain for a long summer and 1965 for a still longer one, both times accompanied by my secretary, Deanie Bullock, who now knows Spain almost as well and loves it as much as I do and, therefore, combined affection with efficiency in dealing with the subject at hand; and the station wagon which by now should be able to go almost without guidance over the Guadarrama Range—or through the new tunnel of which *Castellaños* are so proud!—on its way between Madrid and Ávila. Last year, to our regret, we could find no place where we could keep house in Ávila and we made do with an apartment in Madrid, which, though pleasantly located just off the Castellana in the most aristocratic quarter of the city, had the disadvantages of a refrigerator no larger than a medicine cabinet, an antiquated three-burner stove, a kitchen separated by a long corridor from the dining room, thoroughly undependable plumbing and an elevator so erratic that I was never sure whether I could get to the ground floor, for we were on the sixth story; and the one time I tried to go over the stairs, the consequences to a bad back and two bad knees were disastrous!

However, the elevator was fortunately on its good behavior the days we were invited to the American Embassy, where Ambassador and Mrs. Woodward graciously entertained us; and it did not altogether prevent us from getting out to enjoy the Prado and El Retiro. Besides, we did wedge in several pleasant excursions, outstanding among them a second visit to the historic convent at Ágreda, still actively functioning, where I found my friends, the *Concepcionistas,* deeply absorbed in the cause of *Sor* María's beatification; and two trips to Valfermoso de las Monjas, deep in the Badiel Valley—the nearest approach in isolation and beauty to the Shangri-la of fiction that I had ever imagined, much less seen before. The convent where Inés Calderón received her habit from the Papal Nuncio, Giovanni Battista Pamfili (afterward Pope Innocent X), and later presided as Abbess was badly damaged during the Civil War; but it has been repaired and still harbors thirty Benedictine Nuns, who have fortunately preserved—though in no more worthy a receptacle than a shoe box!—the Papal Bull authorizing the establishment of the convent in the twelfth century and many other documents of almost equal importance. More fervently than I can express in words, I wish I could present this venerable Community with a vitrine suitable to display and enshrine these priceless treasures.

There were also visits to some of the Spanish friends whose hospitality I have found never failing and whose welcome means more and more to me every year. Among these are Don Alfonso and Doña Beatriz de Orléans, respectively the cousin of the late king and granddaughter of Queen Victoria, at the *palacio* in Sanlúcar—a city famous as the port from which Columbus set forth on his third voyage of discovery and Magellan started out around the world: also, as the locale of the dukedom which gave Olivares his second title. Don Alfonso, now in his late seventies, still pilots his plane and goes for a swim every day and, incidentally, is still one of the most charming men I have ever known in my life! And Doña Beatriz, greatly gifted as a designer and painter, is also a botanist of note, and the garden she has created is a lovely sight from the windows of the drawing room where she presides with such grace. I owe much to the generosity of both which, like their hospitality, I have found unbounded; and, on learning that I was working on a book about Philip IV and his Court, they gave me a rare old engraving of the Conde-Duque of Sanlúcar which was then hanging in the wonderful library of the Duke of Montpensier, Don Alfonso's father. Now it is one of the chief ornaments of the Beauregard Memorial Library in New Orleans!

Then there is Señora Primiteva de Norieja, the widow of the famous historian, Agustín de Amezúa, whose death was a great loss to me, both personally and professionally. Her town house on the Calle de Alisal in Madrid, dominated by another fabulous library, and her *dehesa, El Cid,* a few miles from Ávila, are both happy objectives every time I go to Spain. (Literally, a *dehesa* is a pasture ground with no reference to house or landscaping, but in this locality, it is the term generally applied to country estates, large or small; near Segovia, on the other hand, both such estates are called *fincas*.) *El Cid* has been in the Amezúa family one hundred and fifty years; and at least four centuries before that this huge stone house with its own private chapel and dependencies was a stronghold where all the countryside could take refuge in moments of emergency; and which now provides modernized and charming accommodations for an almost indefinite number of grandchildren and their parents, as well as an equally indefinite number of guests. A pleasanter place to spend a day or a week it would be hard to imagine.

The summer of 1965, with its nearer approach to a menacing deadline, put a curb on nearly all leisurely visiting, but we did manage to go as usual to *El Cid* and to lunch at the *Casa de Superunda,* with other old friends, Señor and Señora Caprotti—the former a famous Italian painter, whose train from Paris to Madrid was stalled in a snowstorm at Ávila, and who was so entranced with its glistening beauty that he decided to remain there! This he accordingly did, interpreting with his brush its glories to the delight of thousands and marrying into an aristocratic Avilese family. His studio has been accommodated in the quarters around the patio of their *palacio,* while the living quarters, which include four drawing rooms leading into each other and all magnificently furnished, are reached by a stone staircase of majestic proportions. The dining room is a treasure-trove of rare porcelain and silver and the first dish of a lavish luncheon served there is apt to be *Marmitako,* a delicious soup which, in its indigenous surroundings, is made with sea water. I am proud to have added the recipe for this to several other Spanish dishes which have become mainstays of my own housekeeping.

1 lb. fresh tuna fish*

6 cloves garlic, finely minced

1 onion, finely chopped

6 T. olive oil

6 tomatoes, peeled and chopped

1 red hot and 3 green peppers, cut in strips

6 potatoes, peeled and cubed

Pinch of saffron

Salt and pepper

Water

In the heated oil sauté the onion and garlic until golden; transfer to a soup kettle and add tuna fish, peppers, saffron, tomatoes and potatoes. Add sufficient water to make six servings. Season to taste with salt and pepper and simmer slowly until vegetables are cooked, but not mushy. If the soup becomes too thick, more water may be added.

We also went for *merienda*—the Spanish substitute for both cocktails and tea—with still another old friend, the Marqués de Santo Domingo, whose small exquisite house is set in a huge and luxuriant garden bordered on two sides by the famous walls of Ávila, including eight of its watchtowers. And, through the kindness of Mr. William Walker, Minister-Counselor of the American Embassy, we were privileged to visit the Zarzuela, now the residence of Prince Juan Carlos and his family. The Marqués de Mondejan, Chief of the Household, escorted us through the *palacete,* which is most attractive, as well as around the beautiful grounds; and the excursion marked a red-letter day in a summer otherwise given over almost exclusively to intensive desk work and weighty conferences.

However, the setting for these grueling labors did much to mitigate them. We found a so-called chalet, which bore no relationship whatsoever to its Swiss source of inspiration and, in Spain, was pronounced "shall*ette*." It was about a mile outside of Ávila, with ample grounds and a magnificent view of the walls and the mountains beyond. There was a large fireplace in the living room of which we made frequent use for, contrary to general belief in the United States, summer in Spain is not hot when you get out of the south and into the highlands; and there was a bedroom for Segunda, the

---

*If fresh tuna fish is unavailable, canned, which has been rinsed with boiling water, may be substituted.

faithful retainer who first came into our lives eight years ago, and space in the back yard for her grandchildren to play. This meant that her daughter-in-law Pepita, whose services also date back for eight years, could come in by the day and cook for us.

When we first made the acquaintance of the family, Segunda, Pepita and Pepita's husband Pepe constituted its members; the next year marked the addition of my godchild Paquita and, since then, Deanie's godson Santi and the twins Miguel and Veronica have increased it still further. The children were not the only additions to the household: they brought with them a large dog, her long white coat flecked with black, which bore a general resemblance to that of an English setter. The children had named her Mosca, because they thought the flecks looked like flies (*moscas*), but the name was unworthy of her. She was an altogether charming dog and, when the time came to leave the chalet, it was as hard to part from her as from any human member of the family. And we were indebted to her not only for her own delightful company, but for that of a brindle kitten which she once tenderly brought home in her mouth and offered to us with pride. It was so young that it was barely able to drink milk, not maternally supplied, and we were afraid we could not save it. But, after the first few hungry days, when it mewed piteously all the time, it began to perk up and was soon so frisky that it went darting into every nook and corner of the premises, thus earning the name of Snoopy. As if it recognized a tremendous debt of gratitude to Mosca, it was never satisfied to be separated from its rescuer for more than a few minutes at a time. In its playful moments, it leaped on the dog's back and head and chased her tail quite fearlessly, nor was its confidence misplaced, for Mosca suffered all this gladly; then, exhausted, it snuggled up to her and went to sleep close to her warm body as she lay comfortably stretched out on her side. When the weather grew cold in the evenings and we were forced to abandon the gallery for the living room, Mosca and Snoopy lay in front of the fireplace, slumberous and contented. The memory of them lying there—the black and white dog, the brindle kitten, in the glow of the flames—is one of those I most cherish of all those connected with the writing of this book.

The children played unobtrusively while Segunda and Pepita cooked, cleaned, washed and ironed with perfect good nature and few modern conveniences, though this time we invested in a real refrigerator, a small but serviceable gas stove and a blender; however, there was no washer or any similar equipment, nor was any mention ever made of the necessity for one. Domestically, there was perfect peace and, consequently, long uninterrupted days for writing; scenically, there was such beauty as rarely exists in all this world; and *merienda*—usually just a drink and a sandwich or an *empanadilla*—when the day's work was done, while I watched the sun set and the moon rise, as the lights flooded the walls, was an experience I shall never forget. But there is no perfect place this side of Paradise or, if there is, I have never discovered it. The chalet, for all its superb location, its powerful fireplace and its willing and efficient staff, was not without certain disadvantages which we, as tenants, were supposed either to disregard or to remedy ourselves. For instance, we were not advised beforehand that it was not safe to enter the service bedroom because the floor was caving in! A new floor was our responsibility and before it was in place one of the workmen had fallen through the old one into the cellar. The roof had apparently received no more attention than the foundation; fortunately, it rained only once during the summer, but that storm was what is known in Spanish very accurately as a *tormenta;* a veritable waterfall was released on the dining room table, on my bed and, worst of all, on my desk, for all the papers with which I was working were drenched before I could rescue them; and our landlady remained quite unmoved by our pleas for better shelter and, by that time, we had spent so much money on the new floor, the new stove and a few other extras that we decided to take a chance on the weather and, luckily, we did not undergo another deluge. However, the one bathroom was our most constant problem. Somewhere in the course of the summer I read this description of hell: "It is a place where all the engineers are French, all the cooks are English and all the plumbers are Spanish." I had moments of feeling, as I had the summer before, that the statement must be at least one-third correct. It was impossible to tell, from one day to another, how much confidence we could put in the *taza de fuente*, and there was no spare.

Some problems continued to present themselves to me as an author as well as a housekeeper. None of the older books have indices; this means that you must go through ancient tomes hunting for the reference you want with the same thoroughness as if you were searching for a needle in a haystack. Two researchers on whom I had counted for advice, though fortunately not for much active help, informed me that the seventeenth century was not their "period" and that they could neither work with me themselves nor suggest a single book which would be of service to me. The Acting Director of the National Library, in response to a request for the best general history of Spain covering the reign of Philip IV, sent me the astounding message that there was no such thing, that I would have to make do with Marañón's book on the Conde-Duque (which is an analytical biography and not a history!) and on the "light and long" studies of the reign in José Deleito y Piñuela's series—which I already knew well and have found invaluable, but not as a substitute for a general history. Providentially, our Dominican friend, Father Reyero, was able to supply me from the library of the Convent of Santo Tomás in Ávila with Don Modesto Lafuente's *Historia General de España, Desde los Tiempos Primitivos Hasta la Muerte de Fernando VII* and several other useful volumes which had escaped the attention of the administrator in Madrid.

Another disappointment came in the unavailability of certain authorities in Madrid on whom I had counted. I had been told that the reason I was not able to confer with them in the course of previous years was because I arrived too late in the spring and left too early in the fall: from July 1st to October 1st, I would necessarily draw a blank. So this year I was careful to arrive in June and not leave until well into October. It made no difference. Professional vacations at the University of Madrid apparently began ahead of time and were indefinitely prolonged!

Admittedly, these disappointments slowed me up and, to this day, there are several questions to which I am still searching for answers; but, on the whole, the work progressed satisfactorily in

Spain and, since my return to the United States, more light has been shed on my chosen subject by Dr. Francisco Ugarte of the Department of Romance Languages at Dartmouth College. He has been a great help to me in many ways, including the loan of Pedro Aguado Bleye's *Manual de Historia de España*, but especially by reading the script from beginning to end, by making slight corrections and suggesting some valuable interpolations and by giving his approval from a historical point of view. I am similarly indebted to Eleanor Carroll Brunner who, ever since the days of the old *Delineator*, of which she was Associate Editor, and her subsequent distinguished career as Associate Dean of the School of Journalism at Columbia University and professor at Wellesley, has been one of my best literary advisers, for her editorial suggestions.

Most conversations in the book are imaginary, though all are based on fact and of some we actually have detailed records. I have taken two liberties with dates in slightly advancing that of the opening of the Buen Retiro and that of the arrest of Jerónimo de Villanueva by the Inquisition; both changes were made in the interests of smooth narrative and not with the intention or the result of changing their factual character. I have also included two episodes —that of the King's ride from Zaragoza to Madrid and of his visit to San Plácido—which are based on tradition rather than universally accepted documentation. However, I have always agreed with the great Cardinal, Merry del Val, that "tradition, wisely controlled, even in the absence of written documentation, gives us manifest proofs of the truths of our beliefs" and, in these cases, there were plenty of written documents. The ride is completely in character for the King, one of the most famous horsemen in history and an appreciative and devoted, if not always a faithful, husband; and the invasion of San Plácido by the King at the instigation of Olivares and Villanueva, though treated in different ways by different historians, is regarded as apocryphal by only one—Marañón—who makes this claim about everything unfavorable to his hero, Olivares, and further weakens his case by devoting six pages to the subject of San Plácido, illustrating these with a full-page picture of the key "supposedly" used by the King in entering *Sor* Margarita's cell; and designating her in his index as Philip's *"novia"* (sweetheart)! José de Pellicer, a contemporary pamphleteer, devotes two pages of his *Avisos Históricos* to Villanueva's arrest by the Inquisition and insists that the abbess and three nuns were arrested at the same time. This is long after the first scandal, which resulted in the closing of the convent for several years, and deals with the King's part in the story. Martin Hume, late Editor of the Calendars of Spanish State Papers, Lecturer in Spanish History and Literature at the University of Cambridge, makes the positive statement that "the only part of the story which seems open to question is the continuance of the affair after Philip's remorseful flight." José Deleito y Piñuela, whose seven books on the reign of Philip IV are the most comprehensive survey of it I have found, and who devotes fourteen pages to the story in *La Vida Religiosa Española Bajo el Cuarto Felipe*, states: "It is not possible in the name of scrupulosity to accept the story as authentic while lacking more trustworthy proofs to confirm it. But, truth or fiction, it has such a poetical flavor of the epoch, and so reflects the country's traditions that it is not possible to omit relating it here, with the above reservations. Its narration has inspired not a few stories, novellas, poems and romances." He then mentions the source which he and Marañón consider unauthentic—Mesonero Romanos in his *Antiguo Madrid*—but which R. Trevor Davies, as well as Hume, accepts. Davies considers the story of San Plácido of interest chiefly "as illustrating the social and moral decline that followed the decay of ecclesiastical influence at Court during the regime of Olivares"; but, personally, I feel it is important in showing the great difference in Philip's reaction to a nun who was really a holy woman and to an actress who became one, and to a girl who did not even pretend to have a real vocation and to an abbess whose erstwhile fiancé continued to have free access to her—and of the latter situation, there seems to be ample proof. No question has ever been raised as to the authenticity of the accounts of the so-called "*first* scandal of San Plácido" when the Inquisition stepped in and closed the convent after the chaplain had accused thirty nuns of improper relations with himself. Neither has the authenticity of Villanueva's arrest by the Inquisition, after the reopening of the convent, been questioned.

Moreover, the book given to me on this period by the Count of

Motrico, himself a historian of note, mentions that the nuns at Ágreda, as they watched the King's arrival in their chapel, from behind the grille, are "torn between fear and hope that their fate may be like *Sor* Margarita's." This book is considered wholly authentic by the present abbess at Ágreda, with whom I have twice conferred at length.

The letters ascribed to Isabel in correspondence with her beloved brother-in-law, the Cardinal-Infante, are fictional in form, but are all based on fact. Her account of the "accident" responsible for the birth of a dauphin after Louis XIII and Ana of Austria had been childless for twenty-two years was based on the version of the incident then current and now very generally accepted. However, it is fair to say that at least one eminent French historian—Victor L. Tapié—and probably others with whose work I am not familiar, does not agree with this. In *La France de Louis XIII et de Richelieu*, speaking of Louis XIII, he states: *"On lui avait appris à se défier de la chair. Un essai malheureux qu'on le laissa faire avec la jeune reine, dès leur première rencontre à Bordeaux, alors qu'il n'avait que quatorze ans, éveilla chez lui une répugnance de l'amour physique qu'il mit plusieurs années à vaincre. Son mariage ne fut consommé qu'en 1619."* Tapié admits a certain amount of incompatibility, but says that from then on Louis and Ana "remained husband and wife," several times announcing the prospect of a dauphin; then he mentions a miscarriage which took place in 1622. After that, the incompatibility apparently became an estrangement until the "accident" of 1638 brought it, at least temporarily, to an end; and the birth of a second son, Philippe d'Anjou, in 1640, certainly proves that the "accident" was not unique in the entire married life of this royal pair, as some historians claim!

I am well aware that some of my readers may feel I have not been consistent in using the Spanish forms in naming some people and places and the English form in others; but there was a reason for this, just as there was for including the story of the King's ride and of his intrusion at San Plácido. We have become so accustomed to speaking of some famous people by the Anglicized form of their names that any other usage would be confusing, at least to the average Anglo-Saxon reader and, in some cases, might even prevent identification. For instance, who, in the United States or England, refers to Philip II, III or IV as Felipe? On the other hand, to refer to the Infante Carlos as Charles would cause an equal amount of confusion, since we have Charles, Prince of Wales, as an outstanding character; Mary for María would be almost equally baffling; titles are used in two different ways for similar reasons. To speak of Olivares as the Count-Duke, rather than the Conde-Duque, would be to fly in the face of established custom. In other cases, it is natural and correct to use sometimes the terms Count and Duke, rather than Conde and Duque, though Marqués and Marquesa come more naturally to the average person. In this book, as well as others I have written, I have not felt that consistency is a jewel if followed by a Spanish title. Aragón is the same in English as it is in Spanish; Saragossa has been generally abandoned on up-to-date maps for Zaragoza; and this is equally true of other well-known cities and provinces.

All letters written by Philip IV, as by all kings of Spain from time immemorial through the reign of Alfonso XIII, have been signed: I the King. No comma has been used and, therefore, in quoting his letters, it does not appear in this book, as a direct quote should never be changed. However, the author and her best personal editorial adviser have yielded to the opinion of the publishers that a comma makes for clarity in the title of the book.

Of the letters ascribed to the King, the only one that is fictional is the first—written to Isabel on his accession to the throne. All the others are authentic. Most of these I have translated myself, with expert help. In a few cases, Martin Hume's translations have been used, as have been his rendering of *Sor* María's and the Conde-Duque's letters and most of the quotations from the pamphleteers. My translations of the quotations for flyleaves have been checked and approved by Dr. Richard Chandler, Professor of Foreign Languages at the University of Southwestern Louisiana.

Philip was not essentially a warrior. In fact, he never led his troops into battle until after the fall of his Minister, Olivares, who so bitterly opposed any such action on his part. If the story had centered on either the Cardinal-Infante or Don Juan—and both are worthy of one—the Thirty Years' War in many of its aspects should and would have been an outstanding part of the subject matter. Under the circumstances, however, since no book dealing with such a crowded period can possibly be all-inclusive, I have thought it best to refer to battles only incidentally, as they affected the progress of other events, and to concentrate on Philip's relations with three wonderful women—Isabel, Inés and *Sor* María—and with two ignoble ones—*Sor* Margarita and Mariana. This is the guise in which I visualize him most clearly. I hope it is the guise which will most appeal to my readers.

I may, however, perhaps point out that the writer of historical novels, who may present many imaginary characters and incidents, has a great advantage over the writer of biographic fiction. Unless the latter is unable, despite careful research, to determine the name of a real character, he cannot invent one. (For instance, I do not know the name of Mariana's lady-in-waiting, so I gave her a title once highly regarded in Spain, but now extinct.) And, under no circumstances can you contrive a happy ending when the story you are telling is actually a sad one. You also run into the very great danger, as a perceptive and expert reviewer for *Newsweek* (November 27, 1965) has pointed out, of "missing the forest for the trees, the spirit for the substance." As you dodge the trees and search for the spirit, you can only console yourself by the reflection that some of your readers prefer individual trees to whole forests anyway, and that substance, as well as spirit, is a necessary and vital element.

Work on *I, the King* was done at:

Hotel Wellington
    Madrid, Spain—August-October, 1963.

On board the *Cristoforo Colombo*, both eastbound and westbound, 1964.

Calle de Marqués de Villamejor, No. 4
    Madrid, Spain—July-October, 1964.

On board the *France* eastbound and the *Leonardo da Vinci* westbound, 1965.

Chalet Fuentes Claras
    Ávila, Spain—July-September, 1965.

The Oxbow
    Newbury, Vermont—October-December, 1965.
Sulgrave Club
    Washington, D. C.—January, 1966.
Beauregard House
    New Orleans, Louisiana—February and March, 1966.

Bibliography

In Spanish

Bailly, Augusto, *Richelieu*. Translated by Rosaura Cardoso. Argentina: Ediciones Peuser, 1877.

Sor María de Ágreda, Correspondencia con Felipe IV. Vols. I and II. Selected by Gonzalo Torrente Ballester. Madrid: Gráficas Uguina, 1942.

Sor María de Jesús de Ágreda, *Vida de la Virgen María*. Prologue by E. Pardo Bazán. Barcelona: Montaner y Simón, Editores, 1899.

Bleye, Pedro Aguado, *Manual de Historia de España*. Vol. II, *Reyes Católicos, Casa de Austria (1474-1700)*. Madrid: Espasa-Calpe, S.A., 1954.

Deleito y Piñuela, José, *La Vida Religiosa Española Bajo el Cuarto Felipe*. Madrid: Espasa-Calpe, S.A., 1952.

——, *Sólo Madrid Es Corte (La Capital de Dos Mundos Bajo Felipe IV)*. 1953.

——, *La Mujer la Casa y la Moda* (En la España del Rey Poeta). 1954.

——, *. . . También Se Divierte el Pueblo (Recuerdos de Hace Tres Siglos)*. 1954.

——, *El Rey Se Divierte (Recuerdos de Hace Tres Siglos)*. 1955.

——, *El Declinar de la Monarquía Española*. 1955.

——, *La Mala Vida en la España de Felipe IV*. 1959.

Lafuente, Don Modesto, *Historia General de España, Desde los Tiempos Primitivos Hasta la Muerte de Fernando VII*. Vol. II. Barcelona: Montaner y Simón, Editores, 1888.

Marín, Luis Astrana, *La Vida Turbulenta de Quevedo*. Madrid: "Gran Capitán," 1945.

Marañón, G., *El Conde-Duque de Olivares (La Pasión de Mandar)*. Madrid: Espasa-Calpe, S.A., 1959.

de Maura, Duque, *Vida y Reinado de Carlos II*. Vol. I—*La Minoridad, los Dos Matrimonios; Vol. II—La Sucesión.* Madrid: Espasa-Calpe, S.A., 1954.

Ortega y Gasset, José, *Velázquez.* Madrid: Revista de Occidente, 1963.

de Pellicer, José, *Avisos Históricos.* Madrid: Taurus Ediciones, S.A., 1965.

Pompey, Francisco, *Velázquez.* Madrid: Offo, 1962.

de Salvador, Felipe, *Guía de la Nobleza, Títulos y Corporaciones, Nobiliarias de España.* Barcelona: Gugrañes Hnos., 1956.

Sánchez de Toca, D. Joaquín, *Felipe IV y Sor María de Ágreda.* Madrid: Tipografía de los Huérfanos, 1887.

de Sandoval, Felipe Ximénez, *Un Mundo en una Celda (Sor María de Ágreda).* Madrid—Buenos Aires: Ediciones Studium de Cultura, 1951.

Téllez-Girón, Ricardo Martorell, *Anales de Madrid de León Pinelo, Reinado de Felipe III, Años 1598 a 1621.* Madrid: Estanislao Maestre, 1931.

The Archives of the *Biblioteca Nacional* and the *Academia Real de Historia* of Madrid. The Reverend Florentino Zamora, Presbyter of the *Biblioteca,* and several other persons were very helpful to me.

In French

Descola, Jean, *Histoire d'Espagne.* Paris: Librairie Arthème Fayard, 1959.

Espagne, les Guides Bleus. Paris: Librairie Hachette, 1963.

Espagne. Paris: Pneu Michelin, 1965.

Maurois, André, *Histoire de l'Angleterre.* Paris: Librairie Hachette, 1963.

Tapié, Victor L., *La France de Louis XIII et de Richelieu.* France: Flammarion, 1952.

In Italian

MSS. 8703, *"Ritratto della nàscita qualità costumi ed azioni de Don Juan d'Austria."* British Museum, London.

In English

Atkinson, William C., *A History of Spain and Portugal.* Middlesex, England, and Baltimore: Penguin Books, 1965.

Bertrand, Louis, *The History of Spain, Part I, From the Visigoths to the Death of Philip II.* Petrie, Sir Charles, Part II, *From the Death of Philip II to 1945.* London: Eyre & Spottiswoode, 1952.

The Century Dictionary and Cyclopedia, Vol. IX. New York: The Century Company, 1899.

Chapman, Charles C., *A History of Spain*. Founded on the *Historia de España y de la Civilización Española* of Rafael Altamira. New York: The Free Press; London: Collier-Macmillan Limited, 1965.

Complete Reference Guide to Spain and Portugal. New York: Pan American World Airways, Inc. Trade distribution in the U.S. and Canada by Simon and Schuster, Inc.

Davies, R. Trevor, *Spain in Decline*. London: Macmillan and Company, Ltd.; New York: St. Martin's Press, 1957.

Elliott, J. H., *Imperial Spain 1469-1716*. London: Edward Arnold (Publishers) Ltd., 1963.

Geddes, Michael, *The Life of María de Jesús of Ágreda*. London: B. Barker, A. Bettesworth and J. Batley, and F. Fayram, 1730.

Hume, Martin, *Queens of Old Spain*. London: Grant Richards, Ltd., 1911.

——, *The Court of Philip IV*. New York: G. P. Putnam's Sons; London: Eveleigh Nash, 1907.

Huxley, Aldous, *Grey Eminence*. London: Chatto and Windus, 1956.

Keyes, Frances Parkinson, *The Land of Stones and Saints*. Garden City: Doubleday and Company, Inc., 1957.

Petrie, Sir Charles, *Philip II of Spain*. London: Eyre & Spottiswoode, 1963.

Thomas, Gertrude Z., *Richer Than Spices*. New York: Alfred A. Knopf, 1965.

Toman, Karel, *A Book of Military Uniforms & Weapons*. London: Paul Hamlyn and Allan Wingate, 1964.

The Tourist Guide-Book of Spain. Compiled and edited by Herbert W. Serra Williamson. Madrid: The Times of Spain (The British American Publishing Company).

Wilkinson, Burke. *The Helmet of Navarre*. New York: Macmillan and Company, 1965.

Benavides' Memorial of 1630. Translated by Peter P. Forrestal, O.S.C. With An Historical Introduction and Notes by Cyprian J. Lynch, O.F.M. Washington, D.C.: Academy of American Franciscan History, 1954.

ABOUT THE AUTHOR

Frances Parkinson Keyes is the world-famous author of such best-selling novels as *Dinner at Antoine's, Joy Street, Came a Cavalier* and many other distinguished works of fiction and nonfiction. She was born at the University of Virginia, where her father was head of the Greek Department, and lived for twenty-five years in Washington and nearby Virginia while her husband was in the Senate. She still spends part of every year there, when she is not in residence at Beauregard House in New Orleans or at The Oxbow in Newbury, Vermont, or traveling abroad in connection with her work. She has been five times to Peru, had previously used it as a setting for a book of nonfiction and numerous articles, and spent the entire winter of 1963-1964 there in the interests of *The Explorer*. The summers of 1963, 1964 and 1965 were spent in Spain (a country with which she has been familiar since 1923 and the scene of several previous books) working on *I, The King*.

The latest of her many decorations is the *Sol de Peru*. She has also been decorated with the Order of Isabella the Catholic by Spain and the Legion of Honour by France.